Brides of the Kindred

Book 3: Sought

Evangeline Anderson

PUBLISHED BY:

Evangeline Anderson

Brides of the Kindred

Book 3:Sought

Copyright © 2016 by Evangeline Anderson

License Notes

Author's Note #1: To be the first to hear about new e-book releases, join my new newsletter by going to www.EvangelineAnderson.com. I promise no spam – you will only get email from me when a new book is out for either preorder or for sale.

*Author's Note #2: I'm happy to let you all know that I am going into Audio in a big way. I put **Claimed** , **Hunted**, and **Sought** into the audio format and I had such a great response from readers and listeners, that I have decided to put ALL the **Kindred** books, plus all my **Born to Darkness** books into audio as well as my standalone book, **Purity**. If you have a long commute or you'd like something new to listen at the gym or just around the house, give it a try. The Kindred books are performed by the very talented Anne Johnstonbrown whom I hand-picked to read the series and she really brings the characters to life.*

*Author's Note #3: I'm trying to find out which of my readers are also listeners. For a chance to win a free audio book, sign up for my new **Audio book newsletter** by going to www.EvangelineAnderson.com. It's the same as my e-book newsletter, but only for audio. And as always, I promise not to bother you unless I have a new audio book out or I'm running a contest with an audio book as one of the prizes.*

Author's Note #:You've probably already figured this out but this is the third book in the Brides of the Kindred series. I recommend that you read Claimed and Hunted before attempting to dive into Sought.

Hugs and Happy Reading and Listening to you all,
Evangeline Anderson March, 2016

Table of Contents

Brides of the Kindred

Book 3: Sought

Evangeline Anderson

Chapter One

Kat O'Conner was either dying or flying—she couldn't tell which.

All she knew was that she was hovering above her own body, looking down, and what she saw didn't look good—not good at all.

My God, I'm a mess!

Her long, auburn hair was a tangled snarl around her head and there were deep purple shadows under her eyes, which were closed at the moment. There was a troubled look on her face even in sleep—if it *was* sleep. Kat looked closer, trying to see if her chest was rising and falling, but it was difficult to tell because someone had covered her with blankets. She tried to check her own pulse, but when she reached for herself, she found that she had no hands, arms, or fingers to reach with.

Just like when I joined with Lock and Deep, when we were hunting for Sophie. It had been an exhilarating sensation—the feeling of being a swift, invisible bird able to flit from place to place in space instantly. But she wasn't joined with them now—she could tell. Because, for once in the past several weeks, she wasn't full to overflowing with their overwhelming emotions. And *overwhelming* was the right word.

Anybody who says men don't have feelings is full of crap, Kat thought ruefully as she studied the scene below her. Locks Tight and Stabs Deep, the Twin Kindred warriors who had gotten her into this mess in the first place, had plenty of feelings—enough to make her feel like she was drowning in a sea of emotion whenever they got too close to her. And lately, *anywhere* was too close, at least as far as Kat was concerned.

She'd been trying to avoid them ever since their last joining — the one she'd agreed to in order to find her friend Sophie Waterhouse, who had been kidnapped by the Scourge. The evil race of red-eyed, gray-skinned bastards had attacked Earth a few years ago. Only the intervention of the Kindred warriors — a race of genetic traders from beyond the stars — had saved Kat's home planet.

The Scourge had some kind of prophesy involving an Earth girl that they would stop at nothing to fulfill. At first they'd believed that Sophie's sister, Olivia was their intended target. Then they centered on Sophie. Kat didn't know who was going to be taken next, she was just glad that her friends were safe.

And speaking of Sophie and Liv, where were they? So far Kat had been focusing on her own still body, but now she looked around — if you could look without a head to turn or eyes to see with, that was. God, this was so freaking *weird*. She wondered again if she was dead. If so, wherever she was didn't look much like her idea of Heaven.

The full-figured form which she recognized as her own was lying on one of the floating stretchers the Kindred kept for transporting the sick or wounded. The stretcher itself had been crammed into the back of a space shuttle and there was someone sitting beside her, holding her limp white hand. But it wasn't Sophie or Liv.

Lock, she thought with dismay, watching the large male who was carefully cupping her hand in his. And sitting in the front of the shuttle, at the controls, was his brother, Deep.

Though they were twins, it was easy to tell the brothers apart. Twin Kindred always came in diametrically opposing pairs of light and dark.

The light twin, Lock, had sandy blond hair and eyes the color of melted chocolate. He also had a more optimistic view of life in general than his brother. Of the two of them, Kat found him much easier to tolerate. He was nicer than Deep, for one thing, and she could actually have a conversation with him that didn't turn into an argument. His feelings were easier to deal with, too. Though Lock's desire for her was loud inside her head, it was nothing like the deafening blast of *lust* she felt from his brother whenever he got too close.

Deep, the dark twin, had hair so black it almost had blue highlights and eyes the color of a night without stars. They seemed to burn when they looked at her, making Kat feel naked and vulnerable—feelings she didn't care for a bit. She had enough body issues from having been plus-sized her entire life without an irritating alien male adding to them, thank-you-very-much. The big warrior had rubbed her the wrong way from the moment she'd met him—both literally and figuratively, since he couldn't seem to keep his hands to himself when the three of them did a joining.

Of the brothers, Lock was shorter by about an inch. But since both of them were over six foot six and extremely muscular, it didn't make much difference. They were both huge as far as Kat was concerned—physically, and emotionally.

She should know—she'd had the two of them tramping around inside her head for the better part of a month.

The constant tension of two other people's powerful emotions churning inside her was incredibly tiring and the headache she'd gotten from their joining was beyond painful. Lately she'd been feeling like she couldn't take it anymore. Not that she would ever commit suicide—Kat was a fighter and her grandma hadn't raised her to quit. But the thought of hijacking one of the Kindred shuttles and folding space to put a couple of galaxies between herself and the annoying pair had begun to seem more and more attractive.

The only problem was, she didn't know how to fly a shuttle and she couldn't fold space without the help of the special Kindred technology. Besides, where would she go? Sophie had recently visited Tranq Prime, one of the other worlds the Kindred had initiated a genetic trade with, and she hadn't liked it a bit. She'd come back with stories of roach pudding and clothes that were alive and inclined to play practical jokes that weren't funny. Not to mention extremely snooty natives—at least the ones Sophie had met. No, Kat had no wish to visit Tranq Prime.

She didn't want to go to Rageron either—a savage world filled with blue jungles and vicious predators—which was another Kindred trade planet. And as for Twin Moons—the home planet of Deep and Lock—she *definitely* didn't want to go there. Because that was exactly where the twin warriors wanted to take her. Earlier, on the Kindred Mother ship, she'd caught a few snatches of thought from them that indicated they were homeward bound—and they wanted *her* to come with them.

Not on your life! Kat thought, watching from above as Lock held her hand and Deep steered the shuttle through the blackness of space. *Once they got me there, I'd **never** get away from them. Talk about having the home field advantage!*

But where exactly were they taking her now? As if in answer to her question, Lock spoke at last.

"Are we almost there, Brother? I fear her pulse is weaker than it was."

"Going as fast as I can," Deep growled, throwing an irked glance over his shoulder at his twin. "We just passed through the fold. Home should be just ahead."

"Well, go faster." Lock's voice was urgent. "My touch doesn't seem to be stabilizing her anymore. What if we lose her before we land?"

"We're not going to lose her. We can't—she isn't *ours* to lose." Deep spoke in a lazy drawl but his broad shoulders were bunched with tension as he hunched over the controls.

"I wish you'd stop pretending you don't care." Lock stroked Kat's hand. "Maybe if you'd let her know how you really feel instead of always putting up a wall—"

"There it is." Despite his earlier sarcasm, Deep sounded relieved. He pointed to the viewscreen where a round gold and green orb floated like a Christmas ornament in the blackness of space. "Twin Moons, dead ahead. We're almost home, Brother."

Twin Moons? No! Kat was aghast. *How* had she gotten on board a shuttle with these two and *why* had they been allowed to take her back to their home world? Where were Liv and Sophie when she needed them? The last thing she remembered was talking to her two best friends before everything went black. *And now I wake up dead, on my way to the last place I ever wanted to go? Great, just **great**.*

Kat didn't know how she'd gotten into this mess but *somebody* was going to answer for it. Just as soon as she found out if she was really dead or only sleeping, that was.

As she had the last thought, her vision began to waver.

"Deep—hurry!" she heard Lock say as though from a great distance. "I can't feel her pulse any more!"

"Maximum drive engaged. It's not safe this close to the planetary atmosphere but what the hell," Deep growled. The tiny green and gold orb began to grow in size, filling the viewscreen with a dizzying suddenness.

Kat's strange, otherworldly vision was growing dimmer, but she could still hear what was going on.

A speaker crackled to life and an alien voice spoke loudly in the small cabin. It wasn't speaking English—of that she was sure. But somehow she could understand it anyway. "Unidentified Kindred shuttle, this is Control. Be advised that your approach exceeds upper limits of safe velocity. Please throttle down at once."

"No can do, Control," Deep responded in the same language, his big hands tightening on the steering yoke. "We have a sick female here. Repeat, a sick Earth female dispatched from the Mother ship and she may be..." He cleared his throat and his voice dropped for a moment. "She may be dying."

"Regardless of the circumstances, your vector of approach is too steep. I cannot allow —"

"Did you hear me?" Deep demanded, overriding the voice. "I said she may be *dying*. Requesting clearance to land directly in the Healing Garden."

"Negative!" The voice sounded panicked now. "Clearance denied. Spacecraft are forbidden within consecrated grounds. The gardens are filled with pilgrims at this time of day. To even consider —"

"Then get them out of the Goddess-damned way!" Deep barked. "We're coming in *now*."

The shuttle tilted alarmingly and Kat's vision came back with a jolt. She saw a patch of green rushing toward the viewscreen at alarming speed and had a blurry impression of tiny, Barbie doll-sized figures running to get out of the way. Then her gaze was dragged back to her own still form. Lock was working on her frantically, doing some Kindred version of CPR that looked exceedingly painful as he begged her under his breath to "Live, Kat. Please, *live.*"

"*Almost there,*" roared Deep. "Hold on, Brother. Keep her with us!"

"I'm trying!" Lock's voice sounded close to despair. "But she's so *still.* She's not responding."

"Fucking *make* her respond!" Deep ordered. "And be ready to run the moment we touch down. We're taking her stretcher straight to the center of the garden. Directly to Mother L'rin herself."

"Yes, all right." Lock nodded frantically, still working on her. "Please, lady Kat, if you can just hold on a little bit longer..."

There was a jarring *thump* that rattled everything in the shuttle and Kat saw her body jerk. Then Deep was out of his flight harness and reaching for her. "Go, go go!" he barked, nodding at the opening which had somehow appeared at the back of the shuttle.

"Going!" Lock was still holding her hand as he pushed the floating stretcher toward the pinkish-gold sunlight pouring in through the opening. "Get the other side."

"Got it." Deep grabbed the stretcher with one hand and Kat's arm with the other. "Goddess, she's cold! And her lips are blue."

"I know. I—"

But before she could hear what else Lock was going to say, Kat felt a huge *jolt,* as though she'd been struck by lightning. Suddenly she was no longer hovering above her own still body, but rushing toward it on a collision course.

Wait, she had time to think. *This can't be right. I can't —*

There was a flash of brilliant light and then...

Nothing.

Chapter Two

Mother L'rin was a stern, older woman whom Lock had met only once—years ago when he and Deep had been confirmed with their mentor F'lir as a finder/seeker team. Now she paced in front of Kat's floating stretcher, her bare feet splashing in the golden waters of the holy stream that ran through the center of the Healing Gardens. Mother L'rin practiced holistic healing and drew her powers from nature and the Goddess of All Life. The gardens around them were filled with herbs and plants mixed with flowering bushes and trees, all in shades of pink and gold and pale green.

"I remember you two," she said, nodding at them in her slow, unhurried fashion. "Two more opposite twins I never saw."

"Never mind about us," Deep almost snarled. He was pacing as well, striding up and down the pinkish-gold and green grass that had been allowed to run wild along the edge of the stream. "It's Kat we're here for. She's in trouble."

"Enough trouble for you to land your shuttle in the center of my garden, almost crushing some very devout pilgrims?" Mother L'rin raised one pink-tinged eyebrow at them. She was of the native stock of Twin Moons, with no Kindred blood at all, which explained the way she blended into her own garden.

"Yes," Deep snapped back. "I gave them time to get out of the way."

"Barely." Her voice was mild but her pink and gold eyes flashed. "You must care for her deeply, this *Kat*."

"Not really." Deep shrugged, trying to look unconcerned. "But we *have* been charged with her safety. So—"

"Yes, we care," Lock interrupted his brother. "We care very much. *Both* of us." He squeezed Kat's hand gently and shot Deep a warning look to keep his mouth shut. "Please, Mother L'rin," he continued. "She's already stopped breathing once. I'm not even sure what brought her back, but it could happen again at any time."

Kat was breathing steadily now but Lock knew he would never forget the feeling of relief that had swept over him when he saw her draw that first, shallow gasp as they pushed the stretcher out of the shuttle. He still didn't know why she'd come back to them from the brink of death, only that he was desperate to keep her.

"How did she come to be sick in the first place?" Mother L'rin looked at them. "What manner of illness is this?"

Lock took a deep breath—this was the hard part. "You may have heard that our mentor, F'lir, died a few cycles ago, Mother," he said, inclining his head respectfully. "So Deep and I are without a focus. While aboard the Mother ship, we found ourselves in a desperate position—we needed to use our skills but we had no one to—"

"What my brother is trying to say is that we used Kat here as a focus," Deep interrupted in a bored tone.

Mother L'rin's golden-pink eyes widened. "You used a female as your focus? And an off-worlder at that—one who is alien to us? You had no idea of what a joining with you might do to her mind—to her body!"

"That is true." Lock bowed his head, accepting her rebuke. "We were, as I said, in a desperate position but I know that is no excuse."

"It most certainly is not." Her eyes flashed angrily. "Males must join with males and females with females on the astral plane — anything else is sacrilege. You know that."

Lock nodded. "We know," he murmured in a low voice.

Mother L'rin came to stand at the head of the stretcher and placed her hands on either side of Kat's shining mass of auburn hair. "Very well." She took a deep breath. "What were her symptoms after your joining?"

"Well, the first time —" Deep began.

"The first time?" Mother L'rin's head jerked up and she glared at him. "You used this poor female more than once?"

"We used her twice." Deep lifted his chin arrogantly. "And the second time we cast a net from Earth all the way to Tranq Prime. It doesn't matter that she's female and we're male — Kat's an amazing focus. She has raw natural talent that —"

"That will die with her," Mother L'rin interrupted him.

"What?" Lock's heart fisted in his chest. "Please, Mother L'rin, no!"

"Can't you save her?" Deep's voice was harsh but he was paler than Lock had ever seen him. "Are you saying we brought her to you too late?"

"It was too late the first time you two decided to attempt blasphemy with this innocent child." Mother L'rin stroked Kat's silky hair tenderly. "An elite, too. One blessed by the Mother. Such a pity."

"So she's going to...to die?" Lock heard the break in his voice but he couldn't help it. Gods, to think they'd killed the woman they loved! *Oh Kat, I'm sorry. So very sorry...* From his twin he could feel similar emotions to his own. But Deep's sorrow was shaded with a guilt so intense it was almost despair. *Again,* Lock heard his twin thinking in a rare burst of mental empathy. *I've done it again. Gods…*

"I will do what I can," Mother L'rin said, pulling Lock back from his brother's thoughts. "But I make no promises — you deserve none." She fixed them both with a disapproving glare. "As you know, the bonds between twin males and their female is twofold — there must be a soul bond as well as a physical bond. What you two have done is created an incomplete soul bond with this girl."

"An incomplete bond?" Lock frowned. "I didn't even know such a thing was possible."

"It's very rare. In fact, in all my years of healing I have only seen it happen once before."

"So we're *not* the first male seeker/finders to use a female as our focus," Deep said. "What happened in the other case?"

"The girl died," Mother L'rin said grimly. "I wasn't able to save her."

Lock sucked in a breath and Deep went pale again. "Mother L'rin, please…"

"Her spirit is fractured," she continued. "Which is why she is hovering between this life and the next. You must complete the bond in order to have any hope of healing her."

"How can we bond with an unconscious female?" Deep demanded. "That's called rape and Lock and I don't practice it."

"I didn't say you should complete the *physical* bond." The old woman's eyes flashed again. "I know this is difficult to understand, warrior, as the soul bond and physical bond are usually formed at the same time during bonding sex. But it *is* possible to have one without the other — for a time, anyway."

"What can we do?" Lock said eagerly. "Tell us, Mother, please."

"Her spirit must be tethered to her body. But it must *want* to stay—you have to tempt it with pleasure, lure it back and heal it with your touch."

"Not *my* touch." Deep shook his head. "She's reacted badly to my hands on her since her collapse."

"That's true," Lock said reluctantly, thinking of the way Kat's pulse had spiked after her collapse on the Kindred Mothership. "Her heartbeat increased abnormally and she moaned out loud— something about 'too much' when Deep put his hands on her."

Mother L'rin frowned. "And were you touching her at the same time?"

Lock nodded. "I was. It was my touch that stabilized her the first time. But then, on our way here, it stopped working."

"Because she needs you both. Do not dispute me, warrior," she said when Deep opened his mouth to protest. "I know what I'm talking about. If you want to have any hope of healing this poor girl you and your brother so callously injured, you'll listen and do *exactly* as I say."

"All right." Deep crossed his arms over his broad chest. "What can we do?"

"As I said, you must bind her spirit back to her body. It has to *want* to stay on this plane and be bonded to the two of you."

Lock cleared his throat. "In that case..."

"In that case there's no hope," Deep finished for him. "Kat wants nothing to do with either of us. A fact I've been trying to make clear to you for over a month now, Brother," he said to Lock.

Mother L'rin's pinkish eyebrows shot up. "The three of you had an unwilling joining?"

"Kat only participated in the joining so that we could locate her friend—another Earth girl who was being held captive by the Scourge," Deep said. "She never would have joined with us if need hadn't forced her hand."

"But you said the two joinings you did with her were successful?"

"They exceeded anything we'd ever done with F'lir," Lock admitted. "Deep is right about one thing—the lady Kat is a natural focus. Her ability is unlike anything I've ever seen."

"It's not just her ability—she has an affinity for the two of you, whether she admits it to herself or not." Mother L'rin looked thoughtful. "An affinity I'm sure you felt the first moment you laid eyes on her."

Lock nodded. "That's exactly how I felt."

Deep said nothing.

"So if there is some affinity—some spark between the three of you—there is still hope. You have to bring that spark to the surface. Tempt her spirit back with it and then bind her to you with pleasure."

"If you're talking about sexual pleasure then we're back to where we started," Deep said icily. "Lock and I won't take advantage of an unconscious female."

"Of course she's unconscious," Mother L'rin snapped. "She's is so much pain she can't bear it. One of you must take the pain for her. Only when her agony is gone will she be able to receive your touch. Only then can you heal her spirit."

"I'll do it." Deep stepped forward at once.

"Deep, no," Lock protested. "You don't have to—"

"I want to. And besides, Kat needs your touch to remain stable." Deep frowned. "You stay with her, hold her hand. I'll take care of this."

"Before you accept your lady's pain so easily, you ought to know what it entails," Mother L'rin said quietly. When psychic pain is transmuted to the physical plane, it trebles in strength. And you should know that I sense a great deal of agony coming from this little one." She stroked Kat's hair gently.

"I don't give a damn about that," Deep growled. "Do whatever you have to. Just hurry up and get started."

The wise woman nodded. "Very well." Turning, she motioned to a small clump of golden-pink *flana* bushes on the far side of the stream. "Doby! Bring the whip."

There was a rustling sound in the bushes and then the biggest male Lock had ever seen appeared. He was at least nine feet tall and so heavily muscled it was hard to see how he moved. His mottled pinkish skin proved he was of native Twin Moons stock, the same as Mother L'rin, and he wore only a loincloth made of green and gold leaves to cover himself.

Lock had never seen a native so large—he must be a genetic anomaly. As far as Lock knew, most of the native inhabitants of his home world were tiny. Small but fierce, they mainly lived in the wild lands of the uncharted continent. Mother L'rin was one of the few who had come to live in the more civilized and cultured world the Kindred had created when they first traded with the natives.

As the giant's huge, flat feet splashed in the holy stream the leaves covering his groin fluttered. The flash of leaves caught Lock's eye and he saw that there was nothing but a ragged stump where the huge male's shaft should have been.

Gods! He recoiled at the sight and Mother L'rin saw him and laughed.

"My faithful Doby here is an eunuch. It is the sacrifice he made to come across the golden sea and live here in the Healing Gardens to attend me daily. Such devotion in a male is rare."

"Rare indeed." Lock cleared his throat uncomfortably. "What does he have in the box?" For the huge Doby had produced a lacquered green box from somewhere. He presented it respectfully to the wise woman, holding it in both huge hands.

"A transference device." Mother L'rin opened the box and removed a plain black wooden handle. It was about two feet long and tapered on one end but there was nothing attached to it as far as Lock could see.

Deep must have been thinking the same thing. "I thought you called it a whip?"

"It is. Patience, warrior. All will be made clear." Holding the black handle carefully, Mother L'rin pressed the smooth, round butt of it against Kat's right temple. "Release it, child," she murmured, stroking the shining auburn hair. "Let the pain go. Let it flow. Another has agreed to bear this burden, let me take it from you."

Kat moaned softly and her hand jerked in Lock's. He squeezed her fingers carefully, watching her face for any sign.

Then, slowly, the handle began to change. Wires spouted from it — three long silver wires that seemed to be made of brilliant light. They lengthened and thickened like snakes growing out of the tip of the black handle until they reached to the ground.

Lock watched in amazement as the three tongues of light blazed and sparked like live things at the end of the whip. *Like hungry animals waiting to be fed,* he couldn't help thinking.

"A little more, child. Just a little more," coaxed Mother L'rin. Suddenly the whip's three tongues shivered and bright silver spikes grew from their ends.

Deep's face remained impassive as he stared at the lethal device in the old woman's hand. "And that's a physical manifestation of her pain?"

Mother L'rin nodded. "This is the agony she's been enduring ever since you and your twin used her as a focus. Tell me, Deep, does the sight fill you with dread?"

"Dread? No." His mouth twisted.

Lock spoke for both of them. "What my brother feels — what we both feel — is shame. To think what she went through because of what we did. So much pain..."

"Which is about to be transferred to me," Deep reminded him dryly. "Come on." He jerked his head at Doby and began taking off his green uniform shirt. "I assume you're the lucky one who gets to beat me. I doubt Mother L'rin has much time to practice her whipping technique."

"You're correct in that, warrior. Hands that offer healing must never deal in pain." The old woman nodded at Doby. "Take him to the Stone Throat. Beat him until the whip is nothing more than a handle once more."

"Wait!" Lock put out a hand, fear for his twin squeezing his throat. "How many strokes will that take?"

"As many as it takes," Mother L'rin said calmly.

"That's no answer!" Lock was beginning to be angry. "I know that Deep hasn't been very respectful, Mother L'rin, but to beat him with that...that *thing* is — "

"Fine," Deep finished for him. "Leave off, Brother. It's all right. Think what Kat went through." He nodded at the whip and its spitting, hissing tongues of fiery silver light. "Look at her pain."

"It wasn't your decision alone to let her act as a focus," Lock protested. "I agreed to it as well as you. I should take half the whipping at least."

"Pain cannot be divided between souls, it can only be transferred," Mother L'rin said. "And if the whip isn't used soon, the agony it holds will revert to its original owner."

"In other words, let's get on with it," Deep growled. "Don't worry about me, Brother," he said when Lock opened his mouth to protest. "And don't feel bad—you can tend me afterwards. It's better this way—you're a much better nurse than I am."

"That's true," Lock acknowledged ruefully. "But though you take all the pain, the blame is half mine."

"You can pay me back later." Deep nodded at Kat. "Take care of her," he said roughly.

"I will," Lock promised.

"Go." Mother L'rin handed the hissing, spitting whip to her huge servant. "The Stone Throat. And mind you do the job right. I'll know if you don't—I'll hear it in his screams."

"Yes, Mother." Despite his immense size, the eunuch's voice was as soft and high as a girl's. "All shall be done according to your will."

"See that it is." She waved one wrinkled hand dismissively. "And now, let me see what I can do to keep this sweet child in the land of the living." She stroked Kat's silky red hair and didn't spare another glance at her servant or Deep.

But Lock found he couldn't look away as the massive eunuch led his brother through the tall green and pink grass. Deep's head was held high and he walked casually with no outward sign of fear. And indeed, Lock *felt* no fear coming from him.

Deep was willing, almost eager to take the pain that was about to be inflicted. Because he felt that he deserved it. Every lick of the whip, every drop of blood, every ounce of pain. All earned. All deserved.

He blames himself, Lock thought as his twin's broad, bare back disappeared in the taller grass at the edge of the Healing Garden. *And not just for Kat. Oh Brother, it wasn't your fault—when will you ever believe that?*

But he knew the answer to that.

Never.

Chapter Three

Lauren Jakes walked quickly along the broad sidewalk that led around the edge of Saint Armand's Square. Later on, around lunchtime, the entire expanse of white concrete would be filled with the idle rich—tourists mostly, who had come to see Sarasota, one of the richest small cities in the US. The beaches with their sugar fine sand and tropical blue waters were lovely any time of the year and if the rich got bored with baking their oiled bodies, they could always come here.

The Square was actually many interconnecting squares, all lined with specialty shops and expensive, chic little eateries. Marble statues of Greek gods and goddesses stood like sentries on the well trimmed verge, as pale as ghosts in the dim early morning light. Lauren's shop, The Sweet Spot, was located between the Florida Olive Oil Company which specialized in flavored oils and aged balsamic vinegars and A Little is a Lot, a clothing store that sold only overpriced and undersized bathing suits.

Both shops were dark and quiet as Lauren fumbled for her keys. Neither one would really pick up until the lunch crowd arrived, hours from now. But while her neighbors could afford to sleep in, Lauren couldn't. The Sweet Spot was a specialty cupcake store and she had to get the day's inventory started or she would have nothing to sell. "Everything from scratch, everything fresh, every day," was her motto.

"Should've decided to sell overpriced thongs and banana hammocks to rich old men and their trophy wives instead of baked goods," she muttered to herself as she finally found the right key. "Then I could still be home in bed."

But getting up early was a small price to pay to do what she loved, she reminded herself. She'd always enjoyed baking—her vanilla bean and passion fruit surprise cupcakes had won a national bake-off by the time she was twelve. Her mom had encouraged her to go to college and Lauren had, as a business major. Somehow, though, she wound up baking muffins and brownies for study sessions with her friends more than she actually ended up studying. Her grades weren't great but her cupcakes were.

At last her mother had bowed to the inevitable. She'd helped Lauren finance the shop and given her a place to live in one of the condos she owned, just blocks from the Square. Lauren had only been open a few months but so far The Sweet Spot seemed to be a moderate success. Of course, she'd have to be much more than moderately successful in order to pay back the loan. But her mom didn't seem worried. *"Take your time, my darling,"* she always said. *"Enjoy your life. I just want you to be happy."*

Thinking of her mom always gave Lauren a warm feeling inside. Family was very important to Abigail Jakes—maybe because she'd become estranged from her own family back when she'd become pregnant with Lauren. She didn't talk about it much but Lauren had gotten the idea that her loved ones had hurt her deeply—which made her mom that much more sensitive toward her own daughter. They'd always had a wonderful relationship— even back when Lauren was a teenager. And now as an adult, they were more friends than mother and daughter.

"Although I still want my mom when things don't go right," Lauren muttered, making sure the door was locked behind her. She wished she had her mom with her right now—she would put her to work. Her assistant, Jennie, had quit the day before which meant she had to man the whole shop herself until Lorenzo came in.

Thinking of Lorenzo with his sleek blond hair and tan good looks made her sigh. He was much better at looking good behind the counter than he was at baking. In a moment of weakness, Lauren had let him kiss her and now he thought he owned the place. She'd been putting off his advances ever since and had been planning to replace him before Jennie quit. Now it looked like she was stuck with him for awhile. Still, he *was* good at selling cupcakes. Especially to rich, older women who liked a little eye candy to go with their culinary confections.

Lauren went through the shop, flipping on lights on her way to the bathroom. To hell with the electricity bill—it was creepy being in a dark building all alone. And besides, for the past few days she'd had the feeling that someone was watching her. She knew it was crazy and completely impossible but she kept finding herself looking over her shoulder. Feeling like a pair of invisible eyes was watching her every move.

"Stop being stupid," she muttered to herself as she tucked her long, silky black hair into a hairnet and checked her reflection. The girl in the mirror had smooth mocha skin and large eyes the color of fine whiskey. A tip-tilted nose made her cute rather than exotic, despite the eyes, but her full lips pushed cute to beautiful when she smiled—or so Lorenzo said when he was feeling poetic.

God, what was wrong with her? Why did she always fall for jerks and players? Just once Lauren wished she could meet someone genuine. Someone who was exactly what they seemed to be. But with her work schedule now and trying to keep the shop open seven days a week, she wasn't going to have time to meet anyone but customers.

"Not that I have time for a love life even if I *did* meet someone," Lauren muttered to herself. "As if —"

The words died on her lips. For a moment she could have sworn she saw a pair of eyes behind her in the mirror. *Red* eyes.

She whirled around, her heart pounding, to see…nothing.

"Of course it's nothing. There's no one here but me." The sound of her own voice made her jump and Lauren put a hand to her chest to still her beating heart. It was time to stop being silly and get down to business. Today she had a brand new recipe she wanted to try out — a strawberry hazelnut with cream cheese frosting. She'd tried a small batch in the kitchen in her condo and they had come out nicely but —

Suddenly there was a popping, humming sound like electricity and the air around her seemed to be full of lightning. Every hair on her head stood on end and her nerves twanged like plucked strings. *Danger — you're in danger!* an inner voice shouted. The voice of instinct — the same primitive voice that must have warned the cavemen when a fire or flood was on the way.

Lauren wanted to run — *tried* to run — but everything happened too quickly. The crackling electrical charge seemed to close around her, like a vast hand, and suddenly she felt herself dissolving. Looking in the mirror she could almost see it happening in slow motion — her body had been broken into a million tiny particles that were all vibrating against each other in deadly harmony. Her clothes, however, remained unaffected. In fact, they fell away from her, landing in a heap on the floor.

No! No, what's happening?

There was no answer but suddenly she saw the eyes in the mirror again. Red eyes — blood red and laughing at her pain, her fear. She could almost *feel* the evil in that crimson gaze—the intent to cause harm—the desire to wound and mutilate and kill.

Before she could think anything else, the tiny white tiled bathroom of The Sweet Spot disappeared and she felt herself flying through the air in pieces. It was the most bizarre sensation she had ever felt in her life—as though someone had put her entire body through a cheese grater and shot the results into the air at supersonic speed.

I'm dying. This is dying, right?

Again, no answer. But suddenly she felt herself reforming—all the tiny particles finding their places and sticking together again. *Oh, thank God!* She felt her arms and legs frantically, making sure she was all in once piece. She was naked but she was whole and at least nothing seemed to be missing.

"Here ssshe isss at last. Sssee, my ssson, ssshe bears the mark. The mark the prophesy ssspoke of."

A long, skeletal finger suddenly appeared in front of her and pointed between her breasts. Lauren looked down to her small, pale birthmark reflexively—it was shaped like a star and stood out against her creamy brown skin. She'd always had it and never even thought about it anymore, though it looked strange when she wore a bikini.

A feeling of dread filled her as she looked up, up, up the long arm clothed in billowing cobwebs and into the burning red eyes she'd seen in the mirror.

"Yesss," hissed a voice Lauren knew she'd been hearing in her dreams for the past few weeks. "Yesss, ssshe isss the one. At last I have her. *Ssshe isss mine.*"

Chapter Four

Kat was flying again but this time she wasn't looking down at herself. Instead she was hovering inside a narrow stone tunnel. There was a faint light at one end that illuminated the pinkish brown stones and she could hear footsteps coming, echoing down the long enclosed corridor. *Who's coming? Will they see me?*

Looking down, she realized she couldn't see herself. She was silent and invisible again, just as she had been before. *Maybe I really am dead and this is my funeral. But why would they bury me in a cave?* For some reason the thought held no fear, only fascination. Then the echoing footsteps grew louder. Kat pushed her morbid musings aside when she saw who was coming down the tunnel.

A massive male — she couldn't really call him a man because there was nothing human about him — was leading the way. He had pinkish mottled skin and he was wearing a loincloth of large, flat leaves. In his hand he carried a fiery silver whip that snapped and crackled as though it was made of lightning.

What the hell? The question was driven out of her head when she saw someone familiar following the huge male. Deep was shirtless, his muscular chest gleaming in the light cast by the strange whip. Kat could see the silver light reflected in the black pools of his eyes too, which were otherwise completely impassive.

"So this is the Stone Throat, eh?" he said to the giant who only grunted noncommittally. "I've heard of this place. Never thought I'd see it in person. Not that there's much to see."

The enormous male didn't even grunt this time. He just passed through the stone hallway, ducking his head to avoid hitting the ceiling where Kat was still hovering in her invisible form.

For some reason, she felt a stab of fear. *What's going on? What are they going to do?* Without making a conscious decision to do it, she found herself gliding noiselessly after them down the stone corridor until they came to a thick green wooden door. Deep's guide grasped the tarnished silver ring in its center and pulled it open easily though it looked immensely heavy to Kat.

The door swung to one side revealing a vast, round room made of the same brownish-pink stone as the corridor. The ceiling curved up but instead of forming a perfect arch, it elongated into a tall stone chimney far above. From that small opening, a perfectly round spot of sunlight streamed down to rest on the floor at the exact center of the room. It illuminated a rough obelisk of white stone streaked with reddish-brown mineral deposits.

The obelisk was at least ten feet tall and it pointed up toward the chimney like a jagged, accusing finger. Kat saw that someone had affixed two thick, rusty rings in its center. A feeling of cold dread filled her when she saw the thick chain running through the rings. What went on in this room? Why would anyone need to be chained to the strange white obelisk? She was horribly afraid but she didn't want to let herself acknowledge it.

"Will you be chained or will you stand?" The huge male's voice was high and almost effeminate but it echoed eerily in the vast chamber.

"I'll stand." Deep went to the obelisk without hesitation. Facing it, he gripped one of the rusty rings in each hand. His broad, muscular back presented the perfect target. "I'm ready."

Ready for what? Oh dear God, please no! Kat didn't particularly like Deep — in fact, she thought he was kind of a jerk. He made her more uncomfortable than anyone else she'd ever met in her life. But no one deserved to be whipped with that hissing, crackling silver whip. There were freaking *spikes* on the end of it, for God's sake. Was it some kind of punishment Deep was about to be subjected to? But what had he done? And who had decided he had to be punished?

"Ready yourself," the other male advised, raising the whip.

"I *said* I was ready." Deep's voice held not a trace of fear — only irritation.

How can he not be afraid? What's wrong with him?

Kat watched in horror as the massive arm rose and the whip cracked, lashing around Deep's ribs with a hungry hiss. Deep made a similar sound himself — a low hiss of pain — as the barbed silver tongues bit into his flesh, but no other noise escaped him.

The giant yanked the whip back, splattering crimson droplets against the white obelisk. Suddenly Kat understood that the brownish red streaks on its rough surface weren't mineral deposits. *Blood, my God, it's blood! He's bleeding! Stop it — stop!*

But the whip rose again, ready for another blow. "Scream," the huge torturer advised. "Release your pain into the Throat." He nodded at the stone chimney above. "It will make the agony less."

"Don't want it to be less," Deep growled. "Just get on with it, damn you."

"As you wish." The whip cracked again, biting and tearing the smooth, tan skin of Deep's back, shredding it to bloody ribbons. He barely flinched.

No! Nooo! Kat tried to shriek but no sound came out. Deep didn't cry out either. He stood at the obelisk, grasping the rusty rings in a white-knuckled grip, his jaw clenched and his eyes shut tight. Clearly he was enduring unspeakable agony and just as clearly he was determined not to make a sound.

Kat felt like she was going crazy. Rushing at the giant, she tried to grab his hand and keep the whip from falling again. But she was helpless to stop him—helpless to even *touch* him. It was as though she was trapped in a bad dream, one which she couldn't wake up from.

Please, she begged silently as invisible tears fell down her cheeks. *Please, please don't. Please stop hurting him…*

But nothing she said or did made any difference. The whipping went on and on…and on.

* * * * *

"She's crying." Lock looked down at Kat's still-sleeping face in alarm. "Look, tears are running down her cheeks." He cupped her jaw and brushed them tenderly away with the pad of his thumb.

"So she is." Mother L'rin didn't sound unduly worried.

"But what does it mean?" Lock looked at her anxiously. "What's happening to her?"

"A bad dream, perhaps. I'm more concerned with what's happening with that brother of yours." Her wrinkled face creased in a frown. "I haven't heard a single scream."

"That's because Deep won't scream. He won't give in to the pain that way." Lock wiped Kat's other cheek gently. "He's too damn stubborn." He closed his eyes. "I can feel his pain but he won't share it with me—he's closed tight, turned inward."

Mother L'rin shrugged her bowed shoulders. "His choice. If he'd release the pain into the Stone Throat it would dissipate much more quickly."

"I tell you, he won't scream. He'd probably rather die."

"He won't die." The old woman spoke with certainty. "That would put your life in danger as well and I wouldn't do that, Lock. But he may well wish he was dead by the time the whipping is over." She looked at him. "Are you wishing you could take his place?"

"Yes." Lock swiped away tears of his own, blotting them angrily on his deep green uniform sleeve. "He doesn't deserve this. He thinks he does, but he doesn't. I know he's a bastard a lot of them time but he's my brother and I love him."

"Of course you do." Mother L'rin's voice was suddenly softer and she laid one wrinkled old hand on Lock's arm. "Never fear, you'll both come out of this alive." She looked grim. "I just wish I could promise the same for your lady Kat here."

"Please." Lock felt as though his heart was breaking. "Can't we save her? Won't it be easier for her now that Deep has taken her pain?"

"She'll still be weak and even if you managed to complete the soul bond with her the pain may return in time." Mother L'rin frowned. "You'll need to take her someplace quiet and let her rest for a little while before you attempt that."

"Of course. Deep will be in no shape for any kind of bonding activity for awhile anyway." Closing his eyes again, Lock could feel the echoes of his twin's agony. But Deep was still shut tight, conserving every ounce of his strength to bear the pain.

"His wounds will heal fast," Mother L'rin predicted. "Lashes inflicted with psychic pain always do and Twin Kindred are quick healers anyway. The strokes hurt three times as much as physical wounds but they mend three times as fast as well. When Deep's back is mostly healed, then you may attempt to finish your soul bond with the lady Kat."

"And after we do? What then?"

"Bring Kat back and let me examine her." Mother L'rin put a withered hand on Kat's shoulder. "I'll tell you what to do then if she survives."

She has to survive. Please, Mother of All Life, let her survive, Lock prayed fervently. *Do not let my brother's sacrifice be in vain. Do not let the pain he feels count for nothing.*

Kat was crying again. Tenderly, he wiped the tears from his cheeks, wishing he could ease her pain, wishing he could share Deep's agony. But he was shut out from both of them—unable to help either of the people he loved.

Lock had never felt more alone.

Chapter Five

The human female was troublesome.

It annoyed Xairn the way she cried when he came near her. Later, when he offered her no harm, she began to talk to him and that was even worse.

"Please," she whispered the third time he brought her food and water. "Please, I'm so cold. It's freezing in here and I don't have any clothes." She was huddled in a corner of the bare nine by nine metal cell she was being kept in. Her knees were drawn up to her chin and she had her arms wrapped around her legs but even so her smooth, light brown skin was covered in chill bumps.

"It is the AllFather's wish to keep you as you are," Xairn said stonily. "I only obey his orders."

"But you're not like him." She leaned forward, her eyes wide.

At least they aren't green. Instead they were a brown so light it was almost golden. Amber, maybe. Xairn shook his head. "You're wrong. I am exactly like him. I am his son."

"That doesn't matter. You may have his...his eyes..." She swallowed nervously. "But you don't *feel* like him."

"I haven't laid a hand on you. Nor will I."

"I didn't mean *feel* in a physical sense." She picked up one of the nutra-wafers he'd pushed over to her and began to nibble it. "I meant, whenever he's near me I sense this...this *evil*. Hatred, malevolence—call it whatever you want, but he carries it with him like a cloud. With you..." She shrugged and took another nibble. "I don't feel that."

Xairn thought of telling her she would soon feel a great deal more. The AllFather was only abstaining from taking her until he reached his peak, when his seed would be most potent. It was only a matter of days—weeks at the most—before this human female became the new mother of the Scourge race.

She would probably lose her mind in the process.

It doesn't matter. Nothing matters.

"I am his son," Xairn repeated, not having anything else to say. "I obey his commands and do his bidding."

"Not always," she said softly. "Yesterday I told you I was hungry. Today you brought me three of these cardboard pop tart things instead of just one."

Xairn frowned. "I have to keep you in good physical condition for the AllFather. I have been charged with your wellbeing."

"Still, I want to thank you." She looked at him earnestly. "Maybe someday I can return the favor."

"You will never be in a position to do me any favors." Xairn turned to go.

"Please..." Her voice tugged at him for some reason and he looked over his shoulder.

"What is it? I have other duties besides you to attend to."

"I'm cold," she repeated. "If you could just bring me some clothes. Or even a blanket."

"Your constant complaints are annoying." Xairn reached under his chin and unfastened the black cloak he always wore. It *was* cold on the Fathership—not that any of the vat grown soldiers noticed. Finding a new cloak would be difficult, if not impossible—he'd bought this one by chance from a clothier on a fringe colony. Still, he told himself, being a little chilly was better than listening to her whining. "Here," he said and tossed it to her.

"Thank you." She reached up to catch it and he caught a glimpse of her full breasts and berry brown nipples, tight with cold. The sight bothered him for some reason but he didn't have to see it for long. She huddled quickly beneath his cloak, pulling it tight around her. "I really mean it, thank you so much," she said.

"Keep your thanks," Xairn said coldly. "I'll get the cloak back when the AllFather is through with you."

She drew in a sharp breath and her large amber eyes filled with fear. Xairn didn't wait to hear if she had anything else to say. He slammed the heavy plasti-steel door and keyed in the lock code.

The girl was nothing to him. Nothing.

But as he walked down the bare metal corridor, he couldn't help thinking that amber was almost as troubling a color as green.

Chapter Six

Kat was floating.

Not in the disembodied sense. This time she could feel her body, her limbs heavy with unspeakable exhaustion, her skin tender to touch. She wasn't fully aware of her surroundings but one thing was clear—someone was taking care of her.

Gentle hands lifted her into warm water and strong arms held her securely while someone else washed her hair. The sensations were so soothing she wanted to drift away to sleep. *But I* ***am*** *asleep, aren't I? If not, why can't I wake up?*

The same hands dried her off and put a straw between her lips. Kat sucked reflexively and a delicious, fruity flavor that seemed to be a cross between watermelon, strawberry, and some other fruit she couldn't name filled her mouth.

"That's right, my lady," a deep, somehow familiar voice murmured. "Drink deeply. Nourish yourself. It's almost time to attempt the bond."

What bond? Kat wanted to ask, but she was stuck, held in the same, strange limbo she sensed she'd been in for days. Was it a coma? They said that people in comas retained some consciousness and heard everything that was said to them. But would she be able to drink from a straw if she was truly unconscious? Kat didn't think so. It was all very confusing.

She finished the drink and someone fluffed a pillow behind her head and drew a light blanket over her naked body. "Sleep now," the familiar voice murmured. "I must tend to my brother. He's almost healed so maybe next time…"

But he didn't finish what he was saying.

"Next time what?" Kat wanted to demand. But she felt so warm and comfortable she couldn't be bothered to form the words. Instead she slid into darkness and let herself dream.

* * * * *

"You're healing well." Lock eyed the broad expanse of his twin's back critically. "Of course, there will be scars. Extensive scars, I'm afraid."

Deep, who was sitting at the edge of the large bed they shared, grunted noncommittally. "All warriors have scars."

"Most get them in battle, though." Gently, Lock smoothed some of the healing lotion Mother L'rin had given them over his brother's wounds. Most of them were nothing but pinkish-white lines now, criss-crossing the tan expanse of Deep's back. The wise woman had been right—he was healing remarkably quickly. His body, anyway. Lock feared that he would carry the memory of the beating with him forever. Not that he would admit to caring about such a thing—or anything for that matter. "Do you want to help me attend Kat again tonight?" he asked, changing the subject.

Deep frowned. "She's not going to be happy when she finds out we've been bathing her while she's unconscious, you know."

"We drape towels over her to preserve her modesty," Lock protested. "Besides, we're only acting on Mother L'rin's orders. She said Kat needed to spend plenty of time in the bathing pool—warm water is healing."

"Kat won't see it like that," Deep predicted sourly. "She'll think it's a violation. And she'll think the same thing about completing the soul bond."

"We *have* to complete the bond. Nothing else will heal her fractured spirit."

"Maybe she doesn't want to be healed. Maybe she'd rather be dead than bonded to the two of us," Deep snapped. "Did you ever think about that?"

"I know what you're thinking but Kat isn't like that. She isn't like *her*," Lock said in a low voice.

"So you say." Deep frowned moodily.

"We swore to Sophia and Olivia that we would do everything in our power to protect and heal Kat," Lock reminded his brother.

"We're doing a wonderful job so far, aren't we?" Deep snarled. "We're the reason she's sick in the first place. We should *never* have used her as a focus. Never let ourselves feel…" He shook his head.

"It's too late for those regrets now," Lock said softly, dabbing more lotion on his brother's back. He could feel how tense Deep was—could see it in the way his broad shoulders bunched with misery. The emotion echoed inside his heart, making him ache for his twin. "All we can do is try to heal her, to undo the damage we've done."

"By completing a soul bond with a female who never wants to take the next step and make the physical bond with us as well? What good will it do *any* of us to have half a bond?" Deep demanded.

"It will heal the lady Kat," Lock said firmly, trying to ignore his own fears. "That's all that matters right now."

Deep sighed and his broad shoulders slumped. "Have it your way, Brother. But don't be surprised if she wants nothing to do with you — with either one of us — when this is over."

* * * * *

Four, large warm hands on her body woke her up. They weren't touching her anywhere inappropriate — shoulders, hips, thighs — but they were there, on her bare skin. *Bare skin...oh my God — I'm naked!* And so were the large, male bodies bracketing her own. She could feel their muscular warmth against her back and breasts, surrounding her, invading her, owning her. The familiar current of sexual electricity was running through her body — the feeling she always got when Deep and Lock were touching her bare skin at the same time. When the three of them were...

Kat's eyes flew open and she found herself looking into Lock's melted chocolate gaze.

"Welcome back to the land of the living, my lady," he murmured with a smile. "We're very glad to have you back."

"Lock's right — you gave us quite a scare," Deep's voice rumbled from behind her. "We didn't think you would make it, there for awhile."

"I almost died," Kat blurted, the memory momentarily overcoming her shock at finding herself naked between them. "I was floating above my own body, looking down. I saw you talking about me. And then..." She frowned. "I had another dream. It was terrible but — "

"But it's over now," Lock finished for her, soothingly. "You're getting better, Kat, but you're not out of danger yet."

"In my dream you were taking me to Twin Moons. Where am I?" she demanded.

"I would think that would be obvious," Deep growled in her ear. "You're in our bed, little Kat. And that's where you're going to stay until you're all better."

"What are you talking about?" She struggled to get up but they held her down, gently but firmly.

"Don't be upset," Lock pleaded. "We won't hurt you, my lady. You must know that by now."

"Look, I don't know what you two think you're doing, but I'm not interested in any more joinings. Especially after the way I felt after our last one. I had a headache so bad I felt like my skull was going to split in two."

"We fully comprehend your pain," Lock said.

"Easy for you to say," Kat muttered. "You can talk about it all you want but—"

"It's *not* just talk." Deep's voice was unexpectedly somber. "Lock and I know what we put you through. And we can't tell you how much we regret it."

Kat sighed. "All right—it's not like it's all your fault. After all, *I* was the one who asked for that last joining in order to find Sophie. I guess you could say I got what was coming to me."

"No." Lock shook his head. "We were dabbling in an area we didn't fully understand. We never should have used you as a focus in the first place."

"And we have no interest in doing it again now," Deep continued. "What we're trying to do is heal you."

"Heal me? You're trying to heal me by rubbing your...by rubbing against me?" Kat didn't even try to keep the skepticism out of her voice. "Yeah, right."

"Truly, my lady." Lock's brown eyes were earnest. "Mother L'rin—"

"Who?"

"The healer we brought you to our home planet to see," Deep supplied. "She's an expert in the seeker/finder/focus relationship as well as a master of her craft."

"Okay, let me get this straight," Kat said. "I was at death's door so you two brought me home to the wise old healer lady to be cured. And her 'prescription' was for us to all get naked together in bed?" She twisted around to frown at Deep. "Can you see why I'm not buying this? I mean come, on guys—give me a break!"

"It's true." Deep glared at her, his coal black eyes burning. "Your spirit has been fractured by the stress of acting as our focus. Until we bind it securely back to your body, you're in danger of dying."

"Deep is right," Lock said softly. "Your spirit could become untethered again at any time."

"Well that's a risk I guess I'll have to take," Kat snapped. "I'll let you know if I see a bright tunnel and start hearing the voices of dead relatives telling me to 'go into the light.' Until then, you two can keep your hands and your, uh, other body parts to yourselves."

She started to sit up and this time, as if by mutual consent, they let her. But the moment she was upright, dizziness swept over her, making the world spin and the room dance. She had a vague impression of a large, masculine space lit by soft, glowing lights in the corners. Then she had to put her head in her hands and shut her eyes to keep from getting sick.

"My lady? Are you all right?" Lock's voice was anxious.

"Fine. I'm just...fine," Kat managed to say weakly. But she wasn't fooling anyone—not even herself.

"Little liar," Deep growled. "Lie back down and let us take care of you."

"But I don't want…I can't…" Kat shook her head and wished she hadn't. It made the dizziness worse.

"Come back between us," Lock urged. "Please, Kat, you know we only want what's best for you."

Kat struggled to remain upright a little longer. But when she lifted her head again, the spinning sensation was even worse. "Oh God, I can't take this!"

"Satisfied?" Deep asked. "The only way to make it better is to let us heal you. So stop acting stupid and *let us.*"

"I'm *not* stupid," Kat snapped angrily, even as she allowed Lock to guide her back down to the bed. "That's the main reason I object to letting you two *grope* me as a form of holistic healing."

"What exactly do you think we're trying to do here?" Deep demanded. "You think we want to *fuck* you?"

His rough words made Kat's stomach clench. "I sure as hell hope not for your sake," she said evenly. "You try it and I'll knee both of you so hard you'll be wearing your balls for bowties."

"Bravely spoken, little Kat." Deep had the nerve to sound amused. "But that isn't what this is about at all. We just need to heal you."

"And how…how exactly do you expect to do that?" Kat asked, trying to keep her voice from trembling.

"We have to use pleasure to bind your spirit back to your body." Lock's voice was soothing.

"How much pleasure? What…what exactly are you going to do?" Kat whispered.

"Just touch you." Lock cupped her cheek and looked earnestly into her eyes. "My lady...Kat...please believe me when I say we would never try to take advantage of you. What we're doing here is necessary, I swear it."

Kat opened her mouth to respond but suddenly she remembered something Sophie had told her. After her crash in the mountains with Sylvan, she'd woken up to find him licking her breast. She'd been sure he was up to no good, but it had turned out that he was actually healing her. Could it be that Lock and Deep really *were* on the level—that they were only doing what they had to in order to make her whole again? It seemed crazy but then, a lot of things associated with the Kindred did, she reminded herself.

Blowing out a breath, she nodded reluctantly. "All right. But *no* sex. Especially not bonding sex—whatever that entails with you guys."

"Don't worry." Deep's voice sounded bitter. "Lock and I would never want to tie an unwilling bride to us. The results could be...tragic."

Kat twisted to look at him again. "What the hell is that supposed to mean?"

"Never mind," Lock said quickly. "Deep just means that we would never *physically* bond you to us against your will. So...shall we begin?"

"I guess if we have to." Kat could feel her heart thumping against her ribs. God, how did she keep getting into this kind of situation and how could she avoid it in the future?

"We do," Deep said grimly. "But I don't see how we're going to give you enough pleasure to heal your spirit when you're so unhappy about it."

"Do you really find our hands on you so distasteful?" Lock's eyes were wistful.

"No." Kat closed her eyes briefly. "No, you…you know I don't."

"Then try to relax," he urged. "Please, my lady. Here…" Kat had been lying on her side facing Lock, with Deep behind her. Now Lock turned her gently but firmly until she was lying on her back with both of them leaning over her.

"This is worse," Kat, objected, trying to cover her bare breasts and sex with her hands. "I feel so…so *exposed.*"

"Are you ashamed to let us look at you?" Deep's voice was surprisingly gentle. "You shouldn't be, little Kat. I have never seen such beauty in my life."

"But I'm…" So many words hovered on her lips — *fat, chubby, chunky* — insults from a lifetime of being plus sized in a world where skinny women were the ideal. Living as a size eighteen in a society that preferred a size eight hadn't been easy. "Not thin," she finished at last.

"We know." Lock's voice held only admiration. "You're an elite. The most beautiful one I've ever seen."

That's right — they like big girls here. It was still a novel concept to Kat, who was used to being defensive about her ample curves. "All right," she said at last. "But only because the lights in here are pretty dim. I don't want you to think I'll be parading around in my birthday suit just because you two are into plus-sized women."

"Of course," Lock assured her. "We would never want you to do anything that made you uncomfortable."

Slowly, her heart beating so hard she could almost hear it drumming in her ears, she let her hands drift to her sides. Taking a deep breath, she closed her eyes and tried to relax.

✳ ✳ ✳ ✳ ✳

Deep couldn't stop looking at her. Kat's long, silky auburn hair glistened in the soft light of the glows and her full, creamy breasts rose and fell with each breath she took. They were tipped with deep pink nipples that were tight and erect, just begging to be sucked. And how he longed to do just that—to taste her. The last time they had been together it had been Lock that she allowed to suck her sweet, ripe peaks. Deep had cupped them in his hands but he still hadn't had the pleasure of teasing her nipples with his mouth.

Looking lower, he saw that her voluptuous body was curved in all the right places, her hips and thighs deliciously ample. The small triangle of dark red curls that guarded her sex made his mouth water. He longed to press his face against her there and breathe her in, to inhale the warm, secret scent of her pussy until she spread her legs for him and let him in. He wanted to taste her—to lap her juices from the source and feel her small, delicate hands tugging his hair as she cried his name and begged for more. Just the thought of it made his cock so hard it ached.

Shouldn't be thinking this way. Shouldn't let her affect you so much. But he couldn't help it—she was absolutely gorgeous. Adding to her appeal was the obvious fact that she had no idea how beautiful and desirable she was. Though how an elite could have no idea of her own devastating attraction, he didn't know.

"What are you going to do to me?" Kat murmured and he realized that he and Lock had both been staring too long, drinking in her beauty.

"Touch you," he said, trying to soften his voice which kept coming out too rough. "Bring you pleasure…Make you come."

Her eyes flew open. "You…you have to do that?"

"An orgasm is the fastest way to bind your spirit back to your body." Lock spoke quietly, obviously trying to relax her. "But we'll be gentle, my lady—you know we will."

"But…" Her eyes were wide with fear and uncertainly. "What exactly…?"

"To start with, this." Leaning closer, Deep kissed the side of her neck gently. Her skin was as smooth as silk against his lips and he could feel her pulse pounding out of control just under the surface. Gods, she smelled good! He deepened the kiss, lapping hungrily at her neck.

Kat drew in a ragged breath and he knew he was affecting her. Looking up briefly, he caught his brother's eyes and nodded.

Lock knew what to do. Sliding down, he pressed his mouth to the other side of Kat's neck and began to kiss and lick gently while Deep continued to do the same.

"Oh…" The soft sound fell out of her and she trembled between them. "That feels so *good.*"

"It's about to feel better," Deep assured her, looking up. Cupping her right breast, he thumbed the tight bud of her nipple. Her soft gasp of pleasure and surprise went straight to his cock, making it feel like a bar of steel trapped between his thighs. "Gods, I want you, Kat," he growled, capturing her eyes with his own, not letting her look away. "Want to feel you under me while Lock and I fill you at the same time."

"Deep…" Lock put a restraining hand on his arm. "Don't frighten her."

"I'm not frightened." Kat lifted her chin, her blue eyes snapping in the dim light. "But I'm not willing to go that far, either."

And there's the problem. We're forming a bond with a female who doesn't want to be bonded to us. And we haven't even told her what we're doing—not really. There's going to be hell to pay when she finds out. Deep felt a wave of frustration. "We're aware that you don't want to go too far, little Kat," he growled. "But know this—you *will* spread your legs for us tonight, even if it isn't to get fucked."

* * * * *

Kat's breath caught in her throat at his blunt words. "I don't see why I should…should have to do that," she said, wishing her voice didn't tremble so much.

"Because unless you can come from having your nipples sucked, Lock and I need access to your pussy," Deep said roughly. "Remember how you didn't want to let me open you and stroke your sweet little cunt the last time we were together? Well this time you'll have to."

"It's all right, my lady," Lock murmured, leaning down to kiss her cheek. "We'll go very slowly if you like. And penetration might not be necessary. It might just be enough for us to stroke or kiss you between your thighs"

"Kiss?" Kat's heart skipped a beat. "But I thought…thought that you just wanted to touch me."

"We want to do whatever we can to bring you the most pleasure." Lock cupped her left breast and laid a soft, hot kiss on her nipple. "See, that's not so bad, is it?"

"Not *there*, it's not," Kat said. "But I just don't know…"

"You don't have to know," Deep interrupted. "All you have to do is spread your legs for us and let us touch you and taste you."

"We can try touching first," Lock assured her. "If the idea of being tasted makes you uncomfortable. Here." His hand slid down her trembling abdomen to cup her mound of curls gently. "Like this. Does that feel all right?"

"I suppose," Kat admitted doubtfully.

"Spread her open." There was a hungry look in Deep's eyes as he watched his brother's hand between her legs. "Slip your fingers inside her soft little pussy and see how wet she is."

"May I?" Lock looked at her uncertainly. "Or would you prefer that we suck your nipples some more first?"

"I'll take care of her nipples." Suiting actions to words, Deep leaned over and sucked her right peak deeply into his hot mouth, taking as much of her breast as he could at once.

Kat couldn't help herself, she moaned and arched her back, responding to the fierce suction and the burning desire she could feel inside him. God, he wanted her so badly…

Oh my God, their emotions—I'm beginning to feel them again! Suddenly she realized that she hadn't been filled with their feelings when she first woke up. But now…

"Wait!" she gasped, trying to push them away. "Wait, I can…can feel you again."

Deep looked up, his full lips red from sucking. "Of course you can. We're touching you. Tasting you."

"That's not what I meant," Kat protested. "Your emotions—I can feel them inside me again."

"That's a good sign," Lock told her. "It means your spirit is being bound back to your body. You're becoming part of the physical plane again."

"But…but I don't like it." Kat frowned. "It's so invasive. So uncomfortable."

"You think it's comfortable for *us* to know how *you* feel?" Deep growled. "How frightened you are of bonding with us? Because it's damn sure *not*. I can tell you that."

"At least you're used to it," Kat pointed out, refusing to rise to the bait about her being frightened. "You feel each other's emotions all the time, don't you?"

"When we're not blocking each other out." Lock sighed. "I'm sorry it's so uncomfortable for you to feel us, my lady, but it really is unavoidable. After this is over, I swear we'll go back to Mother L'rin and see if we can find a way for you to put a barrier up between your mind and ours. If that's what you really want."

"Is that even possible?" Kat demanded. "You're not just saying that so you can...keep going?"

"Mind privacy comes naturally to twins," Lock told her. "But it can be taught, too—at least among my people. I don't know about yours."

"Well..." Kat said hesitantly. She was throbbing all over, from the tips of her breasts to the sensitive vee between her legs which made it damned hard to think straight. "I guess so..."

"Then we'd better get on with it," Deep finished for her. "As I was saying, Lock and I need to know how wet you are."

"I...I don't..."

Deep leaned closer, his eyes blazing into hers. "Spread your legs for us, little Kat. Open your pussy and let us see if you're slippery with honey."

Kat had no defenses left—she was being swamped in a sea of lust and only a third of it was her own. Feeling like she was drowning, she spread her legs and allowed them both to look at her.

"Gorgeous," Lock murmured, his admiration radiating against her like sunshine. "So delicate and lovely." He looked up at her.

"May I spread you open, my lady? May Deep and I see your inner folds?"

"I don't understand why you need to," Kat protested feebly.

"We need to know how far we have to go to make you come," Deep growled softly. "If you're wet and ready it might just be enough for one of us to touch you. Unless you *want* to let one of us taste you."

"No, I...not really," she whispered. "All right. Just...be gentle."

"Of course." Lock and Deep exchanged a glance and Lock said, "If we need to taste you, my lady, *I* will be the one to do it."

Kat was flooded with relief. If they had to go that far, she wanted Lock to be the one who went down on her. Letting Deep do something so intimate seemed dangerous somehow. Like trusting a panther to lick your face instead of biting it off. Not that she actually thought he would *hurt* her. He was just so intense it was frightening...overwhelming.

"All right," she whispered again and tried to relax as she felt Lock gently part the lips of her pussy. She jumped slightly when he stroked a fingertip over her swollen clit.

"You're wet, my lady." His deep voice was thick with lust and she could feel his desire filling her.

"Wet but not wet enough," Deep said in a dangerously soft voice. "You need to be tasted, little Kat. Need to have your pussy licked."

Kat's entire body was so tight with tension she felt like she was going to burst. "You're sure?"

"Positive."

"Deep is right." Moving down the bed, Lock positioned himself between her legs. "Open yourself for me, my lady. Don't worry, I'm just going to kiss you."

Biting her lip, Kat watched as he spread her thighs wide with his broad shoulders. Beside her, she could feel the muscular bulk of Deep's large body. His cock was hard and hot against her thigh and the dark spice of his scent made her dizzy.

"Watch him," he growled in her ear. "Watch Lock open you. Watch him taste you."

It was the same thing he'd said during their last joining when Lock was sucking her nipples. "Why…why do you always want me to watch?" Kat demanded breathlessly.

"Because then I know you can't deny it, even to yourself." Deep stroked her cheek, his large hand surprisingly gentle. "If you watch, you have to admit it's really happening, little Kat. And that you're really enjoying it."

Kat had no answer for that. She watched, mesmerized, as Lock parted her pussy lips once more and placed a soft, open mouthed kiss on the throbbing button of her clit. "God!" Her back arched as pleasure raced through her. But she needed more…much more. Lock seemed to understand.

"I need to lick you, my lady," he murmured, looking up at her. "May I have your permission?"

"Tell him yes," Deep directed her in a low voice. "Say, 'Yes, Lock, I want you to lick my pussy.'"

Kat felt her entire body heat with a blush. "Why should I have to say that?"

Deep tilted her chin towards him and looked into her eyes. "Because you need to admit you want it. Admit you *need* it. And because I want to hear you say it. Go on."

"I..." Wetting her lips, Kat forced herself to speak the words. "Yes, Lock, I...I want you to lick me."

"'To lick my pussy,'" Deep corrected her. "Say it right, Kat. Tell Lock what you want."

He still held her eyes with his own and she felt helpless to look away—helpless to disobey his orders. "Lock," she whispered, looking at Deep as she said the words. "I want you to...to lick my pussy. Please."

She felt a surge of lust from Deep and he growled with approval. "Very good. I didn't tell you to add the 'please' but it was a nice touch."

"I will gladly taste you, my lady," Lock murmured. "I've wanted to do this since the first moment I laid eyes on you."

"We both have," Deep said, stroking her cheek again. "Watch now, Kat. Watch and tell me how it feels."

Kat watched as Lock dipped his dark blond head between her thighs again. She honestly couldn't believe she was doing this. Couldn't believe she was lying here with the two of them, naked and spread open, completely defenseless while Lock licked her pussy and Deep watched.

She moaned softly as Lock started at the bottom of her slit and gave her a long, loving taste. His tongue was hot against her sensitive clit—hot and gentle and incredibly intense all at the same time.

"Delicious," he said softly, looking up at her, his mouth wet with her juices. "I love the way you taste, my lady."

"Th-thank you," Kat stuttered as Lock went back for a second taste. God, his tongue felt *incredible* on her. He was tracing her now, circling her clit in slow, intricate patterns that seemed designed to drive her crazy. She could feel herself getting close to the edge almost immediately but she still needed something…something she hardly dared name, even to herself.

"How does it feel?" Deep demanded as Lock continued to lick and suck her inner folds. "Do you like his tongue between your legs? Does it make you feel like you need to be *fucked*?"

Kat's breath caught in her throat. How had Deep known? But of course, he could feel her emotions, the same way she could feel his and Lock's. She knew it must be part of the strange, unwanted link they shared, but that didn't make her feel any less embarrassed.

"I told you, I don't want to go that far," she said breathlessly, trying to frown at Deep.

"You don't have to," he assured her. "What you need is penetration. I can provide that easily enough without using my cock…if you'll let me."

Kat bit her lip. Did she dare? She could see the hunger in his eyes, could hear the longing in his deep voice. But most of all she could feel the need coming off him in waves. *He knows I'm afraid to trust him. He knows he scares me.* And that knowledge hurt him, somehow. Hurt him deeply.

"I know you fear me," Deep said, as though reading her mind. "But I swear I would never hurt you, little Kat. Please…will you let me bring you pleasure?"

"Yes," she whispered, giving in at last. "Just this once, I guess it will be all right."

"Very good." Deep plundered her mouth suddenly in a kiss that took her breath away. When he pulled back he looked at her intently. "If I only get to do it once, then let's make it count."

"Deep—" Kat started to say, but he was already pulling her closer and sliding his hand under her to cup her pussy from below.

Lock stopped licking her for a moment and looked up to catch her gaze.

"It's all right, my lady," he murmured, stroking her inner thigh soothingly. "Deep's going to penetrate you with his fingers. Just open yourself for him and let him fill your pussy."

Kat was drowning again—filled with their emotions as well as her own. But she knew there was no way around what was happening. She had to go through it—had to allow them to do as they wanted in order to come out the other side. *Just once,* she promised herself. *Only once.* She looked at Deep and nodded her head. "All right."

"Very good. That's a good girl, Kat." Slowly two thick fingers breached her entrance and slid deep into her pussy. Deep held her eyes as he penetrated her, watching her intently as he filled her. "Such a good girl to let me fingerfuck your tight little cunt."

Kat lifted her chin. "I'm only doing it because...because I have to," she said, staring back at him challengingly. "Because there's no other way."

"I know." Instead of the anger she had expected, there was a depth of sadness in his voice that made her heart ache for some reason. "But I want you to enjoy it anyway." The sadness faded, to be replaced by lust. "So tell me if you like it. Tell me how you want it."

"I...what do you mean?" Kat frowned, not understanding him.

"Do you want it soft and gentle, like this?" Deep's fingers withdrew and then pumped back into her in a long, slow glide as he kissed her cheek. "Do you want me to be sweet to you and fuck you gently while Lock licks your pussy?" he murmured.

As if on cue, the blond twin went back to lapping her open cunt. Kat moaned out loud at the duel sensations of having one brother's tongue laving her wet folds while the other brother pierced her with his fingers. God, it was too much, how could she stand it? And yet still she needed more.

Deep seemed to sense it. "You want it harder, little Kat?" he asked, his black eyes half-lidded with lust. "You need more? Well, you're going to have to ask for it."

"Damn you." Kat glared at him. "What are you, some kind of a sexual sadist?"

Deep laughed. "No, I'll leave that kind of behavior for the Scourge. "But I want to hear exactly what you want. What you need."

Lock looked up again. "I know it seems like Deep is teasing you, my lady Kat, but truly, he doesn't want to hurt you. He needs to know that you want it before he penetrates you with more force." His brown eyes pleaded with her to understand, to forgive.

Kat thought with exasperation that it was clear why the Twin Kindred always came in pairs. Without Lock to explain and apologize for him, Deep would be completely incomprehensible. He needed his brother to act as an emotional interpreter.

"Fine," she said, glaring at Deep. "I need it harder. Faster. Is that what you need to hear?"

"Yes. *Exactly* what I need to hear. But I want you to say it right."

"Say what?" Kat squirmed impatiently. God, if he didn't start soon...

"Ask me to fuck you." His voice was a soft, lustful growl. "And say my name when you do. I want to hear it on your sweet lips, little Kat. Want to hear you ask me for what you need."

Kat's breath caught in her throat but she had never been one to back down. "All right then..." It took all her courage and her heart was thumping like a jackhammer but she looked him straight in his midnight black eyes as she spoke. "Fuck me, Deep," she said in a soft, challenging tone. "Fuck me *hard.* I...I need you to."

"Gods!" His voice was hoarse with lust as he pumped deep into her open cunt, his thick fingers pistoning in and out of her until she moaned. "So beautiful, little Kat," he growled. "How I wish I was fucking you with my cock instead of my fingers."

For a moment Kat let herself imagine that. The thought of his huge, muscular body covering hers filled her mind. Fucking Deep would be like fucking a tiger — something so fierce and wild it was completely uncontrollable. She would be helpless, able only to spread her legs wide and try to accommodate his thick cock as he pounded into her. As he filled her with his shaft and his seed...

Yes, Deep whispered in her head. *I would ravage you, little Kat. Fuck you hard and long until I filled your pussy with my hot cum. But don't forget, I wouldn't be the only one...*

Another image filled her mind. This time Lock had joined the equation, filling her from behind. He held her and steadied her, helping her take Deep's rough, delicious loving as he stroked slowly into her himself.

God, Kat thought half deliriously. *To be filled by both of them like that. To be fucked by two cocks at once...*

And that's only one of the ways we could take you, Deep taunted her. *Think, little Kat. With three instead of just two, the possibilities are limitless.*

Kat gasped as a barrage of images raced through her overloaded mind. She saw herself on her hands and knees, sucking Lock while Deep took her from behind. Saw Lock fucking her while Deep lapped her open pussy. And then, most frightening of all, she saw them bracketing her as they were now. Both of them were thrusting up and into her and it was clear that they were both piercing her at the same time in the same place...

No! Fear raced through her—surely that wasn't possible. Her stomach clenched but not only with fright.

You want it, Deep whispered in her head. *Want to take us both. To feel Lock and I filling your sweet pussy at the same time...*

No, Kat denied but her mental voice sounded weak, even to herself. Surely he had to be kidding her. There was no way...

"You're close now, my lady. I can feel it," Lock murmured from between her legs, breaking her train of thought. "Just open yourself to both of us and let go. Let us take you where you need to be." Ducking his head, he sucked her clit between his lips and began to lash it with his tongue.

The intensely pleasurable sensations coupled with her forbidden fantasies were too much. "God!" Kat gripped the bedspread beneath her and bucked up, unable to stop herself from moving. The brothers were working in tandem now, neither one of them getting in the other's way despite the close quarters. They seemed to be feeding off each other and her, setting up a mutual rhythm of licking and thrusting that pushed her to the edge of orgasm faster and harder than she'd ever been pushed before.

"You're going to come soon," Deep murmured in her ear, his breath hot against the side of her neck. "When you do, I want you to look in my eyes. I want to see it when you lose control."

Kat wanted to shake her head, wanted to deny him. But somehow she couldn't. Unable to stop herself, she turned to face him and felt herself drowning in the midnight depths of his gaze.

"God," she gasped as the pleasure peaked inside her. "I can't...I'm...I'm..."

"You're coming." Deep's voice was a low, lustful growl as he held her gaze. "I can feel you all around me, squeezing my fingers. Gods, I wish it was my cock instead."

Kat shook her head. "No...not..."

"Don't worry." He frowned. "Lock and I know you don't want to go there with us. With *me*. But a male can dream, can't he?" The image of both of them fucking her at once filled her head again and Kat knew it was more than his fantasy — it was his deepest wish. His most ardent desire.

Kat couldn't speak — couldn't do anything but feel. As the orgasm rushed through her she felt something click into place inside her. It was as though some vital part of her had come loose, but with the rush of pleasure it reconnected, anchoring itself firmly once more. *Is that my soul?* she wondered uncertainly. *My spirit? Am I all right now? Am I whole?*

"We won't know until we take you back to Mother L'rin to be examined." Lock was looking up at her. "Forgive me," he said. "I know we're not in a joining but I couldn't help hearing your questions."

"You think very loudly," Deep agreed, grinning. "But then, so do I. Wouldn't you say, little Kat?"

"I'm sorry," Kat looked away uncomfortably, not wanting to acknowledge the forbidden exchange they'd had moments before. "I'll, uh, try not to *think* so loudly in the future."

She couldn't help noticing that now that her orgasm was over, Lock had withdrawn and was no longer tasting or touching her pussy. Deep, however, still had his fingers buried inside her, filling her in a way that was both uncomfortable and erotic. *How do I ask him to stop? What if I get...excited again? What if— ?*

"Just ask me if you want me to stop penetrating you, little Kat." Deep sounded amused. "And to answer your question, if you get excited again, well, we'll just have to make you come again. Maybe *I'll* get between your thighs and taste your pussy this time. How would you like that?"

Kat didn't know what to say. The idea of letting the dark twin go where his brother had gone still seemed wrong to her — dangerous. "Deep," she said, trying to keep her voice steady. "I need…need for you to take your fingers out of me now. Please."

"That 'please' again, tacked on to the end. So very polite." He didn't sound happy about it but he did withdraw his fingers…very slowly. "Well, until next time."

"There isn't going to *be* a next time," Kat reminded him, frowning.

"Oh?" Deliberately he raised his fingers to his mouth and, keeping his eyes fixed on hers, sucked her juices off with apparent relish. "We'll see what Mother L'rin has to say about that."

Kat wanted to answer but a sudden weariness took her and she could only shake her head. *Later, when I get more energy I'm really going to let him have it.*

I look forward to it, little Kat. Deep grinned at her mockingly. *You have no idea how much.*

Chapter Seven

"Kat's all right—for now at least." Baird was leaning against the doorway, his arms crossed over his massive chest and a serious look on his face.

"Oh, thank God!" Olivia turned from her husband to her sister. "Sophie, she's all right."

"I heard. I'm right here, you know." Half laughing, half crying, Sophie hugged her sister tightly.

"Deep and Lock got her to Twin Moons just in time," Baird continued. "Their healer..." He snapped his fingers. "What was her name?"

"Mother L'rin," Liv supplied for him.

"Right. She did some kind of healing ceremony and now Kat's resting. Lock called and told me a minute ago."

"I'm so glad." Sophie felt like a weight had been lifted off her shoulders. She'd been feeling horribly guilty ever since they'd allowed Deep and Lock to take Kat away to Twin Moons with them. But she and Liv had both trusted Sylvan's decision that it was the only way to save their friend. Kat still wasn't going to be happy to wake up on a strange planet with her two least favorite people in the universe, but at least now they knew she was going to live.

"When can we talk to her?" Olivia asked eagerly.

Baird frowned. "Not for a couple of days according to Lock. She needs to rest. But that isn't the only thing I came to tell you." He cleared his throat. "Do you remember telling me about the sister of your mother, *Lilenta?* The one who died in childbirth?"

"Yes, of course. Aunt Abby." Liv frowned. "What about her?"

"Well, I just came from the view room and you have a call—you and Sophia both, actually. It's a woman claiming to be her—your kin. Do you want to speak to her?"

"What?" Olivia demanded.

"But that's impossible," Sophie protested.

Baird shrugged. "Could be a hoax, I guess. But I don't know why someone would want to pretend such a thing. And..." He hesitated. "Well, she looks an awful lot like you two in the face. Looks like blood kin to me."

To me too, Sylvan suddenly murmured inside Sophie's head. His mental voice was serious. *I'm in the view room now talking to her, Talana,* he continued, using his pet name for Sophie. *I think you and your sister should come see her.*

On our way, Sophie sent back. "Come on," she said, hopping up and pulling Liv to her feet. "Let's see what she has to say."

"All right." Olivia still looked shocked but she followed Sophie out of the suite to the viewing room which was used mainly for long distance conversations. Hesitantly, they looked around the corner at the huge viewscreen mounted on the wall.

Oh my God, Sylan was right! Sophie was shocked. The woman had black hair and light brown eyes but the face on the viewscreen could have been a slightly older version of hers and Liv's. Or their mother's.

Olivia was obviously thinking along the same lines. "She looks just like Mom. Oh, Sophie." She nearly crushed Sophie's fingers with her grip.

Sylvan, who had been standing in front of the viewscreen talking, motioned for them to come all the way into the room. "It's all right, *Talana*, I believe she is who she says she is. Sophia, Olivia, meet your Aunt Abigail."

"Aunt Abby?" Sophie could hardly believe her eyes.

"Yes, that's me." The woman nodded and for the first time, Sophie noticed that her lovely eyes, which were a brown so light they were almost amber, looked red from crying. "You must be Sophia and Olivia. I...I'm sorry we had to meet for the first time under these circumstances," the woman continued.

"What circumstances?" Olivia put a hand protectively over her belly. She was still in her first quadmester and wasn't showing yet, but her mothering instincts were already in high gear.

"Your husband didn't tell you?"

"Tell us what?" Liv frowned. "First tell us why you aren't dead. No offense, but that's what our mom told us before...before she passed away."

Aunt Abby closed her eyes for a moment as though holding back tears. "Yes, I heard about that. I can't believe I never got to say goodbye to her. I always thought there would be time but I was afraid, so afraid she wouldn't want me back in her life. And now it's too late. She's gone and Lauren is gone...I've lost everything. Everyone."

"What do you mean 'she's gone' and 'Lauren's gone'? Lauren was our mom's name," Sophie protested.

"And it was the name of my daughter too. The one who disappeared. Look." She pressed a button and suddenly her face was replaced with the image of a lovely girl with creamy mocha skin and eyes the same amber color as Aunt Abby's. The girl was laughing, her long silky black hair being whipped in the wind and the sun shining through palm trees behind her. She was wearing a pink striped bikini top and shading her eyes with one hand. There was something about the picture that bothered Sophie but she couldn't quite put her finger on it.

"She's beautiful," Liv said when their aunt reappeared again. "She has your eyes."

"And her father's skin," Aunt Abby said grimly. "Which is why your grandparents decided to kick me out when they found out I was pregnant. I didn't know they'd told your mom I was dead, though."

"They said you died having her—having Lauren." Sophie spoke through numb lips. "Mom never liked to talk about it much. It made her too sad."

Aunt Abby shook her head. "Your grandfather paid me a great deal of money to sever all ties with my family. I took it and did well with it—I'm a wealthy woman now, for all the good it does me. I was carrying twins, you know, when I first got pregnant with her. And then I lost Lauren's sister when I gave birth. But I told myself as long as I had Lauren…" Tears began to leak down her cheeks. "And I don't even have her now. I don't know where she is or even if she's alive."

"Oh, Aunt Abby, I'm so sorry!" Sophie wished she could give the woman a hug. "What happened? Is there anything we can do to help?"

"I hope so." Their aunt wiped her eyes with a tissue. "I only tracked the two of you down a month or so ago. I was going to contact you first and see if you were interested in having some kind of relationship before I told Lauren. She always wanted to have more family." She sniffed. "But I'm contacting you now for a different reason. I was hoping that since you're both with the Kindred, maybe you might be able to help locate her in some way."

Sylvan and Baird had been standing quietly in the background but now Sylvan stepped forward. "Tell us about the circumstances of her disappearance and we'll see what we can do."

"All right." Aunt Abby sniffed again. "She disappeared from her shop almost a week ago. It's the strangest thing—the police can't find any blood or hair or fibers that might lead to the…to the attacker at all." She cleared her throat, obviously forcing herself to continue. "In fact, there was nothing but a pile of clothes in the bathroom. But the way they were layered on top of each other, the clothes on the shoes… It wasn't like she'd taken them off—more like she'd just…*disappeared* right out of them."

Sophie felt her breath catch in her throat and she saw Sylvan's face tighten. *The molecular transport beam. Could it be?* "Aunt Abby," she said. "Could…could you show us that picture of Lauren again?"

"Of course." Their aunt's image disappeared to be replaced with the laughing picture of Lauren in the pink striped bikini top.

"There," Olivia said, striding up to the viewscreen and pointing. "Right there. Do you see it? Between her breasts?"

"The star shaped birth mark," Sophie breathed. *That* was what had been bothering her about the picture. She looked at Liv. "The prophesy," she whispered, aware that her aunt could still hear them if they spoke too loud. "The Scourge prophesy."

"Lauren is the one." Liv's face was pale and she was whispering too. "Oh my God, the poor girl!"

"Should we tell her?"

Sylvan shook his head. "Not yet," he murmured. "Let's see if we can do anything first."

"Sylvan's right. There's no point it giving her news like that until we look into it and make sure," Baird said in a low voice.

Aunt Abby appeared once more. "Well?"

"We'll do everything in our power to help you." Sylvan put a hand over his heart. "Any kin of our mates is a priority with us. You can believe that, Ms. Jakes."

"Thank you." Aunt Abby looked like she was going to cry again. "You can reach me through the HKR building in Sarasota, Florida. That's where Lauren was living when she was…was taken." The last word turned into a sob and suddenly the viewscreen went blank.

"What can we do?" Sophie looked at Sylvan frantically. "The Scourge have her, Sylvan—I just know it. Oh that poor girl!" She and Liv both knew first hand what it was like to be captured and interrogated by the evil AllFather. Sophie wouldn't have wished it on her worst enemy.

Sylvan looked grim. "I don't know if there's anything we *can* do, short of attacking the Fathership to take her back by force."

"And I don't think the High Council is gonna go for that," Baird rumbled, frowning. "Not unless we get some kind of incontrovertible proof that they have her and that's where she's being held."

"Where else could she be?" Liv demanded.

"Anywhere." Baird shook his head. "The Fathership isn't the only Scourge stronghold, you know, *Lilenta*. They have a home planet too. It's a Deadworld now—they killed it with their greed and pollution. But they still have impregnable fortresses there they can go back to in a pinch."

"So you're saying we just have to *leave* her there?" Liv was beginning to cry. "Leave her with that…that *monster?*"

"I'm saying let us talk to the Council first before you go gettin' all upset." Baird stroked her shoulders soothingly. "This news has a bigger impact than just the fact that your kin has been kidnapped."

"Baird is right." Sylvan nodded. "If the Scourge have finally found the key to their prophesy, something big may be about to happen. The Council will want to consider all complications and repercussions before they act."

"Which means she'll be dead or as good as dead by the time we get to her," Liv said dully. "*If* we get to her. Oh, poor Lauren."

"Poor Lauren," Sophie echoed. Putting her arms around her sister, she held her tight and prayed for the cousin neither one of them had ever even known they had. *Let her be strong. Let her be able to stand whatever the AllFather throws at her.*

But she knew from experience how terribly difficult that could be.

Chapter Eight

Kat woke up feeling weak but rested. She was glad to find herself alone in bed — and, it seemed, alone in her own head, at least for awhile. Either Lock and Deep were far away, or neither of them was having any really strong emotions at the moment. Whatever the reason, Kat was glad to have some peace and quiet inside her skull for once.

Sitting up she stretched and yawned. God, she was starving! Was there anything to eat around here? The area she found herself in didn't appear to have any food. It was a bedroom, from the look of it, with white walls and a green wooden floor. The huge Twin Kindred bed which dominated the entire center of the room was low to the ground. The spread was a warm green and gold that matched the floor and the sheets were a pale off-white color and softer than any linen Kat had ever felt. She pulled one of them around her as she got out of bed, because she had no idea where her clothes were.

Walking slowly, she made her way to the huge rectangular window across from the bed. It was covered with an indigo shade that gave the shadows in the room a bluish purple tinge Kat rather liked. She wanted to see out the window but the shade wouldn't move and was firmly anchored in all four corners of the window.

"Stupid thing," Kat muttered to herself, reaching high to run her fingers over the topmost edge of the shade. "How the hell does it open?" Just as she was about to give up, her seeking fingertips encountered two small buttons. "Okay, let's just see what these do."

She pressed the top button but instead of opening slowly, the shade suddenly snapped up sharply, leaving the entire window bare.

"Oh!" Kat stepped back as a flood of brilliant pinkish-gold sunlight bathed the room. She was momentarily blinded and had to shade her eyes with one hand while she clutched the white sheet to her chest with the other. Finally her vision adjusted and she was able to look out and see what was going on.

Kat had never been to Europe but she'd seen plenty of docu-dramas about it on TV. Now, looking at the narrow, crooked streets and tall, leaning buildings of the Twin Moon's settlement, she couldn't help thinking that it looked a lot like a quaint European town. It seemed to have an old world charm that was lacking in her home town of Tampa.

There were some differences, of course. Instead of being whitewashed, the buildings were made of some pinkish-gold stone and the streets weren't paved with cobblestones. In fact, they seemed to have some kind of short pink and green vegetation growing in them—an idea that was reinforced when she saw several Take-mes grazing on the edge of the road. The two-headed animals were a pain to ride but if she remembered correctly, Liv had told her that they were native to Twin Moons. Although why anyone would want to domesticate something that looked like the push-me/pull-you from the Doctor Dolittle books was beyond Kat.

Far beyond the quaint, crooked houses she saw something that looked like a vast sheet of undulating gold. It took her a moment to realize it was water—an ocean in fact. *An ocean of golden water. Beautiful...* The sight took Kat's breath away. There were small wooden boats with red and blue sails rocking on the glassy, gold surface of the water and people walking up and down the docks.

Despite her fair skin, she'd always loved a day at the beach. She made a mental note to get Lock to take her as soon as possible.

Dragging her eyes from the enticing sight of the seashore, Kat looked down at the street outside her window and saw vendors selling some kind of meat on a stick and others selling fruit or bread. *Wonder what that long purple looking thing is?* she thought, stepping closer to the window for a better look. Was it a fruit? Some kind of Twin Moons pastry? Whatever it was, it was shaped like a banana but as large as a watermelon. Just the thought of ripe, juicy melon made Kat's mouth water and she realized for the first time in ages that she was actually hungry.

She was just about to look around for some clothes so she could go find something to eat, when the vendor selling the purple banana thing looked up and saw her. He shaded his eyes and then a broad grin broke over his face as he waved at her. He nudged the vendor beside him and *he* looked up and waved as well.

Smiling, Kat waved back. *What nice people. I wonder if it's some kind of custom to greet newcomers even if you don't know them?* A handful more of the vendors and a few shoppers were waving at her now and she felt she had to wave back in order to be polite. She held her sheet firmly in place for modesty's sake and waved until her arm was sore. She started to wonder how long the welcome ritual lasted.

"Okay, people," she said under her breath when her stomach started growling and her arm felt like it was going to fall off. "I don't mean to be rude but I have to get going and find something to eat before I fall over." Nodding and smiling, she backed away from the window and went to find something to wear.

There was a long, low box in one corner of the room that could double as a bench if you had really short legs. Kat opened it up and found a green shirt with a blue and pink pattern depicted in short, shiny feathers. "Very *fancy*," she murmured, picking it up. It was obviously made for a very large man—probably it was some kind of Twin Kindred dress clothing. She looked around but didn't see any pants to match it or any other clothing options. *Looks like it's this or the sheet.* Shrugging, Kat put on the shirt, which fell almost to her knees. Well, at least she was decent, unless the Twin Moons inhabitants frowned on women showing their bare legs. In which case, too bad. She was hungry.

Rolling up the sleeves, she made her way out of the bedroom and down a long hallway with the same green wooden floor. There was a spiral staircase on the far end of the corridor which led directly down into a sunny food prep area. All the standard Kindred appliances were there—the glass-front refrigerator and the Kindred stove called a wave. Liv had showed her how to use it, but Kat was still afraid she might burn some fingers off if she messed around with the alien appliance. Then she noticed the kitchen was occupied.

A tall, slender woman with light brown hair was standing in front of the sink. She was wearing a pink toga-looking garment and washing some juicy blue-green fruit about the size of large grapes. Kat had eaten those before—they were twin fruit. You couldn't eat the outside though—it was bitter and sour. You pealed the succulent looking outer flesh off and ate the nut inside which tasted kind of like peaches and pecans mixed together. The woman appeared to be engrossed in her task and hadn't heard Kat come down the stairs.

Kat cleared her throat, trying not to startle her. "Um...hi," she said hesitantly.

The woman looked up at once and smiled at her. "Veelash abra boolash," she responded pleasantly.

"Oh dear." Kat frowned. "Uh, I don't suppose you speak any English like Deep and Lock, do you?"

"Deep vun Lock crabash le taber." The woman made a walking gesture with two fingers and pointed at the door which appeared to lead out to a garden.

Kat assumed that she meant the brothers were out doing…whatever it was they did while they were home. She wondered if the tall, slender woman was in any way related to Deep and Lock. She looked a little too young to be their mother but not quite old enough to be an older sister. Maybe she was just a maid?

"Um, okay," she said hesitantly, wishing she'd gotten an injection of translation bacteria the way Sophie had before she visited Tranq Prime. "I guess I'll just—" To her mortification, her stomach growled loudly, interrupting her hesitant speech. "Oh my God, I'm so sorry!" Thoroughly embarrassed, she put a hand over her tummy, only to have it growl again.

The woman threw back her head and laughed. "Cheela! Noosh. *Noosh*," she said, taking Kat by the arm. She pointed at the sink where Kat could now see there were several fruits or vegetables— she couldn't tell which—laid out. The woman pointed at them and then looked at Kat and raised her eyebrows. It was clear she was asking which one Kat wanted.

"Uh…" Kat looked over the variety uncertainly. Aside from the twin fruit there was a twisted purple root and a greenish-yellow object with orange dots, about the size of a lemon.

Neither of the other choices looked really appealing. Kat was about to go for the twin fruit by reflex, when a warm, rich, ripe scent tickled her nose. She lifted her face and sniffed—what *was* that smell? *Whatever it is, it smells amazing! Like a cross between pineapple and raspberry with something salty thrown in. Maybe buttered popcorn?* The delicious aroma seemed to be coming from a bowl of triangular fruit about the size of her palm.

Looking closer, she saw the individual fruits were shaped a little like a strawberry, though they were considerably larger. Each was a tempting golden peach color with just a blush of pink on its smooth skin. They had purple stems at the top that were so pretty they could almost double as flowers. But Kat had never seen flowers that she wanted to eat, and suddenly her mouth was watering to try one of the three-sided fruits.

"Could I...would you mind if I tried one of those?" she asked, pointing to the bowl which was sitting to one side of the sink.

The woman looked surprised. "Kala?"

"Yes." Kat nodded eagerly. "Kala—I'd like to try some of that. If it tastes half as good as it smells I'll think I've died and gone to heaven."

The woman looked doubtful at first but then she shrugged and handed Kat one of the fruits.

Kat took it by the stem carefully. She had a fleeting thought that she might be about to eat something that was perfectly fine for Twin Moons inhabitants but poison to an Earthling like herself. But when she brought the peachy-pink triangular fruit to her nose and took a deep sniff, all her fears disappeared. Nothing that smelled so good could be bad for you, could it? *Still, I'll go slow, just in case.*

Experimentally she took a tiny nibble from the pointed end of the fruit. A flavor unlike anything else she'd ever had exploded in her mouth. It tasted like it smelled—fresh pineapple, juicy raspberry, and hot buttered popcorn—but there were other, more subtle flavors as well. A hint of hot chocolate, a taste of honeydew melon, and the tiniest bit of smoked cheddar cheese. Really, the fruit had too much going on—the strange and different flavors should have fought with each other. Instead, they blended harmoniously in her mouth in a way that made Kat's eyes roll back in her head with pleasure.

In no time she had finished the first fruit—right down to the purple stem—and the woman handed her another.

"Oh my God, this is *amazing*," Kat said around mouthfuls of the juicy, tender flesh. The triangle fruit, as she was beginning to think of it, had a texture like a peach but with little crunchy lumps in it that were chewy and crispy at the same time. She finished the second as well and looked hopefully at the bowl. "Um, I don't want to make a pig of myself or anything but..."

Laughing, the woman pushed the entire bowl into her hands. Then she surprised Kat by giving her a hug and a kiss on the forehead.

"Oh. Uh, okay. Thanks." Kat was caught off guard by her sudden affection. But the triangle fruit was so good she probably would have put up with much weirder things than a hug and a kiss in order to get a whole bowl of it.

Still smiling at her, the woman led Kat to a small, sunny alcove in the corner of the kitchen where large, flat pillows were arranged on the floor. She seated Kat on a blue and purple one and then made motions at the bowl of fruit. "Noosh. Noosh."

That must mean 'eat.' Kat nodded politely. "Yes, noosh. Don't worry, I will absolutely noosh. Thank you." She picked up another triangular fruit and took a bite. "Mmm, good!"

This seemed to satisfy the woman. She smiled at Kat, said a few other things in the Twin Moons language, and went back to washing fruit at the sink.

Left alone with the bowl of succulent fruit, Kat got busy. She told herself sternly she ought to take it easy—after all, who knew what effects the alien fruit might have on her system? But it had been days since she'd done more than pick at her food and she was ravenous. Before she knew it, she was down to the last two fruit in the bowl and wishing she'd gone slower. She was about to take a bite of the next-to-last-fruit when Deep and Lock came through the door.

Immediately Kat was flooded with emotions that weren't hers, and none of them were good.

"What in the seven hells were you doing this morning?" Deep demanded, striding over to her.

Kat was immediately on the defensive. "I don't know what you're upset about but you can just back off. You two went out and left me here in a strange house, in a strange town, *on a strange planet* where I don't even know the language. I had to muddle through on my own."

"We're very sorry, my lady." Lock, who had been speaking rapidly in Twin Moons dialect with the tall woman, came over to where Kat was still sitting with the mostly empty bowl. "We had to run some errands and we didn't think you'd be up before we got back."

"Oh, she was up, all right. Up and giving the vendors at the market a show," Deep snarled.

"What are you talking about?" Tired of craning her neck to look up at him, Kat stood and put a hand on her hip. Of course she still had to look up, just not quite as far.

"I'm talking about the way you were showing yourself out the window this morning—the entire township is talking about it." Deep glared at her.

Kat frowned. "I couldn't find any clothes when I first got up but I wrapped a sheet around myself. I looked out the window and some people waved at me so I waved back. What's the big deal?"

"The 'big deal' is that you shouldn't be showing your body to strangers." Deep eyed her possessively, making her feel suddenly naked.

"I *wasn't*," Kat protested, wishing the weird, feathered shirt she'd put on was longer. "I was very careful to keep the sheet wrapped around me the entire time, I swear."

Lock cleared his throat. "Apparently, the light shining in the window rendered your sheet, ah, transparent."

"What?" Kat felt a heated blush sweep over her. "Are you serious? So all those guys who were waving and smiling at me weren't just being friendly?"

"They'd like to be a whole lot more than *friendly*," Deep growled. "Do you know how often the average male here on Twin Moons gets to see an elite? Almost never. And to see an elite without her clothing, her lush curves revealed, her—" He stopped abruptly and frowned at the triangle fruit Kat was still clutching in one hand. *"What* are you eating?"

"I don't know," she admitted. "She gave it to me." She pointed at the tall woman who had been standing at the sink and watching their conversation with a worried look on her face.

Lock turned to her. "Mumzell? Chara vena Kat Kala ala noosh?"

She nodded her head rapidly. "Ja, ja! Shiba ava Kala ala noosh." Then she hugged Lock and stood on tiptoes to kiss his forehead.

"What? What is she saying?" Kat demanded.

Deep frowned. "She's saying you asked for it. She thinks you wanted it because..." He broke off, shaking his head.

"Because what? What does it do?" Kat asked, worried. Had she poisoned herself with the strange fruit? Or had she somehow eaten something she wasn't supposed to eat for religious reasons? Damn it, she didn't know *anything* about this stupid planet. She *had* to get herself some translation bacteria!

Lock finally finished speaking to the older woman. He turned back to Kat and spoke in a low voice. "What you ate are Kala fruit— what we call bonding fruit. They have uh…a special significance to our people."

Deep snorted. "That's an understatement."

"Deep, please." Lock gave him a warning look. "Will you just let me explain?"

"They're not poisonous or anything, right?" Kat asked. "I mean, I'm sure the nice lady wouldn't have let me eat them if they were but—"

"That 'nice lady' is our mother," Deep said harshly. "And she now believes that you intend to mate with Lock and myself. *Immediately*. Because why else would anyone eat an entire bowl of bonding fruit in one sitting?"

"What?" Kat felt a sudden rush of panic. "No, no," she said to the woman, shaking her head rapidly. "It's not like that with us. Really, it's not." She turned back to Lock. "What exactly are 'bonding fruit'? Do they have some kind of religious importance to your people?"

"Not religious exactly…" He hesitated for a moment as though trying to think how to explain. "Bonding fruit is usually eaten by unmated women right before they bond with the twin males they have chosen to be their mates."

"Oh." Kat was relieved. "So it's just a misunderstanding. She thinks because I ate the fruit, you and I and Deep were going to…but we're not, of course." She laughed nervously. "So just explain it to her and tell her I'm sorry I gave her the wrong idea and we can forget about it, right?"

"I'm afraid not." Deep shook his head. "I don't think any of us is going to be able to just 'forget about it' for quite a while."

Kat frowned at him. "Look, I'm sorry, okay? I didn't mean to profane your weird eat-fruit-before-you-get-busy custom but it was an honest mistake. If you can't get over it then that's your problem, not mine."

"That's not what Deep means, my lady." Lock shook his head apologetically. "You see, there is a reason that females eat bonding fruit before they get mated. It has special properties."

That sounded ominous to Kat. "What *kind* of special properties?" she demanded.

Lock looked uncomfortable. "Well, it increases your elasticity in certain, uh, areas."

"What?" Kat demanded. "What are you trying to say?"

"It makes you able to take two shafts in your pussy at the same time," Deep said bluntly. "Is that clear enough for you?"

Kat was horrified. Her eyes went immediately to the sink where the twins' mother had been standing, but luckily, she had left the room.

"Don't worry. Mumzelle can't hear us. And even if she could, she can't understand English, remember?" Deep laughed but it wasn't a happy sound. "I can feel how upset you are. Why don't you say something?"

"I just…I can't…why the hell would anyone want to…to do *that*?" She looked at Lock appealingly, ignoring Deep though she couldn't help remembering the images he'd sent her the night before. Of both of them inside her, thrusting, filling her...*But I never thought it was really possible. Never thought they would really want to –*

"It's how we perform bonding sex, my lady," Lock said gently, breaking into her frantic thoughts. "Deep and I thought you knew that."

"Especially after our exchange last night," Deep growled, giving her a piercing look.

"I didn't think you were for real." Kat shook her head, her mind filled with painful, scary images. "Never thought you'd really want to..."

"Of course we want to," Deep said harshly. "It's the way of our people."

"But I thought...I guess I thought you did it, uh, one at a time. Or at the very worst, one in front and one in, uh, the back." She could feel herself blushing but she couldn't seem to stop. God, she *really* didn't need to be thinking about this right now. Especially considering what the three of them had been doing the night before and the images Deep had sent her.

"We do share a female in many different ways." Lock nodded. "And we can form a *limited* kind of physical bond if one of us fills your, um, *front* and the other one fills your *back*, as you put it. But for true bonding sex to occur..."

"Both our cocks have to be buried to the hilt in your pussy at the same time," Deep finished for him in a low voice.

"Oh my God." Kat shook her head. "But you guys are *huge.* I, uh, felt you against me last night. There's no way anyone could –"

"Certainly you could. Especially after eating an entire bowl of bonding fruit." Deep smirked at her.

Kat rounded on him, suddenly furious. "Why do you keep making such a big deal about how much of it I ate? I was *hungry*, damn it!"

"Brides-to-be usually start slowly, eating just a few bites of the fruit each day to increase their flexibility. They only eat a whole fruit on the day of their bonding ceremony," Lock explained. "Just *one* whole fruit. I'm afraid since you ate considerably more than one, the effects will be multiplied." He shook his head. "I really wish Mumzelle hadn't planned the party for tonight."

"What effects? What is this stuff going to do to me?" Kat waved one of the two remaining triangle fruits in his face.

"The bonding fruit doesn't just make you more flexible," Lock said carefully. "It also makes you more…what's the word?"

"Horny." Deep grinned at her but it wasn't a happy expression. "I've been practicing my Earth vernacular again. Did I get it right?"

Kat's hand itched to slap him but she somehow restrained herself. "You bastard," she said in a trembling voice. "You're telling me that I ate some kind of aphrodisiac? Didn't just eat it but practically overdosed on it? And you think it's *funny?*"

"Not at all." The grin faded from his face and he looked at her intently. "In a very short period of time, *none* of us is going to think it's funny."

"What do you mean none of us? How can it affect you two?"

"We can feel your emotions, remember?" Deep tapped the side of his head. "Everything *you* feel, *we*, feel."

"But it won't just be us—though we'll be affected most deeply." Lock had a grim look on his face. "It's going to affect every male in your immediate vicinity."

"Okay, I get the emotions thing. But *how* is it going to affect everyone else?"

"Your scent," Deep answered for his brother. "You already smell like a female in heat whenever you're around Lock and me. This is only going to make it worse—*much* worse." He started to pace as he talked. "You already *look* irresistible and now you'll *smell* irresistible as well. We're going to have to warn off every other male at the party tonight."

Lock shook his head. "I just hope it doesn't come to blows."

"What party?" Kat was becoming thoroughly exasperated. "And why can't we just skip it if it's going to be such a problem?"

"The party our mother planned in your honor," Lock said quietly.

"Which is why none of us can just 'skip it,'" Deep snarled. "We have to attend and every other high ranking male in town is going to be there as well. The mated ones won't be a problem. But the unmated males…"

"You're going to have to stay very close to us," Lock told her seriously. "Of course this wouldn't be a problem if…" He hesitated.

"If what?" Kat said. "Come on, spit it out. If you know a way to keep every single guy in the immediate vicinity from humping my leg just because I ate the wrong fruit, then by all means, please share."

Lock sighed. "If you'd let Deep and I mark you with our mating scents…"

"But you *did*," Kat protested, in a low voice. "When you…you know, *licked* me. Didn't you?" The memory of Lock's head buried between her thighs while Deep growled in her ear and pumped her pussy with his thick fingers made her feel hot all over.

"I did mark you some," Lock admitted. "I couldn't help it. But I wasn't tasting you to mark you, my lady—my aim was to bring you pleasure, so I wasn't very thorough. And besides, my scent alone won't keep other males away from you. Deep needs to add his scent as well."

Kat put a hand to her throat. "And how exactly…"

"We need you naked and open between us." Deep's eyes raked her body, making Kat shiver.

"What…what do you mean *open?*"

"The same position we started in last night." Lock's voice was calming but somehow Kat didn't feel soothed. "But you'd have to open your legs. To allow our shafts to rub against you. Against your—"

Kat had heard enough. "Huh-uh. Sorry guys, but no way." She backed away from them, shaking her head. "I am *not* up for that. That's too close to…Anyway, I'm not going there."

"All right. It's all right." Lock held up his hands in a gesture of truce. "Deep and I would never do anything to you that you didn't want us to do, my lady." He looked at his brother. "Would we, Deep?"

Deep looked at her speculatively. "Not unless it was for her own good. Which this very well may be, as you know, Brother. After all, we can't let her be attacked by every stray male who smells her scent just because she's a little squeamish about letting us mark her."

"No!" Lock held up a hand to stop him when he started to approach Kat. "Stop it, Deep. You know you wouldn't act against Kat's wishes, so stop pretending you would."

"Who's pretending?" Deep growled. "I absolutely *would* act against her wishes if I thought her life was in danger and what I was doing was in her best interest."

Kat glared at him. "Thanks for the vote of confidence. I guess I'm just too *stupid* to know what's good for me."

"No, you're just too damn tempting for your own good." Suddenly Deep was right in front of her, cupping her cheek and looking down into her eyes. "You have no idea how alluring you are, do you, little Kat?" he said softly. "With your full curves and your hot scent. No male in the universe could be near you without wanting to fuck you."

"Leave me the hell alone." Kat jerked away from his touch. "I've had enough of you for one day." Turning, she marched to the spiral staircase.

"You're going to have to put up with a lot more of me during the party tonight. A lot more of both of us," Deep called.

Kat didn't bother to answer. She still had one of the triangular bonding fruits clutched in her hand. Acting on a sudden impulse, she flung it at his broad chest. The fruit hit him squarely above the heart and splattered all over his deep green uniform shirt, making what Kat hoped was a permanent stain. She was hoping to piss him off as much as he had irritated her. But to her intense annoyance, Deep only looked at her and laughed. Looking her in the eye, he drew one finger through the pulp that stained his shirt and stuck it slowly in his mouth.

"Juicy, little Kat," he rumbled. "Juicy and succulent and oh, so sweet."

Kat refused to dignify his leering with an answer. He was still laughing as, with one last glare in his direction, she climbed out of sight.

* * * * *

Lock sighed and reached down to pick up the remaining bonding fruit and the carved wooden bowl Kat had left on the cushions. He knew his mother only kept such fruit in the house to remind her of their fathers. Though she had loved their stepfather dearly, the same Kindred male who had been Baird and Sylvan's true father, she had never forgotten her first mates — Twin Kindred who had died in battle with the Scourge.

She had been overjoyed when he and Deep had brought an unmated female home with them. After what had happened with Miranda, she seemed to have lost hope that they would ever call a bride. So of course when Kat had reached for the bonding fruit, she'd gotten the wrong idea about what was going on between the three of them. *I wish it was the right idea,* Lock thought longingly. *Gods, how I wish it.*

Putting the fruit in the bowl, he straightened up to see Deep staring moodily up the stairs where Kat had disappeared. The ruined bonding fruit was dripping down his shirt but he didn't appear to notice or care.

"Why do you do that?" he asked, unable to keep his frustration from spilling over. "Why do you antagonize her? Why do you push her away?"

Deep turned to look at him. "In case you didn't notice, Brother, I'm not the only one pushing."

"Kat only pushes you away because you push first," Lock accused him. "Why don't you tell her how you really feel? Why don't you tell her what you did for her? How you took her pain?"

Deep was on him in a flash, both hands fisted in Lock's shirt. "That is *not* your secret to tell, Brother," he snarled. "We haven't come to blows since we were children but I promise if you tell her about the whipping —"

"Fine." Lock pushed him away roughly. "You don't have to threaten me. I don't know why you want to keep it from her, but I'll keep your secret if it means so much to you. I'd no more tell her what you did than I would tell her about Miranda."

"See that you don't." Deep frowned and straightened his shoulders. "I'm going to try and get some rest before the party tonight. If you're smart, you'll do the same."

"I can't rest now," Lock said wearily. "I have to talk to Mumzelle and try to explain that the bonding fruit was a mistake. Then I'll try to make peace between you and the lady Kat—if that's even possible."

"Why should you care if we get along or not?" Deep demanded. "Just let it go, Brother. You know the minute we take her back to Mother L'rin she'll be asking for a way to break the connection between us. Hell, she doesn't even know it exists and she's already angry. What is she going to do when she finds out we have a soul bond with her she didn't ask for?"

"I don't know," Lock said, running a hand through his hair. "But I don't think now is the time to tell her. Right now I just want to keep her from hating you. From hating *us.*"

"Too late, Brother." Turning, Deep left him alone in the kitchen, clutching the last remaining bonding fruit. "Too late."

Chapter Nine

Kat was a mess. She sat on the bed with her arms wrapped around herself and shivered. God, she hated to admit it but those two got under her skin—especially Deep! What was it with him, anyway? Why did she let him get to her so much?

"Drives me *crazy*," she muttered, running a hand through her hair. It was surprisingly glossy and clean, despite the fact that she'd been out of it for so long before she'd woken up between Deep and Lock the night before. Vaguely, she remembered dreams she'd had. Dreams of large male hands bathing her and washing her hair—but those were just dreams, right? The thought of the brothers handling her naked body while she was unconscious made her really uncomfortable.

And what about the damn bonding fruit? Her hands still smelled of the triangular, palm-sized fruit. The scent was tempting and incredibly delicious but Kat had no desire to eat any more now. What was going to happen to her when the weird, alien aphrodisiac kicked in? And how was she going to make it through a huge formal party if she was horny out of her mind?

*Not that I'd ever get horny enough to let Deep and Lock try **that** on me.* Just the idea of both of them trying to fit their huge shafts inside her at the same time gave her the shivers. There was just no way that any fruit, no matter how "special," could make that kind of three-way action anything but painful. *How would you even get in the right position to do that?* It made her head hurt just to think about it. *Then don't think about it.* But the image wouldn't leave her head. It was the same one Deep had sent her the night before while she was swamped in lust. Then it had seemed almost plausible and extremely hot. But now...Kat shivered and shook her head. *No way. No way in* **hell**.

Sighing, she got up to pace back and forth in front of the wide window. Then she looked down at her bare legs and had a sudden thought—who knew if what she had on would be considered decent or not? She didn't need to be putting on another show. Quickly, she shut the shade, plunging the room into bluish-purple gloom, but not before she saw several men on the street below smiling and waving at her. Kat did *not* wave back. *God, some of those jerks will probably be at the party tonight!*

The thought made her wince. Her time on Twin Moons was really getting off to a great start. She hadn't even been awake for one whole morning and she'd already given a peep show to strangers and eaten a whole bowl full of horny fruit by mistake. What the hell was she going to do tonight? And what—

"My lady?" A soft rapping on the door interrupted her mental tirade.

"Yes?" Kat sighed with resignation. "Come in."

"Thank you." Lock came in and shut the door behind him. He was alone, Kat saw with relief. She didn't think she could handle another dose of Deep just now. "I just wanted to talk to you," Lock said, coming over to the window where she was standing. "I wanted to tell you—"

"Have you been washing my hair while I was unconscious?" Kat blurted.

"Um..." Lock coughed and looked down at his boots. Then he looked up and nodded. "Yes."

"You and Deep both or just you?"

"It was my idea," he said softly, looking into her eyes. "But I did get Deep to help me."

"God!" Kat started pacing again. "I *knew* it. I knew it wasn't just a dream." She rounded on Lock. "Do you know how creepy that is? I mean, I was *unconscious,* for God's sake! You two could have been doing *anything* to me."

"We only bathed you," Lock said in a low voice. "Deep and I are honorable males. We would never take advantage of you as you slept."

Reluctantly, Kat shook her head. "No, I guess not. *You* wouldn't anyway."

"Deep would not take undue advantage either," Lock said, obviously taking her meaning. "And we draped you in towels to preserve your modesty if that makes you feel any better."

Strangely enough, it did. Kat sighed and nodded slightly. "I guess, maybe a little."

"Try to understand." Stepping forward, Lock took her hand in his. "We were charged with your safety and well being. We were acting as any males would toward the female they cared for." Bending his head, he pressed his lips to the back of her hand and gave her a soft, lingering kiss.

Kat felt her heart skip a beat at the old fashioned gesture and the feel of his warm lips on her skin. He looked so handsome standing there, so earnest and hopeful as he kissed her hand. When he looked up, his whole heart was in his chocolate brown eyes.

"Lock…" she said, not knowing how to continue.

"My lady," he murmured. "Forgive me for offending your modesty. Please know that I acted only out of affection and the most earnest desire to see to your needs."

He had needs of his own. Kat could feel them. She could feel the yearning inside him—the wanting so strong it brought tears to her eyes. And all of it, all his desire and need and love and lust, all was centered on *her*. "Oh, Lock..." Somehow she found herself hugging him, wrapping her arms around his muscular torso and holding him close.

"My lady... Kat," he murmured into her hair, returning the hug carefully.

Kat breathed in his scent without speaking, knowing it was his mating scent but not caring for once. It was warm and calming—a mixture of hot coffee on a cold morning and fresh laundry straight from the dryer. Under it was a hint of masculine spice that tickled her nose and made her nipples and the tender vee between her legs throb. But despite her desire, hugging Lock was wonderfully comforting. His arms were hard and strong around her and she realized for the first time that she liked him—liked him a lot.

He liked her too. She could feel the warm iron bar of his cock against her thigh, but she didn't pull back. It seemed right somehow—or at least, not scary. Her irritation and worry seemed to melt away and for a moment she allowed herself to just feel good in his arms.

"Kat," he breathed and she looked up. His brown eyes were half-lidded and she realized he was going to kiss her.

I shouldn't be doing this. I'm probably only feeling this way because of all the damn fruit I ate. But she couldn't help remembering the gentle way he'd tasted her the night before, the sweet way he'd made her come with his tongue. The memory made her hot and cold all over and she shivered in his arms. She tilted her mouth up to meet his—

"Brother, I—" Deep's voice at the door made her jerk away, but not before the dark twin's coal black eyes had taken in the way she and Lock were wrapped in each other's arms.

"Deep." Lock raised a hand to his brother. "The lady Kat and I were just—"

"I see what you were *just* doing." Deep's eyes flashed. "Don't let me interrupt you."

"Stop," Lock pleaded. "You know it isn't like that. It *can't* be. Without you—"

"I'd say you're doing just fine without me." Deep nodded at both of them coldly and left, shutting the door behind him.

Lock sighed and stepped back, away from Kat. "I shouldn't have done that. I shouldn't have been *able* to do that."

Kat frowned. "What do you mean?"

"We're bonded twins." Lock ran a hand through his hair. "Touching a female in the way I was touching you should have been excruciatingly painful for me without my brother somehow involved." He sat heavily on the edge of the bed. "It hurt me to take you in my arms without Deep touching you as well, but I *was* able to do it."

"It *hurt* you to hold me?" Kat looked at him, her eyes wide. "Really? How...how does it feel?"

"Like a low-level electrical shock running through my body. But just the fact that I was able to do it at all..." He shook his head. "We've grown apart lately. Ever since—"

"Since what?" Kat asked but he only shook his head.

"Never mind. I owe you an apology."

"It's all right," Kat said softly, sitting beside him. "I wasn't exactly trying to get away. I should have, though—I don't want to lead you on."

He gave her a look from the corner of his eye. "Meaning you still have no interest in us."

"I think I could if I let myself—I could have feelings for *you*, anyway," Kat said honestly. "I mean, you're sweet and kind and caring and gorgeous—what more could a girl want?"

"But?" Lock raised one dark blond eyebrow at her.

"But…" she said reluctantly. "You come with an awful lot of baggage. You know what I mean."

"Yes." He nodded heavily. "Yes, I do. But my lady, if you could just give Deep a chance…"

Kat was already shaking her head. "I'm afraid not, Lock, it would never work. Deep and I—we're like oil and water—we don't mix. We can't even have a single conversation without it turning into a shouting match."

Lock's broad shoulders slumped. "I know he's difficult to get along with. But he truly does care for you."

"Then why don't I feel it?" Kat asked. "I get all these strong emotions from you two but what I mostly feel from him is lust and annoyance. He wants me but mostly I *irritate* him."

"You're only feeling what he lets himself feel," Lock protested. "But under all that, he cares. I *know* he does."

"Maybe you just want him to," Kat said gently. "Because you two come as a package deal and I can't take one without the other. Look, I can tell how hard it is for you and I'm sorry—really I am. But aside from the whole feeling both of your emotions thing and the, uh, way you perform bonding sex which is scary to say the least…" she shivered and wrapped her arms around herself. "Aside from that, the fact is, I just can't let myself get involved with two guys when one of them can't stand me." She shook her head. "God, that sounds so weird."

"No, it sounds like common sense." Lock looked down at the green wooden floor between his black boots. "I can't blame you for what you feel, my lady. But I can't help what *I* feel, either."

"I'm so sorry." Kat put a hand on his knee to comfort him. Then she pulled it away quickly. "Oh, I didn't think. Did that hurt you just now? Me touching you without Deep being here?"

"A little." Lock gave her a sad smile and put her hand back on his knee. "But it's worth it."

"That's sweet." He looked so dejected and his feelings of sadness and loss were so overwhelming, Kat felt like she was going to cry if they sat that way much longer. Clearing her throat, she rose and began pacing in front of the bed. "So when do the effects of this, uh, bonding fruit I ate kick in? And how long do they last?"

Lock shook his head. "The fruit should be in full effect in a few hours. As for how long it will last, it could be days."

"What?" Kat rounded to face him. "Are you telling me I'm going to be feeling…uh, amorous for *days?*"

"No, no." He shook his head hastily. "That will be the first effect to fade. But your scent will remain enhanced for a long time. As well as your…" He coughed delicately. "Flexibility."

"Oh, well…" Kat crossed her arms over her chest protectively. "I don't think we need to worry about it then. As long as I can get through tonight at the party…"

"You'll be all right," Lock finished for her. "And I promise we'll take you back to Mother L'rin tomorrow. She wanted to examine you after we healed you, anyway. And maybe she can help you to shield yourself against some of our emotions."

"I certainly hope so," Kat muttered. "But about the party, tonight—before we go, I *really* need a shot of those translation bacteria that Sophie got. I mean, this whole mess could have been avoided if I could have talked to your mom instead of just pointing at the fruit I wanted. I don't want to get into any more trouble."

Lock shook his head. "I'm sorry, but those are only available on the Kindred Mother ship."

"Really? Damn!" Kat sighed and raked a hand through her hair. "You know, I don't get it. Back when you two were bringing me here in the spaceship I heard Deep talking in another language and I could understand it. But when I talked to your mom I didn't catch a word."

"You weren't conscious in the ship," Lock protested. "In fact you almost...almost died." His face had gone pale and the last word came out in a whisper.

Kat nodded grimly. "I figured it was something like that. I was floating above my body looking down. And I saw you doing some kind of weird CPR on me. But the talking...I don't see how I could understand the Twin Moons language then and not now."

"Maybe you were dream-sharing with us." Lock looked thoughtful. "It might explain why your spirit didn't drift away entirely and also why you could understand our language. However tenuously, you were linked to our minds, seeing and hearing as Deep and I saw and heard."

"Well I wish I could have a little of that now," Kat grumbled. "This is going to be some fun party. I'll be high on horny fruit and I won't have any idea what anyone is saying to me." Then she thought of the males who had seen her in only a sheet that morning. "Come to think of it, maybe that last part won't be such a bad thing."

"There will be a few people there you can talk to," Lock told her. "Some of the ambassadors and their mates have had the translation implants so they'll understand you. And they'll be safe—your scent won't affect mated males."

"So I should stick with the couples." Kat nodded. "Got it."

"Only if you should get separated from Deep and myself," Lock said. "But I don't think that will be a problem. We'll be shadowing your every move."

"Oh joy," Kat said dryly. "I can't wait."

It certainly was going to be a party to remember.

Chapter Ten

"What's the matter, honey? You look like you just lost your last friend."

At the sound of English being spoken, Kat looked up eagerly. The party, which was being held at a huge structure that was reminded her of an opera house, with frescoed ceilings and elaborate carvings, had been horrible so far.

It wasn't so much that she didn't know the language — although that was a big part of it. But she also felt like a prisoner, being flanked at all times by Deep and Lock. She was on an alien planet for the first time — she wanted to go explore. There were amazing works of 3-D art all over the walls and vast rooms full of strange and exotic things to look at. Not to mention all kinds of new foods to try — though Kat was being careful about that. But instead of wandering through the crowd checking things out, she was stuck staying where it was "safe." At least according to her two captors.

Kat couldn't see that it was so very unsafe at the huge, bustling party. It was true that just about every male in the place seemed to be eyeing her hungrily, but none of them had made any off-color gestures or remarks. Kat assumed it was just the scent she was supposedly giving off. And come to think of it, she wasn't even sure about *that*. She didn't *feel* any different and she'd sniffed herself several times without smelling a thing. Could it be that Deep and Lock were making up the whole bonding fruit thing — or at least exaggerating it — in order to keep her close to them?

Entirely possible, she thought, eyeing Deep, who was scanning the crowd warily for possible threats. But at least now she had someone to talk to. The woman who had spoken to her looked to be about five years older than Kat and she was voluptuous in the extreme, her full curves draped in a peacock colored toga-type dress which seemed to be the traditional Twin Moons style.

*Speaks English **and** she's plus sized!* Kat smiled at her, feeling like she'd just won the jackpot. "Hi," she said, nodding gratefully. "I'm Kat. Kat O'Connor."

"Piper." The woman held out an elegant hand dripping with diamonds and Kat took it. "Oh, who am I kidding? Come here!" Piper pulled her into a warm embrace and held her for a moment before letting go. "Sorry." She grinned unrepentantly at Kat. "It's just that I've been out here on Twin Moons with my husbands for so *long.* I'm so glad to see another face from Earth I could cry."

"That's okay." Kat grinned back. On Earth she would have been put off by such effusiveness but not here, under these circumstances. "I know how you feel," she said. "I haven't even been here that long and I'm already homesick."

"Of course you are! I mean, it's wonderful here. But sometimes you just want to go to McDonalds and get a Big Mac and some fries. And knowing the closest Mickey D's is seven light years away can make a gal feel mighty lonesome." Piper sighed and patted her honey-blonde hair which was piled on her head in an elaborate up-do. "Where are you from, anyway?"

"Tampa," Kat said, smiling. "You?"

"Houston, honey. Born and raised." Piper smiled wistfully. "You know, it's a big, dirty, ugly city and around here it's all quaint little fishing towns and unspoiled beauty—couldn't be more different. I'll be the first to admit it's gorgeous and all, but sometimes I miss the traffic and the smog. Isn't that strange?"

"Not at all," Kat said earnestly. "I haven't been here for long but before that I was stuck on the Kindred Mother ship. I miss downtown Tampa and the Tampa picture show—it's this old theater that's been running for the last hundred and fifty years. The acoustics are horrible and the seats are so hard they hurt your behind, but my girlfriends and I used to go there and watch all the indie movies that none of the multiplexes would play." She sighed. "They have this old fashioned popcorn machine and they use real butter—not that nasty fake stuff."

"Oh, don't get me started on Earth food." Piper's lime green eyes lit up. "What I miss the most is good barbeque. You couldn't get decent pulled pork on Twin Moons to save your life! I don't even think they have an animal that's anything like a pig. Everything is so lean and healthy and good for you." She shivered.

"Which is probably why everyone's in such good shape and all the women look like supermodels," Kat said, looking around. Every Twin Moons woman she had seen was tall and thin with perfect cheekbones. They glided around the room, taking nibbles from the mountains of fruit which were piled on low pillars, and looking perfect in the warm lighting.

"Oh no, honey." Piper shook her head. "You and I, *we're* the supermodels here. And that's the one thing Twin Moons has over dear old Earth."

"Uh, because we're 'elites'?" Kat dropped her voice, not wanting Lock and Deep to hear her discussing it. "I mean, the guys I'm with, they're always talking about how curvy women are valued here—"

"Valued? Honey—we're the cat's pajamas! Just look at the way they're looking at us." She motioned to the hungry glances that were coming from several different sets of twin males scattered around the large gallery. "Why, every single man in this room would be on us like a duck on a junebug if we weren't already mated!"

"I'm not though—mated, I mean," Kat said.

Piper's perfectly shaped eyebrows lifted in surprise. "Not mated? Then what are you doing here?"

"It's a long story." Kat glanced up again to see if Deep or Lock was listening. She really wanted to pour her heart out to a sympathetic ear but she didn't want them hearing everything she said.

Piper seemed to understand the situation. "Come on, honey, let's go powder our noses and you can tell me all about it," she said, hooking her arm through Kat's.

Suddenly Deep was blocking the way. "Where do you think you're going?" He frowned at Kat.

Piper looked at Kat. "I thought you said you weren't mated?"

"I'm *not*." Kat frowned unhappily. "Look, Deep, this is Piper and as you can see she's female. We're going to the ladies restroom—" She looked at Piper. "Uh, they *do* have a ladies restroom here, right? I mean, it's not unisex or anything?"

"Heavens no!" Piper smiled sweetly at Deep and Lock who was now standing beside his brother. "You two just run along for a little while. I promise I'll keep your little gal safe."

Deep didn't budge. "Oh you *will*, will you?" he murmured, one black eyebrow cocked in obvious disbelief.

Lock cleared his throat. "Forgive me, my lady, but we don't even know you."

"I'm Piper. I'm the mate of Ambassadors Knows Much and Thinks Swiftly." She patted Lock on the arm. "You two just go on over and talk to Much and Swifty, as I call 'em," She nodded her head at a pair of Twin Kindred who were standing off to one side. "While we run along to the ladies room."

"Her mates are males of renown," Lock said, talking to Deep.

"Well, if you're just going to the room of convenience..." Deep was still frowning.

"That's all. I promise." Piper nodded at both of them. "It's okay — we just want a little Earth girl talk."

"We'll accompany you," Deep decided.

Kat sighed as the two of them flanked herself and Piper and they moved in a unit through the milling crowd. It felt like all eyes were on them and she couldn't help feeling embarrassed. *This is so stupid! Like I'm some helpless little girl who can't go anywhere without her bodyguards.* Finally they came to a large pink and gold archway set in the back wall. It was right beside a flamboyant hologram display which appeared to be naked people covered in red, green, and brown paint pretending to be trees.

"From Earth," Piper said, nodding at it. "You wouldn't catch any native Mooners doing nonsense like that but they think our stuff is just to die for."

"Mooners?" Kat raised an eyebrow.

"That's just what I call 'em." Piper nodded at the crowd of Twin Moon natives before turning to Lock and Deep. "All right now," she said, giving them a bright smile and a nod. "You two just run along. We're going to be in here a little while."

"When will you be back?" Deep wanted to know. He was still scowling, presumably at the idea of having to leave Kat alone.

"When we're damn well good and ready," Piper snapped, apparently losing patience. She towed Kat into the pink and gold entrance which curved off to the right, putting them out of sight of the main room. "Lord, those two are overprotective! And you say you're not even mated to them yet?"

"No and I'm not going to be either." Kat looked around the large, parlor like room they found themselves in. "Hey, this is really nice."

It looked like an old fashioned power room down to the deep, plush chairs and red velvet wallpaper. Though when she took a closer look she saw that the wallpaper was some kind of moss, not velvet, and the chairs had an almost organic look—as though they'd been grown instead of made. There were also hanging plants, dripping exotic looking pink and gold and pale green blossoms everywhere.

As if in contrast to the organic appearance of the room, the walls were filled with wide angle, full length 3-D viewers for checking your makeup and dress. Kat saw dozens of herself reflected in the viewers. The new deep green toga-dress Lock had picked out for her complimented her auburn hair, which she'd decided to wear down for once.

"It *is* nice, isn't it?" Piper looked around, smiling fondly. "Of all the Kindred trade planets, Twin Moons is the closest you're gonna get to Earth. The islands, anyway—all bets are off on their continent but nobody goes there, so who cares?"

"You've been to the other trade planets?" Kat asked, interested.

Piper nodded. "Oh sure, honey—not that they're much fun. Rageron is just this horrible, humid blue jungle full of critters so scary they'd make a gator cry. And on Tranq Prime they all live in caves and eat bugs." She shivered. "Can you imagine? Of course here on Twin Moons they have the Grieza worms, but I can handle those since they taste like chocolate."

"Those *are* good." Kat had eaten some at Liv's wedding and really enjoyed them despite their unappetizing appearance. "I haven't eaten much Twin Moons food yet," she confessed. "And what I *did* eat...well, I really shouldn't have eaten it. I just..." She trailed off, not sure how much she wanted to reveal.

But Piper's curiosity was clearly piqued. "What, honey? You can't just leave a girl hanging like that—what did you eat?"

"Bonding fruit," Kat admitted in a low voice. "Almost a whole bowl full of it. That's why my guys—uh, Deep and Lock—are being so overprotective. They say I'm giving off some kind of a, uh, scent, because of it."

Piper's vivid green eyes widened. "You ate a *whole bowl* in one sitting? Was it a big bowl? How many did you eat?"

"Five or six," Kat said with a sigh. "I'd just woken up from a long, uh, illness, I guess you could call it, and I was famished. But so far I don't *feel* any different."

"Oh you will, honey. You *will*," Piper assured her. "But if it's the first time you've had bonding fruit, it will probably take a little time to kick in—that's how it is with us Earth girls. But once it does— watch out! You're gonna be hotter than a firecracker on the Fourth of July."

"Seriously?" Kat frowned unhappily. "I was hoping that Deep and Lock were just exaggerating. Or maybe that it didn't work on me."

"Oh, it'll work all right. But if you're lucky it won't start until after the party when you can be alone with your men." Piper grinned at her and shook her head. "If you're not bonded yet you sure as hell will be pretty soon."

"What?" Kat began to feel panicky. "But I don't *want* to be."

"Is it the whole two poles in one hole thing, honey?" Piper clucked her tongue sympathetically. "Don't let that worry you. Now I'm not gonna lie to you, it *is* kind of a tight fit. But once that bonding fruit gets working on you, you'll be feeling no pain. It's like a mixture of Spanish fly and valium—you'll be hopped up and cooled out at the same time."

"No, it's not that. Or not *just* that," Kat protested. "I don't get along with them at *all*—one of them, anyway."

"Now let me guess—that would be your dark twin. Am I right?" Piper raised an eyebrow at her and Kat nodded.

"Lock is really sweet. But Deep...we just can't get along." She looked down at her hands. "My parents divorced when I was twelve and my grandmother raised me but before then, they were constantly yelling and screaming at each other. I just...I don't want to be stuck for life in a relationship like that and..." She looked up. "And I don't even know why I'm telling you this when I just met you."

"That's 'cause I'm easy to talk to." Piper smiled at her. "*Everybody* says so. I was a bartender back on Earth back before my men called me as a bride. Worked at a club in downtown Houston called Foolish Pride. I bet I listened to fifty sob stories a night and you know what? I kinda miss it."

"You're good at it." Kat smiled at her. "Did...do you have the same problem with your, uh, guys? Not that Deep and Lock are mine or anything," she continued hurriedly. "I mean, we kind of all got stuck together by accident and now I'm having a really hard time getting away."

"Isn't that just the way?" Piper nodded sympathetically. "As for dark twins—they're *always* a problem. Ask any female on God's green Earth who's mated to one. They're contrary and irritating and just plain ornery and yours seems to be worse than most."

"He certainly is," Kat agreed, thinking of Deep's tendency to get under her skin. "He's sarcastic and moody and dark..." She sighed. "But he's very protective, too. And loyal and gentle when he wants to be. And..."

"And you're really confused," Piper finished for her.

Kat nodded gratefully. "I really am. But I *do* know I don't want to be bonded to anyone until I'm ready. And I am so far from being ready right now it isn't funny."

"Then stay away from them tonight when the bonding fruit kicks in," Piper said seriously. "Ask for a private room or lock yourself in the bathroom but whatever you do, *don't* wind up between them or it's gonna be game, set, and match. I promise you that."

"Okay, thanks for the warning." Kat crossed her arms over her chest. "Damn it, all this could have been avoided if I'd had a shot of translation bacteria before I came. Now I'm stuck here on a strange planet with no idea of what anyone is saying. It's so *frustrating.*"

Piper smiled. "I don't know what to tell you about your man problems but the translation thing is something I *can* help you with." Reaching into a fold of her toga, she pulled out a tiny little clutch purse the exact color of her dress. "Now let me see, I'm sure I have one left...ah-ha!" Triumphantly, she pulled out what looked like a small green caterpillar with a head on either end and long purple hairs growing out of its hide. "Here you go," she said, handing the half-inch long, wriggling creature to Kat.

"Uh, thanks." Kat took it very reluctantly—she'd never liked bugs or insects much. She wasn't afraid of them like Sophie, but she was more likely to step on them than make them pets.

Piper took a look at her expression and burst out laughing. "You don't have any idea what it is or what it's for, do you?"

"No," Kat confessed. "I don't."

"It's a convo-pillar. You put it in your ear and it picks up whatever you hear and translates it into your own language for your brain. It works the other way, too—just think what you want to say and it'll send thought messages to your speech center and help you talk the other person's language. Isn't that great?"

"Uh, did you say you put it in your *ear*?" Kat frowned. "Look, I don't like to sound squeamish but I've seen *Wrath of Khan*. I mean, it's an oldie but a goody right? And anything alive that goes into your ear is bad news as far as I'm concerned."

"Oh, please, honey," Piper said a touch impatiently. "If you're afraid you won't be able to get it out again, don't be. Look how easy it is." She tugged twice at her left earlobe and a small orange caterpillar with pink hairs crawled out of her ear and onto her finger. "See?" she held it out to Kat. "Easy as pie."

"How come yours is orange and pink and mine is green and purple?" Kat asked doubtfully.

"That's cause the one I gave you is a new breed—special." Piper smiled. "Supposed to be almost no lag time at all between thought and translation with that little bugger. I was saving him for a special occasion but I'd say you need him more than me."

"Well, thank you." Kat was still reluctant to put something alive in her ear but she didn't see how she could refuse now without offending her new friend. "Uh, what happens when they, you know, *die?*"

"Oh, they stop working *long* before that," Piper assured her. "When you stop understanding what people are saying, just tug your earlobe, get him out, and get a new one. If you can, that is. I don't know of a supplier on Twin Moons—I get mine from a colony near Rageron." Lifting her hand, she allowed the tiny creature to crawl back into her ear canal. "Now you. Go on."

Wincing, Kat lifted the green convo-pillar to her ear. *Oh God, I really don't want to do this!* The tiny hairs tickled horribly as the little creature crawled in her ear canal and she had to curl her hands into fists to keep herself from yanking it out again. It was hard to overcome the instinctive response to scream and freak out at the feeling of something living going where it very clearly didn't belong. But she squeezed her eyes shut and reminded herself grimly of the benefits of having it there. She'd be able to understand everyone around her now and avoid any more disastrous mistakes like the one that had led her to eat an entire bowl of bonding fruit. And she could apologize in person to Deep and Lock's mother, who had been looking at her sadly ever since Lock had explained to her that they weren't really a threesome after all. And—

"Okay, it's in. You can open your eyes." Piper sounded like she was laughing. "I know it takes some getting used to but believe me, in a minute or two you won't even know it's there."

Kat wasn't sure about that, but at least the little creature wasn't moving around any more. It seemed to have found a comfortable position and was staying still. Instead of the feeling of having a hairy bug in her ear, Kat felt more like someone had plugged it with a piece of cotton. "It makes it kind of hard to hear on one side," she said uncertainly.

"No it doesn't," Piper said confidently. "You think so because of the way it feels but actually the convo-pillar conveys sound as naturally as your own eardrum does."

"You're right." Kat nodded. "My ear *feels* like it's plugged up, but actually I can still hear just as well on that side."

"Of course you can." Piper hooked her arm through Kat's. "Come on—let's go try it out."

Kat frowned, suddenly worried. "Uh, I'm not sure how Deep and Lock are going to feel about this."

"*Please*, honey." Piper made a shooing gesture. "What they don't know won't hurt 'em. Here—we'll go out the back way." She tugged Kat toward the opposite end of the large room where there was a small door.

"We're just going to leave without telling them?" Even though she'd been longing to go off on her own, Kat was still reluctant.

"Of course. Aren't we bad?" Piper giggled and tugged at her arm. "Come on, it'll be an adventure. And don't worry—we'll get back to your boys before you know it."

"Well...okay." Though she still had some doubts, Kat allowed herself to be led out the much smaller, back exit from the ladies room.

She just hoped the convo-pillar worked. If she had to wear a live insect in her ear, it had damn well better be worth it.

Chapter Eleven

"Are these the only thing you guys eat or are they just prison food?" Lauren lifted one of the cardboard pop tarts questioningly after the tall man with the red-on-black eyes slid it across to her. "I mean, not that I'm not grateful," she went on hurriedly. "Because I am. I was just wondering."

He had been heading for the door to the cell they were keeping her in, but he turned back with obvious reluctance. "Nutra-wafers are specially formulated to provide all the protein, vitamins, and nutrition a warrior needs in a single work cycle. They should keep you in good health until the AllFather is ready for you."

Lauren cringed at the mention of his father but she was determined not to let fear shut her down. Her jailor was the only person she ever saw—her only hope of escape. She *had* to form a connection with him.

"I was just wondering if you guys had any kind of junk food," she said, trying to smile. "You know, Cheetos, Doritos, cupcakes?"

He frowned. "What are those? What is 'junk food?'"

Lauren sat forward and wrapped his cloak more securely around herself. "It's food you eat just for fun. It's usually not good for you but it tastes really good."

He shook his head. "We have nothing like that. What would be the point?"

"Pleasure is the point," Lauren said, looking up at him. "For instance, I own a cupcake bakery called The Sweet Spot back on

Earth. Nobody who comes in my shop actually *needs* one of my delicious cupcakes but they buy them for pleasure."

"I still don't understand. Why should one take pleasure in eating?" He was still just standing there, staring down at her. Lauren wished he would sit down. If she could just get him to stay with her a little while she might have a chance of connecting with him.

"You wouldn't ask that if you could taste one of my deep, dark chocolate devil's food cupcakes," she said enticingly. "The cake itself is dense and moist and it just fits in the palm of your hand. Well..." She looked at his large, rough looking hands. "*You* could probably hold two or three. But anyway, when they first come out of the oven they're hot and sweet and sticky—they practically melt in your mouth."

"That sounds...strange."

"Not strange—*delicious*. Stay and talk to me a little while. I'll tell you all about it."

He frowned. "Why should I stay? I have duties to attend to."

"Because I'm lonely." She didn't have to lie about that—it was the absolute truth. "Please...just talk to me for a minute," she whispered, almost pleading.

"I shouldn't." But he settled himself slowly in the opposite corner of her cell and made a motion with his hand. "Go on—tell me more."

"I frost them twice," Lauren said, her heart thumping. "With homemade butter cream frosting. First, when they're hot out of the oven, I put on a thin layer that just melts right down into the cake. After they cool, I frost them again. I pipe out a thick, creamy dollop right on top and then cover them with chocolate sprinkles that crunch when you take a bite." She closed her eyes, remembering the deep, chocolate flavor wistfully. "They're so good people come from all over to get one."

"All the flavors and textures you describe...I've never had anything like that." He shook his head. "We have no such 'pleasures' aboard the Fathership."

"You don't know what you're missing," Lauren sighed. "And that isn't even my best seller. I make a raspberry filled vanilla bean cupcake with cream cheese frosting that's out of this world." Remembering her surroundings, she gave a sad little laugh. "Well, out *my* world, anyway."

"You're very passionate about your work. These things you make — the cakecups —"

"Cupcakes," Lauren corrected gently, studying him from under lowered lashes as she talked.

Despite his frightening eyes and strange, gray skin, he had strong, noble features that looked like they had been carved out of granite. His profile looked almost Native American and she had an idea that the coal black hair he kept in a club at the back of his neck might be soft and thick if he ever let it free.

"Cup...cakes," he repeated slowly. "You enjoy making them for others to consume?"

"Yes, I enjoy it very much. I love baking — creating things that give other people pleasure." She smiled at him. "I wish I could bake one for *you*."

"Me?" He looked startled. "Why would you wish such a thing?"

"To see you eat it. To watch your face when you first bite into it — I love to watch people the first time they taste one of my cupcakes."

"You do?" He sounded perplexed.

Lauren nodded. "Yes—it's always the same. The smell gets them first—warm and fragrant and then they *have* to take a bite. Even the ones who swear they're on a diet—they just can't resist."

He leaned forward a little. "Yes? And then?"

"And then the flavor hits them. It rolls over their tongue, sweet and perfect as the cupcake just melts in their mouth. Their teeth sink through that moist, delicious texture and crunch on the sprinkles. Then their eyes roll up in their head and most of the time they moan."

"They moan?" He frowned, his red eyes narrowing. "I thought you said it was a pleasurable experience."

"It *is*. They moan because it tastes so good—feels so good in their mouth. Haven't you ever had anything that made you feel so good you just had to let it out?" Lauren asked.

He shook his head. "No, never."

She sighed. "Then I *really* wish I could give you one of my cupcakes. If we were on Earth, in my shop right now I would hand you one and say, 'Here you go, Mr...'" She paused and tilted her head to one side. "I just realized I don't know your name."

He frowned. "I suppose there's no harm in telling you. I am called Xairn."

"Is that your last name or your first?"

"I have only one name."

"All right. Zzzairnnn." She rolled the name on her tongue and looked up at him. "And I'm Lauren—but you probably already know that."

"Your name is known to me," he acknowledged gruffly. "Not that it makes any difference."

Lauren refused to be sidetracked. "Xairn, I wish I could bake you a special cupcake to thank you for what you've done."

"What have I done but capture and imprison you?" he demanded.

"You've given me more to eat when I asked for it. You gave me your cloak." She nodded down at the thick black fabric which kept her from freezing in the cold and lonely cell. "And you've given me your time and attention when I needed to talk and to hear someone's voice. I don't feel so alone because of you."

He scowled. "You don't mean that—any of it."

"Yes, I do," Lauren protested. "Please don't be angry. I'm just trying to get to know you."

Xairn seemed to loosen up a little bit—at least some of the tension went out of his broad shoulders. He really was huge, Lauren reflected. Every bit as big as the Kindred warriors who came to Earth now and then to call their brides. "What do you want to know?" he asked.

"I don't know…what are your hobbies? What are your dreams?"

He shook his head. "I have neither. I was born on the Fathership and I will most likely die here. I do not aspire to anything else."

"That's so sad," Lauren blurted. "I mean, to never have any hopes or dreams."

"I have work that must be accomplished or I will be punished," he offered.

She shook her head. "Uh-uh, work doesn't count. What do you do for *fun?* You know, for enjoyment?"

Xairn shook his head again. "Nothing. I told you, we have no pleasures here."

"Nothing at all?" She leaned forward eagerly. "You don't play games or read books or watch vids? Don't you have any pets?"

But she seemed to have said the exact wrong thing. Suddenly his face, which had been almost open to her, closed, and he stood up abruptly. "None of what you mention is permitted here. I must go."

"Wait!" She reached for him, upset at the sudden change when everything had been going to so well. "Please don't go — I'm sorry if I said something wrong."

Xairn looked at her, his eyes narrowed to black and crimson slits. "Cover yourself," he said coldly. "I have no desire to see your flesh."

Looking down at herself, Lauren realized that his cloak was gaping open, showing her bare breasts. "I'm sorry," she whispered, pulling it closed quickly. "It was an accident. I...I didn't mean to offend you."

"I must go," he repeated. At the door, he turned to look at her, his face impassive. "Eat your nutra-wafers. They may not be as good as your *cupcakes* but they will keep you strong until the AllFather sends for you."

And then he was gone.

Lauren watched the heavy metal door close and heard the muted sound of the locking sequence being keyed in from the other side. *Damn it, damn it, damn it!* Tears of frustration rose in her eyes and she sobbed aloud before she could stop herself. So close! She'd been so close to making a connection with him — she could feel it. And then...nothing. *What did I do? What did I say that upset him? That drove him away?*

She sobbed again and then blotted her tears with the corner of his cloak which still carried a warm hint of his scent. It wasn't just the lost chance that upset her — she genuinely didn't want him to go. He was the only person she ever saw, the only one who would talk to her. Her only link to the outside world in this claustrophobic metal prison. *Watch it girl — you're stuck on an alien ship, a prisoner of the Scourge — the ultimate bad guys. The last thing you need is a bad case of Stockholm syndrome on top of everything else,* she warned herself.

Lauren knew it was true but she couldn't help herself. Xairn was the only one she had to talk to. She missed him when he was gone.

* * * * *

Xairn stood outside the heavy plasti-steel door and listened to her sob. He told himself that he felt nothing but it wasn't entirely true. For some reason he wanted to open the door again and go to her. And then he would...*What? What would you do?*

He didn't have the faintest idea.

It was a foolish thought, anyway. Better to keep your mind on your duties.

Yes. He had much work to accomplish if he didn't wish to be punished. And just because the AllFather was no longer able to feed off him didn't mean he couldn't devise some cruel and cunning physical penalties. He could have Xairn thrown in the drowning tank, for instance, as he had when Xairn was young. Just the memory of that made him cringe inside. After all these years, he still feared deep water, though he knew how to swim.

I need to get back to work, he told himself, turning away from the soft sounds of distress on the other side of the plasti-steel door. *I won't visit her again. I'll instruct one of the vat-grown to bring her meals.*

The thought of never seeing her again seemed to stab at him, to touch a place inside that ought to be untouchable — frozen like the rest of him. Xairn ignored it. There was work to be done and punishment to be had if the work was not completed. He had no time for the human girl—*For Lauren,* whispered a voice in his brain—no matter how strangely she made him feel.

Chapter Twelve

"Here we are! These folks are prominent locals right here in town," Piper said, ushering Kat up to a middle aged threesome who smiled and nodded at her kindly. "This is Twila and her two mates, Fishes Often and Catches Many. Go on, say hi," she urged, nudging Kat with an elbow.

Kat looked at the smiling, nodding people and felt suddenly shy. "Uh, should I just talk in English and the Twin Moons language will come out of my mouth?"

"That's right honey." Turning to the threesome, Piper spoke in a language that was clearly not English but somehow Kat understood her anyway. "My friend is new to Twin Moons. Her name is Kat and she would be pleased to make your acquaintance."

At once, both of the males each took one of Kat's hands and their female mate came forward and gave her a kiss on the forehead. "Welcome. Welcome to our world," she said, smiling broadly.

"I...thank you," Kat said haltingly. "Thank you very much." She could tell that the words coming out of her mouth were some foreign language but somehow it seemed to be comprehensible to the Twin Moons threesome.

"See?" Piper grinned. "Works like a charm! Let's see now, who else can we introduce you to?" Nodding goodbye to the smiling threesome, she grabbed Kat by the arm and towed her deeper into the milling crowd.

Kat followed her, trying not to step on any feet. It seemed that the party had gotten even more crowded while they were in the ladies room and she wondered where all these people had come from. Had Deep and Lock's mother invited the entire town or were some of them just crashing the party? Speaking of Deep and Lock, she craned her head to look for them, but the Twin Moons inhabitants were too tall to see over. She felt like a little kid lost at the mall and looking for her mother. There was another feeling too, starting at the tips of her breasts and between her legs—something strange and ominous that made Kat uneasy. But before she could give it much thought, Piper was talking again.

"Here we are," she said, nudging Kat into position in front of her. "These two own the local vegetable and fruit market here in town. It's a very lucrative business they inherited from their fathers." She nodded at two males who appeared to be around Lock and Deep's age and spoke again in the Twin Moon's language to Kat. "This is Large Tasty and this one's Rigid Juicy."

"Excuse me?" Kat said, startled. "I'm not sure I caught those names right."

"I said they're—"

"Oh my goodness, Piper—thank the Goddess you're here!" A distraught looking Twin Moons woman suddenly appeared and grabbed Piper by the hand.

"Mina, what is it?" Piper's easy smile was replaced by a frown of concern.

"It's the Take-mes, they're at it *again*. I *knew* it was a bad idea to bring a breeding pair, especially since Ju-ju is coming into heat. But those stupid mates of mine wouldn't listen. Can you come help me? You know they always mind you so much better than me."

"Of course I'll come." Piper squeezed the woman's hand and turned to Kat. "Sorry, honey, but this is sort of an emergency. I'll be right back, okay?"

"But…but I don't really know anyone here," Kat protested.

"You've got your convo-pillar—you'll be okay. Look, hon, I really have to go. You've never seen a mess like Take-mes in rut. They're as mean as a bull with a porcupine up his ass." Piper patted her hand. "You just stay right here and I'll be back in two shakes."

And then she was gone.

Not knowing what else to do, Kat turned back to make polite conversation with the two large twins Piper had been introducing before she got called away. "Um, how do you do?" she said, trying to smile.

"We are well to do, thanking you, my lady." The one Piper had introduced as Large Tasty had light blond hair and pale blue eyes. Clearly, he was the light twin. The other, Rigid Juicy, had dark brown hair and green eyes that reminded Kat of emeralds. *He must be the dark twin,* she thought, trying not to feel uncomfortable as that glittering green gaze raked over her body. The two of them looked somehow familiar but she didn't know why.

"I'm not sure I understood your names correctly," she said slowly, thinking how strange it was to hear a foreign language that she really didn't know come out of her own mouth. "Could you please repeat them?"

"I am Large Tasty," the light twin said, taking her hand and kissing it. "A name which tells of me—I have an immense fruit of succulent quality."

"Uh, okay," Kat said doubtfully. *I really hope he's talking about the fruit he sells at his stand!*

"And I am Rigid Juicy." The dark twin took her other hand and kissed it slowly, his eyes never leaving hers. "Because of my fruit, which is full of flavorful juices for the sucking."

"Umm." Kat *really* didn't know how to answer that. But the way they spoke seemed strange. Was her convo-pillar not working? "I'm Kat O'Conner and I'm new to Twin Moons," she said, smiling uncertainly at both of them. "It's very nice to meet you."

"Already we have seen you," Large Tasty said, nodding pleasantly.

"You have?" Kat frowned. "When?"

"In the light of morning, as the sun rose up, the day to greet," his brother answered for him. "We rose our eyes to the window and see a star wrapped in shadows."

"Huh?" Okay, her convo-pillar *definitely* wasn't doing its job — this conversation was becoming more and more incomprehensible but Kat didn't know how to end it.

"It was you, my lady," the light twin, or Large, as she was beginning to think of him said. "Your sheet like a cobweb to cover the curves of a goddess."

Suddenly, Kat got it. *Oh no! No **wonder** they look familiar — they were two of the guys who waved at me this morning when I was only wearing a sheet.* She began to feel intensely uncomfortable and not just because of what Large and Rigid were talking about. The strange prickling sensation she'd had earlier in her nipples and pussy was back and this time it was multiplied.

Shifting uncomfortably, she blurted, "Well, I'm glad you enjoyed the show but I didn't do it on purpose. I mean, I didn't know you could see through the sheet with the sun shining on me that way."

Large frowned but then nodded, as though understanding her. "But though you showing curves of luscious tastiness without intention, still the seeing of an elite was a thing more beautiful than skies aflame by burning sun."

Clearly it was a compliment so Kat nodded politely and murmured a soft, "Thank you." She really wanted to get away from this embarrassing predicament and find out what was going on with her tingling body parts, but when she turned to leave, Rigid took her hand.

"The Goddess has blessed you with enough delicious to burn a male with desire," he rumbled, his green eyes blazing into hers. "Good thing, come with us. Please enjoy evening entertainment of our tongues on every scrumptious curve."

"Huh?" Kat tried to pull away but the dark twin was gripping her hand too tightly and refused to let go. "Look," she said carefully. "I don't think we understand each other very well, but I am *not* going to have sex with you and your brother. Is that clear?"

"Fine lady." The light twin took her other hand and stared earnestly into her eyes. "Forgive this brother of mine. His tongue is rough like a boot to the rear. His meaning is this—you go with us and discover the joys of meat?"

"Meat?" Kat said doubtfully. Maybe they were just asking her out to eat. Not that she wanted to go anywhere with this weird tingling sensation going on in the most sensitive parts of her body. Still, she felt she ought to be polite. "Uh, well, I *do* enjoy meat. The only thing I've had to eat so far on Twin Moons is fruit."

"Bonding fruit." Suddenly Rigid pulled her close and pressed his face to her neck. Kat tried to push him away but he held her tight, inhaling deeply. To her dismay, the heated lump she felt pressed against her thigh proved that he really lived up to his name.

"Hey, let me go!" she gasped, pushing at his broad chest. It reminded her of the way Deep had scented her when they first met but this was different—*strange*. She couldn't explain it but it felt utterly and completely wrong to have someone who wasn't Deep or Lock touching her. Especially this intimately.

"Hands off, you son of a bitch," a deep, familiar voice behind her growled. "This female is spoken for."

"Deep?" Kat turned her head and saw him standing there, his black eyes blazing with barely controlled fury. "Oh, thank God! Help me—they won't let me go!"

"That's because you just agreed to spend the night with them, teasing their cocks with your talented tongue."

"I said *what?*" Kat gasped as Deep pulled her away from the very irritated Rigid. "I did not! They just asked me if I liked eating meat and I said that yes, I did enjoy it."

"Is *that* what you heard them say?" Deep frowned as he hustled her away through the crowd.

"Well, not in so many words," Kat said, trying to keep up with him. "I mean, it was more like, uh…" She tried to think of exactly how Large had put it. "Something about discovering the joys of meat."

Deep raised one black eyebrow at her as he dragged her along. "You mean the *pleasures of the flesh?*"

"Oh my God!" Kat shook her head. "But I had no idea that was what they meant. Look, could you please slow down? I—" She stopped abruptly as she tripped over someone's foot and nearly fell. Only Deep's grip on her hand saved her, but her stumble pushed them both into a silvery fountain which was spouting some kind of pale green alcoholic beverage. Kat only got a few drops on her dress but the entire front of Deep's shirt was thoroughly drenched.

Cursing, he straightened up and plucked at the sodden mess. He was wearing the same kind of shirt Kat had found in the chest that morning and the tiny little feather designs that decorated the front of it dripped with alcohol.

"I'm sorry," Kat said. "I didn't mean to trip but if you hadn't been dragging me along so fast—"

"Come on." Grabbing her hand, he began pulling her through the crowd again. Kat expected that he was taking her back to Lock but she saw no sign of the light twin as they pushed through the people milling around the large room.

"Where are we going?" she demanded when Deep started pulling her up a broad spiral staircase that led to the upper levels.

"Away from unmated males for one thing," he snarled, throwing a glance at her over his broad shoulder. "You smell entirely too luscious for your own good."

"I do?" Kat wanted to stop and sniff herself but she wasn't at all sure that she would be able to smell what was clearly so apparent to Deep's sensitive Kindred nose. She concentrated on climbing the spiral staircase which was beginning to seem never ending. Deep had already pulled her past several upper levels and showed no signs of stopping. With each step she felt more and more sensitive and irritated between her thighs and she was beginning to have the urgent feeling that she needed to go somewhere private and *do* something about it, even though she wasn't entirely sure what she could do. "How...how much further are we going?" she asked, trying not to sound out of breath.

Deep ignored her breathless question. "How did you even understand enough of the language to talk to those two without translation bacteria?" he demanded in a low voice, looking back at her.

"Piper gave me a convo-pillar," Kat gasped. His pace was so relentless it was like being on the stairclimber at the gym set on maximum. "She...she had one too but hers worked... better than mine. I could...could barely understand what they were saying."

"A convo-pillar?" He threw a glance over his shoulder. "You know those are illegal on most Kindred colonies?"

"No, of course I didn't." Kat felt a stab of panic. "Why? Do they cause some kind of disease or infection?"

Deep barked out a laugh. "Nothing like that. But they're notoriously unreliable. The Kindred High Council determined they cause more problems than they solve." He pulled her higher and higher until finally the never ending staircase came to an abrupt halt in a narrow hallway. At the end of it was a small, plain wooden door. "In here," he growled, pulling Kat through it unceremoniously.

It turned out to be another restroom but one far less elaborate than the ladies room down in the main gallery. There were a few sinks with small 3-D viewers mounted above them and some blowers that she assumed must be for drying hands. And, to her intense relief, she could see a row of small, round curtained-off areas which must be the Twin Moons equivalent of bathroom stalls. The strange sensations in her body had increased until she was *dying* for some private time.

"Um," she said, edging toward the row of round curtains. "I had a lot to drink earlier so I'm just going to—"

"Go on." Deep released her hand. "And don't worry—I won't listen."

Kat wanted to say something about there not being anything to listen *to,* but she was in too much of a hurry to get some privacy. Trying to walk normally even though her pussy was throbbing, she made her way to the last curtain at the very end of the row. It reminded her of an old fashioned shower curtain back on Earth— the kind people had used with those free-standing claw foot bathtubs. Her grandmother's house had one in the downstairs bath.

Behind her she heard Deep laugh. "All the way down to the end, huh? I *told* you I wouldn't listen."

Kat refused to dignify his remark with a reply. Instead she slipped inside the small, round space and closed the curtain firmly behind her.

Inside was an extremely low toilet with a padded purple seat and some strange looking nozzles poking out at different angles. *Some kind of Twin Moons bidet?* Kat wondered, but she really didn't care about the facilities.

Lifting her dress, she pressed trembling fingers down the front of her panties. God, she was on fire! Her pussy so hot and wet with need she was surprised her juices weren't running down her inner thighs. At the first tentative touch a moan rose to her lips. Kat managed to clamp it off by biting her lip but it was a near thing. Already she was right on the edge—it seemed like the lightest touch might make her come.

Have to be quiet! Can't let Deep hear! The idea of him finding out what she was doing was too embarrassing—Kat knew she would just *die* if he caught her touching herself. But she was finding it really hard to keep quiet when every gentle movement of her fingertips over her swollen clit sent intense jolts of pleasure through her entire body. Just as she thought she couldn't keep from groaning or gasping one more minute, the loud sound of the blower cutting on provided the answer to her problems.

Thank goodness! Deep must be drying his shirt—now I can be as loud as I want to.

Wishing she had something to lean against, Kat spread her thighs wider and stroked her sensitive clit more firmly. An orgasm rolled through her and then another, arching her back and forcing a low moan from between her lips as her pleasure crested again and again. But with each successive orgasm, instead of decreasing, her desire seemed to intensify. Until finally, she was coming almost continually and getting more and more turned on each time.

What's wrong with me? she thought hazily, her heart pounding and her head swimming. *How can I be getting **more** horny every time I come? Shouldn't I be feeling better by now?* But she wasn't — not at all.

Though it was incredibly difficult, Kat forced herself to stop. Clearly the effects of the bonding fruit had kicked in completely and what she was doing wasn't working. What she needed was to go home and sleep it off. *As if I could sleep like this. I feel like I'm going to crawl out of my skin! I'm so empty inside. I need to be filled. Need...no!*

Panting, Kat pulled her hand out of her panties and straightened her dress. *I can't go back to the party like this. I can't. I'll go insane.* She would have to get Deep and Lock to take her home and then shut herself up in the bathroom, just as Piper had recommended. *And then what? Make myself come all night until I'm so sore I feel like my pussy is broken?* It sounded ridiculous but she didn't know what else to do.

Taking a deep breath, she straightened her shoulders and tried to look calm as she pushed back the curtain. She might be in desperate straights, but she was damned if she'd let Deep know about it. The last thing she needed on top of this crazy predicament was to have him mocking her.

To her relief, his back was to her when she exited the small circular stall. He was leaning over one of the blowers, holding his shirt up to dry it off.

Kat frowned as she walked closer. There was something on his back—its broad, tan surface was covered in long, pinkish-white marks. Kat had seen him shirtless before during a joining and she knew the marks hadn't been there before. Suddenly, she realized what they were.

"Scars," she whispered, putting a hand to her mouth. "My God, so many *scars*. But how—?"

Deep whirled around to face her, though she would have sworn he couldn't have heard her horrified whisper over the roaring of the blower. "Feeling better now, little Kat?" he asked, giving her a knowing smirk as the blower cut off.

"What happened to your back?" Kat asked, ignoring the innuendo.

He shrugged lazily. "An old battle wound."

"More like *wounds*. Those are fresh scars—how did you get them?" The sight of his back had stirred something inside her—some memory so disturbing she'd somehow repressed it. Maybe a dream she'd had? Kat didn't know—she only knew seeing the cruel white and pink scars covering his broad back upset her terribly.

"They're old. You just haven't noticed them before." Deep went back to examining his shirt. "I think I got most of the fermented *narr* juice off so if you want to go back to the party—"

"Hey." Kat grabbed his arm. "Don't brush me off or act like I'm stupid—a vagina and a brain aren't mutually exclusive, you know."

He raised one black eyebrow at her. "Are you accusing me of being sexist?"

"Among other things. I've seen you shirtless before and your back never looked like that. *What happened?*"

Deep's bottomless black eyes narrowed as he stared pointedly at her hand on his arm. "It's none of your concern. Now if you're finished *pleasuring* yourself, maybe we can find my brother and get the seven hells out of here."

Kat felt her cheeks heating in a blush but she refused to back down. "Why won't you tell me?"

"Why don't *you* tell *me* what you were doing talking to two strange males when I specifically told you what effects the bonding fruit would have on you? Do you *want* to be raped? Or were you just looking for anyone besides me to scratch your itch?"

"You bastard!" Before she could stop herself, Kat slapped his cheek as hard as she could.

Deep caught her hand before she could pull it back. "Very nice, little Kat." Slowly, he drew the two fingers she'd used to touch herself between his lips, sucking and licking gently as though trying to get every last trace of her juices.

Kat felt her heart skip a beat and then start to pound crazily against her ribs. Like it or not, she had to admit that the feel of his warm mouth on her flesh and the hot way he was looking at her was having an effect on her overheated body. "St-stop it," she stuttered, trying to pull away. "Let me go."

"For now." He released her hand and began shrugging back into his shirt. "But you'll pay for that little love tap, my lady. I promise you that."

Kat wanted to respond in kind but somehow the words wouldn't come. She watched mutely as he rebuttoned his shirt and tucked it into his tight black pants. Then, taking her hand firmly, he pulled her out the door.

"Wait," she said, finally balking as they reached the head of the stairs. "I...I can't go back to the party. I have a...a problem to take care of. I need to get home."

"Of course you do." Deep's annoying smirk left no doubt that he knew exactly why she didn't want to go back to the crowd. "I've alerted Lock. He'll meet us at the back entrance and we'll leave from there. We'll go straight home and help you with your *problem* together."

Kat began to panic. "I'm not bonding with you tonight!" she said, trying to pull her hand out of his. "I don't care how much of that damn fruit I ate—there's no way I'm letting you two get me between you."

"Oh, you'll be between us all right," Deep snarled, keeping a firm grip on her hand as he dragged her down the spiral stairs. "That choice has been taken from you. You gave it up with your first bite of bonding fruit, little Kat."

* * * * *

"What in the seven hells did you do to her? She's scared to death and angry too." Lock paced in front of the locked bathroom door. Kat was on the other side of it and she refused to answer his calls or pleas.

Deep shrugged lazily. He was leaning with one shoulder against the wall, a look of apparent unconcern on his dark face. "I simply told her that you and I would take care of the problem the bonding fruit had given her."

Lock faced his brother. "And how *exactly* did you tell her we would do that? She probably thinks we're waiting out here to pounce on her and bond her the minute she opens the door."

"That's *exactly* what I think." Kat's voice was muffled but audible through the thick wooden panel of the door. "Which is why I'm not coming out for the rest of the night until this damn fruit wears off."

"My lady…" Lock paused, trying to think how he could put what he had to say delicately. "Forgive me," he said at last. "But the, ah, effects of the fruit won't just wear off on their own. Deep may have put things in the wrong way when he spoke to you, but he was right about one thing — you're going to need help."

"That's not what Piper told me," she protested.

"Piper also gave you an illegal life form to put in your ear. Look where *that* got you," Deep pointed out sarcastically. "Now are you going to come out and let us help you or not?"

"Forget it. I know what your idea of help is — both of you skewering me at once. I'm not about to become a sexual shish-ka-bob for the rest of my life just because I ate the wrong fruit by mistake."

"It doesn't have to be like that," Lock pleaded. "Please, my lady, we can help you without making love to you or bonding you to us — I swear it." To his surprise, Deep sighed and came to stand beside him at the door.

"Lock is right," he said, putting a hand on the wooden panel. "Come out, Kat. I didn't mean to frighten you, I was just…" He stopped and cleared his throat. Looking down at his boots, he continued. "I was angry when I saw you talking to those two unmated males."

There was silence on the other side of the door and then, finally, it opened a crack. "Is that your version of 'I'm sorry?'" Kat asked, one blue eye appearing warily in the narrow opening.

"It is." Deep nodded, tightlipped and frowning. "And I don't say it often."

"Or ever," Lock murmured, earning a glare from his brother.

"All right." Kat opened the door all the way and stood there, her arms crossed protectively over her breasts as she shifted from foot to foot. "I'm listening. I wouldn't be if the stupid fruit I ate wasn't driving me crazy, but it *is*. So talk. How can you *help* me without the three of us doing the hokey-poke-her?"

"The what?" Deep frowned. "As much as I study Earth vernacular, sometimes I still find you completely incomprehensible, Kat."

"Oh yeah?" She frowned up at him. "Well that goes double from me back to you, Deep. So come on, boys—what's the plan?"

* * * * *

Lock had that look on his face, like he was trying to pick his words carefully so Kat was pretty sure she wasn't going to like what he had to say. In fact, the only reason she was willing to listen to him and Deep at all was because the *symptoms* from the bonding fruit were getting completely out of control.

She'd thought she was uncomfortable at the party but that was *nothing* to how she was feeling now. From the minute she'd locked herself in the bathroom she'd been doing nothing but touching herself—she couldn't help it. But, like before, giving herself pleasure had only made the problem worse. She was desperate— though she'd be damned if she would admit it.

So she stood there with her arms crossed over her breasts, trying to sound level-headed and cool when it felt like every inch of her skin was throbbing with unquenchable desire.

Facing them with their mating scents washing over her didn't help either. Lock's was warm and comforting—the fresh coffee/clean laundry scent that tempted her to relax and trust him completely. Luckily, Deep's mating scent counteracted it and put her on high alert. He exuded something that smelled like pure sex dipped in dark chocolate—sensuous, alluring...and dangerous as hell. It got into her head and made it hard to think. Any female in her right mind would think twice before trusting a scent like that, Kat thought, frowning up at him.

"You need two things to get over the effects of the bonding fruit, my lady," Lock said at last, apparently deciding to just come out with it. "To be touched and to be penetrated."

Kat put a hand to her throat, her eyes drawn unwillingly to Deep. "You mean the way you did the other night. With…with your fingers?"

Lock shook his head. "I'm afraid not."

"You've had bonding fruit, little Kat—a *lot* of it." Deep's voice was surprisingly soft. "You need deep penetration."

Kat had heard enough. "No thanks." She started to shut the door in their faces but Deep caught it with one hand and held it open easily, though she was shoving against it with all her strength.

"I said you needed to be penetrated—I didn't say it had to be with a cock," he rumbled. His eyes narrowed. "You need to be fucked, Kat. But there are other ways of doing that than the traditional method."

"What you two consider 'traditional' counts as porn on my planet," she pointed out. "And I'm not about to star in the Twin Moons version of *Debbie gets a Double Dicking*."

"We'll keep our pants on—both of us. Will that help?" Deep raised an eyebrow at her.

Kat stopped pushing against the door and stood still. "I suppose…" She really wasn't sure *what* would help at this point but she knew she needed *something*.

"Good. Then come on." Deep took her by the hand and Lock took the other. Kat shivered as the familiar rush of sexual electricity rushed over her. She wasn't at all sure she was doing the right thing...but she didn't know what else to do.

Chapter Thirteen

They led her to the bed and Lock undressed her gently while Deep rummaged in the chest-like bench she'd found the feathered shirt in earlier that morning — which now seemed like a lifetime ago. Kat still felt shy about being naked in front of them but they had dimmed the lights and Lock murmured soothingly to her, telling her how beautiful she was and how he loved her body until she felt a little better.

Finally Deep came back but the object he held in his hand didn't do a thing to assuage Kat's fears. "My God!" she said, sitting up and crossing her legs protectively. "What the hell do you think you're going to do with *that?*"

"I'm going to fuck you with it, little Kat," Deep growled, getting on the bed with her and Lock. Kat noticed that he left his shirt as well as his pants on, though Lock had removed his own dress shirt and was bare-chested.

"I don't think so," she said, eyeing the long, extremely thick, carved wooden phallus he held in one hand. "I don't know what you're thinking but I can tell you right now there is no way in hell *that* is going to fit inside me."

"This is only a little smaller in circumference than our shafts put together," Deep assured her, his black eyes blazing. "Which is why I bought it specifically for you this morning, after we found out how much bonding fruit you'd eaten."

"Leaving aside the question of what will and won't, uh, *fit...*" Kat cleared her throat. "Isn't it kind of strange for you two to have your, you know—*equipment*—touching like that? I mean, most straight guys that I know wouldn't like it at all."

"Touching my brother is like touching myself," Lock said, answering for both of them. "We have sexual feelings only for the woman between us—for you, my lady."

"That's really nice but—"

"You're stalling, Kat." Deep sat on the bed beside her and handed her the phallus. "Here—take it in your hand, look at it, touch it. Get used to it. Because I promise you, before the night is out, it's going deep in your pussy."

"I...I don't..." Kat shrank away from it but Deep took her hand and wrapped her fingers firmly around the wooden shaft. It felt smooth and hard and cool in her palm and Kat couldn't help looking at it with equal parts fascination and dismay. "I'm telling you," she said, looking up at both of them. "It's *not* going to fit."

"Oh but it will, little Kat. I promise you, it will," Deep assured her. He moved up to the head of the bed. "Let's talk a little while first," he murmured in her ear. "Here, sit with me." He coaxed her into position between his thighs but Kat found it hard to relax at first. With his hard chest against her back and his legs on either side of hers, she felt completely surrounded by him—possessed in a way that was both frightening and compelling.

"Relax," Deep urged, stroking her hair with surprising gentleness. "I won't hurt you, sweetheart. You can feel safe with me."

"All...all right." Kat wasn't sure she would ever feel *safe* with him, but she did manage to lean back against him and let some of her tension leak away.

"That's very good." Deep's breath was warm against her ear. "We'll let Lock do the actual penetration and fucking if that makes you feel better. I know you feel safer with him in charge."

Kat couldn't deny that his words were true so she didn't try. She just bit her lip and tried to loosen up as Lock kissed her cheek and the side of her neck. "Slowly, my lady. Gently," he murmured as he slid down her body.

"Do you want Lock to lick your pussy, little Kat?" Deep asked softly. "He can if you think it would help get you ready."

"It would be my very great pleasure," Lock said, looking up at her. "I love tasting you, my lady."

"No...no thank you." Kat shook her head. "I'm just so sensitive right now. I think it might make things worse."

"What things?" Deep asked, one large hand sliding over her bare shoulder. "What are you feeling right now, Kat? What do you need?"

Kat bit her lip but she knew there was no use trying to avoid the question. "I need...I need to be filled," she said in a low voice. "It's like an ache inside me—an emptiness I can't help or control."

"Your body is crying out for ours," Deep told her. "To really be fulfilled, you need both of our cocks buried to the hilt in your pussy—need to have both of us fucking you and coming in you, filling you with our seed."

Kat stiffened against him. "I told you, we are *not* going there."

"Not tonight," Deep assured her. He was caressing both her shoulders now, his large, warm hands moving up and down her bare arms in a soothing massage. "I'm just telling you what your body needs—not what it's actually going to get. Even *one* of us inside you would be better than a carved piece of wood, but I take it you're not prepared to go there either?"

"No." Kat shook her head firmly. "I don't want to take a risk. My pills ran out while I was on the Mother ship — I'm not protected right now."

"There is no birth control pill that works with a Kindred male," Deep said. "But you wouldn't need protection anyway — there's no way you could conceive if only one of us made love to you. In order to become pregnant by Twin Kindred, both of us have to fill you at once."

"That's very comforting," Kat said dryly, hoping her voice didn't tremble and give away her fear. "But I think I'll skip it anyway."

"Let me urge you to reconsider," Deep said seriously. "Penetration with the phallus will ease some of your symptoms. But only being filled with the seed of either Lock or myself will truly end your pain — the deep need you feel to be taken."

"I can't," Kat whispered, shivering. "Can't let myself go that far."

"Not even with Lock?" Deep rumbled in her ear. "He can be very gentle and slow, little Kat. You could just lean back against me and let him fuck you."

His words brought an inescapable image to her mind's eye — one so vivid Kat couldn't help seeing it. She saw herself, leaning back against Deep's broad chest, her hair spread like a red shawl over his shoulders. He was murmuring in her ear, telling her to relax, to open herself, while Lock covered her, his cock thrusting slowly into her, pumping in a gentle rhythm until he filled her with his seed.

For a moment she wanted it — wanted it so badly her entire being ached with the need to have one or both of them inside her, to be pinned between them and penetrated with no hope of escape.

But that was the bonding fruit talking, Kat was sure. She pushed the need away and shook her head. "No," she said. "Not even with Lock. I'm sorry," she added, looking at the light twin. "I just can't."

"I understand." Leaning down he placed a soft, warm kiss on the top of her knee. "I've told you before, my lady, that I don't wish to do anything you don't want me to do."

"Thank you," Kat said gratefully. "I believe you. And I trust you. I...I trust both of you."

"You don't sound entirely sure about that." But Deep sounded amused rather than offended. "Very well, little Kat, let's see what we can do to make you feel better. First I need you to spread your legs."

Kat had known this was coming but it was still incredibly hard to part her thighs completely and let Lock get between them. She forced herself to do it, though, knowing there was no other way.

"Easy, my lady," Lock murmured, rubbing his cheek against the inside of her right thigh. "I swear I'll be gentle with you."

"I know you will," Kat said tightly. "It's just...that thing is so *big*."

"Lock will take things slowly." Deep spoke softly in her ear. "As slowly as you need him to." His hands slid down to find hers and he entwined their fingers. "Hold on to me if you need to."

Kat found she *did* need to. She gripped Deep's fingers tightly as Lock positioned the smooth wooden head between her thighs.

"I'm just going to wet it with your juices, my lady," he said. "For easier penetration." He stroked the head of the phallus between her swollen pussy lips, sliding over her clit. Kat moaned, her hips jerking involuntarily at the bolt of almost painful pleasure that shot through her.

"Sorry," she gasped. "I'm just so damn *sensitive*."

"It's all right." Lock looked concerned. "Did I hurt you?"

"You didn't hurt her, you made her come." Deep's voice was a low growl in her ear. "Look how tight her nipples are. And her pussy is coated in honey. Did it feel good, Kat?" he murmured in her ear. "Or do you need more?"

There was only one answer Kat could give. "More," she whispered breathlessly. "Please, *more.*"

"Put it in her," Deep directed his brother. "Slowly, though. Make sure she's open enough to take it." He kissed Kat on the cheek. "Lock is going to enter you now, Kat. Are you ready?"

"I think so." Kat squeezed his fingers harder. "Just...be gentle."

"Always," Lock assured her. "Always, my lady."

Kat felt him position the head of the carved wooden cock against the entrance of her pussy. Then slowly but firmly he began to slide it into her.

Thought she tried not to, she couldn't help tensing up. On Earth, every time she had a pelvic exam, her doctor always had to use the extra small speculum—she was that tight. And the damn wooden thing Deep and Lock seemed determined to use on her was freaking *huge.* Sure enough, she could feel herself stretching as the wooden shaft slid deeper and deeper into her...but somehow it didn't hurt.

"See?" Deep murmured in her ear. "That's not so bad, is it? And Lock's already got half of it inside you."

"No, it's not," Kat admitted. "It feels...kind of like it's opening me up."

"It is," Deep told her. "But don't worry, it's not permanent. The bonding fruit allows you to be more flexible but everything goes back to normal the minute penetration is over."

"And when...when will it be over?" Kat asked breathlessly as Lock slid the wooden phallus home inside her. She could feel the head of it pressing against the end of her channel and thought she had never been so full in her life.

"Not for a little while," Deep said, kissing the side of her neck possessively. "You need to be fucked hard and deep, little Kat. Need to spread open your pussy and let Lock fill you until you've had enough."

"How will I know when I've had enough?" she protested, her breath catching in her throat as Lock pulled the wooden cock halfway out of her and then thrust it back in again.

"When you stop coming," Deep growled in her ear. "Now let go of my hands for a minute. I want to tease your tight little nipples while Lock fucks you."

Kat released his hands and moaned softly as he reached around her and cupped her bare breasts. "So full and ripe," she heard him mutter hoarsely. "So delicious, my curvy little elite. Fuck her, Brother," he told Lock, who was in a semi-reclining position between Kat's thighs. "Do it for both of us. Give it to her long and hard, the way she needs it."

"God!" Kat's back arched as Lock obeyed his brother's orders.

"That's right, Kat." Deep's voice was hoarse with desire. "Just lean against me and let it happen—let Lock fuck you. Gods but you look beautiful like this—so open and hot."

Kat couldn't answer. She could feel the wooden cock moving inside her, could see it sliding in and out of her pussy, slick with her juices, but she still couldn't believe it. The fact that she was doing this with them—allowing this—seemed both strange and a little frightening at the same time. But right too—undeniably right. The pleasure rolled over her in waves building higher and higher with each stroke, rocking her to her core and making it hard to think. Making it hard to do anything but feel.

She fisted her hands in the material of Deep's black pants, clinging for dear life as he twisted her nipples and Lock fucked her with the wooden cock. "God...*God...*" she moaned almost desperately. She could feel her pleasure coming to a peak and somehow she knew it would help—but not enough. *Need more. Need both of them in me...*but no, she couldn't think like that. It was dangerous.

Deep seemed to know how she was feeling because he began murmuring in her ear. "It feels good, doesn't it little Kat? To be opened...to be *fucked.* But this isn't really what you need. What you need is to be between Lock and me. To open yourself for both of us at once and let us fill your cunt with our cocks."

"No," Kat managed to say.

"Yes." Deep twisted her nipples almost roughly, sending sparks of painful pleasure from her breasts to the place between her thighs where Lock was pumping into her. "You need it," he continued. "Need to feel us thrusting inside you, filling you together until we coat the inside of your pussy with our cum. Only then will you feel true relief, only then will you get what you really need."

"I don't...I can't..." But Kat couldn't talk anymore. Suddenly the pleasure crested inside her, swamping her like an enormous tidal wave that came crashing down around her, nearly drowning her with its intensity. "God!" she cried, her back arching and her fingernails digging into Deep's knees. "Please!"

"Please what?" Deep demanded, his breath hot against the side of her neck. "Please stop fucking you? Or please keep it up?"

Kat couldn't answer. She had never felt so overwhelmed in her life. At least Lock had stopped thrusting into her, though. He withdrew the wooden shaft and sat there waiting, his chocolate brown eyes half-lidded with lust, as she struggled to catch her breath.

"My God," she whispered at last. "That was...incredible."

"Just think how much better it would be with the real thing," Deep said and Lock frowned at his brother.

Now that the tsunami-like orgasm was over, Kat was feeling much more self conscious. She tried to sit up but Deep pulled her back against his broad chest.

"Let me go," she protested. "Aren't we done here?"

"Oh no, little Kat." He sounded like he was smiling as he kissed the side of her neck again. "It takes much more than one deep orgasm to dissipate the effects of the bonding fruit. We're just getting started."

Kat groaned but already she could feel her body wanting more...wanting to be filled again. It was going to be a very long night.

Chapter Fourteen

"You're sure it's been enough time? The results will be accurate?" Sophie stared at the small silver machine which whirred quietly to itself in the corner of Sylvan's home office. He had brought it back to their suite from the med station at her request, because she didn't want to be someplace impersonal when she got her results.

"Ninety-nine point nine percent accurate." Sylvan's deep voice was hushed and Sophie couldn't help biting her lip as she looked at the man she loved. *What is he thinking? What is he hoping for?*

"And...here it is." The machine emitted a few beeps and the lights on its front panel blinked. Sylvan reached into the small slot where he had put the vials of blood he'd drawn from her arm earlier. Sophie was no longer afraid of needles—though she still didn't love being stuck. But this time she had barely felt the needle, she was so anxious to get the results of the test Sylvan was running.

She held her breath as he closed his large hand over the contents of the slot and held it out to her. "What is it?" She was nearly dancing with impatience when he unfolded his fingers to reveal...a small white flower.

"White." Sylvan spoke gently, saying it aloud. "You're not pregnant, *Talana.*"

"Oh." A strange combination of relief and sorrow rushed through Sophie. *So I'm not going to be a mom after all. Not now, anyway.* Then she looked up at Sylvan's face. Though his features were impassive, she knew him well enough by now to see the disappointment in his ice blue eyes. She opened her mouth to speak…and a sob rose in her throat.

"Sophia?" Sylvan leaned down, a worried look on his face. "Are you all right?"

"I…I think so. I don't know why I'm crying." But she couldn't seem to stop.

"You don't know why?" He took her by the shoulders and looked at her worriedly.

"Yes, I do. I know," she said through the sobs that shook her. "It's because I know…know you wanted a son. One who could grow up and play with Liv and Baird's little boy. I'm sorry, Sylvan. So sorry I disappointed you."

"You didn't disappoint me!" He swept her into his arms and held her close, his face pressed to her neck. Pulling back, he looked into her eyes. "You could never disappoint me, *Talana*. I have *you*, and you're all that I need."

"But I know you want a family too," Sophie said, sniffing. "We can try again as soon as you want."

"We weren't trying in the first place," Sylvan pointed out, giving her his little one-sided grin.

"No, I know." Sophie blotted her eyes on her sleeve. "I guess I just got so used to the idea in the past few days. And Liv is so happy to be pregnant."

"Olivia is *ready* to be pregnant," Sylvan said. "I get the feeling you're not. Not quite."

"Maybe I'm not." Sophie looked down at the little white flower which indicated a negative pregnancy test. "But I *want* to be ready. When I look in your eyes and see how much you want a son, I want so much to give you one. A little boy with blond hair and blue eyes, just like you."

"No, he should have green eyes and brown hair with red highlights—just like his mother." Sylvan smiled again and swept a strand of her hair behind her ear. "Or, you never can tell—we might have a daughter. It's extremely rare but it *does* happen from time to time."

Sophie shook her head. "I'd rather have a little boy. I think I would worry about a boy less than a girl."

"I doubt you'd worry less if you knew some of the things *I* got up to as a child."

"Yes, well you were killing abominable *vrannas* by the time you were nine. I hope you wouldn't expect to let our son do anything like that."

"No." Sylvan looked thoughtful. "There aren't any *vrannas* aboard the ship. I suppose we could devise a different manhood ritual for him, though."

"Over my dead body!" Sophie pushed away from him. "Listen, Mister, if you think for one minute I would let you take any son of mine into that kind of dangerous situation—" She broke off because Sylvan was laughing softly. "What?" she demanded.

"Nothing. I'm just thinking what a wonderful, protective mother you're going to be when you're ready to have children. When we're *both* ready." He pulled her close again and Sophie buried her face in his broad shoulder and breathed in his familiar, comforting scent.

I love you, she sent through their link, because it was so much more intimate to use mind-to-mind communication. *Love you so much. Thank you for understanding.*

Talana. Blood of my blood... He buried his hands in her hair and eased her head to one side, baring her throat for his teeth.

Sophie offered her neck eagerly, wanting to feel the rush of pleasure as he bit her and injected her with his essence. Before they had gotten bonded, she had been under the impression that Blood Kindred only bit at the moment of climax. But it turned out, biting—at least the deep, intimate biting done between a warrior and his mate—was almost like deep kissing for them. And now that he knew she truly didn't fear it anymore, Sylvan was prone to sinking his fangs into her any time they had a moment alone. The sharp little prick of his four sharp points penetrating her flesh was like foreplay for her now. In fact, just the feel of his double set of fangs tracing her sensitive skin was enough to make her shiver with desire.

I want you, Sylvan said through their link, tracing his tongue over the delicate blue veins pulsing in her throat. *I want to take you to bed and fill you all night. Want to pump you full of my essence and my cum over and over.*

I want that too. Sophie thought her mental voice sounded rather breathless but she couldn't help it—Sylvan made her weak in the knees, literally. She could barely stand, she wanted him so badly.

Obviously sensing her dilemma, Sylvan swung her up into his arms. Sophie gasped and then snuggled closer to his broad chest. She loved how strong he was—and how gentle he could be despite his immense strength.

"You're strong too, you know," he whispered, apparently catching her thought. "Stronger than you know. You're going to make a wonderful mother when the time is right."

"Maybe it's right tonight," Sophie suggested, kissing him eagerly. "We could try."

"We could," he agreed. "I'm not adverse to 'trying' all night long, if you wish, *Talana.*"

"Yes," she murmured, kissing him again as he carried her from his office to the bedroom. "Yes, let's try."

The only thing that bothered her as he laid her on the bed and began undressing her was the thought of Kat. *I'm not pregnant. I should have gone with her. She's all alone and it's my fault.*

Then Sylvan's hot mouth closed over one of her aching nipples and all coherent thought left her as he bonded her to him again...

* * * * *

"So you're not preggers." Liv looked down at the small, white flower, looking slightly disappointed.

"Afraid not." Sophie handed her twin a plate before sitting down beside her on the couch. Today Liv was craving pancakes and nobody made better blueberry buttermilk pancakes than Sophie—or so she had claimed over the Think-me when she begged Sophie to come make her some. "Anyway, I wasn't when we did the test. After last night, all bets are off again."

Liv laughed. "You decided to try again?"

"And try...and try...and try..." Sophie laughed and then suddenly sobered. "I feel bad about it, though."

"Why should you?" Olivia took a bite and closed her eyes to savor the delicious taste. "Mmm, you've outdone yourself, Sophie!"

"I'm glad you like them. Wasn't that what I was making the morning Baird first claimed you? Blueberry pancakes?"

"Could be." Liv took another bite. "Mmm. But I seem to remember that Kat wanted to make some kind of quiche. Something with way too many ingredients...ugh."

"Kat is always so crazy in the kitchen." Sophie sighed. "Poor Kat… That's what has me feeling so bad. I'm not pregnant, Liv—I *should* have gone with her."

"You couldn't have known," Liv said reasonably. "It was too early to take a test and we couldn't wait to make the decision. It was send her to Twin Moons or lose her—personally, I still feel like we did the right thing."

"I'm worried about her, though. When will we ever get to talk to her?"

"Soon." Liv took a drink of milk. She had told Sophie she still couldn't get Baird to try it. He didn't like the idea of drinking something that came from a bag between a cow's legs, though he ate cheese like it was going out of style. "Baird said that he had a call from Lock a little while ago," she continued. "He and Deep are taking her back to see the holistic healer woman—Mother L'rin—again. They're going to call us on their viewscreen on the way back." She shrugged. "Who knows—if Kat gets a clean bill of health she could be back aboard the Mother ship with us before you know it."

"I hope so," Sophie said earnestly. "And I hope she can forgive us for sending her off with Deep and Lock in the first place."

"Tweedle-dum and Tweedle-dee?" Liv grinned and cut another wedge of pancake with a particularly plump blueberry right in the middle. "Don't worry about them. This is Kat we're talking about—she can hold her own against anyone. I'm sure she'll have some interesting stories to tell us when she gets back, though."

"No doubt," Sophie said, taking a nibble of her own pancake. "Not to change the subject but have you heard any more about Lauren? When I think about what might be happening to her…" She shivered.

"I know," Olivia agreed soberly. "Baird's been working with the High Council but so far they've determined that we can't make any overt moves on the Scourge without having proof of where they're holding her." She sighed and put her plate down on the coffee table. Apparently, the thought of their unknown cousin being subjected to the probes of the AllFather took her appetite away.

"Well, have you heard any more from Aunt Abby? I don't know how much longer we can keep what really happened to Lauren from her," Sophie said.

"As long as possible," Liv said grimly. "Think about it. What's worse — thinking that your only daughter has disappeared into thin air? Or *knowing* that she was kidnapped by an evil, malevolent...*thing* for purposes too horrible to think about?"

"I see your point." Sophie nodded sadly. "But poor Lauren! I was looking her up on-line, you know, wishing we could have gotten to know her. She looks so happy and bright in all her pictures. And did you know she dropped out of business school to start a specialty cupcake shop in Sarasota?"

"Specialty cupcakes? Mmm." Liv nodded. "Sounds like a woman after my own heart."

"Or a woman after your pregnant stomach." Sophie gave her sister a little smile. "I just hope she's all right somehow. And that someday we get to meet her."

Olivia nodded. "I hope so too. I feel so bad for Aunt Abby, though. She still thinks Lauren is on Earth and she's certainly sparing no expense to try and find her."

"What do you mean?" Sophie took another nibble of her pancake.

"We got another vidcall last night. I meant to tell you earlier but I forgot," Liv said. "Baird took it. It was a private investigator Aunt Abby hired — a specialist in finding missing persons."

"Really? What did he want?"

Liv shrugged. "More information and Kindred cooperation. Baird said he was a real hard-ass. But he seemed to think that was a good thing. You know — like he respected him."

Sophie sighed. "Sounds like an alpha male thing to me."

"Of course." Olivia smiled. "And we should both know about that, right womb-mate?"

"Yup." Sophie allowed herself a small smile. "And to think, I used to believe an alpha male was the last thing I wanted."

"You just had 'alpha male' confused with 'asshole,'" Liv said comfortably, picking up her pancake plate again. "They don't always have to be the same thing, you know."

"I know that *now*," Sophie agreed. "But it took Sylvan to show me."

"And Baird to show me." Liv sounded thoughtful. "I wonder what Kat is learning from Deep and Lock?"

Chapter Fifteen

"You're telling me we have *what* kind of a bond?" Kat stared at the two of them in disbelief.

"A soul bond," Lock said quietly. "It's only half a bond, really — incomplete without the physical aspect."

"Which, as you may remember, we have all agreed we're *not* going to pursue," Deep said dryly, his arms crossed over his broad chest. "It's really not that important."

"If it's no big deal then why are you telling me now?" Kat demanded.

"We thought that since you're going to see Mother L'rin again today —" Lock began.

"We thought you'd rather hear it from us than her." Deep frowned. "Speaking of which, if we don't get to the shuttle soon, we're going to be late. They're not going to let us land in the middle of the Healing Gardens again, you know. We're going to be doing some walking to get to her."

"Oh no, you're not brushing this off so easily." Kat put a hand on her hip. "I want to know more about what you two did to me and why you didn't tell me first."

"Let's talk and walk, then," Deep suggested. He was being infuriatingly calm about the whole thing — as though he and Lock bonding her to them against her will was of no importance whatsoever. Which of course made Kat suspicious.

"Please understand, my lady — we were saving your life," Lock pleaded as they all left the house and headed for the waiting shuttle. It had taken the form of a smallish car, as all Kindred shuttles did when not in use for flight. "Mother L'rin told us it was necessary. Your spirit had fractured — forming a bond with you was the only way to mend it."

"I don't know if I believe that," Kat snapped as she climbed into the back of the shuttle.

Deep turned from the driver's seat, his dark eyes narrowed. "Are you calling us liars?"

"Well, it's not like you can actually *prove* what you're saying," she pointed out. "I mean, if I'd broken my arm and woke up with a cast on it, I could buy that. But this whole 'fractured spirit' thing—"

"Came straight from Mother L'rin herself," Deep said, frowning. "She can explain all about it when we get to the Healing Gardens. Until then, don't call us liars until you know what you're talking about."

"Deep, please, I'm sure the lady Kat didn't mean to offend," Lock said quietly from the passenger seat. "She's just upset, that's all."

"Damn right, I'm upset." Kat glared at both of them. "After all that high-sounding talk about how you would 'never bond an unwilling female to you...'"

"We meant a *physical* bond," Deep growled. "Which we could have formed last night if we'd wanted to instead of—"

"Don't start." Kat lifted her chin. "I told you I didn't want to talk about...about what we did last night." In fact, she preferred not to think about it either. *Stupid bonding fruit!* She'd been completely out of control, letting the two of them fuck her with that huge wooden dildo. It made her cheeks hot with shame just remembering it. *Don't think about it,* she told herself. *Just put it behind you and never let it happen again.*

"Don't want to talk about it, hmm?" Deep's eyes were angry in the rearview reflector. "Why not, little Kat? Don't you want to discuss the way you spread yourself for us? The way you gave it up so sweetly while Lock fucked you—"

"That's enough!" Lock's voice was almost a shout. Kat and Deep both stared at him, surprised. "Why," he continued in a lower tone. "Can't the two of you just get along for two minutes? Why can't you stop fighting and admit that you care for each other the way...the way I care for both of you?"

"Because we don't," Deep said coldly, before Kat could answer. "I know you have this sweet, pathetic fantasy that the three of us are going to end up together, Brother but it's not going to happen."

Lock shook his head. "Don't," he said in a low voice. "I thought after last night..."

"You thought wrong." Deep's eyes clashed with Kat's in the rearview again and then he turned his attention back to the curvy, winding road.

"I'm sorry, Lock." Kat reached up to put a hand on his broad shoulder. "I didn't think—"

"And you don't care, either." Deep's eyes were still angry and the emotions coming from him were like a black cloud, filling the interior of the car. Filling Kat herself with hurt and anger and misery.

"Deep..." Lock's voice held a warning note but Deep shook his head.

"She doesn't, Brother—not the way you want her to. So leave it alone. The sooner we get to Mother L'rin and have her dissolve our partial bond the better."

Kat couldn't have agreed more. But she still felt horrible as the little car made its way to the Healing Gardens. *I never wanted it to be like this,* she thought miserably. *Never wanted to care for either one of them. I don't know how my life got so screwed up.* Well, it was about to get straightened out, she comforted herself. According to Deep and Lock, this Mother L'rin person could fix everything.

Kat just hoped they were right because at the moment, a lot more than just her spirit felt broken.

* * * * *

"Looking better today, you are." The wizened old woman with strange, jewel-like eyes and pink-tinged skin circled Kat slowly, watching her sharply as though looking for some invisible defect. "But deceiving appearances can be."

"Oh really?" Kat said politely, glad she could understand what was being said. She'd forgotten all about the convo-pillar still stuck in her ear until Mother L'rin had started speaking. Deep, of course, had wanted her to take it out. He'd said he or Lock could translate for her, but Kat had refused and demanded to speak to the healer alone.

She wanted to be able to talk confidentially with the old woman the twins said had saved her life. There were things she wanted to say and questions she wanted to ask that she didn't feel comfortable having Deep and Lock hear. Besides, she was *dying* to get away from their suffocating emotions. After the fight she'd had with them, riding in the tiny shuttle car all the way to the Healing Gardens had been like breathing in choking lungfulls of second hand smoke. Putting some distance between herself and the two brothers was a breath of fresh air.

Now she was sitting in a lovely little meadow with flowering bushes all around and a golden stream tinkling musically to one side and she felt much calmer. She didn't know where Deep and

Lock had gone — she just hoped they stayed away for a good long while.

"Very ill, you were. Nearly dead, mm-hmm." The old woman nodded wisely and Kat nodded back. The convo-pillar seemed to be working much better today, though it *did* kind of make Mother L'rin sound like Yoda.

"Deep and Lock say you saved my life," she said. "I wanted to thank you for that."

"Healing my profession is. Necessary thanks are not."

"Uh, okay." Kat nodded uncertainly. "They also say you told them to form a soul bond with me — whatever that is."

"Half of a true bond, a soul bond is — the joining of three spirits as one."

"And the other half is the physical bond? When you...?" Kat trailed off, blushing.

"Have sex that is bonding," Mother L'rin finished for her, eyeing her sharply. "But this you have not done."

"No, of course not," Kat blurted. "Look, I never meant to get involved with Lock and Deep in the first place and now everything is all messed up and my whole life feels out of control! I can feel their emotions filling me up until I think I'm *drowning.* Can you help me block them? Lock said you might be able to."

Mother L'rin shook her head. "Only with a full bond is mind privacy possible."

Kat's heart sank. "So you're saying in order to have any kind of peace I'd have to tie myself to them for life?"

The wise woman nodded solemnly. "Bonded to them you must be."

"But I can't be. I don't *want* to be," Kat protested.

"Until you are, weak you will be." Mother L'rin poked a finger at her. "The pain...return it will."

"It will?" Kat felt sick. Come to think of it, she hadn't felt anything like the symptoms she'd had while she was aboard the Mother ship since she woke up. But just the *thought* of enduring that splitting headache again was hideous.

"You must touch them—one at least. Both is better." Mother L'rin nodded sagely. "As greater your weakness grows, the more deeply must you touch."

"You mean like a..." Kat cleared her throat. "Like a *sexual* touch?"

"Yes, yes." Mother L'rin nodded vigorously. "The bond it strengthens. Your pain will ease."

"But I don't *want* to be bonded to them," Kat said, feeling like a broken record. "I mean, Lock is really sweet and I like him a lot but Deep is so *angry* all the time—"

"Much loss has Deep suffered," Mother L'rin interrupted her. "Took your pain he did."

"What?" Kat stared at her, confused. "You mean the headaches and dizziness I was having?"

"Yes," Mother L'rin said simply.

Kat was still confused. "How could Deep take my headaches away?" The sharp, stabbing ache behind her eyes had been intensely painful but she couldn't imagine how it could have been transferred to another person.

"Show you, I will." Mother L'rin raised her voice. "Doby! The whip."

There was a rustling in the nearby bushes and a giant with pink mottled skin appeared. He was taller than a professional basketball player and about three times as broad. His loincloth was made of large, flat leaves and he carried a green wooden box carefully in his huge hands. For some reason he looked familiar to Kat. *That's silly. How can a nine foot tall giant in a leaf loincloth look familiar?* But she couldn't shake the feeling and the sight of him made her vaguely uneasy.

"Here I have it, Mother," he said in a high, almost feminine voice.

"Good. Accompany us to the Stone Throat you will." Turning, Mother L'rin marched off through the long green and pink grass at a surprisingly fast pace. Kat had to scramble up and almost run to keep up with her.

The lovely wilderness of the Healing Gardens was a blur around her as they walked quickly through the grass and flowering bushes. Kat was feeling more and more uncomfortable though she couldn't put her finger exactly on why. But when they came to the mouth of a cave made of brownish-pink stone, the feeling grew even stronger.

"Wait a minute," she said, when Mother L'rin started into the low stone entrance. "Where is this place? I have the strangest feeling of deja-vu but I know I've never been here before."

The old woman only gestured toward the cave. "Inside we must go." She went in and the pink giant followed her, leaving Kat no choice but to join them.

They walked down an echoing stone hallway with Kat feeling worse all the time. By the time they came to the green wooden door with the tarnished handle in its center she was shivering and it wasn't from cold. But it wasn't until Doby swung the door open, revealing a vast, round chamber with a red-streaked white obelisk at its center, that Kat nearly lost it.

"Oh my God! This room!" She walked into the echoing chamber on unsteady legs. "I dreamed this. I saw…" She whirled to Mother L'rin. "I saw him." She stabbed a finger at Doby's mottled pink hide. "He took Deep in here. And he…he…" She couldn't go on. Mutely she went to the white obelisk, pointing like an accusing finger toward the narrow stone chimney above. The red streaks were there, just as they had been in her dream. But now she knew what they were. "Dried blood," she whispered. "My God, he whipped Deep. Whipped him until he bled." She turned back to Mother L'rin. "I saw it all in my dream. What does that mean?"

"Dream sharing you were," the old woman said quietly. "Saw everything you did."

"You mean what I saw was *true?*" She had a sudden mental image of the night before—Deep's broad back, covered in a twisted pattern of white scars. "Oh my God—it *was* true!" Suddenly she felt so faint and dizzy she couldn't stand up anymore. She started to fall and Doby put out a huge hand to catch her. "Get away from me." Kat pushed away from the giant, feeling sick to her stomach. "You're the one who did it to him."

"No, *you* are." Mother L'rin pointed a crooked finger at her. "*Your* pain he took."

"But I don't understand. How could he—?"

"The whip." Mother L'rin nodded at Doby who opened the green lacquered wooden box he carried. Inside was a plain black handle which Kat found sickeningly familiar.

"I…I've seen that before," she said weakly. *Only last time it had long silvery tongues attached to it. With* **spikes** *on their ends.*

"Transfers pain, the whip does," the old woman explained. "Someone had your pain to take."

"And *Deep* volunteered?" For some reason Kat found tears in her eyes. "Why?"

Mother L'rin put a hand on Kat's arm and looked into her eyes. "Why do you think, child?" she said gently.

"I d-don't know." Kat sniffed and blotted her eyes against the long sleeve of her toga-dress. "I honestly don't. He *hates* me. Or at least he doesn't like me very much."

"Himself he hates," Mother L'rin said, releasing her arm. "Cleansed of his hate he must be before you bond."

"But I *can't* bond with him and Lock. Don't you see? It would never work out." Kat thought of her parents—the constant shouting, the cold silences, the ugly accusations and names. Her father calling her mother "a fat, lazy whore" and her mother telling him, "Every time I see you, I hate you more. I wish you were dead." And all that was *before* the beatings started.

Up until they'd finally gotten divorced and her grandmother had taken her in, the only peace she had was when she went to Liv and Sophie's house. *Their* parents had loved each other and it showed in the little acts of affection, the kindness and consideration they showed each other. But Kat's home had been a war zone. And though neither parent had ever physically laid a hand on her, only each other, she still carried the scars of their many battles.

"You don't understand," she told Mother L'rin, aware that she was crying again but unable to help herself. "I can't be with them. I can't be with *him*."

The old woman shook her head and put an arm around Kat's heaving shoulders. "Child, come," she said, leading Kat back to the green door. "If bonded you cannot be, then a journey you must make."

"A…a journey?" Kat blotted her eyes on her sleeve. If this kept up, she was going to have to change clothes because her entire freaking dress would be soaked in tears. God, she hated to cry! "A journey to where?" she said, sniffing and trying to get hold of herself.

"The *fifilalachuchu* blossom you must seek."

"The *what?*" Kat was convinced that her convo-pillar was acting up again but Mother L'rin repeated the name and she realized she'd heart it correctly the first time. "But what good will this uh, *fi-fi* flower do? Will it break the bond between us?"

"Seek it you must," the wise woman repeated firmly. "Back to me you will bring it. Medicine I will make for you."

"Okay." Kat nodded. The strange sounding flower must be the only way to break the soul bond between herself and Lock and Deep. "Uh, where can I find it?" she asked, as they left the cave and walked back to the meadow with the golden brook.

"Find what?" Deep and Lock came forward. Clearly they had been waiting for Kat to come back.

"Some kind of rare flower." Kat found she could barely look at Deep. Why had he taken her pain? Was it out of pride? A sense of responsibility? She knew that a Kindred warrior took his oath to protect any female in his care very seriously. Could that be why Deep had submitted to the vicious beating for her? She wanted to ask him about it—to thank him for what he'd done. But one glance at the scowl on his dark face told her now wasn't the time.

"The *fifilalachuchu* blossom," Mother L'rin said firmly, pulling her thoughts back to the present.

"You mean the Moons blossom? But those are just a legend," Lock protested.

The old woman shook her head. "In some legends, truth lies. Find it on the continent you will."

"The continent?" Deep raised one eyebrow at her. "You want us to cross the golden strait in search of a mythical flower that only blooms when both full moons are in the sky?"

Mother L'rin marched up to him and poked him in the chest with one knarled finger. "At once you *must.*"

Though she was so tiny she barely reached his waist, Deep took a step back and nodded respectfully. "All right, all right. As you say, Mother."

"Very good. Enough time have I wasted with you." She nodded at her giant, silent assistant. "Doby, come."

"Yes, Mother." He shambled after her. Before long, both the tiny figure and the huge one had disappeared into the long pink and green grasses that lined the far side of the stream.

"Well." Lock looked somewhat nonplussed. "It seems we have a quest to fulfill."

Deep snorted. "It seems so. Though what she expects us to find on the continent besides filth and ignorance, I have no idea."

"You heard her—she said to find the Moons blossom." Lock straightened his shoulders. "We'd best get going if we want to make arrangements to leave immediately."

"Immediately?" Kat asked, startled. "As in *tonight?*"

"If we can," Lock said grimly. "You heard Mother L'rin—she said we had to go at once. It may be a matter of life and death." He looked at Kat. "What did she tell you?"

"A lot of things." Kat studied the ground, afraid that if she looked up she would catch Deep's eyes and see the silver whip reflected in their midnight depths.

"What did she say about *you?*" Deep's voice was harsh. "Are you completely well? All healed?"

Kat thought of what the wise woman had told her. That if she didn't touch at least one of the brothers—or preferably both—her pain and weakness would come back. She opened her mouth to tell them…but somehow she just couldn't. Not after the fight they'd had. How could she ask them to touch her when she refused to bond with them? It seemed rude and wrong—like she was using them. Besides, she had her pride. She didn't want to sound like she was begging.

"Are you well, my lady?" Lock said and she realized she'd been silent too long.

"I'm fine." She shrugged, trying to sound unconcerned. "What you two did for me cured me. So…thank you."

Deep raised one black eyebrow. "So you *admit* the soul bond was necessary. You're not so quick to call us liars now, hmm?"

A sharp retort rose to Kat's lips but she bit it back when she remembered what he'd done for her. Mother L'rin's voice echoed in her head. *"Himself he hates."* Lifting her chin, she looked at Deep. "I'm sorry if what I said hurt you," she said, staring unflinchingly into his angry eyes. "But it looks like we're stuck together a little while longer. So I'd like to offer a truce—no more fighting. No more backbiting. No more hurting each other. Deal?"

He raised an eyebrow. "For the duration of our little 'quest' as Lock puts it?"

Kat nodded. "Yes. Will you agree?"

Deep shrugged, a look of apparent unconcern on his face. "If you like. Though fighting with you is much more amusing than fighting with Lock."

"None of us ought to be fighting," Lock said in a low voice. "We're going to need to stick together when we get to the continent—if we ever want to get off of it again, that is."

That sounded ominous to Kat. *Like we're going to the dark side of the moon or something. It's all on the same planet—how bad can the 'continent' be?*

She was afraid she was going to find out.

Chapter Sixteen

"Kat! You look wonderful!" Liv was so glad to see her friend's face on the viewscreen she nearly *squeed* with joy. Beside her, Sophie was practically hopping up and down with excitement.

"Kat-woman! We miss you so much!"

"I miss you guys too. You have no *idea* how much."

"I'm so sorry we let you go alone," Sophie said breathlessly. "We didn't want to but pregnant women can't go through folded space."

Kat looked startled. "So *you're* pregnant too?"

"No, no." Sophie shook her head rapidly. "But at the time I thought I might be. Because Sylvan and I had been…you know, practically every spare minute and my period was late."

"Well don't worry about it, I forgive you." Kat smiled at both of them.

"But you're okay?" Liv asked her. "You're managing, right?"

Kat made a shooing gesture. "Don't worry about me, girls. There's nothing on Earth I can't handle if I put my mind to it. Or on Twin Moons, either."

"You look good," Liv said, not quite truthfully. Honestly she thought Kat looked tired and not quite herself. But at least she was up and about instead of passed out on the floor—which was the state she'd been in the last time they'd seen her.

"How do you feel?" Sophie wanted to know.

"Better than I did," Kat said. "But still not a hundred percent. The headache is gone at least."

"That's a start," Liv said firmly. "So when are you coming home? Just say the word and Baird will get them to fold space."

Kat grimaced. "If it was up to me I'd be there *yesterday* but…unfortunately, I can't come back for a little while yet. There's something I have to do—have to get—before I can leave Twin Moons."

"What?" Liv and Sophie chorused together.

Kat laughed. "It always cracks me up when you guys do that—say the same thing at the same time. Well, it's kind of a long story…"

"And we've got nothing but time," Liv said. "C'mon, Kat—spill."

Kat sighed and raked a hand through her long auburn hair. "God, how do I put this without sounding crazy…?"

"Don't worry about the crazy part—that's a given when it comes to the Kindred," Sophie ordered. "Just talk."

"Fine." Kat took a deep breath. "Apparently joining with Lock and Deep the way I did, to act as their focus, 'fractured my spirit.' And the only cure for a fractured spirit is to form a soul bond with a willing Kindred…or two. So…"

"Oh my God!" Sophie clapped a hand over her mouth.

"You mean you're *bonded* to Lock and Deep?" Liv demanded.

"Not entirely," Kat said quickly. "Only about halfway, if that makes any sense."

"Not a bit," Liv said. "But go on."

"Well, with Twin Kindred the bond comes in two halves—the soul bond which is kind of a spiritual connection—and the physical bond. Which is what you get when you have bonding sex." Kat made a face. "And girls, you would not *believe* how the Twin Kindred do it."

"One at a time?" Sophie guessed.

"One in the front and one in the back," Liv said.

Kat shook her head. "Nope. I met a new friend here by the name of Piper who comes from Houston. And as Piper so charmingly put it, they put 'two poles in the same hole.'"

"No!" Both Liv and Sophie were aghast. "Jillian never told me that," Liv protested.

Kat shrugged. "Well, it's true."

"But that's barbaric," Sophie protested. "Unless they have...do they have really tiny equipment?"

"From what I've seen and felt, they're every bit as *endowed* as all the other Kindred warriors," Kat said dryly. "Remember how we used to joke that all Kindred were hung like Clydesdales?"

"Oh *no*." Sophie looked horrified.

"It's not as bad as it sounds," Kat said, apparently worried by the way they were looking at her. "They have this stuff called bonding fruit that, uh, makes you more *flexible* in certain areas. If you know what I mean."

"And that's supposed to make it okay?" Liv demanded.

"I don't know about 'okay,' but supposedly it keeps the whole *process* from hurting." Kat's cheeks were pink. "Not that I want to find out first hand."

"Kat, that's awful! You can't let them do that to you. You have to get away from them!" Liv leaned forward, wishing she could reach through the viewscreen and drag her friend to safety.

"That's what I'm trying to do," Kat protested. "But first we have to find this rare flower—it only grows in a certain part of Twin Moons."

"Seriously?" Liv raised an eyebrow at her. "You can't come home because you and Lock and Deep are going to go *flower picking* together?"

"We *have* to. It's the only way to dissolve the bond." Kat sighed. "We're going to bring it back to Mother L'rin and she's going to make some kind of special bond breaking medicine or something."

"Well," Sophie said doubtfully. "I guess if that's the only way you can get free of them…"

"It *is*." Kat ran a hand through her hair. "Look, I told you it sounded crazy, didn't I? But I have no choice. And I swear as soon as I get the stupid bond dissolved I'll be on my way back."

"Well, if you have to, you have to." Sophie sighed philosophically. "Just try not to take too long. You *do* realize I can't plan my wedding without you."

"Or my baby shower," Liv put in.

Kat shook a finger at them. "You'd better not!"

"Of course not." Liv smiled. "So how are things otherwise? Are Tweedle-dum and Tweedle-dee behaving themselves?"

Kat shook her head. "I just don't know. Lock is a sweetheart, as always. But Deep…well, Deep is Deep. And I mean that both literally and figuratively."

Sophie frowned. "Meaning what—that you two are still fighting?"

"We have what you could call an uneasy truce right now," Kat said. She looked behind her and then leaned closer to the viewscreen and lowered her voice. "But I found something out about him. Something he did—"

"Kat," a deep male voice said from somewhere off screen. "The ship leaves very soon. You need to hurry."

"Just a minute!" Kat looked harassed. "We have to leave on the flower hunt tonight and the guys are waiting outside the shuttle so I can talk to you two privately. But I guess they're getting impatient."

"Forget about them," Liv said. "Tell us what you found out. Is he an axe murderer? A gigolo?"

"No," Sophie cut in. "She said it was something he *did*. What did he do, Kat? Was it awful?"

"Kat!" said the deep male voice again. "We have to go *now*."

Kat sighed. "Sorry, I guess I'll have to tell you later. But believe me, you will *never* guess in a million years. Love you both." She blew kisses at the viewscreen and Liv and Sophie did the same.

"Kat, just tell us—" Liv started to say but then the viewscreen went blank as their friend's picture flickered out.

"Crap!" Sophie sounded disappointed. "What do you suppose she was about to say? What did Deep do?"

"I have no idea." Liv frowned. "But knowing him, I'm guessing it wasn't random acts of kindness. I just hope Kat will be okay."

Sophie looked troubled. "I hope so too."

Liv gave her twin a comforting hug. "I'm sure she'll be home soon and then we can get the scoop directly from the source."

"I guess." Sophie didn't sound convinced. "But I think I'll ask Sylvan what he knows about Deep...just in case."

Liv nodded thoughtfully. "I'm going to grill Baird too. And we can compare notes later."

She just hoped she didn't find out anything too awful about the dark twin's past. If Kat was already halfway bonded to him, there was no telling what might happen to their friend.

Chapter Seventeen

"So we're actually going to sail to this continent place on a *boat?*" Kat eyed the green wooden boat with the pale pink sail doubtfully. It looked very picturesque rocking on the golden water—but not very safe. And despite living in Florida all her life, Kat had never learned to like sailing—she was always afraid she'd fall off whatever boat she was on, into shark-infested waters. "Why can't we take the shuttle?" she asked Lock. "We could just fly there, find the *fi-fi* flower, and be back in a couple of hours."

"It isn't permitted to take advanced technology to the continent, my lady," he said, shaking his head. "The natives who live there are very superstitious. They might take it for black magic and want to kill us for offending their gods."

"Wait a minute—there are *natives?*" Kat's heart skipped a beat.

"Angry, *hostile* natives." Deep, who had been loading their gear spoke up.

"Not if you don't antagonize them," Lock said quickly. "And honestly, there aren't that many of them. Hopefully we'll be able to avoid them all together."

Kat shook her head. "I don't understand. Twin Moons seems like such a civilized place. How can you have a whole continent of superstitious savages?"

"It has to do with the genetic trade," Lock explained. "When the Kindred first came to Twin Moons, hundreds of cycles ago, they introduced themselves to the inhabitants of the islands. There are over three hundred islands of different sizes and shapes in the archipelago, you know. Anyway, the Kindred made their trade with the islanders. Being fishermen, traders, and explorers, they were more open to new ideas and to change."

"I get it." Kat nodded. "So the islanders got all the technology and advances..."

"Not to mention the genetic advantages of the Kindred," Lock said. "While those who still lived on the continent—"

"Remained ignorant savages." Deep smirked at her. "Ignorant and *depraved* if you can believe the rumors. It's said they have the most barbaric sexual habits."

Kat raised an eyebrow. "More barbaric than never having sex unless you have at least *three* people involved?"

Deep grinned. "Point taken. But no, they still have two males to one female—that's normal. For *our* world, of course. I'm well aware it's considered immoral and disgusting on yours." He laughed, as though making a joke, but Kat could feel a wave of bitterness coming from him that belied his apparent good humor. It settled harshly on her tongue like a bad tasting medicine she couldn't spit out.

"Over the years attempts were made to bring the natives into the trade, but they were put off by the change in our physical appearance," Lock explained. "The Kindred genes make us much larger and more intimidating. And they changed our skin and hair color too, making us resemble the natives less and less each passing generation. Until at last, we are an entirely different race of people."

"That's kind of sad," Kat said thoughtfully. "To lose contact with your roots that way."

"Believe me, if you saw them, you wouldn't think so," Deep said. "They still live in grass huts and perform sacrifices to their gods on full moon nights. Some even say they practice cannibalism."

"Ugh." Kat made a face. "I *really* hope we can find the *fi-fi* flower and get back without running in to any of those guys."

"That's what we all hope, my lady," Lock said soberly. "But the sooner we get to the continent, the sooner we can find the Moons blossom and come home." He looked at Deep. "Are we ready?"

The dark twin nodded. "Everything's loaded." He stepped from the pier and over the side of the rocking boat. Looking at Lock and Kat he said, "Come on. Time's wasting."

"Very well—come, my lady." Lock climbed aboard also and then held out a hand to Kat.

Kat looked at the swaying golden water uneasily. It was very beautiful, certainly. But who knew what it hid in its depths? Just watching the way the waves swelled and slapped against the wooden side of the boat made her stomach roll. Still, she had to get aboard. Taking a deep breath, she reached for Lock's hand. But just as she was leaning over the narrow gap between the pier and the side of the boat, a wave of dizziness hit her.

"God!" She put a hand to her head, swaying and would have fallen if Lock hadn't quickly grabbed her hand.

"My lady?" he asked, looking at her with concern. "Are you all right?"

"Fine, I'm fine." Kat blinked, trying to clear the bright spots that were dancing in front of her eyes. *"Weak you will be,"* whispered the voice of Mother L'rin in her head. *"The pain...return it will."* But that couldn't be happening yet, could it? She was probably just weak because she hadn't eaten much today and her blood sugar was low. *That must be it,* Kat told herself. *Please God, that **has** to be it. I can't* *deal with this right now. I just need to be strong enough to go get this damn flower and get back again.*

"Are you sure you're all right?" Deep was frowning down at her, his bottomless black eyes filled with some emotion she couldn't read—it roiled inside him like a cloud of smoke, nebulous and confusing. "What happened, anyway?" he asked.

"Nothing," Kat lied. "I just started to trip but Lock saved me. No big deal."

"It had better not be. If I find out there's something you're not telling us…"

"Leave her alone, Deep." Lock frowned at his brother. "Go make sure the boat's ready to sail. We need to go if we're going to catch the crosswind."

"Yes, *Captain.*" Performing a mock salute, Deep turned to go. But not before he pierced Kat with another impenetrable look.

"So how long is this, uh, voyage going to take, anyway?" she asked, ignoring him as they got under way. "Not too long, I hope. This isn't a very big boat."

"It's the sailing vessel our fathers left us," Lock explained, doing something to one of the many ropes that were all around the boat. "We used to come out in it often before they died."

"I'm so sorry," Kat said. "I didn't mean to offend you."

"You didn't," Lock assured her. "It was a long time ago. And to answer your question, the trip to the continent is only a few hours with a good headwind. We'll be there before you know it."

"Oh good." Kat felt relieved. "I was afraid we were going to be gone for weeks."

"We might be," Deep said. "The flower Mother L'rin is sending us to find is rare—some say it exists only in legends and fairy tales."

"What?" Kat frowned. "Then how are we supposed to find it?"

"We'll start in the hill region," Lock said. "That's where the legends that talk of it come from. And it's only a day's hike from where we'll be landing."

"Hiking?" Kat raised her eyebrows. "Nobody said anything about *hiking*. I know you guys have on boots but I'm still wearing these." She nodded down at the dainty, strappy sandals Lock had gotten for her at the local bazaar. She had to admit he had good taste and was excellent at judging her size, but the sandals were hardly suited to days of rugged mountain climbing.

"Don't worry," Deep told her. "The continent is covered in *belsh*. It's a soft, velvety moss that cushions your feet at every step."

"It's so comfortable to walk on barefoot that the natives have never worn shoes," Lock explained. "The whole concept of footwear is entirely foreign to them."

"Well...all right." She nodded. "But if we're going to be there awhile, where are we going to stay the night? I'm assuming there aren't any Hiltons or Holiday Inns on the continent."

"We'll sleep under the stars," Deep said. "And there's a tent if it rains." He raised an eyebrow at Kat. "Though it might be a tight fit for three."

"Guess we'll be hoping for clear skies then," she said dryly. Although a night snuggled up between the two of them was probably exactly what she needed to keep from getting too weak to function. *What I want and what I need are two different things*, Kat told herself firmly. *Besides, there's no point in being worried over nothing. We'll find the flower and come back in no time. I'll be fine.*

She hoped.

* * * * *

Kat thought later in her life that the trip in the little wooden boat over the golden sea was one of the things about Twin Moons she would never forget.

Because Twin Moons' sun was a red dwarf, the sunlight had a golden-pink glow that sparkled on the water. It was so clear she could see fathoms and fathoms down to the ocean floor where rainbow colored fish flitted playfully among spiny corals and waving anemone-type creatures. There were larger creatures too, moving in the depths. Some longer than their boat and about twice as wide, with round, glassy eyes and rough purple skin. Lock told her not to worry about them, though. He said they were peaceful plant eaters that wouldn't harm her even if she fell overboard. Kat planned to stay firmly in the boat anyway—she had no interest in finding out how "tame" and "harmless" the huge creatures were firsthand.

At last they landed on the sandy shore of a vast tract of land— the continent. Deep and Lock anchored their boat firmly in a natural cove they knew of and the three of them took off their shoes and boots and Kat hiked up her dark blue toga dress before they splashed ashore.

The pink, sugar-fine sand of the beach soon gave way to rolling hills covered in a soft green velvety moss that felt wonderful under Kat's toes. It was sprinkled with yellow and periwinkle blue flowers which she gathered as they walked and wove into a crown to wear in her hair. It was a game she and Liv and Sophie had used to play—queen of the castle—and she wished they could be there to see her now and admire the scenic beauty of the land she found herself in.

To her surprise, Kat was actually enjoying herself. She was more at peace than she could remember feeling since before Liv's wedding. *Before I met Deep and Lock, that is,* she told herself. But even the twins seemed to be feeling peaceful. Or at least, Kat wasn't filled to overflowing with their angst and hunger for once. Everything was quiet here on the continent—even their usually overwhelming emotions. It was very pleasant, though she knew it could change in an instant.

The sky was a vast lavender-blue bowl above her head without a single scrap of cloud. *Looks like our sleeping arrangements won't be too crowded tonight then,* Kat thought, gazing up at it. *Good thing I'm still feeling fine.* It was true she was a little tired, but a lot had already happened that day—it was to be expected that she would get somewhat fatigued, she told herself. Lifting her chin, she ignored the ominous beginnings of a headache behind her right eye, and kept walking.

"So what are we looking for, anyway?" she said after they'd been hiking for about an hour in silence. "I mean, what does this *fi-fi* blossom look like?"

"The Moons blossom has two flowers on a single stem," Lock said. "One light and one dark, like the moons that fill our sky at night."

"One moon—*Dakir* is always in the shadow of the other—*Lanare*," Deep explained. "So *Dakir* shows up as a black disk in the sky rather than a white or light one like *Lanare*. "When both are fully visible at once, then it's said the Moons blossom will bloom."

"Is it a full moon night tonight then?" Kat asked, shading her eyes to look up at the sky. The large pinkish sun was already descending, dropping behind the purple peaks brooding in the distance.

"The moons are coming to their zenith tomorrow night," Lock said. But they should be close enough to full tonight for our purposes. Legend says that the Moons blossom hides in plain sight—its stem blends into the *belsh* and the flowers don't unfurl until the light of the moons touches their petals."

"So...they could be anywhere and we'd never see them?" Kat asked.

"Not until the moons come out." Deep frowned. "Actually, we should probably be finding a place to camp. There's a likely looking copse of trees over there about a hundred yards away." He nodded at the small area of dense vegetation which reminded Kat of the bushes and trees in the Healing Gardens. "We might as well get comfortable and find a place to rest since we're going to be up half the night hunting for *fi-fi* flowers, as Kat calls them."

"Very funny." Kat put a hand on her hip. "But that's as close to pronouncing that weird long name that Mother L'rin said. Come to think of it, my convo-pillar wouldn't even translate it. Why is that?"

Deep raised an eyebrow at her. "Possibly because it's the biological equivalent of a shoddy piece of technological equipment? I believe in Earth vernacular you would call it a 'piece of crap.'"

"Nice try," Kat said. "But I'm not giving it up. I don't like being dependant on anyone else to communicate for me."

Deep put a hand to his chest. "It touches my heart, little Kat, that you're so very *trusting*."

Kat knew she shouldn't let him get to her, but her head was really beginning to throb. "Maybe if you'd *talk* to me instead of keeping secrets," she said furiously. "If you'd give me a *reason* to trust you—"

"Stop!" Lock frowned at both of them. "Kat's convo-pillar couldn't translate Mother L'rin's name for the Moons blossom because it comes from the Elder Tongue."

"The what?" Kat asked.

"The Elder Tongue," Lock repeated. "It's the root of all languages on Twin Moons and impossible to translate by biological or technical means. You have to study it for years to understand even a tenth of it."

"And have you?" she asked. "Studied it?"

"Unsolvable riddles and obtuse, unlearnable languages are my dear brother's passion," Deep answered for him. "It's one of the reasons he puts up with me so well."

"Exactly," Lock replied, smiling. "Because no one else in the universe speaks Deep's language but me. Not really."

Kat could well believe that was true, but it was interesting to hear them admit it out loud. *So they know what they are to each other and how they appear to other people. Deep knows that he makes it hard for Lock and Lock forgives him and loves him anyway. Fascinating.*

"Come here, Brother." Deep grabbed for his twin and threw an arm over Lock's shoulders, pulling him close for a brief embrace. "What would I do without you to translate for me?"

"You'd have died long ago. Most likely at the hands of an angry mob." Lock grinned and hugged his twin back.

For a moment Kat forgot her growing headache in the pleasure of their positive emotions for each other. The love that flowed between the brothers spilled through their three-way link and flowed over her skin like the warm glow of a fire on a chilly night. *Wow,* she found herself thinking. *See, if they felt like this all the time, I wouldn't mind sharing their emotions at all. It's really kind of nice.*

It was so nice, in fact, that she didn't notice the large green bush with vivid pink flowers that was creeping up behind her. Nor did she see the hand holding a knife with a strange, clear blade until it was at her throat.

By the time she felt the sharp prick on the side of her neck, it was too late. "So still — not moving. A frightened creature ensnared. Lovely prisoner," whispered a throaty voice in her ear.

"What?" Kat started to look around in panic but the sharp point dug deeper into her neck.

"Goddess of full curves. I do not wish to harm you. Be still in my arms," the voice commanded as a hard arm encircled her waist.

"Deep?" she gasped, holding perfectly still. "Lock? Guys, I think we have company."

The twins turned in unison and she saw their faces change from happiness to worry and rage. "You dare..." Deep took a step toward her and her unseen captor, his eyes turning red and his huge hands balled into fists. "You *dare* touch our female? Take your hands off her *now* or suffer the consequences!"

"Deep, no!" Lock put a restraining hand on his brother's shoulder. "Going into *rage* won't help."

"It can't hurt, either." Deep took another step forward. He was looking over Kat's shoulder, clearly addressing the male who was holding her captive. "Let her go now and I *might* let you live."

"This elite beauty. Sunfire hair, throat so white. One wrong step kills her," hissed Kat's captor.

Despite her terror, Kat couldn't help wondering about his speech. *Is my convo-pillar acting up again or is this guy actually speaking in haikus?* If she hadn't been so afraid it would have been funny. *Oh well, better haiku than iambic pentameter,* she thought, feeling slightly hysterical. *I always sucked at that whenever we did Shakespeare in class.*

Deep advanced on her captor, a low growl rising in his throat.

"Deep, stop!" Lock sounded desperate now. "He has a crystal knife — they dip them in *shagra* venom. One scratch could be fatal to the lady Kat."

Deep's eyes narrowed and he took a step backward with obvious effort. "All right, fine." His voice still sounded rough with barely suppressed fury. "Tell us what you want and then leave us alone."

"This holy meadow. You trespass here un-asking. Death is your reward." The knife at Kat's throat poked a little harder but somehow it still didn't break the skin. From the corner of her eye she could see a strange sight—the bushes they had seen in the small copse of trees where Deep had wanted to camp for the night were all moving toward them. As they came closer, people emerged from behind them—strange looking people with mottled pinkish skin and large, golden-pink eyes. Their hair was black with a purple tinge and they had thin lips and delicate, pointed ears that made her think of elves or fairies. They were all wearing leaf loincloths and every single one was short—none of them was even as tall as Kat's own five foot six.

With their diminutive stature and strange, jewel-like eyes, Kat thought they looked an awful lot like Mother L'rin. And their leaf couture reminded her of the wise woman's huge and silent attendant, Doby. But their appearance didn't worry her nearly as much as the fact that there appeared to be about fifty of them and all of them were armed with long, clear knives.

Oh my God... She felt faint and queasy. *Is this how it ends? Killed by angry alien natives who speak in haikus? I never should have left Earth...*

But then Lock began speaking rapidly, saying something that her convo-pillar couldn't even begin to translate. He gestured at Kat and then made a pleading motion with both hands, his palms outstretched. Kat didn't know what he was saying but slowly, the male holding the knife at her throat relaxed and finally he withdrew the sharp point all together.

Kat nearly cried in relief but from the look on Lock's face, they weren't out of trouble yet. He was still talking for all he was worth, gesturing eloquently, as though trying to make a point. The male behind Kat, who was holding her arm, replied but she got the feeling that Lock wasn't convincing him to let them go.

Her feeling proved to be justified when her captor came around in front of her and looped a thick strand of rough rope around her wrists.

"Lock," she asked, careful to keep her voice low and nonthreatening. "What's going on?"

"I'd like to know as well," Deep growled. He was eyeing the short, stocky male who had captured Kat in a most unfriendly way and the pupils of his eyes were still more red than black.

"They're taking us to meet their chief," Lock said in a low voice. "Apparently we stumbled into their holy meadow and the usual penalty is death. But I told him the lady Kat was a lost sun goddess looking for Moons blossoms to cure her illness."

"Very poetic of you, Brother," Deep said, frowning. "But a *sun* goddess?"

"She has sunfire red hair and she's an elite," Lock shot back. "It was the best thing I could think of at the time."

"So that's it?" Kat asked as the natives bound both Lock and Deep's wrists with the same rough, faded pink rope. "We're just going to go with them?"

"I'm afraid we have little choice, my lady," Lock said ruefully. "They all have poisoned knives. One scratch will introduce a neuro-toxin into our systems so deadly we would never get home alive."

"All right." She nodded and swallowed hard, trying not to think of how close the knife point had come to cutting into her throat. "But what will they do to us when we get to their chief?"

"I think I'll be able to talk to their chief," Lock said. "They seem impressed that I know the Elder Tongue. Hopefully I'll be able to make some kind of bargain."

"Hopefully," Kat echoed faintly. *When I get out of this, I'm going to have some story for Liv and Sophie.*

She just hoped she lived to tell it.

Chapter Eighteen

They threw Kat into a cave. Not just any cave, either—a dark, dirty cave full of very sharp rocks. The only light was from some glowing blue fungus that grew on one wall. There was a large flat boulder not far from the luminescent wall and Kat dragged herself to it and collapsed on it.

*Oh God, my head...my **head**.* The pain was back, just as Mother L'rin had predicted and this time it felt even worse than Kat remembered. She wished now that she hadn't been too proud to tell Lock and Deep what the wise woman had said and ask for help. *Stupid...I'm so stupid.* But it was too late to be sorry. The brothers had been taken somewhere else and she was on her own.

Kat tried to think about escape but really, where would she go? Even if she could bear to stand upright and try to sneak past the guards at the mouth of the cave, what then? Of course, a heroine in one of her favorite romance novels would have been feisty and smart enough to hatch a plot to save both of her guys and get them all away to safety. *But I'm not smart,* Kat thought with a groan. *Or I would have told Deep and Lock what was going on to begin with. And I'm pretty much the exact opposite of feisty right now. I'm miserable and weak and drained.*

She didn't know how long she lay on the cold, flat boulder. The pain in her head and the weakness that had come over her were so debilitating she could barely move. Her consciousness seemed to come and go in waves and the glowing blue wall at her side flickered in and out like a bizarre kind of neon sign.

"Kat?" The deep voice echoed in the darkness some unknowable length of time later. "Kat? I know you're in here—I can feel how upset you are."

"Here," she managed to whisper feebly. "Who…?"

"It's me." Deep came suddenly into view, picking his way toward her over the fallen rocks. "Lock and I felt your distress and he managed to convince the natives that one of us had to be in here with you at all times. Sorry it turned out to be me, but he has to keep talking to their chief so I'm afraid you're stuck with—" He broke off abruptly, obviously getting a good look at her for the first time. "Gods, Kat! Are you all right?"

"Just peachy." Kat managed a weak smirk. Despite her pain she was still reluctant to admit the extent of her disability to Deep.

"Why are you lying there like that? What's wrong?" he demanded, crouching beside her.

"Just getting a little rest." *This is stupid—just tell him!* But somehow she couldn't. "Being kidnapped at knifepoint by aliens who speak in obscure forms of poetry always tires me out." She tried to smile but it was apparent Deep wasn't fooled.

"Stop being so goddess damned brave and tell me what's wrong." Tilting his head to one side to look into her eyes, he cupped her cheek gently. "Please, Kat. Tell me."

Even that one simple skin-to-skin touch made things a little better—drove the pain behind her eyes back a bit. Kat couldn't help herself, she moaned softly in relief.

"I'm sorry!" Deep pulled his hand away as though he'd been stung. "Forgive me, I didn't mean to hurt you."

"You didn't." When his hand left her skin, the pain returned. This time it felt like someone was driving a rusty iron spike into her brain. Kat squeezed her eyes shut, a single tear slipping down her cheek though she tried to hold it back.

"Kat?" He sounded genuinely distressed. His hand hovered over her cheek again but didn't quite connect—as though he was afraid by touching her he would make her worse.

"You didn't hurt me," she forced herself to say again. "This…the pain is back, that's all."

"How? How could it come back?" Deep demanded.

"Doesn't matter." Kat tried to shake her head and groaned. "Knew…knew it would come back. Mother L'rin…warned me."

Deep scowled. "I *knew* she'd told you more than you were letting us know. Tell me now, Kat—what did she say?"

Kat was still reluctant to talk but it seemed she couldn't avoid it any more. "She said…she told me that I still needed…needed to touch you and….Lock." The rusty iron spike was digging into the tender flesh behind her eyes now, making it hard to think. "Incomplete bond means…pain…weakness…."

Deep ran a hand through his hair distractedly. "Why didn't you tell us?"

Despite her pain, Kat lifted her chin defiantly. "Didn't want…your pity. And after the fight we had I didn't…didn't think you two would want to touch me anyway."

"You mean you didn't think *I* would want to." Deep shook his head. "Goddess damn you, Kat, for your stupid, stubborn pride. Don't you know I'd do anything to keep you from pain?" Standing, he began stripping off his shirt.

But when he reached for her, Kat had a sudden thought. "Wait," she protested as he bent toward her. "Lock said…said it hurts you to touch too much if…if the other one isn't there." She gestured weakly at his bare chest. "Too much skin-to-skin contact...without Lock...will hurt you."

"You think I give a damn about that?" Deep's voice was an angry growl but he gathered her into his arms with surprising gentleness. "Come here, damn you. Let me hold you," he murmured, settling himself on the flat boulder with her in his lap.

Kat couldn't help it—she didn't want to give him pain, but the immediate relief she felt when his broad, warm chest came in contact with her cheek was too wonderful to deny. His arms around her were so comforting and strong and the scent of his skin made her feel safe—protected. Suddenly, though she didn't know why, she was crying.

Stop crying, stupid! It's bad enough that holding you hurts him, he doesn't want you crying all over him too! But she couldn't stop. And to her surprise, Deep didn't say a thing. No sarcastic remarks or biting observations—he just held her closer and stroked her hair in a gentle rhythm that somehow calmed her down.

"I'm sorry," she said at last, when her tears slowed. "I didn't mean to cry like that."

"Were you crying because it still hurts?" Pressed against him as she was, his voice rumbled through her in a way that was oddly comforting.

"No," Kat said honestly. "I think...I think I was crying because it finally *stopped* hurting. I know that doesn't make any sense..."

"It doesn't have to." Deep stroked her hair. "There's no rhyme or reason to pain—it just is."

"I'm feeling better now," she said cautiously, raising her head to look at him. In the dim otherworldly glow from the luminescent moss he looked like a dark angel. "I...I should probably be all right for a little while now."

He shook his head. "Can't wait to get away from me, can you?"

"It's not that," Kat protested. "But I know this is *hurting* you. Every minute you touch me without Lock touching me too—he told me it was like an electrical shock running through you. That can't be comfortable."

"It's not," he said shortly. "And yet, I would hold you a little while longer, if you'll permit it."

"Oh, uh…okay." Kat tried not to let the surprise show on her face but clearly he could feel it through their link.

"It surprises you?" Deep asked, settling her more firmly against him. "That I would want to touch you—to be near you—for any kind of nonsexual reason?"

"It's not sexual?" she blurted. "I mean, you *do* have your shirt off and I'm wearing a really thin dress with no bra—"

"Does this feel sexual to you?" He shifted his hips, pressing up against her. The intimate contact made it obvious that he wasn't hard.

"Uh no," Kat admitted. "No, I guess not."

"It can't be sexual—not without Lock. And I don't want it to be," Deep said softly. "Don't want you to think that's all there is—to think that's all I want from you."

"What *do* you want?" Kat looked up at him, honestly confused.

"Right now? Just to hold you." He kissed her gently on the forehead.

"But the pain—"

"Believe me, little Kat, the pain of *not* holding you is much worse than any discomfort I get from a little skin-to-skin contact." Deep stroked her back. "Do you believe me?"

"Yes." She nodded slowly. "I don't understand but...I do believe you."

"Thank you. Now relax and be still."

They sat in silence for a long while—how long, Kat didn't know. There seemed to be no time in the dark, cool cave. Just the sound of their breathing and the faint thunder of Deep's heart in her ear. She could smell his mating scent—the warm, dark chocolate sex smell which had made her feel so threatened before. But it didn't scare her now. She breathed it in gratefully, glad for its soothing effect on her nerves. *Safe*, it seemed to whisper deep in the primitive part of her brain. *As long as you're in his arms you're safe. This male will kill or die to protect you. Safe.*

Kat relaxed and though she never would have believed it possible, she felt strangely content. She didn't feel anger or hurt or irritation coming from Deep, either. He seemed to somehow be perfectly at peace—as though something had calmed the roiling storm of negative emotions that seemed to constantly fill him. Something or *someone*. Could it be her? Was *she* the reason he was calmer now, at peace? But how could that be right? Could it be that Deep cared for her...even loved her the way she knew Lock did?

The thought was so wholly foreign that Kat pushed it away at first. *Why would he feel that way about me? He can't stand me—we get on each other's nerves.* But then why had he taken her pain? Why was he, even now, allowing himself to be hurt for her sake? Could it be more than his Kindred sense of duty toward a female he had sworn to protect?

Experimentally, Kat shifted in his arms. Leaning even closer, she put her right arm around his waist and rested it lightly on his broad back. Deep stiffened at first but he didn't tell her to stop, even when she traced one of the raised, ridged scars with a careful finger.

"Tell me about these," she said softly, looking up at him. "Please?"

He shifted uncomfortably. "What do you want to know?"

"How you got them. *Why* you got them."

"I told you—"

"And tell me the *truth*," she said, before he could finish the lie. "I already know it—I just want to hear it from you."

"If you already know, why do you want me to say it?" he demanded. "How did you find out, anyway? Did Mother L'rin tell you?"

"More like she reminded me of it. I...I saw it in a dream," Kat confessed, not sure how he would take it. "I think it was while I was unconscious—when you two first brought me to the Healing Gardens."

"So...you were dream sharing with us? With *me?*" Deep sounded shocked.

"I guess so." Kat looked up at him. "Does that upset you?"

"It surprises me." He peered down at her. "I guess I thought there could never be that kind of connection between us."

"Why?" asked Kat, honestly curious. "I mean, why not? After the connection we shared during the joinings we did, it doesn't seem so strange."

"One doesn't necessarily equate with the other. Just because we—"

"Deep," she interrupted softly. "We're getting off the subject. Why did you take my pain?"

"Someone had to." His voice was rough and low and he wouldn't look at her. "Mother L'rin said you'd die otherwise. I...couldn't let that happen."

"Why not? Because you and Lock had been charged with my safety?"

"If you like. It's as good a reason as any other."

"No, it's not." Kat sat up in his lap and frowned at him. "I need to know the *real* reason."

He raised an eyebrow at her. "Why? Why do you care?"

"Because I need to know how you feel about me—all right?" Kat pushed away from him and stood there trembling, her hands on her hips.

"How can you not know?" His voice was hoarse and he sat there unmoving before her, his hands on his thighs. "We share emotions, remember? We feel each others feelings constantly."

"But all I ever *feel* from you are negative emotions—anger, pain, sorrow, irritation…" Kat shook her head. "Lock tried to convince me that you cared about me, but you weren't admitting it to yourself. Except, I don't know if I can buy that. How can you not let yourself feel if you care for someone?"

Deep scowled and looked away. "Feeling too much can be a dangerous thing, little Kat. Especially if you know the other person doesn't feel for you as well."

"You have to give the other person a *chance* to feel." Kat couldn't believe she was having this conversation with him, but somehow the words kept coming out. "You have to let them *believe* you could ever be interested in them."

He gave a short, sharp laugh. "How could anyone *not* be interested in you? You're an elite with curves like a goddess."

"Which is exactly why plenty of the guys on my planet *wouldn't* be interested," Kat said quietly. "I don't know how much you understand about Earth but most cultures there—especially *my* culture—don't go for full figured girls in a big way. They want skinny women—the skinnier the better."

"What?" Deep stared at her, obviously startled. "So they *reject* you because of your curves instead of revering you for them?"

Kat couldn't help smiling. "I know—it's bizarre, isn't it? I mean with a body like this, you'd think I'd have the world at my feet." She made a gesture at her full hips and breasts.

Deep's gaze flickered over her body hungrily. "That's *exactly* what I would think."

She laughed. "I was being sarcastic."

"I wasn't," he said softly.

"I can tell." She looked at him seriously. "Look, I've been plus-sized all my life. And barring some miracle breakthrough in skinny drugs, it looks like I'm *always* going to be a size eighteen instead of a size eight. But that's okay, I'm used to it. I'm just…not the kind of girl you and Lock would be dating back on Earth. You're big, muscular, good looking guys—you could have your pick. And I guarantee it wouldn't be me."

"If you think either one of us would rather be with some stick-thin bag of bones—"

Kat laughed again. "Hey now, no need to get down on the skinny girls. They need love, too."

"Not from me and my brother." Deep looked at her, a small frown on his face. "Kat, you're beautiful—gorgeous. Is that really so hard for you to believe?"

"Not as much as it was," she said carefully. "But then, I've always known you and Lock found me attractive. I could, uh, feel it pretty clearly when I was between you."

"You mean the way our bodies react to yours," he murmured. "Of course. How could we help it?"

Kat cleared her throat. "To be perfectly honest, I wouldn't kick you two out of bed for eating crackers either. So the physical aspect isn't an issue."

Deep shook his head. "I don't understand your reference. Are you trying to say you find my brother and me attractive?"

"Very much so." Kat ducked her head, having a hard time looking him in the eye. "But you already knew that."

"I knew that your body reacted to ours," he said softly. "But physical attraction doesn't always equate with compatibility."

"Exactly." Kat took a deep breath. "Which is why I still don't know why you took that beating for me. Did you do it out of a sense of duty? Or just because you wanted me—felt lust for me? Or was there another reason?" she said, before he could answer. "A deeper reason?"

"Come here." He reached for her and Kat went willingly into his arms. He was so tall that, even though he was still sitting and she was standing, they were pretty much eye-to-eye. "You have to understand," he said hoarsely. "You're so beautiful...so high above me. What good does it do a male to love a goddess? I might as well love the sun or the stars or anything else that's forever out of reach."

"I'm not completely out of reach," she said quietly. "I'm just *frightened*. Feeling your emotions all the time—that's pretty overwhelming. And you...you can be pretty scary sometimes." She lifted her chin. "Not that I'm afraid of you."

He studied her for a long moment. "Maybe *I'm* afraid of *you*—did you think about that?"

"Why?" Kat frowned. "You're a hundred times stronger than me. You could probably break me in half with your pinky finger."

"It isn't physical pain that frightens me," he said hoarsely. "That's nothing. It's—"

At that moment five or six of the pink-skinned natives came into the cave, voices echoing in the darkness with their strange language. Kat caught parts of several different haikus, though none of them made much sense.

"Deep," she said apprehensively.

"Stay behind me." Deep dropped her hands and stood protectively in front of her. He was so big she had to peer around him to catch sight of their captors.

Suddenly a new voice rang in the cave. "It's all right. Deep— Kat—don't worry." Lock suddenly appeared behind the armed natives. "It's all right," he said again. "They're just moving us to the guest hut."

"The guest hut?" Deep sounded skeptical. "Why are we going there?"

"I convinced the chief that we're not going to run away." Lock reached them at last. Then he nodded and said something to the natives who grunted back and began to lead the way out of the cave.

"So are we stuck here?" Kat started to head for the entrance but her foot slipped on a loose stone and she nearly fell. "Whoa!"

"Be careful!" Deep caught her by the arm. "Are you all right?" he asked frowning. "Still weak?"

"A little weak but I'm fine," Kat assured him.

"Perhaps I should assist you, just in case." Lock came up on her other side and took her hand.

"A good idea, Brother," Deep said, letting her go at once. "Be certain she doesn't trip — the ground here is treacherous."

"Yes, it's very dangerous." Kat reached for the dark twin and took him by the hand. She saw Deep's startled look as she entwined their fingers and she gave him a tentative smile in return. "So dangerous that I need both of you to help me."

"If you're certain..." Deep looked down at their hands as though he couldn't believe she was touching him when she didn't have to.

Kat could scarcely believe it herself. Now that all three of them were touching skin-to-skin, she could feel the familiar tingle of sexual electricity traveling through her body. But strangely enough, she had no urge to pull away and end it as she always had before. Instead she held both brothers' hands tightly and smiled at both of them as they exited the cave.

It wasn't far from the rocky cave in the hillside to a small village of grass huts, enclosed by a high wall of sharpened green stakes. Their captors led them past the gates and through the middle of the native town.

Kat tightened her grip on the twins' hands and tried not to notice how people were gawking at them. Apparently having strangers in town was big news — especially if they were aliens from another land. She saw family units, all with two males and one female, and numerous pink children running around and playing in the lush *belsh* that carpeted the ground. The women stopped drawing water from the well and the children ceased their chatter as Kat and her men walked past. *Well, I always did want to be a show-stopper,* she thought wryly, smiling at one of the many children who were staring gape-jawed at them.

At last they reached a circular grass hut near the outskirts of town and their guards motioned for them to go in.

"Thank you." Kat ducked inside, grateful to be out of the public eye. She wanted to explore the grass hut they found themselves in but she was already tired again. "So what kind of deal did you make with the chief?" she asked Lock, as she sat on a straw-stuffed cushion covered in the same velvety *belsh* as the ground. "God, I'm wiped."

"Are you all right?" Deep, who had been checking the hut, his eyes narrowed for possible threats, looked at her with concern.

"Fine." She waved a hand at him. "Still just a little tired, that's all."

"You mean weak." He came to sit beside her and nodded at his brother. "Lock, come. Kat needs both of us now."

"With pleasure." Lock settled himself on her other side. "Is there a problem?"

"Kat's weakness and pain will come back if we don't touch her enough," Deep explained.

Lock looked worried. "Mother L'rin told me that might happen but I had hoped she was wrong."

Deep frowned. "When did she tell you that?"

"When we first brought Kat to her. While you were being—" Lock seemed to catch himself just in time. "When you weren't there."

"It's all right, Lock," Kat said in a low voice. "I know about what Deep did for me and he knows I know it."

"You do? Good." Lock looked relieved. "I'm glad not to have to hide it anymore."

"I think the three of us should stop hiding a lot of things from each other," Kat said firmly. "For instance, I notice that you still haven't answered my question—what kind of deal did you make with the chief?"

The light twin looked uncomfortable. "Tomorrow night is their full moons festival. I had to promise that we would make a sacrifice to their gods."

"A what?" Deep frowned. "Brother if you think—"

"Not a sacrifice of blood," Lock interrupted. "Don't worry about that—no one needs to get hurt."

"Then why are you feeling so upset about it?" Kat asked. "Just tell us, Lock—how bad can it be?"

Lock blew out a breath and raked a hand through his dark blond hair. "I'm upset because I know *you're* going to be upset, my lady. I...I had to promise them a sacrifice of pleasure. We're going to be acting out the courtship of the sun and the moons for the, ah, private edification of the chief."

"Lock!" Deep looked angry. "Couldn't you offer them anything else?"

Lock turned on his brother. "Not without spilling blood! We trespassed on their holy meadow—we're lucky we're not all *dead* right now."

"Okay, all right you two." Kat held up her hands. "Look, it's a lot more comfortable being between you when you're not angry with each other."

"I hope you're willing to be between us in a much more literal sense then, little Kat," Deep growled. "Because that's what my brother has promised these savages."

"What?" Kat went cold all over with apprehension. "What do you mean?"

Lock sighed. "It has to do with the legend of our sun, *Nyra*, and her two lovers the moons, *Dakir* and *Lanare*. She had to choose between the two of them."

"Oh?" Kat raised an eyebrow, her heart pounding. "And which did she choose?"

Deep gave her a level look. "Both."

Chapter Nineteen

"I want to hear more about your home world. More about Earth." The words were demanding but his tone was soft and his blazing red-on-black eyes were almost gentle.

Lauren was so relieved to see him again, to hear his deep voice, that she didn't care what he asked her. *As long as he talks to me. As long as he comes back.*

For a time the tasteless nutra-wafers had been brought to her by strange, emotionless creatures that scared her. They had flesh and gray skin like Xairn's but they reminded her of robots out of a science fiction movie. Their eyes were dead — both the white and the iris were bottomless black pits and when she looked into them, she saw nothing. Nothing at all.

Pushing away the awful memory, she concentrated on the man in front of her. "What do you want to know?"

"Tell me about your life, your...family." He frowned. "Is that the correct word for the people you live with?"

"Well I don't live with anyone right now," Lauren said cautiously. "And I don't have a whole lot of family — really it's just me and my mom. But we're very close."

"You...love her?" He said "love" as though it was a word in a foreign language that he didn't fully understand. *It probably is,* Lauren told herself. *I'm lucky he speaks English at all.*

"Yes," she said softly. "Yes, I love her very, *very* much."

"And she feels the same for you?" He was leaning forward now, a look in his strange red-on-black eyes that was hard to define. Hunger? Need? Longing?

"My mom loves me more than anything else in the world," Lauren said with unshakable certainty. "She would die for me without thinking twice." *And she's probably dying a little every day right now, wondering where I am.*

She could imagine her mother's frantic, worried face, could picture the way she was probably searching everywhere to find Lauren. Everywhere but in the right place. Because how could she ever suspect what had happened? *Oh Mom, I miss you so much!* A sudden longing to see her mother, to hear her familiar soft voice and know that everything was okay, came over Lauren so strongly that tears rose in her eyes.

"If she has so much love for you, why are you crying?" He still pronounced "love" like a foreign word but the look he was giving her was one almost of concern.

"Because I *miss* her. And I know she's probably looking *everywhere* for me. She's probably frantic with worry and I...I'll probably never see her again. "

"It would hurt you that much to be forever separated from her?" He sounded curious.

"Of course it would!" Lauren blotted her eyes on his cloak and took a deep breath, trying to slow the tears. She knew from past experience that crying was a sure way to drive any man away and she wanted Xairn to stay. "I'm sorry, but wouldn't *you* be upset if you were never going to see your father again? I mean, I know he's really scary and weird but he's still your dad. Right?"

Xairn looked away. "I feel nothing for him. And he feels nothing for me."

"Oh." Lauren bit her lip, uncertain what to say. "I…I'm sorry."

"Don't be." He shook his head. "It has always been so."

"But don't you…" Lauren hesitated, uncertain of how to phrase her question, afraid she might drive him away again. "Haven't you ever had anyone love you? Or had anyone to love?" she asked at last.

"Once." His deep voice was remote. "It doesn't matter now."

"It *does* matter," Lauren said earnestly. "My mom always says that everyone just needs three things to be happy — something to do, something to look forward to, and someone to love."

He laughed tonelessly. "Why would you think that happiness is a priority aboard the Fathership?"

"I guess it's not." Lauren twisted her fingers together. "But don't you *want* to be happy?"

"I don't *want* anything." His voice sounded dead. "I merely exist."

Lauren wanted to point out that "merely existing" was no way to live but she sensed this was no time to trade philosophy with him. *If I want to keep him with me, I have to keep him interested.* It made her think of Scheherazade, the heroine from *The Arabian Nights,* which she'd read as a little girl. Scheherazade had been married to a king who took a new wife every morning and killed her every night. But she told the king stories every night, stories that led into other stories and kept him too interested to kill her.

I have to be like that, Lauren told herself. *I have to keep him interested.*

She cleared her throat and smiled at Xairn. "Let me tell you something else about Earth. Have you ever heard of ice cream?"

* * * * *

Xairn listened to her speak, her soft, harmonious voice rising and falling as she told him about her world. She talked on and on, about the strange foods the humans ate and the soft white sands and warm waters of the beaches in the place where she lived. She talked about entertainments called movies and plays and explained that they read stories called "books" for pleasure.

The concept was foreign to Xairn. He knew how to read in two hundred different languages and dialects, including her own English, but the idea of reading something for anything other than information was a novelty to him.

Lauren answered his questions about books and then spoke about her childhood, growing up alone with only her mother for company. Much as Xain had had only his

father — the AllFather. But it soon became clear that their childhoods had nothing else in common. She spoke with love and tenderness about her mother, talked about how she had taken care of Lauren even in difficult circumstances. As far as he could tell there had been discipline, but nothing like the kind of punishments the AllFather could devise. Lauren had never known cruelty or hatred from the one who was supposed to love and care for her.

Xairn wondered why his heart throbbed while he listened. It was a weakness, he supposed — the same weakness that had caused him to come see her again, even though he had sworn not to. But still, he lingered and he listened, unable to pull himself away.

At last he realized the time. It was late — much later than he'd intended to stay. Already he had missed some crucial tasks for which he would doubtless be punished.

"I have to go." He rose as he spoke and her eyes—lovely and golden in her light brown face—followed his movements.

"Do you have to?" Her voice was soft and pleading. "Can't you stay a little while longer?"

Xairn shook his head. "I've already neglected several of my duties too long. I will probably be whipped—my father will order it done."

"Oh no!" Lauren put a slim hand to her mouth. "I'm so sorry! I didn't mean to get you into trouble."

Xairn shrugged. "It doesn't matter."

"Yes, it does," she insisted. "You'll hate me for it when you're being punished. And then you'll never want to come see me again."

"That's not true." Not knowing why he did it, Xairn stooped and placed a hand awkwardly over hers. "I take responsibility for my own actions," he said softly. "I wanted to stay with you and so I stayed. I don't hate you."

She looked up at him with uncertainty and fear in her eyes and suddenly he saw how he must look to her. He was huge, hulking— monstrous. His shoulders were fully twice as broad as hers and his skin, which had seemed normal to him until now, was rough and discolored next to her smooth, creamy brown. And his eyes...his eyes were the worst of all. He had studied some Earth mythology and he knew what they must look like to her. *A demon — isn't that the word? She must think I have a demon's eyes.*

"You're not a demon," she said softly and he realized he must have spoken the words aloud. "I don't think that about you, Xairn."

The momentary lapse startled and troubled him. "That's because you don't know me," he said roughly. He stood abruptly. "I must go."

"Will...will you come back?" She looked up at him, hope shining in her amber eyes. "Please, you're the only one I have to talk to. Please don't leave me alone again with those...those *things.*"

"They are Scourge, the same as me," he said, frowning. "They're simply grown in the artificial wombs we call vats."

"No." Lauren shook her head. "They're not the same as you. They're nothing like you. I can see it in their eyes — they're empty inside. Soulless."

"So am I."

"No," Lauren said again, more softly this time. "You're not soulless, Xairn. You're just locked up tight inside. So tight even *you* don't know how to find the key."

"I have no time for your Earth metaphors," he said harshly. "I must go."

"Go on, then." She looked at him appealingly. "But please...please come back."

"I make no promises," he said. The disappointment in her eyes made him add, "But I will try."

"Thank you," she said simply. "I'll look forward to our next conversation. Maybe...maybe you can tell me something about *your* life."

"I could." Xairn laughed humorlessly. "But I doubt you'd wish to hear it. I have no pretty little stories of when I was young, Lauren. The only tales I could tell you —" He broke off, shaking his head.

"What?" she urged softly.

"Nothing." He turned for the door. "I'll come back again if I'm able."

"I'll look forward to it."

And though he knew she was only acting out of self preservation, he could have sworn that she actually meant it.

Chapter Twenty

"Tell me again what we have to do," Kat said, wishing she felt a little less weak and nervous. She'd spent the night cuddled between Lock and Deep, in a nice, nonsexual way. The contact should have boosted her energy, but somehow she still felt off her game. At least the headache hadn't come back, though—she didn't think she could stand to go through what they were about to do with that rusty iron spike in her brain.

They had spent the day being feasted and stared at by the natives. Then, as evening drew near, all of them had bathed separately in the sacred golden waters of the holy stream in preparation for the night. Kat had been avoiding the thought of the coming ceremony, but she couldn't help thinking of it now as she arranged the ceremonial outfit she'd been given to wear.

Her native haute couture appeared to be made mostly of leaves and flowers and was tied on by vines. It made her feel like Jane from the old Tarzan movies and not in a good way. She was nervous because she didn't have on anything under it. So any strong breeze was likely to equal a wardrobe malfunction of epic proportions.

Deep and Lock had on leafy loincloth things too, but on *them* the leaf look was somehow hot. Their broad, sculpted chests and long, muscular legs seemed made to be exposed. They looked like Greek gods that had come to life right down to the strategically placed fig leaves. Of course, pretty soon she was going to be looking under those fig leaves. *Don't kid yourself, Kat—you're going to be doing more than looking,* whispered a little voice in her head. Kat tried to push it away but it wouldn't go. She couldn't quite believe what she was about to do, but it seemed to be their only way out, so she had no choice.

"We'll be reenacting the courtship of the sun and the moons," Lock said, interrupting her nervous musings. He patted her shoulder comfortingly. "The chief will be reciting the legend in their common speech so hopefully your convo-pillar will be able to translate. Just do exactly as the chief says and everything will be all right."

"Yes, but what exactly is the chief going to say?" Kat asked, vainly trying to rearrange her leaves for maximum coverage. *God, this is ridiculous! I feel like I'm wearing a salad—I'd get more coverage from a g-string bikini.*

"We discussed this last night—you know the legend," Deep growled. "It's mainly going to be a lot of kissing and tasting but there's likely to be penetration too. It just depends on these people's version of the tale."

"Will we…" Kat swallowed hard. "Is this going to seal the bond between us?" The prospect wasn't as frightening as it had been. She and Deep seemed to be on better terms now, though she wished their talk in the cave hadn't been interrupted. But she still wasn't sure about the idea of being tied to the brothers for life.

Deep seemed to sense her hesitation. He frowned. "That shouldn't be necessary. Though you may have to allow us to penetrate you."

Kat swallowed hard. "Both at…at the same time?"

"No." Lock shook his head firmly. "We won't go that far, my lady, I swear it. At most Deep and I will enter you one at a time and then only briefly, for the purpose of the reenactment."

"We won't fuck you or come in you if that makes you feel any better," Deep said harshly. His blunt words made Kat's heart skip a beat.

"Oh my God. Okay. All right." Kat took a deep breath. "I can handle this. I *can*."

"Of course you can." Deep's voice went from harsh to unexpectedly gentle. "You know Lock and I would never hurt you, little Kat."

"Yes, I know." Kat had a sudden thought. "But won't it hurt *you?* I mean, to be so…uh, intimate with me if only one of you is involved?"

"As long as we're both making contact with you it won't matter that one of us is touching you more…intimately than the other." Lock coughed. "If you know what I mean."

"I think so." Kat nodded.

"So if Lock has to penetrate you, I'll be holding you," Deep explained. "The same way we did the night after you ate the bonding fruit. Remember?"

"How could I forget?" Her uninhibited behavior that night still made Kat's cheeks hot. *But I'm about to get a whole lot more uninhibited now,* she told herself unhappily. *We're about to put on a live three-way sex show here for Chief Pervert and his band of merry men. Crap, how am I going to do this?*

"My lady…" Lock took her by the shoulders and looked into her eyes. "It's going to be all right," he murmured. "We're going to get through this together."

Kat saw the sincerity in his deep brown eyes and felt a little of her anxiety melt along with her heart. Why did Lock have to be so sweet and easy to trust? It made refusing to be with them permanently even harder. "Yes, all right," she whispered. "I know."

"And though it may strengthen the bond we already have — the soul bond, I swear it won't form a physical bond," Deep added, also looking at her. "I know that's what you're afraid of, but you don't need to worry."

Kat wasn't sure what to say to that. She could feel the hurt radiating from Deep, the longing she had felt after their first joining, when he'd asked her to stay the night with him and Lock. Part of her wanted to hug him and give him hope — to let him know that she was becoming more open to the idea of bonding with them. But another part — a deeper part — was cautious.

She well remembered the times in her parents' marriage when her father and mother would seem to make up. For weeks — once even for months — the constant bickering would stop and there would be peace between them. Kat would always get her hopes up that this would be the time they would learn to love each other...and then everything would blow up and things would be worse than before.

I can't risk that, she thought, seeing the need in Deep's black eyes, feeling the desire from both of them. *I have to be absolutely sure before I let myself get into something I can never get out of.*

"I'm sorry," she said at last, looking up at Deep. "Really sorry."

"You have nothing to apologize for." Lock stroked her cheek gently. "We know how you feel, my lady. And neither of us blames you for it."

But Kat was very much afraid that Deep *did* blame her — and there was nothing she could do about it. He was silent, however, as he bent and kissed her forehead.

Then their guards came to the door of the hut and motioned. "The full moons shine down. The chief awaits your pleasure. Come do her bidding," said the short, husky one who had taken Kat prisoner in the first place.

Her? Kat decided her convo-pillar must be acting up again. She nodded at the guard, trying unsuccessfully to smile. *God, if I never hear another haiku again it'll be too soon!*

"All right, we're coming." Deep and Lock put her between them. Then, with Lock leading the way and Deep bringing up the rear, they left the grass hut and followed the guards.

The sun had just finished setting and there was still a warm pinkish-orange glow in the deep purple sky as they walked. A soft breeze played over her face, caressing her with the exotic scent of foreign flowers. Kat wondered where the twin moons were— she still didn't see anything in the sky but the white pinpricks of the stars.

Somewhere out there is Earth, she thought. *I've never been so far away from home in all my life.* The thought made her feel lonely and homesick so she tried not to dwell on it. *After all, I'll be going back soon. Back to the Mother ship to see Liv and Sophie. As soon as we do this little show the natives will set us free. Then we'll find the stupid fi-fi flower, get the meds from Mother L'rin, and I'll be back with the girls eating Ben and Jerry's and catching up on the latest gossip before you know it.*

She tried not to imagine how she would feel once she took Mother L'rin's medicine and was truly and permanently separated from both Deep and Lock. Even two days before she would have felt only relief to be parted from them. Now she wasn't so sure...

Kat refused to let herself think about it. Instead she looked around at the lush, Twin Moons landscape and thought about how oddly familiar their surroundings looked. Come to think of it, where they were looked exactly like...

"Hey," she said in a low voice. "Aren't we back in the holy meadow?"

Lock looked around. "It would appear so."

"So this is where we're supposed to, uh, do our thing?"

Deep shrugged. "I guess so."

Kat put a hand on her hip, thoroughly pissed off. "So their precious meadow is too holy to walk on but it's okay to have a three-way screw session on it?"

"It's not just a 'three-way screw session,'" Lock said, mild reproof in his deep voice. "The legend we're enacting is holy to all of us on Twin Moons—not just the natives. It explains how we became the people we are—why we are born as twins and need to share a single female between us."

"Sorry," Kat felt abashed. "I didn't mean to make fun of your Adam and Eve story. Or I guess in this case, Adam and Eve and Steve. Or whatever."

"It's all right." Lock smiled at her. "I just wanted you to know that what we're doing tonight is more than just the chief's erotic whim. It's sacred to us—a beautiful thing, if you can bring yourself to see it that way."

Kat swallowed. "I'll try," she said softly. "But I didn't know we were performing a sacrament. I'm afraid I'd make a lousy alter boy."

"A *what* kind of boy did you say?" Lock frowned.

"She's just making a joke because she's nervous," Deep said, coming unexpectedly to her rescue. "Go easy on her, Brother. This is hard for our little Kat."

Harder than you know, Kat thought, but didn't say aloud. Their native guards were gesturing at them now and pointing to a circular clump of bushes to one side of the meadow. She and Deep and Lock walked over to the leafy clump and Kat was surprised when there was a sudden rustling and three pink skinned natives appeared from behind the bushes.

Two of them were male warriors with the usual leaf loincloths. But the third was clearly female. Despite her diminutive stature, she stood straight and tall, with the regal bearing of royalty. She had thick, lustrous black hair that reached to her ankles and she was wearing the same kind of leaf/flower/vine dress that Kat had on. In her hand was a green wooden scepter tipped with the deadly clear crystal all the native warriors had in their knives.

"Behold." Lock bowed low to the regal female. "The chief."

"A woman?" Kat asked doubtfully as she and Deep followed Lock's lead and bowed. "But I thought the chief was a man."

Deep frowned. "Why would you think that? We *are* a matriarchal society, you know — even the natives."

"*Especially* the natives," Lock murmured softly, watching as the chief conferred with the two males Kat assumed must be her mates. "They worship and revere their females almost as goddesses. Which of course, is as it should be."

Kat shook her head. "You guys...I swear, if more Earth girls knew about Twin Moons, your whole planet would be completely overrun with desperate females looking to be Kindred brides."

"I don't think so." Deep's voice was unexpectedly harsh. "We frighten your kind, Kat. Frighten them to death."

"What is *that* supposed to mean?" she demanded in a low voice. "If you have something to say —"

His eyes flashed. "Nothing you want to hear, I'm sure."

"Be silent." Lock's voice was unusually sharp. "The chief wishes to speak."

"Visitors from the land beyond, we bid thee welcome," the chief said in a low, melodious voice.

Kat counted the syllables silently. *Good – no more haikus! Maybe because she's a woman? Who knows…*

"Thou art indeed most welcome, though thou camest as trespassers upon our holy soil," the chief continued and Kat sighed inwardly. Apparently, the convo-pillar had traded Japanese poetry for Old English mumbo-jumbo. *But at least she's understandable. And she doesn't sound like Yoda – that's always a good thing.*

"We are pleased to do your bidding, blessed one," Lock said, bowing deeply again. "If by our sacrifice of pleasure we can make your full moons festival more sacred, then we gladly give of ourselves."

Speak for yourself! Kat thought. From the dark look on Deep's face, he was thinking much the same. The two of them remained silent, however and Kat couldn't help thinking it was a good thing they had Lock to do the talking. He was really sweet and kind and honest but he could also, apparently, be a silver-tongued negotiator when he put his mind to it. It gave her new respect for the light twin, who could be sometimes overshadowed by his brother's dark moods.

"Thy coming was foreordained by the stars," the chief said, nodding her head at Kat. "A sunfire goddess searching for the sacred blossom, and her mates, light and dark, as the moons above." She lifted her hands to the heavens and Kat looked up instinctively. What she saw nearly took her breath away.

High above them were two huge moons. One was a brilliant, silvery white and the other was so black it looked like an onyx orb in the sky. Both were many times bigger than Earth's moon and the white one shed an eerie, otherworldly light over the holy meadow.

Kat couldn't understand how she hadn't seen them before. They had either risen very quickly or she had been too involved in the conversation with Deep and Lock and the chief to notice. But now that she had seen them, she couldn't look away.

"Oh," she whispered reverently. "They're *beautiful*."

"*Dakir* and *Lanare*," the chief said softly. "The twin lovers of *Nyra*, our beloved sun. But how came the fiery maiden to choose them both? Tonight shall we speak of these things and show them again for the pleasure of all."

"You mean *we're* going to show them," Deep muttered, frowning.

The chief caught his words and nodded. "Indeed, warrior. Your brother has told me of your quest. Know this — if thou please the gods with thy sacrifice, the holy meadow shall burst into blossom and the *fifilalachuchu* flower shall be thine."

"Really?" Kat looked around the meadow eagerly, but she saw nothing except the little yellow and blue flowers she'd woven into a crown the day before. "Where are they?"

"They shall not bloom unless thy sacrifice is pleasing." The chief sounded stern. "See to it that it is."

"Of course we shall," Lock said smoothly. "How do you wish us to perform, oh blessed one?"

"My mates and I shall sit here, behind the screen of leaves." The chief gestured to the flowering bushes behind them. "I shall speak the sacred words and thou must act upon them. See that thou givest proper sacrifice — the gods themselves are as we shall be — seeing but unseen." She nodded at them regally and then stepped back behind the bushes. Her mates followed her and, after a brief rustling of leaves, the three of them were completely concealed.

Seeing but unseen, Kat thought. *Well, at least that's a little less intimidating than if they were all standing over us watching. I guess if we **have** to do this —*

"In the dawn of time, from the emptiness of the great black void, was born a beautiful elite maiden, with the curves of a goddess and fiery red hair," the chief's low, musical voice began, interrupting her thoughts. "Her name was *Nyra.*"

"Oh, uh…" Kat wasn't sure if she was supposed to act out being born or what. But luckily, the chief was already speaking again.

"She moved through the void seeking for her mate, seeking in all directions."

Feeling like she was back at summer camp, playing charades, Kat shaded her eyes with one hand and pantomimed looking everywhere.

"Two males she found—brothers, one light, one dark. The light brother was named *Lanare* and the dark one, *Dakir.* *Nyra* cared for them both and she found it difficult to choose. *Lanare* was loving and warm. He made her smile and feel at ease and *Nyra* found his kisses most pleasing."

Kat thought uncomfortably that the legend was hitting a little too close to home. Then Lock was taking her in his arms. Smiling, he pressed a feather-light kiss to her forehead and then to both her eyelids, and finally, to her lips.

Despite their unseen audience, Kat felt herself warming in his arms, feeling completely at ease with him, as she always did. At her back she could feel Deep, his large body like a line of fire down her spine. He was touching one of her shoulders, making sure the kiss wasn't painful for his brother. Kat was glad—knowing that the intimate contact wasn't hurting the light twin enabled her to completely relax and enjoy it. But just as she was really getting into the kiss with Lock, the chief continued her narrative.

"But though *Lanare* filled her with peace, *Dakir* filled *Nyra* with fire. He was harsh and unforgiving with the soul of a thunderstorm but when he took her in his arms, she could think of nothing but him."

The hand on her shoulder gripped tighter and suddenly Deep spun her around to face him. He took Kat in his arms, pulling her against him, holding her close so that she could feel the hard ridge of his cock branding her thigh. For a long moment he simply gazed at her, his black eyes burning. Kat could feel the lust rolling off him in waves. They crested around her, threatening to drown her with their overwhelming intensity.

"Deep—" she started to say, and then he was crushing her mouth with his.

Kat gasped at the sudden flare of heat that went through her. Hardly knowing what she was doing, she locked her arms around his neck and stood on her tiptoes, giving as good as she was getting.

Not to be outdone, Deep bent her over one muscular forearm. His tongue caressed the seam of her lips until Kat moaned and opened for him. She was dimly aware of Lock's hand on her shoulder as the light twin performed the same service for his brother that Deep had done for him, but most of her attention was focused on trying to stay afloat on the sea of emotions she felt emanating from Deep.

Finally, after kissing her dizzy, Deep released her. As suddenly as the kiss had started, it was over.

Kat wanted to moan in frustration and disappointment. Her nipples were throbbing behind the strategically placed leaves and her pussy felt wet and swollen. But soon she became aware that the chief was speaking again, going on with the legend.

"The brothers could not agree upon which of them was to have *Nyra* and she confessed herself to be incapable of choosing one over the other," the low, hypnotic tone continued. "Thus did they devise a contest, to see who could bring her the most pleasure and so earn a place by her side. *Lanare* went first, suckling her breasts and teasing her tender nipples with his tongue until she moaned."

If she hadn't done this with Lock before, Kat would have been freaking out. But she knew the light twin would be gentle. Smiling at him, she allowed him to untie the vines that held her top together. It fell off and landed in a little pile of leaves at their feet. Kat stood bare breasted under the stars and the two huge moons, feeling vulnerable.

"Beautiful," Lock breathed, smiling at her. "Such full, luscious breasts, my lady."

"Then suck them, Brother." Deep's voice was hoarse with desire. "Give our little Kat what she needs."

Lock cupped the under-curves of her breasts gently and Deep stepped up behind her, until Kat could feel his broad, muscular chest pressed against her bare back. She felt surrounded by them — just as she had when they were in a joining — but in a good way.

"My lady..." Lock looked at Kat, an unspoken question in his true brown eyes and she knew he was waiting for permission. Not speaking a word, she thrust her chest out, pushing her breasts into his hands and giving him his answer.

"Suck her, Brother," Deep commanded. "Suck her ripe tits and make her moan. Make her moan for both of us."

Lock obeyed, his mouth enclosing on one tight nipple in wet heat that made Kat gasp breathlessly. "God," she whispered. "God, Lock… feels so…"

"It feels good, doesn't it?" Deep murmured in her ear. "Feels good to be bare breasted in the moonlight, letting Lock suck your sweet nipples. Give in to him, little Kat. Just relax and let him suck you."

Kat didn't see how she could have done anything else. With a low moan, she pressed forward even more, offering Lock her body.

The light twin took her offer eagerly, sucking first one tight nipple and then the other until Kat thought she would die of pleasure. The sexual electricity traveling through her body was becoming too much to bear and yet she realized that the three of them had barely started their erotic journey together. Suddenly she heard the chief's voice again.

"*Lanare* brought *Nyra* much joy by sucking her nipples, but then it was *Dakir's* turn and he vowed to double and even treble the pleasure his brother had given *Nyra* by the use of his tongue."

By the use of his tongue? What exactly — But the question scarcely had time to form in her head before Deep was turning her to face him again. Then, as Kat watched, he went down on his knees before her. His face was on the same level as her leaf skirt and Kat suddenly understood what was about to happen.

"Little Kat," Deep murmured, looking up at her. "I know you feared me in the past, but I swear I would never, *never* hurt you. Will you allow me to taste your sweet pussy?"

A shiver went through Kat, a strange feeling of apprehension mixed with desire so strong it took her breath away. Deep was right—she *had* been afraid of him in the very recent past. And she still wasn't nearly as at ease with him as she was with Lock. But the pleading look in his eyes and the need she felt radiating from him seemed to melt her defenses.

"It's all right, my lady," she heard Lock murmur, as he pressed his chest to her back, surrounding her with his comforting warmth. "Deep only wishes to give you pleasure. Just open your thighs and let him in."

Kat felt helpless to do anything else. Biting her lip, she watched as Deep untied the vines that held her skirt in place and let it drop to the ground beside her leafy top. She was completely naked now and she should have been feeling incredibly exposed. Instead, she felt surrounded and protected by the two men. With Lock at her back and Deep in front of her, she knew that no would dare try to hurt her. And if they did try...

"We'd kill them," Deep murmured, obviously catching her thought. "We'd do anything to protect you...and anything to pleasure you." Bending his head, he nuzzled her thigh and kissed the top of her mound.

"Deep..." Kat shifted uneasily but Lock stroked her shoulders soothingly and whispered in her ear.

"Easy, my lady. Deep won't hurt you. He simply wants to learn your scent before he tastes you."

Speaking of scent, Kat felt surrounded by both of theirs. Lock's—warm, fresh, and comforting, and Deep's—dark, dangerous, and completely intoxicating. She breathed them in, feeling dizzy with fear and desire.

Deep kissed the inside of her thigh with surprising gentleness. "You smell so sweet, little Kat," he growled softly. "And you're already so hot and wet..." With one fingertip he traced the slit of her pussy, making Kat moan as he brushed lightly over her throbbing clit. Deep looked up at her. "You need this," he said, his eyes meeting hers. "Need to be opened and tasted. I can feel it coming off you in waves."

Much to her shame, Kat couldn't deny it. She wasn't sure if it was because of the incomplete bond between them or simply because she was so turned on but it was true—she didn't just want Deep to taste her, she *needed* him too.

"Please," she whispered, not sure what else to say. "Please, Deep, I..."

"Yes." He answered her unspoken request. Lifting her leg, he placed it over his broad shoulder. "Yes, sweetheart, I'll give you what you need."

The new position spread her open, parting her pussy lips and putting her inner folds on display. If Kat had remembered that they had an unseen audience, she might have been embarrassed. But at that moment, in the lovely, unearthly moonlight, it was easy to forget that anyone else but the three of them existed.

"Little Kat," Deep murmured and then he parted her even further with his thumbs and took a long, loving taste of her pussy. He started at the bottom of her slit and licked up, pressing the flat of his tongue to her heated inner cunt, dragging upward in a slow, teasing taste that made Kat feel like she was melting from the waist down.

"God!" Her hips bucked forward involuntarily and she might have fallen if Lock hadn't been there to hold her up.

"Is it good, my lady?" he said softly in her ear. "Does it feel good to let Deep taste you?"

"Yes," Kat breathed, unable to lie. "God, yes, it does. So much..."

"Get ready, little Kat," Deep growled, looking up at her. "Because it's about to feel even better." Pressing his face between her legs, he lapped her again and then sucked her swollen clit into his mouth and teased it mercilessly with his tongue.

Kat cried out and found that she was clutching his head, her fingers clenching in the thick black silk of his hair. When she realized what she was doing she tried to let go, but somehow her fingers wouldn't uncurl. And besides, her frantic grip seemed to actually add to Deep's pleasure. She felt a fresh wave of lust from him, licking over her entire body like flames, and then he growled low in his throat and redoubled his efforts.

"Deep...Oh God, *Deep*," she gasped as he lapped her pussy mercilessly. One minute she could feel his hot tongue invading her and the next moment he was pressing two thick fingers deep in her cunt as he lashed her clit, licking and sucking as though he was determined to drive her completely mad.

Through it all, Lock held her steady, talking softly about how beautiful she was when she surrendered herself and how he loved to watch her open herself for his brother. The constant low murmur of encouragement and the feelings of need, desire, and lust coming at her from all directions were pushing Kat to a higher peak than she'd ever been to before.

I'm going to come, she thought deliriously as Deep pressed his tongue deep inside her yet again. *Going to come so **hard**...*

But just at that moment, she heard the voice of the chief again and Deep stopped his relentless oral assault.

"*Nyra* received pleasure such as she had never felt before from the dark brother's tongue, but still she could not choose between them," the low, melodious voice intoned.

Damn it! Kat was so aggravated she wanted to scream. *I was so close...so **close**...* But the chief's next words almost drove her sexual frustration right out of her head.

"So it was that *Lanara* proposed a last contest, to see which of them should stay at the lady *Nyra's* side forever. He said that it should be decided which should claim her by seeing which of their shafts fit the best inside her and gave her the most pleasure."

Oh my God, here we go. Kat suddenly felt as though she'd swallowed an entire bucketful of ice cubes. Could she really do this? Could she really let Lock penetrate her pussy for an audience — even an unseen one?

"It's all right, my lady," she heard the light twin whisper in her ear. "I swear I'll be gentle with you. And I'll withdraw after only a few strokes."

"All...all right," Kat whispered, knowing she really had no choice. "But just a few..."

"Of course." And then the twins were switching positions and the three of them were down on the soft, inviting *belsh* covered ground.

"It's all right." Deep was behind her, holding her as he had been when Lock had used the carved wooden shaft on her. "It's all right, little Kat. Just relax and let Lock fuck you."

Kat leaned back against the dark twin's broad chest and watched, wide-eyed, as Lock insinuated himself between her thighs.

"I'll be slow and gentle," he promised, leaning down to kiss her gently on the mouth. "You'll barely feel me in you."

As he spoke, he fitted the broad, mushroom-shaped head of his cock to the slippery entrance of Kat's pussy. Then, with one long, smooth thrust, he pressed inside her.

Despite his promise that she would barely feel him, Kat couldn't help moaning. He was thick and despite the bonding fruit she'd had recently, she could feel him stretching her open as he entered her.

"Easy, sweetheart," Deep murmured, stroking her hair. "Just relax. Lock only needs to thrust once or twice to fulfill the legend."

"Okay," Kat gasped as the light twin pulled almost all the way out of her and thrust in again. He was keeping his thrusts shallow and wasn't hitting bottom inside her, doubtless trying to make her feel more at ease. But Kat was getting used to the feel of him inside her now, getting used to the thick cock stretching her pussy, and she found that she liked it—liked it a lot. Her pleasure was building again, reaching closer to the peak with each slow, careful stroke and she wanted more...*needed* more...

"So *Lanare* withdrew from her, having showed that he fit well within her," the chief said and suddenly, Lock pulled all the way out of her, making Kat feel empty inside.

Damn it, what is wrong with this woman? she thought, glaring in the general direction of the bushes. *Does she have a sixth sense about screwing up other people's orgasms or what?* And then the chief was speaking again.

"But *Dakir* vowed that he could outdo his brother. He asked *Nyra* to open herself to him in order that he might prove it was so."

Oh God. Kat felt her apprehension rising. It was Deep's turn in her pussy—the dark twin's turn to fuck her. And despite the fact that she was feeling much more comfortable around him lately, she still wasn't completely relaxed about the idea of spreading her thighs and letting him thrust his long, thick cock deep inside her.

Deep must have sensed her fear because he turned her slightly and lifted her chin so they were eye to eye. "It's all right, Kat," he murmured hoarsely. "You don't have to be afraid. Just a few thrusts and I'll be done. I won't come in you."

"All right." Kat looked down, unable to meet his intense gaze. Could she really do this? Yes, she decided. And not just because she had to. *I want him in me,* she thought with some surprise. *Want to feel him thrusting inside me just the way Lock was. It doesn't feel right, doesn't feel...**balanced** if only one of them does it.* She looked back up at Deep. "All right," she repeated in a stronger voice. "Do you want me to lean against Lock?"

"Yes, but not the way you're thinking." Deep urged her up until she was kneeling on her hands and knees, her bare breasts swaying like ripe fruit beneath her.

Kat looked over her shoulder. "But—"

"I'll take you from behind," he growled, caressing her bare ass with one large, warm hand. "That way you don't have to see me do it."

Kat heard the faint hint of bitterness in his voice and knew what he was thinking. *He still thinks I don't want him – that I don't feel for him like I feel for Lock.* "Deep—" she started to say, but then Lock was in front of her, urging her to rest in his arms and lean her head against his broad chest as Deep got into position behind her.

"It's all right, my lady," he murmured soothingly. "Just spread yourself open and let Deep enter your pussy."

Kat shivered as she felt the broad, blunt tip of Deep's cock slide over her slick, swollen folds. Clutching Lock tightly, she pressed her face against the broad planes of his chest, trying to be ready for what was coming.

"I'm afraid I can't be quite as delicate as my brother," Deep said from behind her. "I want you too badly, little Kat. Need to be inside you, even if it is only for a few thrusts."

"Don't frighten her," Lock said sharply, hugging Kat tightly to him. "You know you won't hurt her, Deep, so don't make her think you would."

"Hurt her? No." Deep's voice was a hungry growl. "But I can't be satisfied with a few shallow thrusts, either. I need to be deep in her pussy, Brother. Need to fill her completely and feel her sweet little cunt clenching around my shaft."

"Then do it." Kat turned her head to look at him, looming over her in the moonlight. Taking a deep breath, she parted her thighs even wider, trying to be open enough for him. "Just...just do it," she said breathlessly. "Go on, Deep. Please."

"Your wish is my command." And then he breached her suddenly, driving the full length of his thick, hot shaft deep inside her open pussy.

Kat cried out and clutched wildly at Lock who held her tight and close. The light twin's entry had been as smooth as silk but Deep's was rough and demanding. He didn't just thrust into her — he pressed deep, plumbing her depths and grinding hard until the head of his cock kissed the mouth of her womb. Then, instead of pulling out again, he held himself there, rock solid and steady inside her.

"Feel that, little Kat?" he growled softly, pressing even deeper. "That's me inside you, my cock deep in your tight little pussy. How do you like it, sweetheart? Does it feel good?"

Once again, Kat couldn't lie. "Yes," she moaned, pressing her cheek to Lock's chest. "God, yes. I can't help it...it *does*. It feels so *good*."

"The only thing that would feel better is to have both of us inside you at once. Just imagine it..." As he spoke, Deep began to pump, setting up a slow, deliberate rhythm in her pussy that made Kat feel like she was going insane. "The two of us together, filling you. You think you're full now? Think my cock is thick? Just wait, little Kat. If Lock and I entered you together, you'd be more open than you've ever been in your life."

"She doesn't want that," Lock reminded his brother, stroking Kat's shoulders as she shivered against him. "Doesn't want both of us inside her at once."

"Doesn't want both of us? Hells, Brother, she doesn't even want *me*." Deep laughed bitterly. "But she's got me, for a few more strokes at least. Isn't that right, little Kat?"

"Deep…" She wanted to tell him he was wrong, wanted to let him know that she wanted him every bit as much as Lock. But somehow the words wouldn't come. "Deep, please…" she whispered as her pleasure built once more. Close…she was getting so *close*…

"Just a few more thrusts inside your hot little pussy, sweetheart," he growled, obviously misunderstanding her. "If this is going to be my only chance to fuck you, I want to do it right. Want you to always remember how it felt to have my cock buried deep in your tight little cunt."

"You've had enough." Lock sounded almost angry. "Enough now, Brother. Stop it and pull out—the lady Kat doesn't want you to come in her."

"Please!" Kat wanted to cry at the thought of him stopping now. True, it was frightening and intense to open her pussy and let Deep fuck her. But she could feel her orgasm building again, getting closer and closer like a thunderstorm over her head, about to break and drench her in pleasure. *I have to come,* she thought deliriously as she clenched the thick length of Deep's shaft inside her. *Have to come this time or I'm going to go crazy. I **need** to come.*

"Please," she said again and then forced herself to turn her head and look at Deep. The expression on his dark face was utterly focused, completely intent as he drove himself into her. She had the feeling he could go on all night—if only she let him.

"Please what, little Kat?" he demanded. "Please pull out of you now and leave you alone?"

"No." She shook her head, forcing the words out with an effort. "I'm so close. Please, Deep, I…I need to come."

Deep's black eyes, so hard a moment ago, softened at once. "Of course you do," he murmured, caressing her back with surprising tenderness. "And I swear I won't stop until you do." Looking up, he met Lock's eyes. "Touch her, Brother," he demanded hoarsely. "Pinch her nipples. Stroke her pussy. Do whatever you can to help—little Kat needs to come."

"With pleasure." Lock kissed her forehead tenderly and then two large, warm hands cupped Kat's breasts and he began to tug and twist her nipples in the same rhythm that Deep was thrusting into her. "Is that good, my lady?" he asked as Kat moaned and writhed between them.

"Is it?" Deep demanded, before she could answer. "Do you like to feel Lock play with your nipples while I fuck you? Is that what you need?"

"Yes but *more*," Kat gasped. She felt like her entire body was on fire, like she couldn't get a deep enough breath. And she was close, right on the edge of coming. She just needed a little more stimulation…

"This is what you need, isn't it?" Deep growled and Kat felt one large hand slide from her hips down between her legs where they were joined. It didn't take much—two strokes of his fingertips against her swollen clit and then she was coming, coming so hard she saw stars flashing in front of her eyes as the thundercloud finally burst, drenching her in the warm, sweet rain of pleasure.

It was intense — more intense than anything Kat had ever felt in her life. She felt herself clenching around Deep, her pussy gripping his shaft like an impatient fist. At the same time she pressed her face into Lock's chest, holding onto him for dear life as the pleasure took her to mindless heights of ecstasy, climbing higher and higher until the sky swirled dizzily above her and she couldn't tell the light moon from the dark one.

Lanare or Dakir, she thought deliriously. *Which one should I choose? Why can't I have them both?*

And then the light flicked and went out, leaving her floating in the smooth blackness of space.

* * * * *

Deep's heart nearly stopped in his chest when she suddenly went limp. "Gods!" he gasped, sliding out quickly and gathering her in his arms. "Kat? *Kat?*"

"My lady?" Lock was distressed as well as he patted Kat's cheek anxiously. "My lady, come back to us. Please!"

My fault, Deep thought numbly as he and his brother cradled her still form between them. *I was too rough — too harsh. I overloaded her with my need, my desire. I knew she wasn't feeling well. Hell, just yesterday she was so sick she could barely move. But I still couldn't stop myself from taking her too hard, couldn't keep from rutting inside her like a beast...*

In that moment he hated himself more than he ever had. Even more than after what had happened to Miranda. It was apparent that Lock felt his pain and self loathing because he looked up briefly and shook his head.

"No, Brother, don't feel so. She wanted more from you — she asked for it. It's just the incomplete bond between us that made her too weak to withstand the pleasure you gave her."

"The bond is no excuse," Deep said roughly. "I hurt her. I killed her —"

"Hey, you guys, I'm not dead yet." It was Kat's voice — faint but unmistakable.

Deep felt a surge of hope. Gazing down into her lovely blue eyes he saw that she was looking up at them with a worried look on her face.

"What happened?" she whispered.

"You fainted for a moment," Lock murmured, stroking her flushed cheek tenderly.

"Are you all right?" Deep demanded. "How do you feel?"

"Pretty good for someone who just took a trip to la-la land." Kat struggled to sit up between them and Lock helped her. Deep sat back and kept his hands to himself, fearful of what might happen if he touched her again.

"Are you certain you're all right, my lady?" Lock asked anxiously.

"Fine, except..." She looked down at herself blushing and then crossed her arms over her breasts. "Uh, that was all really intense but now I'm kind of embarrassed."

"You have nothing to be embarrassed about," Lock assured her. "You were simply giving your all, participating in the reenactment of the legend."

"What I'd like to be participating in right now is getting dressed," Kat said. "I mean, I know you guys have seen me in my birthday suit but I'm still shy about putting on a show for anyone else."

Lock shook his head. "Birthday suit? You have special clothing you wear on the day of your birth?"

"Birthday suit means nude," Deep explained, glad to finally understand a piece of the confusing Earth vernacular Kat was always speaking. "Where are her clothes?"

"If you can *call* them clothes," Kat muttered, still covering herself. She looked at both of them, frowning. "Hey, are you sure I fainted? I mean, I don't feel dizzy at all. In fact, this is the best I've felt since before the first time we did our first joining to find Sophie and Sylvan."

"You fainted, all right," Deep said dryly, as he helped her fasten on the discarded leaf garments. "Only for a moment but it was long enough."

"Long enough for what?" Kat asked. "What happened while I was out? Did she finish the story?"

As if in answer to her question, the chief's soft, melodic voice floated out into the still night air again.

"And then *Nyra* declared that she could not choose between the brothers for she loved them both. And she took both *Dakir and Lanare* as her mates and slept between them every night, giving her light to the world every day as she shone in the sky."

She might have loved them both but only one of them was good for her, Deep thought, eyeing the gentle way his brother was caressing Kat's cheek. Ever since he'd walked in on them kissing, he'd had the sense that they belonged together—that Kat and Lock would be better off on their own, without him. The way she'd fainted while he was fucking her seemed to confirm that belief.

But she cares for me now — not just Lock. She cares for both of us, whispered the soft voice of hope in his head. *And maybe Lock is right — maybe it's just the incomplete bond that makes her weak. If the three of us were bonded completely maybe she could withstand the pleasure I give her, maybe I wouldn't hurt her anymore. If only...*

His thoughts were interrupted by a soft gasp from Kat. She was staring down at the ground around them, her eyes filled with wonder. "Oh my God! Look!"

"Look at wha — ?" Deep started to say and then he saw.

Flowers had suddenly bloomed everywhere, covering the soft green *belsh* in fragrant beauty.

"They're gorgeous!" Kat leaned down to examine one. "And look — they each have two blossoms coming from one stalk."

Deep looked and saw that it was true. The flowers were large — about the size of his palm. And every stalk had two of them — one a pure, milky white and one a deep, velvety black. In the heart of each blossom was a crimson center — like a single, perfect drop of blood. *But they weren't here just a moment ago,* he thought. *Did they appear the minute the chief finished speaking the legend? They must have.*

"The Moons blossom," Lock breathed reverently. "So it *does* exist."

"Not only does it exist, it's our ticket out of here." Kat leaned down to sniff one pure white flower. "Mmm, they smell good too."

Deep started to respond and then he felt Kat's rush of relief. His fragile hope that she had learned to love him as well as Lock crumbled in that instant.

She's glad, he thought, his mouth twisting. *So glad we've found the blossoms. Because now we can take them back to Mother L'rin and Kat can be rid of us forever. Rid of me.* He had no doubt that Kat would have happily joined with Lock if he himself hadn't been in the picture.

He'd lingered outside the bedroom door after seeing their kiss for a moment, intending to go back in. And he knew what Kat meant when she told Lock that he "came with a lot of baggage."

More Earth vernacular, he thought bitterly. *Just another way of saying I'm not the one she wants.*

He'd fooled himself into thinking that she cared for him—that she loved him as he had so stupidly allowed himself to start loving her. But it wasn't true—she couldn't wait to get the Moons blossom and leave—he could feel the impatience to be away coming from her already.

It doesn't matter anyway, Deep told himself grimly. *I'm no good for her—just look at my past. At what happened to Miranda. I don't want that to happen to Kat, even if she doesn't care for me. I couldn't bear it if...*But he couldn't make himself finish the grim thought. Instead he watched as his brother helped the woman they both loved gather the rare, mystical blossoms. They were laughing as they did and Kat was tickling Lock under the chin with one of the two-headed flowers.

Lock is good for her, Deep realized. ***He's** the one she ought to be with. Not me and not both of us. Just **him**.* The concept of one of them having a female without the other was so foreign to him it was hard to contemplate, but he knew it was true.

It didn't matter who he thought Kat belonged with, though. They had the Moons blossoms—or *fifi* flowers, as she called them. Mother L'rin would be able to brew a potion to separate Kat from both of them.

By this time tomorrow we will be two and one again instead of three, Deep thought. *That's a good thing—good for all of us.* But though he tried, he could feel no joy at the idea. All he felt was achingly empty.

Chapter Twenty-one

Sophie turned on her side again and flipped her pillow, hoping the new position would help her fall asleep. It didn't, though she was tired enough. She'd started her new part time job at the elementary school aboard the Mother ship and the little ones had just about worn her out.

Sylvan had told her she could just stay home and concentrate on her art but Sophie had decided she needed an occupation outside the home to keep from going crazy. Besides, she adored kids and teaching them to paint and draw and use modeling clay was great.

But it wasn't her new job that was on her mind now. Something else was keeping her restless and wakeful.

With a sigh, Sophie turned over again, facing Sylvan's broad, bare back. He was breathing deeply and she knew he must have had a hard day at the med station. There had been a big influx of wounded that day from a scrimmage with the Scourge and he'd been going from morning until night with barely a pause.

Sophie sighed softly. If only the thoughts and images would leave her alone. If only —

"Sophia?" Sylvan turned over to face her, his eyes glowing a faint blue in the dark. "Are you all right?"

"I'm sorry," Sophie said contritely. "I didn't mean to wake you up. I know how tired you are."

"It's all right." Reaching out, he cupped her cheek gently. "I can tell you have something on your mind."

"It's nothing," Sophie protested. "Go back to sleep."

"I'm awake now so you might as well talk. Come on, *Talana.* Tell me what's troubling you."

Sophie sat up and ran a hand through her hair. "It's Lauren—I can't get her out of my head. I keep imagining what that horrible AllFather must be doing to her and I feel so bad. I mean, that could have been *me*. It *would* have been if you hadn't found me in time."

"Sophia…" Sylvan sat up beside her and drew her close to his side. In the darkness he felt warm and solid and his muscular arm around her shoulder was very comforting. "I know you feel bad for your kin but you can't dwell on it," he said softly, his deep voice rumbling through her. "There's nothing we can do at the moment—no way to trace her."

"I wish Deep and Lock were here," Sophie said mournfully. "Maybe they could locate her doing their seeker/finder thing."

"That's very doubtful if not completely impossible," Sylvan said. "They don't have a properly trained focus and without one, their only hope to find Lauren would be to join with someone who knew her intimately. And you saw how that ended for Kat."

"That's true." Sophie nodded. "But it just seems like there should be *something* else we can do."

"You're not the only one who thinks so," Sylvan said dryly. "Baird told me he got another call from the detective the sister of your mother hired to find Lauren today. He was angry when Baird put him off."

"He was?" Sophie frowned and sat up. "But why? What does he know?"

"I'm not sure." Sylvan shook his head. "But I don't think we can keep evading his questions forever. The male has good instincts—he seems certain that we know more than we're telling him."

That reminded Sophie of something. "Sylvan," she said, looking up at him. "Speaking of keeping secrets, can I ask you something?"

"Of course, anything." He looked at her. "But I hope you don't think I'm keeping secrets from you."

"No, I know you're not—this isn't about you. It's about Deep."

"What about him?"

"Well, Kat seemed to think that there was something he'd done in the past. Something…troubling. She didn't get a chance to give us any details but Liv and I were worried about it."

Sylvan sighed and raked a hand through his spiky blond hair distractedly. "What you're asking me, *Talana*…it's a secret that really isn't mine to tell."

His actions put Sophie on high alert—she almost never saw her cool, collected male so obviously agitated. *Whatever it was, it must have been bad!*

"Please," she pleaded. "This is Kat we're talking about—she's my best friend in the world besides Liv. If she's in any kind of danger when she's with Deep I need to know."

Sylvan was silent for a long moment, apparently debating with himself. Then he shook his head. "I'm sorry but I can't reveal another warrior's past—not even to you, *Talana*. Not when it concerns something this delicate."

"Sylvan—"

"I *will* tell you that Kat is not in any danger," he said, interrupting her protest. "And that Deep didn't do anything wrong…though that's not how he sees it."

"Do you have any idea how frustrating this is?" Sophie demanded. "You keep throwing out these little half hints and then refusing to tell me the whole story."

Sylvan looked serious. "The whole story, as you put it, is a grim tale—not something I want to talk about in the dead of night."

"Not even with me here to keep you safe?" Deciding to let the matter drop for now, Sophie snuggled against him.

"There are other things I'd rather do with you at night than talk." He kissed her, taking her mouth in a way that made her moan softly.

"Sylvan..." she protested. "About Deep—"

"I don't want to talk about that. About grief and sorrow and loss." His deep voice was unexpectedly rough. "Don't you know I have dreams—nightmares—where I don't reach you in time? Where I break into the Scourge ship to find you already...already gone?"

"Well, I'm not gone—I'm here with you." Sophie pressed closer to him. "You got to me in time—you saved me, Sylvan."

"No, *Talana*," he rumbled, kissing her again. "It was *you* who saved *me*. Without you I'd be dead inside."

"Hmmm," she whispered, stroking his thigh. "You feel pretty alive to me."

"I'm going to get a whole lot livelier if you keep that up," he warned.

"That's okay," she murmured. "I don't mind. I..." But she couldn't finish—Sylvan was licking a long, slow trail down her neck.

Sophie's heart began to race as his warm, wet tongue caressed her sensitive skin. His big, hard body felt so good against hers and his mating scent was rising, enveloping her in pure lust. She tilted her head to one side, baring her throat. "Do it, Sylvan—I want to feel you in me."

"I never get tired of biting you," Sylvan growled softly, lifting her so that she was straddling his hips. "Or kissing you...or tasting you...or *fucking* you."

"Sylvan..." she whispered breathlessly as he lifted the lacy hem of her nightie and parted her thighs. Hearing dirty talk from him when he was usually so cool and logical never failed to turn her on.

"Yes, *Talana?*" he murmured, sliding the broad head of his shaft against her wet folds. "Was there something you wanted?"

"Nothing but you. *God,*" she moaned as he sank his fangs and his cock into her at the same time. "Sylvan!"

"I love it when you call my name while I'm inside you," he sent through their link. *"Love the soft, helpless little sounds you make when I take you."*

"Take me harder...more!" she begged. And the part of her mind that wasn't drowning in pleasure wondered how he always knew exactly what she needed. All the troubling thoughts that had been bothering her were swept away on the tide of pleasure as he made her his once again.

But though Sophie knew she would sleep well after their loving, she was also certain she would return to her worries eventually. Lauren was still out there, somewhere and as for Deep's dark past...well, she would have to compare notes with Liv and see if she'd gotten anything out of Baird.

Later...

Chapter Twenty-two

"We're here! And we brought the *fi-fi* flowers." Kat presented the bouquet of blossoms triumphantly to Mother L'rin.

"Have them, you do," the old wise woman acknowledged, nodding. She was sitting quietly in the middle of the Healing Garden, doing something with a fluffy bunch of pink and purple herbs. "And still you wish to use them?"

"Of...course we do." Kat looked uncertainly at Deep and Lock who were standing on either side of her. Well, standing might be too strong a word—Deep was actually slouched against a nearby tree studying his fingernails. "That is...I think so."

"My lady..." Lock gave her a pained look. "Kat...I wish to say that the time Deep and I have spent bonded to you—even partially—has been an experience I shall never forget. Neither of us will," he added, looking at Deep.

"How *could* we forget it? It's been one disaster after another from the start." Deep spoke in a bored tone. "But I suppose there's no use rehashing it now that we're almost free."

"Almost *free?*" Kat couldn't help the sharp pang of hurt and rejection that raced through her, though she told herself it was ridiculous. "Is *that* how you feel?"

"Isn't it how *you* feel?" he countered, looking up to give her a smoldering glare.

"I...I don't know." Kat's voice sank to a whisper. "I just don't know."

She'd been overjoyed to find the Moons blossom—ecstatic almost. But now she realized the reason for her joy wasn't that she was going to be parted from Deep and Lock—it was because the lovely black and white flowers represented her ticket home. In her mind, they had come to symbolize everything she missed—Earth and Sophie and Liv and a culture where she spoke the language and didn't have to rely on a partially defective fuzzy caterpillar to translate for her. Somehow that was all she'd been thinking of when she gathered the *fi-fi* flowers—she'd conveniently managed to forget that the sacred blossoms also meant the end of her partial bond with the brothers.

"Strange that you don't know how you feel when it's abundantly clear to *me*," Deep snapped, breaking her train of thought. "I felt your relief when we found the blossoms. I'm sure Lock did too. Mother L'rin," he said, turning to the old woman. "We would be most grateful if you'd use these blossoms to brew the potion that will separate Kat from my brother and me."

Mother L'rin shook her head. "Separate you it will not. No potion such a thing can do."

"What?" Kat said flatly. "I *really* hope my convo-pillar is acting up again. It sounded like you just said the *fi-fi* flowers *won't* break the soul bond."

"That they cannot do."

"But you told me," Kat cried. "You said if I brought you the flowers—" She stopped abruptly. What *had* the wise woman said? Had she ever really promised that the flowers would break the soul bond? Or had Kat just inferred it because she had been so eager to get away from Deep and Lock?

"Break the bond the flowers cannot," Mother L'rin said. "But ease your pain they will, as nothing else."

"Ease her pain? What do you mean?" Lock demanded. "Why should the lady Kat need special blossoms to ease her pain?"

"Because come back, it will" the old woman said calmly. "Half-bonded a female cannot be forever. But the *fifilalachuchu* blossoms her torment will ease—for a while, at least."

"What?" Kat's heart was suddenly in her throat. Surely she must have misunderstood the old woman? But from the grim look on Deep's face and the concerned look on Lock's, they had heard the same thing she had. "But...but I don't *want* to live in pain the rest of my life," she whispered through trembling lips. "And I don't want to be dependant on some magical flower in order to function."

Mother L'rin rose and poked her hard in the sternum. "Then bonded *you must be*. No way to break the soul bond there is and so—"

"Yes, there is." Deep stepped forward, frowning. "There is a way to break the bond between us—one that has nothing to do with flowers and foolishness."

"What are you talking about?" Lock said, frowning. "There's clearly no way around this—Kat will have to be fully bonded to us."

"You'd like that, wouldn't you?" Deep's bottomless black eyes narrowed to slits. "Yes, you'd *love* it, dear brother. The problem is, that little Kat here, would *not*." He turned to Kat. *"Would* you?"

Kat's heart clenched in her chest. "Up until recently I would have said I absolutely didn't want to be with the two of you," she said quietly. "But—"

"But now you've had a change of heart and you've decided you want to be with us forever?" Deep said sarcastically.

"I didn't say that," Kat protested.

"Of course you didn't. "Because that's not what you want. *We're* not what you want."

"Deep," Lock said warningly, stepping toward his brother.

Kat waved him back. "No, let's try and talk this out. Deep," she said softly, taking a step toward the dark twin. "Why are you acting this way? After how we talked in the cave, I thought..."

"I thought a few things myself." Deep's hot glare turned suddenly cool and distant. "All of them wrong. But as I was saying, there *is* a way to break the soul bond and let the three of us go back to living our normal lives."

"Of what do you speak?" Mother L'rin demanded.

Deep frowned down at her. "The Scourge. *They* developed a way to break bonds between warriors and their mates. The psychic knife, they called it—a machine they developed on their home world."

Lock stared at him, obviously appalled. "You can't be serious. That *machine*, as you call it, was a torture device."

"Why shouldn't I be serious?" Deep demanded. "The breaking of an incomplete bond wouldn't hurt any of us. I'll admit the machine was invented for diabolical purposes, but why shouldn't we use it to our advantage?"

"Maybe because it's on the *Scourge home world?*" Lock raised an eyebrow at his brother but Deep was not so easily deterred.

"Please, Brother, their planet is a deadworld now. Since the last battle of Berrni nothing lives there and no one goes there—the entire place is abandoned. We could walk in, break the bond, and fly off-planet and no one would ever be the wiser."

"The Goddess would know." Mother L'rin rounded on Deep, waving a crooked finger in his face. "Sacrilege you speak of."

Deep frowned. "No, what's *sacrilege* is bonding an unwilling female to you." He looked at Kat. "Wouldn't you agree?"

Kat's chest was tight but she lifted her chin and looked him in the eyes. "Yes," she said, nodding stiffly. "I would."

"Good, then it's settled." Deep clapped his hands together once, in a motion of finality. "We'll go at once."

"Not without permission from the Kindred High Council, we won't." Lock glared at his brother. "Or have you forgotten that it's a forbidden zone?"

"We'll find a way around that," Deep said casually. "You know Baird has friends on the Council."

"But what about lady Kat's pain?" Lock demanded. "Or don't you care about that, anymore?"

"Of course I care." Deep's voice was suddenly gruff. He turned to Mother L'rin. "How long will it take you to brew that potion?"

"No potion will I make for you!" Mother L'rin threw the bouquet of black and white blossoms on the ground and trampled them into the dirt with her tiny feet.

"Hey, wait!" Kat protested. "We went to a lot of trouble to get those! And anyway, I thought they were sacred!"

"Sacred they are. But better they should be crushed than used by such as you. Blasphemers!" She spat at Deep's booted feet. "If pain your lady has, ease her yourself." Then she stalked off into the tall pink and gold grass muttering angrily.

Kat felt her heart sink. "Wait! Please, Mother L'rin," she called and started to go after her.

"She's just going to tell you that the only solution is to let Lock and I bond you to us forever," Deep said. "Is that really what you want to hear?"

Kat stopped. "No," she said, giving him a cool look. "No, most definitely *not.*"

"I didn't think so." He smiled but it wasn't a happy expression. "So it's settled. We'll head straight back to the Mother ship and get permission to go to the Scourge home world where we can break our annoying little bond. We'll be free of each other before you know it."

"Wonderful," Kat said flatly. "As easy as one, two, three."

"Exactly." Deep nodded. "And if your pain comes back, just tell Lock or I. We'll take care of you."

"You're *too* kind," Kat said, glaring at him. "But I feel fine — better than fine, actually. Great. Especially now that I know I'll be getting away from *you*."

Turning, she stalked away. Tears were rising in her eyes again and she didn't want to cry in front of either of the brothers. Especially not Deep — the heartless bastard.

* * * * *

"Why did you do that?" Lock's voice was soft and desolate. When he looked at Deep, the hurt in his brown eyes was almost too much to bear. Deep wanted to shield himself against his brother's suffering, but he didn't deserve not to feel it. Instead of closing himself off, he opened himself to the painful emotion.

"I did what was best for her," he said evenly. "You know that's true, Lock."

"No, you did what was best for *you*." Lock's pain turned suddenly to rage. He rounded on Deep, his hands clenched into fists, his eyes blazing. "Because you *always* do what's best for you. And because you think if you push her away first, she won't have a chance to hurt you."

"She's had her chance," Deep said in a low voice. "Don't worry about that, Brother."

"Well, I haven't had mine!" Lunging forward, Lock punched him on the jaw.

Deep saw it coming but he didn't back away or try to defend himself. He took the punch full on. And the next and the next, until his face was as bloody and numb as his heart.

Finally Lock stopped and stood there panting. His hands hung limply by his sides, the knuckles blood-spattered and raw. The blows had hurt him as much as Deep—the echoes of their shared pain, both emotional and physical—flooded the closed loop between them.

Deep wiped blood from his lower lip and winced. "Are you finished? Or do you want to hit me some more?" It was the first time since they were children that Lock had struck him. He was hurt but not surprised—not really. *I had it coming.*

Lock looked down at his hands, examining his bloody knuckles with dead eyes. "No...I'm done."

"Good." Deep straightened his shoulders and sighed. "Let me get some gel packs on my face before it swells while you go find Kat. If we hike fast and the tide is right, we can be folding space before the sun sets."

"If we hurry," Lock repeated dully. "Because the faster we get back, the faster you can get us separated from the only woman I've ever really loved. The only woman *either one of us* has ever really loved."

Deep raised an eyebrow. "Aren't you forgetting Miranda?"

"We shared a few dreams with her," Lock said wearily. "Not our lives—not like Kat."

"So she doesn't count because we never actually got to meet her in person?" Deep demanded.

Lock looked up at him wearily. "What happened to Miranda was terrible, Brother. It was a grief deeper than anything I have ever felt—until now." He sighed. "But Miranda is gone and Kat...she's right here. She's lovely and intelligent and perfect in every way. So of *course* you have to drive her away."

Deep looked his brother in the eyes. "If you truly love her, then you'll help me in this. I'm no good for her, Lock—for any female. I'll poison her life if we get too close."

"Just the way you've poisoned mine." Lock ran a hand through his hair and blew out a breath. "I wish I could cut the tie between us. Not just between the two of us and Kat—between you and me. I wish...I wish we weren't brothers." He glared at Deep. "I'd rather be dead than spend one more day as your twin."

Despite his outward composure, Deep's breath caught in his throat. He knew his brother—Lock never spoke unkindly and he never lied. If he said a thing, it was true from the bottom of his heart. "Brother..." he said uncertainly.

"Don't call me that." Lock threw him one last glance over his shoulder before he walked away. "Not anymore."

Deep watched him go, his heart aching in his chest. He was only doing what he had to do, but it still hurt. *It's for the best though,* he told himself. *For Kat. For all of us.*

But seeing misery in the set of his brother's hunched shoulders, and feeling the echo of both his pain and Kat's, it was hard to believe.

Chapter Twenty-three

"So you're going to the Scourge home world?" Sophie's green eyes were as wide as saucers.

"Apparently." Kat took a scoop of the ultra-premium vanilla bean ice cream and plopped it unceremoniously onto the homemade chocolate chip cookie. Then she jammed another cookie on top and sighed. "If Baird can get us permission from the council."

"He got it." Olivia came into the food prep area and lifted her nose. "Mmm, you can smell those cookies all the way down the corridor."

"Liv! These were supposed to be a surprise," Sophie protested. "We're making you homemade chocolate chip ice cream sandwiches but we're not nearly done yet. These have to go into the freezer for at least an hour before..."

"Before what?" Olivia said, around a mouthful of cookie and ice cream. Her eyes rolled up in her head and she moaned, "Soooo good!"

Despite her inner turmoil, Kat couldn't help laughing. "I swear, she's getting worse all the time! Liv, honey, I don't want to hurt your feelings but you need to ease up on the sweets or you and I will be able to swap clothes after the baby is born."

"Uh-uh." Liv shook her head and grabbed a napkin to wipe her chin. "That's one of the nice things about carrying a Kindred baby — you don't have to worry about weight gain."

"You don't?" Kat frowned. "Who told you that?"

"Sylvan," Sophie said promptly. "He says when an Earth woman is carrying a Kindred fetus, she requires so many extra calories that she could live on Krispy Kreme donuts and Godiva truffles and not gain an ounce — the real problem is to keep yourself from *losing* too much weight."

"Seriously?" Kat could scarcely believe it. But it was true that though she ate from morning until night, Liv didn't appear to have gained a single pound. Which was really kind of unfair when you thought about it.

"Uh-huh." Liv nodded and took another bite of the drippy ice cream sandwich. "Of course I try to get plenty of fruits and veggies too. But I'm not holding back on the stuff I like, either." She turned to Sophie. "And these are *heavenly*. Thank you so much!"

"Well, you *did* say you were craving something sweet." Sophie gave her a one armed hug since she was holding a dripping ice cream scoop in the other hand.

"When am I not?" Olivia laughed and nodded at the plate. "Well, go on you two — might as well dig in. I can't eat them all but I might be tempted to try if you don't help out."

"Oh, all right." With a sigh, Sophie put down her scoop and picked up a sandwich. "But you're *supposed* to freeze them first." She looked at Kat. "Have one. You better get them quick before Baird and Sylvan get home — Baird has a sweet tooth almost as bad as Liv's."

Kat shook her head. "You two go ahead. I'm not hungry."

"Oh *no*." Sophie put down her cookie at once and gave Kat a worried look. "Are you sick again? Did the pain come back?"

"And how did it go away in the first place?" Olivia demanded. "Was it that wise woman they took you to see or what? Now that you're home and we're finally all together again you have to spill."

"I'm fine," Kat told them, more or less truthfully. "I'm a little weak but there's no pain." *Not yet, anyway.* But she didn't say that aloud—no point in worrying her friends when there was nothing they could do about it. "As for how the pain went away in the first place…well, remember that I told you Deep did something you'd never guess?"

Liv and Sophie gave each other a look she couldn't interpret. "We remember, all right," Liv said. "But neither Sophie or I could get anything about it out of Baird of Sylvan."

Kat frowned. "Baird and Sylvan? How would they know?"

"I don't know but they do—only they won't tell us," Sophie said. "Sylvan said he couldn't reveal the past of another warrior or something like that."

"Baird said the same thing," Olivia chimed in.

Kat shook her head. "Well, it's nice that they're so trustworthy, but I really don't see how either one of then could know that Deep took my pain."

"What?" Liv asked just as Sophie said,

"He took your *what?*"

"He took my pain," Kat repeated. She went on to tell her two best friends about the dream she'd had of Deep being whipped in the cave and how Mother L'rin had showed her that it was real. "So you see," she ended in a low voice. "He's the reason my head doesn't hurt anymore."

"I don't think it's your *head* we have to be concerned with right now. It's your heart." Liv put down her sandwich and wiped her fingers on a napkin before putting an arm around Kat. "Am I right, Kat-woman?"

"I d-don't know." Kat brushed at her eyes angrily. "I'm sorry—I don't know why I let him affect me like this. He's such a *bastard.*"

"He does put the ass in asshole," Liv agreed calmly. "But it sounds like he's not *all* bad."

"He's the reason we're going to the Scourge home world in the first place," Kat said, sniffing. "He doesn't want to be bonded to me—not even partially bonded. We're supposed to find some machine the Scourge invented called 'the psychic knife' to cut ourselves apart."

"What a jerk!" Sophie said indignantly. "Don't you listen to him, Kat. Any guy would be lucky to have you!"

"Speaking of other guys, how does Lock feel about all this?" Olivia asked. "It seems to me that he's always in the middle of you two—that can't be easy for him."

"I don't know." Kat shook her head. "We didn't talk on the trip back home at all. None of us. But...I'm pretty sure the two of them were fighting after our argument on Twin Moons."

"Really? How could you tell?" Liv looked interested.

"I'd say Deep's face was a pretty good indication. He looks like he slammed head-first into a concrete wall. And the knuckles on Lock's right hand are all cut and bruised."

"A *fist* fight?" Liv shook her head. "Really? Because I was under the impression that Twin Kindred never strike each other—under *any* circumstances. I think it hurts them just as much to hit their twin as it does to be hit...like they share the pain they inflict or something like that. That's what Baird told me, anyway."

"Well, I'd say they made an exception to the no-knuckle-sandwich-between-brothers rule," Kat said dryly but she couldn't help being troubled. "I guess...I guess they were fighting over me."

"Lock loves you, doesn't he?" Sophie said sympathetically.

Kat nodded. "And I could love him too if—"

"If Deep wasn't in the way," Olivia finished for her.

But Kat shook her head. "No, that's not what I was going to say. I *could* love Lock — hell, I could love *both* of them if there was any chance of my love being returned."

"But what about having their emotions in your head all the time?" Sophie asked. "I thought you hated that."

Kat thought of the warm, happy feelings she'd gotten from both brothers just moments before they were captured by the natives. "It's not so bad when they're in a good mood. But Deep..."

"Is never in a good mood," both Liv and Sophie said.

Kat nodded sadly. "You know, for awhile there back on Twin Moons, I really thought we were almost on the same page. I found out what Deep had done for me and then we talked and it seemed like the three of us were getting really close. Especially after —" She broke off abruptly, blushing.

"After what?" Sophie and Liv demanded together. "Come on, Kat — *give.*"

"Oh God, you guys, do I *really* have to say it?" Kat looked at them, pleading with her eyes. "You're married women now — or practically married. You get enough hot sex of your own without hearing about my measly sex life."

"Are you kidding me? We might get hot sex but *you* my friend are getting some genuine *ménage a trois* action," Liv said. "Or *are* you?"

Kat sighed. "Well...kinda."

"Kinda? What does that mean?" Sophie frowned. "When I think how you two pried out the details of how Sylvan healed me and marked me in that cabin..."

"All right, all right…" Kat held up her hands in a gesture of defeat. "I'll tell all. But you can't laugh."

"Why would we laugh?" Sophie grabbed the platter of oozing cookie sandwiches. "Come on, let's move this into the living room."

"Before I start," Kat said, once they were comfortably settled on the large leather couch. "I want to get one thing straight—what was it that you guys *thought* Baird and Sylvan knew about Deep before I told you about how he took my pain?"

"We told you—we' don't know," Liv said and she and Sophie gave each other an uneasy look.

"It's something about Deep's past," Sophie said. "Something really bad, I think. Sylvan said you aren't in any danger from him though, if that's any consolation."

"Not much." Kat's stomach did a flip. "God, I wonder what it was? And even if Deep won't tell me, why doesn't Lock?"

Sophie shrugged. "Who knows? Why didn't he tell you about how Deep had taken your pain?"

"Baird says there's a huge stigma among the Kindred in being involved in a tragedy involving a potential mate," Olivia said.

"A potential mate? And *tragedy?* That's the word he used?" Kat raised an eyebrow.

"Yup." Liv nodded. "It's like a blot on their character—a shame they can never live down. Maybe Lock is *ashamed* to tell you about whatever it is."

"Maybe," Kat said thoughtfully. "Or maybe Deep won't let him." She sighed. "He never has wanted to let me in—not even a little bit. He blocks me constantly."

"Well, you won't have to put up with it for much longer," Sophie said comfortingly. "But...do you really think it's safe, going to the Scourge home world?"

"Baird says it's completely deserted," Liv said. "There was this big battle there about fifty years ago and the Kindred annihilated almost everyone living there—which were all men, by the way, since the Scourge have no females. The few that were left packed up and flew off in the Fathership. They've been growing more warriors in these huge, disgusting vats ever since but they can't have any babies naturally because they have no women."

"I wonder if that has anything to do with that weird prophesy they're always talking about?" Sophie said in a low voice. "And with cousin Lauren. You don't think she's...they took her to...to...uh, replenish their race, do you? I mean, because when they had me in that ship they were talking about...about *breeding* and—" She broke off, clearly too upset to finish.

Olivia shivered and gave her sister a comforting hug. "I know it was awful, Sophie but it's over now. And as for what they want with Lauren, maybe Kat can find out. That's the excuse Baird used to the Council," she explained turning to Kat. "You guys are going to hunt for traces of Lauren and also see if you can get any more information on the Scourge prophesy."

"So we're on a fact finding mission that just happens to double as a psychic soul-divorce," Kat said dryly. *"Lovely."*

"It's better than being tied to a man who doesn't love you," Sophie said, straightening up. "You know that, Kat."

"Yes, I know." Kat sighed and ran a hand through her hair. "I thought about that a lot while we were on Twin Moons. Mostly because of, you know, my mom and dad."

"They…weren't very happy together, were they?" Sophie asked tactfully.

"Our house was a war zone," Kat said flatly. "They were always screaming insults at each other, throwing things…hitting each other. That's why I was always over at *your* house." She shook her head. "I swore to myself that I would never be with a man I didn't love with my whole heart, who loved me the same way. I *can't* be with someone I'm constantly fighting with—someone who doesn't want me."

"Of *course* you can't," Sophie exclaimed. "Just wait until they cut you lose, Kat, and find some other nice Kindred. Try a Blood Kindred like Sylvan—they're wonderful."

"I would have to put in a vote for a Beast Kindred," Olivia said, grinning. "Not only are they the best lovers, they're the best cooks too. Baird has been making me something new every night."

"Better than his first attempt at pizza, I hope?" Kat said, trying to smile.

Liv grinned. "*Much* better. Baird's come a long way from the days when he thought fruit cocktail was a good topping option."

Kat sighed. "They sound great and both of your husbands are wonderful men…"

"I hear a 'but' coming," Sophie murmured.

"But, I'm just not interested." Kat sighed and put her head in her hands. "I don't know, maybe when this is all over with I'll just go back to Earth and try to find a regular human guy. One who doesn't force me to feel his painful emotions all the time, one without a tortured secret past, one who doesn't freaking have to have his brother in bed with him to have sex."

Liv snorted. "Uh, sorry Kat but that came out sounding really *wrong.*"

Kat waved a hand. "You know what I mean. It's not sexual—not between *them,* anyway. But they seriously can't touch me unless the other one is too, or it hurts them."

Sophie shook her head. "That's so *weird.*"

"Weirder than being bitten every single time you have sex?" Liv said, frowning. "Weirder than any of the other stuff that goes with being a Kindred bride?"

"Well, I *guess* not," Sophie said, shrugging. "But you have to admit, it's not what we're used to."

"Different isn't always bad," Liv said. "And love comes in all shapes and sizes. Maybe Deep is *afraid* to let himself love you, Kat. Maybe because of whatever it was that happened he feels *unworthy* of your love."

Kat frowned. "He *did* say something about me being unattainable—like the moon or the stars or something like that." She crossed her arms over her chest. "But then he went right back to being a jerk."

"He went back into his protective shell," Olivia said. "I'm telling you, Kat—I bet he loves you just as much as Lock does—in his own way."

"Yeah? Well he could have fooled me," Kat said sarcastically. "He can't *wait* to get rid of our bond. He…" she trailed off, shaking her head. She was feeling weaker and weaker as she spoke but she didn't want to show it.

"He what?" Sophie asked.

Kat sighed wearily. *Need to get out of here and go lie down.* "He—"

Just then the holo link buzzed, interrupting her.

"Oh, hang on a minute. Hold that thought," Sophie said. She ran to the link and hit the accept button. Immediately a winking blue dot appeared about a foot above the black cube of the holo link. It slowly expanded to show the stern features of a Blood Kindred warrior.

"Excuse me, mate of my commander," he said formally, nodding at Sophie—a gesture which looked odd since only his head was being projected. "Communications officer Bastian here. Forgive me for interrupting you at home but I'm afraid there is a planet to ship call coming in for you from Earth in the viewing room."

"Oh?" Olivia came to stand beside her sister. "Who is it?"

"A human male by the name of Detective Adam Rast. He claims to have spoken to both your mates before, but now he wishes to speak to you as well." He nodded at Liv and Sophie, including them both.

"Well, you can tell him to just—" Liv began.

"Wait!" Sophie put a hand on her twin's arm. "He's the one searching for Lauren. We'll take it," she told the communications officer. "We'll be in the viewing room in five minutes."

"Very well. I will inform him." The holo head nodded again and then winked out.

"Why did you do that?" Olivia demanded, frowning. "What can we possibly tell him?"

"The truth." Sophie's face was paper-pale but she looked determined. "It's not fair to do anything else."

"Sophie, we can't just—"

"Look, girls, you two are going to have to work this out between you. I'm beat." Kat rose carefully, trying not to let them see how weak she was. She hoped neither of her friends noticed how white her knuckles were as she gripped the arm of the couch for support.

"You're going?" Sophie asked. "But you haven't even told us the dirty details of your time on Twin Moons yet."

"And you're folding space for the Scourge home world tomorrow morning," Liv added.

"Sorry girls." Kat tried to laugh but it came out as more of a croak and she had to turn it into a cough. "Looks like you'll have to grill me later."

"Kat, are you *sure* you're okay?" Liv looked at her critically. "I mean, you still don't seem like yourself."

"Of course she doesn't," Sophie jumped to her defense. "Her soul is still tangled up with Deep and Lock's. She won't be back to her old self until she gets all that straightened out. Right, Kat?"

"Right." Kat nodded. God, she was *so* tired. *Have to get out of here.* "And as anyone knows, a good night's sleep is really important before getting a soul-divorce. So I'm going to hit the hay."

Sophie gave her a hug. "We'll be there to see you off, tomorrow," she promised.

"You don't have to do that," Kat protested. "I'm sure we're leaving at some ungodly hour."

"Doesn't matter." Olivia hugged her too. "We wouldn't miss it."

I hope I don't miss it either! Hope I'm not too weak to get there. Or in too much pain... The beginnings of a headache were throbbing behind her eyes ominously. Kat tried to smile. "Okay, you win. I'll see you both tomorrow."

It took every ounce of strength she could muster to stand straight and walk out the door as though nothing was wrong. But somehow she managed. She even managed to get to her own suite without falling over. Once there, however, she collapsed on the bed and put a hand over her eyes.

*Oh God, the pain...*The rusty iron spike was back, digging into her brain just behind her eyes. Kat knew she ought to call for help but the only two people who could help her were Deep and Lock.

And after the scene the three of them had been through on Twin Moons, she knew she would rather die than ask. *We're getting our divorce tomorrow,* she told herself, gritting her teeth. *Surely I can make it until then...*She hoped.

Chapter Twenty-four

Detective Adam Rast was a big, imposing man with dark green eyes and golden brown hair, cut short and neat. From his image on the viewscreen, he looked to be in his early to mid thirties. If Liv hadn't spent so much time around the Kindred, he might have intimidated her. But though he was nearly as tall as Baird and built like a linebacker, she was used to big males now. And besides, he was back on Earth—there was nothing he could actually do to them.

Though it certainly looked like he wanted to try.

"I'm sick of these evasions and half answers." His deep voice was a menacing growl. "Your aunt hired me to find your cousin and I *know* you know more about her disappearance than you're telling me."

"What makes you think that?" Liv asked coolly. "My husband tells me the Kindred have cooperated with you fully."

"He's also not telling me everything he knows." The detective gave them a frustrated look. "Look, I know you girls have never met your cousin but she may be in real danger so—"

"She *is* in danger," Sophie said quietly, looking up at the viewscreen.

"What?" He frowned at her. "What do you mean?"

Liv sighed. *Here we go.* But if Sophie had decided to let the truth come out, she had to support her. "We believe Lauren was taken by the Scourge," she said clearly.

Detective Rast glowered at them. "Why wasn't I told this immediately?"

"Because there's nothing you can do about it," Liv said. "Hell, there's nothing *we* can do about it." She pointed a finger at the viewscreen. "And don't think for a *minute* that we don't care just because we've never met Lauren. Both Sophie and I have been held by the Scourge and we're well aware of what a horrible experience it is."

"Which is why we didn't want to tell you—or Aunt Abby," Sophie added. "We thought it would be better for her to go on thinking that Lauren was just missing rather than actually *knowing* that she's a prisoner of that...that..." She shook her head, her eyes filling with tears. "Poor Lauren."

The anger in Rast's face faded to be replaced by concern. "And you're sure they took her?"

"Not positive, no," Liv said. "But the way she was taken—with all her clothes left behind—is consistent with the way the Scourge kidnapped Sophie here. They have this device called a molecular transfer beam that can only transport living tissue—that's why the clothes get left behind."

"And she has a mark between her breasts," Sophie added, sniffing. "We saw it on the pictures Aunt Abby showed us."

Rast frowned. "What does that have to do with it?"

"We're not completely sure," Liv said. "But the Scourge have a prophesy that seems to have something to do with an Earth girl who has a special mark between her breasts. They checked both me and my sister for the mark when they kidnapped us. Lauren is related to us and she has it—we're pretty sure there's a connection."

"What can we do? How can we get her back?" Rast asked.

"We can't," Liv said bluntly. "I'm sorry, but we're not even sure where they've taken her. Although we *do* have some Kindred warriors who are going to go to the Scourge home planet tomorrow," she said, wanting to give him hope. "They're going to be looking for any traces of Lauren and also, they want to find out exactly what the Scourge prophesy says."

"What good is that?" Rast demanded. "Isn't it more likely that they have her in their ship?"

"The Fathership? Possibly," Liv said. "But it's practically impregnable and the Kindred High Council has determined that they can't make an attack on it and risk the safety of the entire Earth just for one girl." She sighed. "I'm sorry, Detective Rast."

"Please don't think we don't care about Lauren," Sophie pleaded. "She's all I've been thinking about lately. I feel so *bad* for her because I know what she's going through."

"And that's all you can tell me? You're not holding anything else back?" Rast looked back and forth between them.

Liv nodded. "I'm afraid that's it. I hope you can see why we've been hiding it. We thought not knowing was a better option for Aunt Abby than telling her that her daughter had been abducted by the Scourge."

"It's a tough call, all right." Rast blew out a breath and ran a hand through his short golden brown hair. "But I need to let her know. I can't keep taking her money when there's nothing I can do."

"Hold off on telling her just a little while longer," Sophie pleaded. "Maybe Deep and Lock—the warriors that are going tomorrow—will find out something about where she's being kept or...or what they want her for."

"We might even be able to arrange for you to come up here to the Mother ship and talk to them after they get back in person," Liv said, having an inspiration. "I could ask my husband to ask the Council for a special dispensation."

"I fail to see how taking a tour of your ship will help me locate Lauren," Rast growled. "But I *would* like to conduct interviews in person rather than over this damn viewscreen."

"Let me see what I can do," Liv said smoothly.

"And in the mean time, can you hold off on telling Aunt Abby?" Sophie pleaded.

Rast sighed. "I'll think about it. As I said, I don't like taking her money without doing my job."

"But you *are* doing your job," Liv pointed out quietly. "You didn't quit until you got answers about where Lauren is."

Rast got a stubborn look on his chiseled features. "Your aunt hired me to find Lauren and bring her home safely. Until that's accomplished, my job isn't done." He nodded briefly. "I'll let you go now, but I'll be in touch. If you find out anything, the communications officer I spoke to has my contact information. Call me any time of the day or night and I'll come straight down to the Human/Kindred Relations building to talk on the viewscreen."

Sophie nodded. "All right, thank you, Detective."

His face softened slightly. "Thank *you* for telling me the truth. Now we just have to hope to God that the warriors you're sending find something."

"I'm sure they will," Liv said, making a mental note to talk to Lock about it. Just because he and Kat and Deep were mainly visiting the Scourge home planet to get their "soul-divorce" as Kat called it, didn't mean they couldn't also dig for clues. She knew the light twin would take the assignment very seriously if she asked him to.

Rast nodded once more and then the viewscreen flickered and went blank.

"Wow, he's really dedicated," Sophie murmured.

Liv nodded. "I can see why Baird respects him so much." She sighed. "Well, the cat's out of the bag, now. I wonder how long he'll wait to tell Aunt Abby."

Sophie looked troubled. "Maybe...maybe *we* should tell her. It doesn't seem fair to put that decision on him. And we *are* family."

"You were the one begging him to wait," Liv pointed out. "And besides, I think you were right. Kat and the guys *might* find something worth knowing. If they could even get the exact wording of the prophesy, we might have a clue about exactly what they want Lauren for and where they might be taking her."

Sophie nodded reluctantly. "All right. I just feel so bad that we're keeping it from Aunt Abby. But it still seems worse to just come out and tell her that the AllFather has Lauren without being able to offer her some kind of hope." She looked at Liv. "Do you think if we can somehow prove she *is* aboard the Fathership the Council will approve an attack or some kind of rescue attempt?"

"I don't know." Liv sighed. "That would mean full scale war which would probably have some serious fallout effects on the Earth. It's one of those "the lives of the many are worth more than the lives of the one or few" kind of things."

"But Lauren is blood! She's our cousin." Sophie's eyes filled with tears. "Oh, poor girl. I wish I knew where she was right now."

"Me too." Liv gave her sister a comforting hug. "Me too, Sophie."

Chapter Twenty-five

"The girl will have to be moved. Ssshe will come with usss to the home world."

"The home world?" Xairn frowned at his father, who was seated on the black metal throne etched in glowing green runes. He was surrounded, as always, by four enormous vat grown soldiers he'd had specially made for his own private guard.

"Yesss." The AllFather nodded, his shadowy hood billowing with the movement to reveal burning red eyes. They did not glow quite so brightly as they had in the past—since he had lost his primary source of sustenance, Xairn's father seemed to move more slowly and speak with a little less vehemence.

He is weakening before my eyes. Xairn supposed he ought to feel pity for the male who was his father but since he, Xairn, had been the AllFather's main source of nourishment, he couldn't find it in him to care. In fact, he cared about nothing lately—which was the reason the AllFather could no longer feed on his negative emotions. He had none.

"We mussst go back," the AllFather hissed. "There are facilities there to augment my power."

"You need more power?" Xairn kept his voice neutral.

"Imbecile! You know that I do!" the AllFather raged in a weak voice. "Now that your pain no longer nourishesss me, I have only the vat grown to feed on. And their emotionsss are vague ssshadows—not nearly enough to sssustain me."

"What of the humans you took just yesterday with the beam?"

The Allfather made an irritated gesture. "Too weak. They are already sssucked dry."

"I'm sorry you can no longer harvest my pain, Father," Xairn said blandly. "Perhaps you should have taken more care not to destroy your primary source of sustenance." When he had been forced by his father to kill his beloved pet, Sanja, Xairn's emotions had died with her. He was empty inside thanks to the AllFather's cruelty. Not that he cared.

"Never mind. Sssoon I ssshall have no need of your pain." The sunken eyes glowed a dull red. "My peak approachesss—the time when my ssseed will be most potent. I ssshall have more than enough pain to sssustain me when I breed the girl."

Xairn felt a flicker of uneasiness which he quickly extinguished. The human female was nothing to him—was she? *Of course she's not,* he told himself firmly. "When will you reach your peak?" he asked.

"Tomorrow—I feel it building." The AllFather rubbed his skeletal hands together in anticipation. "Which isss why we must prepare to fold ssspace at once."

"The Kindred instruments will pick up our movements," Xairn objected.

"They would—if we were fool enough to fold in this sssector," The AllFather said. "We will be taking the adjunct ssship sssome distance away and using a thinner fold. If they detect usss at all, they will think it a sssimple anomaly."

"Very well." Xairn bowed. "When do you wish to leave, Father?"

"At once, asss I sssaid. Have the girl moved and the adjunct ssship primed for take-off within the hour."

Xairn felt a dark impulse stir within his soul but he quickly repressed it. "And are we to be the only passengers? You and the girl and myself?"

The red-on-black eyes flashed bright crimson for a moment. "Do you think me a fool? My guardsss will come asss well." Reaching out, the AllFather patted the massive forearm of the nearest vat-grown solider. Though Xairn well knew how repulsive his father's touch was, the huge male didn't even flinch.

"But the home world is deserted," Xairn pointed out. "What need will you have of them?"

"I may find a use for them." Grasping the soldier's arm more firmly, the AllFather pulled himself to his feet. "They will ssserve me well, won't you, Alpha?" he crooned in his high, evil voice.

"Yes, AllFather." The vat grown male looked straight ahead, never blinking.

"You sssee?" The AllFather nodded.

Xairn shrugged. "As you wish. I will get the girl."

"Sssee that you do. And let her know what isss in ssstore for her. Tell her how I ssshall ssspread her legs and breed her." The red eyes gleamed hungrily. "Her terror when I take her will be all the sssweeter for the anticipation."

For some reason Xairn's large hands curled into fists. *She's mine! I'll never let you* – He frowned and pushed the thought away. Where had such a foolish, possessive impulse come from? What the AllFather wanted, he got — it had always been so. And if he wanted to breed Lauren to fulfill the prophesy, then he would have her. It was as simple as that.

Yet, for some reason Xairn's chest felt tight when he imagined the Earth female's delicate form pinned beneath the AllFather's shadowy black robes as he ravaged her. *Stop being so stupid,* he told himself. *You feel nothing.* But still...

"Xairn?"

He looked up to see the AllFather eyeing him hungrily. "Yes?" He kept his voice carefully neutral.

For a long moment those hateful red-on-black eyes, so like his own, seemed to pierce right through him. Then the AllFather shook his head. "Nothing. For a moment I thought I felt...but I sssuppose I was wrong."

"Yes, Father." Xairn bowed again and turned to leave. But he couldn't help throwing a glance over his shoulder as he descended the broad, black steps that led to the throne.

The AllFather seemed shrunken and depleted, leaning for support on the arm of his Alpha guard. But Xairn could still read the malice in his eyes, could still feel the hunger and dread emanating from him like a poisonous miasma. His father might be weak, but

he was still strong enough to do what he wanted—to take Lauren.

And though Xairn knew he shouldn't care, he couldn't stop his jaw from clenching or his hands from curling into fists again. *Mine,* whispered a voice in his head. *She should be mine...*

* * * * *

Lauren looked up in surprise when her cell door clanged open. Xairn had just been to see her a few hours before, to bring her morning ration of cardboard pop tarts, as she thought of the nutra-wafers. He shouldn't be back again until supper time, which was when they usually got to talk. Or rather, *she* talked. Xairn mostly listened.

His face was expressionless as he looked down at her, but somehow she knew something wasn't right.

"What is it?" she asked, clutching his heavy black cape tightly around her shoulders. "What's wrong?"

"Get up." His deep voice was charged with tension.

Lauren scrambled to her feet. She gasped as he clamped one huge hand around her upper arm in a grip tight enough to hurt. "What's happening? Where are we going?"

"To the home world."

"What? Why?" she asked desperately as he dragged her out of the cell and down a long metal corridor.

"Why do you think?" He threw her a glance, his red-on-black eyes burning.

"I...I don't know," Lauren faltered.

"Yes, you do." He dragged her along so fast she had to run to keep up with his long strides. The interior of the ship went by in a dull-gray blur around her but she had eyes only for his face. His expression remained impassive but his eyes blazed.

"Please, Xairn," she begged. "You're hurting me."

"Not as much as you're going to be hurt." He glanced at her briefly as they rounded a curve and went through a low archway. "Here we are."

"Where is here?" Lauren looked around uncertainly. They were in a vast room filled with ships of all sizes and shapes. Most of them were long and narrow and sleek, their outer skins an oily, inky black that was hard to look at for some reason. Xairn chose a larger ship and herded her toward it.

"The docking bay. We're taking the adjunct ship to the home world."

"Do you mean your home planet—the place you came from?" she asked as he dragged her through the echoing space to the chosen ship. The metal floor was freezing under her bare feet.

"It was never my home. But it is the place my people originated, yes." He placed his large hand against the inky black side of the ship. Lauren watched in amazement and fear as his fingers seemed to sink right into the strange black metal—as though he'd put his hand into a puddle of oil. The ship shivered and *oozed* open—there was no other word for the way the gaping hole suddenly appeared in its side.

"But...why are we going there?" she asked as he half pushed/half boosted her into the strange ship. *Why are you taking me so far away from Earth? From my mom and everyone I love?* She didn't dare to say it aloud but the fear that she would never return rose in her throat, almost choking her.

"The AllFather needs to draw power from his place of origin." Xairn's voice was tight as he pushed her to the back of the ship where Lauren could see a holding cell. It looked much like the one she'd been kept in on the Fathership except it was smaller—*much* smaller.

"Please!" She turned to face Xairn when he would have pushed her into the cell. "Please, *wait.*"

"We don't have much time. The AllFather will be here soon and he will expect the ship to be primed and ready."

"Just tell me one thing," Lauren said, trying to control her panic and keep her voice level and calm. "Why does he want me?"

"He wants to breed you. You are the fulfillment of a prophesy—the female we have been searching for." He looked down at her, his eyes blazing. "Only you can replenish our race. Only you can bear daughters born of the AllFather's seed."

Lauren had been afraid something like this was to be her eventual fate but she hadn't allowed herself to think about it. Now, faced with the truth, she knew she could do one of two things — panic and give up hope, or save herself the only way she could.

"Why does it have to be him?" she asked in a low voice.

Xairn frowned. "What do you mean? What are you asking?"

"I said, why does it have to be him who, you know, *does it?*" Taking a deep breath, she took a step toward Xairn. His broad chest was at the level of her face and she had to look up to see him looming over her. But she didn't flinch, not even when his red-on-black eyes bored into hers.

"I don't understand you." He shook his head.

"Why can't it be you?" Slowly, gently, Lauren raised her hand and cupped his cheek. His skin was warm and slightly scratchy under her palm though she had never noticed any beard shadow on his face. Up close she could smell his scent — the same warm, exotic spice that permeated the cloak he had given her.

"Me?" His deep voice was hoarse.

"Yes, *you,*" Lauren said patiently. She hoped desperately that she wasn't overplaying her hand but this was all she had and she would rather die than submit to the hideous AllFather. "You're his son. You have the same blood — the same DNA. Why can't it be you who…who breeds me?" The word stuck in her throat but she forced it out anyway.

Xairn jerked back from her light touch as though he'd been burned. "Are you asking me to rape you?"

Lauren swallowed hard and let her hand drop to her side. "It doesn't have to be rape," she said in a low, steady voice. "Not if you're gentle. You can be gentle, can't you, Xairn?"

For a moment his face twisted and then he shook his head. "I have no gentleness in me. Only cruelty and brutality."

"You've never been cruel to me," Lauren protested. "Please, Xairn. If…if someone has to do *that*, I want it to be you. Not him. Never him." The tears were filling her eyes but she blinked them back, not allowing herself to cry. *Have to stay calm. In control.*

"Even if I wanted to breed you, I couldn't." His deep voice was cold but his eyes blazed. "Those desires are buried in me—never to emerge."

"You're saying you can't do it because you don't want me? You don't find me attractive?" she asked.

"I…" Xairn frowned. "Certainly you're very beautiful. But beauty means nothing to me. My sexual urges are dormant and shall remain so."

"Oh?" Lauren had no idea if she was doing the right thing or not. She only knew she was desperate. Taking a deep breath, she unfastened the neck of the long black cloak and let it drop. It pooled at her feet in a heap of fabric. She felt horribly naked and vulnerable without it, but she refused to cover herself.

"What are you doing?" Xairn's voice was a harsh whisper now.

"Look at me," she murmured, holding her hands out to her sides. She was no Victoria's Secret model but she had curves in all the right places and she knew it. Her bare breasts were high and full and firm and her berry-brown nipples were tight in the cool air. The neatly trimmed thatch of black curls between her thighs was soft and inviting.

"Why should I?" he demanded but his eyes burned over her body, devouring her hungrily, making her feel even more naked.

"I want you to see me," Lauren said clearly. "Not just as a sex object or a female animal with the right bloodlines. See *me* – see *Lauren*. The girl you've been talking to for so long."

"I see you." His eyes stopped roving over her body and he looked into her eyes. "But I still don't understand."

"I'm asking you to help me," Lauren said softly. "And I think you will."

"What would lead you to believe that?" He sounded uneasy.

Lauren took a step closer until she could feel the heat of his large body against her bare skin. "Because you clothed me when I was cold and fed me when I was hungry. Because you comforted me when I was sad. You care, Xairn – I *know* you do. So please, *help me*."

"I cannot. I must not." But he didn't move away from her this time.

"You *can*," Lauren assured him. Taking his hand, she placed it carefully between her bare breasts, pressing his palm to the smooth skin of her chest. "Feel my heart. Look into my eyes. You can have me if you want – I won't fight you. Just don't...don't let *him* have me. Please."

Xairn looked down at his large hand between her breasts and then back up into her eyes. "I – "

The sound of boots echoing outside cut him off.

Lauren looked toward the door in the side of the ship with alarm. "Who – ?"

"Quickly!" Stooping, Xairn retrieved the cloak, wrapped it around her, and pushed her into the small holding cell almost in one motion. "Be silent," he warned in a low voice. "Don't bring attention to yourself."

"But will you help me?" she whispered, looking up at him, pleading with her eyes. "Please, Xairn!"

"We'll speak of it later." He slammed the door in her face and she heard the locking mechanism being punched in.

There was nothing in the small cell but a tiny triangular bench affixed to one corner and a harsh, overhead light. Trying not to cry, Lauren wrapped his cloak tighter around herself and huddled on the bench. Did Xairn care for her enough to save her from his hideous father?

She was afraid she wouldn't find out until it was too late.

Chapter Twenty-six

"This is stupid," Kat mumbled to herself. "Not...not gonna kill myself for pride." Through a haze of pain, she fumbled for the button on her holo-link, which was sitting on the nightstand next to her bed. She wished she could use a Think-me, like Liv and Sophie did but as an unmated female, she wasn't permitted to use the Kindred version of a telepathic cell phone. It wasn't a sexist rule—more of a practical one. Without a Kindred mind bonded to and shielding her own, she might transmit her thoughts anywhere—including to the listening ears of the Scourge. *Not that the AllFather wants to hear about my splitting headache,* she thought wearily. *He's probably too busy cooking up his next nasty plot to care about one stupid Earth girl who accidentally got herself soul-bonded to the wrong guys by mistake.*

She hated like hell to call Lock and Deep, but she could tell the pain wasn't going away any time soon without them. Already it was almost as bad as it had gotten back in the cave on Twin Moons. And how was she ever going to get through the psychic divorce if she was completely incapacitated?

Maybe I'll just call Lock. No, it'll hurt him to touch me without Deep. But damn it, she *really* didn't want to have anything else to do with Deep right now. Especially after their last encounter. Her finger was hovering indecisively above the send button when she heard someone pounding on the front door of her suite.

"Coming," she groaned, dragging herself off the bed. "I'm coming, just hang on." She slapped the switch and the door slid open with a soft *whoosh* to reveal a very worried looking Lock.

"My lady?" He came inside just in time to catch her as her legs collapsed. "Kat!" He looked at her anxiously. "Are you all right? I could feel your pain and distress—it worried me."

Kat smiled at him weakly. "Just the same old thing. You'd think I'd be used to it by now." She sighed. "Where's Deep?"

Lock's handsome features tightened. "I don't know and I don't care to know."

"What? So you two really are fighting?" she asked as he carried her back to the bedroom and laid her gently on the bed.

"It goes beyond that." Lock stripped off his shirt and climbed into the bed beside her.

Kat sighed in relief when she felt his warm hand on her arm. She didn't even protest when he pulled her blouse gently over her head, leaving her bare from the top up except for her bra. "We should call him, even if you are fighting," she said as Lock pulled her close, pressing his broad chest to her back. "Don't want to hurt you."

"The pain is nothing," Lock assured her gently. "It's more than worth it to be near you, my lady. Especially when..." His voice faltered for a moment. "When I'm going to lose you so soon."

"Oh, Lock..." Kat could feel his sorrow welling up, a sense of loss so great it nearly smothered her with its intensity. Still, she didn't draw back or try to get away. Instead, she turned in his arms so she was facing him and drew him into a tight embrace. "I'm sorry," she whispered into his shoulder. "So sorry."

"So am I." It sounded like Lock might be crying. His large form shook against hers and Kat held him tighter, wishing she could comfort him better. "I love you, Kat," he whispered brokenly. "And the idea of being torn apart from you tomorrow—of losing what little bond we have between us—it feels like death to me. Like the end of everything."

"I love you too," Kat admitted. "And...I feel like I *could* love Deep. If only he would let me. If only he wanted me to."

Lock stiffened in her arms. "He won't. He doesn't. There's no point in even considering it. No hope." A low growl rose in his throat. "Gods, I wish I wasn't tied to him."

"Don't say that," Kat said softly. "You're brothers—twins. You ought to be close."

"How can I want to be close to him when he's killing the only relationship that ever mattered to me?" Lock demanded. "What he's doing to you—to *us*...I cannot forgive it."

"Of course you can't." The new voice startled them both.

Kat jerked her head up to see Deep lounging in the bedroom doorway, one broad shoulder pressed against the door jam. There was a mocking look on his dark face but his eyes were fierce. "Well, well," he murmured. "You two look so *cozy*. I'd join you but I don't think that bed is big enough for three."

Lock sat up, shielding Kat protectively with his arm. "What are you doing here?" he snarled.

"The same thing you are, dear brother. Little Kat's pain called to me—dragged me like a magnet all the way across the ship from the Unmated Males section."

Lock's brown eyes flashed. "What were you doing there? You're not unmated!"

Deep raised an eyebrow. "I practically am. Anyway, why should you care?"

Kat looked back and forth between them uneasily. She wasn't sure exactly what went on in the Unmated Males area—but she thought there must be some kind of sexual element to it. She'd never heard of prostitutes aboard the Mother ship but vague whispers and rumors seemed to indicate that there was *some* form of release available to the unmated warriors. Which made sense when you considered the uncharted amount of testosterone in the average alpha male Kindred.

"I care because it's disrespectful to the lady Kat," Lock growled. "But why should I expect anything different? You disrespect everything and everyone. You don't care about anyone but yourself."

Deep threw up his hands. "That's me—I'm just a self-centered bastard, pissing on everything you hold dear. Ruining your life."

"Yes, you are!" Lock's hands were curled into fists and his normally mild expression had turned to one of hatred. He started to get off the bed but Kat stopped him with a hand on his arm.

"Don't," she whispered, shaking her head. "Please, don't."

"Let him." Deep gestured to the half-healed bruises on his face. "If the only way he can express his emotions is through his fists. Why not?"

"Because." Kat hated how weak she sounded, how her voice trembled. She wanted to say something cutting or witty. Wanted to defuse the tension somehow, the same way she had sometimes when she was a little girl and her parents fought. *If you can make them laugh or make them hate you instead of each other, they'll stop fighting,* whispered a little voice in her head. *And maybe they won't hit each other anymore...* But nothing came to mind. "Please," she repeated softly. "Please, just don't."

"I won't, my lady, forgive me." Lock gathered her protectively into his arms. "I'm sorry we upset you," he murmured into her hair.

Kat closed her eyes, feeling bombarded by their emotions. Lock was feeling *sorrow/worry/protectiveness* and Deep was filled with *despair/rage/hatred.*

*No, not just hatred...**self-hatred.*** Kat opened her eyes to see the dark twin smirking at her, an insolent expression on his handsome features. But underneath that look of indifferent scorn, she thought she saw a flash of something else. A sorrow so deep it was nearly unbearable. A desolation so dark it made her heart knot like a fist in her chest.

"Guess I'll leave and let you two finish comforting each other," he said.

"Wait!" The skin to skin contact she'd had with Lock gave Kat the strength to jump out of bed and run after Deep as he was turning for the door. "Wait," she demanded again, putting a hand on his arm.

"What is it now?" Deep growled, turning to face her.

Now that she was facing him, Kat didn't know what to say. She wanted to shake him, to demand he stop acting this way and admit his true feelings. But part of her was still shaken by the fight—or almost fight that had just occurred. Part of her was still the scared little girl, huddling in the corner, listening to hatred and insults fill the air and praying that the people she loved wouldn't hit each other this time.

"Well?" Deep demanded and she realized she'd been standing there silent for too long.

"Don't be this way." She looked at him pleadingly. "Please, Deep. I...I know you care about me. And I know you love Lock—he's your brother. Please don't act like you don't."

He raised an eyebrow at her mockingly. "You think I care? How very touching. And, unfortunately, how very wrong."

"You *do* care," Kat insisted. "Why else would you take my pain? The scars on your back prove it."

"They prove nothing, other than my honor as a warrior," he snapped. "I couldn't let a female whose safety I'd been charged with die. That is the *only* reason I did what I did. Nothing more."

Kat felt herself freezing inside. Despite her outward self-confidence, she'd suffered a lot of rejection in her life. It was hard—incredibly hard—to stand there, insisting that a huge, gorgeous, muscular man who would have been dating a supermodel if he was human and lived on Earth—loved her. Especially when he was saying in no uncertain terms that he *didn't.*

Still, she tried one more time.

"I know something bad happened to you in the past," she said quietly, meeting his eyes.

"Oh you do, do you?" Deep's black eyes blazed. He looked up at Lock. "Thank you, Brother, for revealing my most private and painful shame."

"I said nothing," Lock growled.

"I'm just saying that I know about it, not that I know any details or that I judge you for it," Kat said hastily. "I was thinking that whatever it is, maybe it had something to do with the way you're acting now."

Deep shook his head. "What happened is in the past—over and forgotten. It has nothing to do with what I feel for *you*, little Kat."

Kat lifted her chin, her heart pounding. "And what *do* you feel for me?"

Deep leaned down until they were almost close enough to kiss. Looking into her eyes, he murmured, "Nothing. I feel *nothing* for you."

Kat sucked in a breath. It felt like someone had punched her in the gut and she couldn't get enough air. "Oh," she whispered.

Deep nodded and straightened up to his full height. "Are you satisfied now, sweetheart? Can I go?"

"You can go, all right." Tears of pain and rage filled Kat's eyes but she blinked them back fiercely. "Go straight to Hell!"

Deep winked at her. "I prefer the Unmated Males section. There are so many more...*distractions* there."

"I don't care where you go—as long as you're back in time for our trip tomorrow." Kat kept her voice steady though she wanted to sob. "So we can go get this damn bond cut once and for all."

Deep grinned insolently. "I wouldn't miss it." He sauntered out of the bedroom and through the suite.

Kat held herself in until she heard the front door *whoosh* shut behind him. Then the tears came—tears of shame and pain and embarrassment. Tears of rejection that stung worse than all the others put together. *He really doesn't care. Doesn't want me.* Putting a hand over her mouth, she sobbed.

Lock was there suddenly, enfolding her in his arms and raining soft, consoling kisses on her hair. "Oh my lady," he whispered brokenly. "I'm so sorry. So very sorry."

"I shouldn't let him get to me." Kat blotted her eyes against the back of her hand. "But I feel so stupid. Liv kept saying tonight that maybe he was just afraid to love me or that he felt unworthy." She shook her head. "I'm the unworthy one."

"No, you're not!" Lock took her face in his hands and looked at her earnestly. "You're beautiful and intelligent and *perfect*. If only I could be free of him, I would bond you to me as quickly as I could. If you'd have me, that is."

Kat sniffed and straightened up. "Thank you, Lock. I wish I could," she whispered. "But I can't be with a man who doesn't want me and there's no way to separate the two of you. I'm sorry."

A look of sorrow passed over Lock's face. "Will you let me hold you tonight, at least?" he asked softly. "Since tonight is the last night I'll ever be able to do so?"

Kat knew by now that he didn't care about the pain the physical contact would cause him. "Yes." Turning her head, she kissed his broad palm. "Yes, I'd like that very much."

"Thank you, my lady." Lock swung her up into his arms and carried her back to bed.

Kat laid her head on his shoulder and closed her eyes, trying to forget the hurt and humiliation she'd endured. But in her mind's eye, she just kept seeing Deep's mocking grin and hearing him say over and over, *"Nothing. I feel nothing for you."*

She wished she could say the same about him.

Chapter Twenty-seven

Deep didn't go to the Unmated Males area. In fact, he barely made it back to the suite he shared with Lock. Just inside the front door, he collapsed, sliding down the wall to sit with his knees drawn up to his chest.

She hates me now. Utterly and without a doubt. Hates me. Well good — that was what he'd wanted. Wasn't it?

Self loathing rolled through him in waves like nausea until he knew he was going to be sick. Heaving himself to his feet, he just made it to the bathroom in time to void the contents of his stomach.

When he was empty, he splashed water from the sink in his face and rubbed his cheeks and mouth vigorously with a towel. Looking up into the viewer, he saw emptiness — a male with nothing left to lose. Nothing left because he'd just thrown away the most precious thing in his life. Thrown it away like a piece of garbage to lie rotting and festering in a dump.

"I killed it," he said aloud, addressing the hated face in the mirror. "Anything she felt for me is dead now."

But that was good — that was how it had to be. Closing his eyes, he remembered again the moment of total panic he'd experienced when she fainted during their love-making. *I would have hurt her. Would have been the death of her — the same way I was with Miranda. She's better off without me. Better off with Lock.*

Yes — that was the truth of it. The real heart of the matter. Deep knew he didn't deserve to love and be loved in return by such a beautiful, intelligent elite female. But Lock did. And Lock would take care of her, he would shelter Kat and protect her from the fiercest danger. *He* was the one she needed to be with. But how?

I know a way. Deep thought of the schematics for the Scourge torture device called the psychic knife. He'd been studying them before he was called away by Kat's pain. When he'd first suggested using it, Deep had fully intended to simply sever himself and Lock from Kat once and for all. But after reading over the specs, a different plan was emerging in his head.

Forgive me, little Kat, he thought, wiping his face one last time and going in to the bedroom to study some more. *Forgive me for hurting you but you'll see – it will be for the best in the long run. I promise it will.*

* * * * *

Kat was dreaming. At least, she *thought* she was—she seemed to be floating disembodied in an empty room. *Where am I?* she thought, looking around. The room seemed familiar—the large leather sofa built for three, the small, cozy fireplace, the pictures on the wall of a world with golden oceans… *Deep and Lock's suite,* she thought. *But what am I doing here?*

Her question seemed to be answered when Deep walked in and settled himself at the desk in one corner of the room. Opening a drawer, he pulled out a long, thin tube and unrolled it to form a personal memory pad. Kat watched with interest as the liquid crystals within the pad's black surface came to life and began to form shapes. What was he doing? The dark twin didn't strike her as the introspective type—the idea that he might keep a memory journal surprised her greatly. But then, a lot of things about Deep surprised her. And not all of the surprises were pleasant.

Deep looked over his shoulder for a moment, almost as though he could sense that someone was watching him. Then, having satisfied himself that he was alone in the room, he leaned closer to the pad. "Enable memory five-two-six. Replay nonstop. Allow no interruptions," he murmured.

There was a soft clicking and then the display screen enlarged substantially as the crystals expanded. By the time the memory began, it was large enough that Kat could have seen it from across the room.

The memory looked like a scene shot with an old fashioned handheld camera. It was clearly from Deep's point of view and seen though his eyes because Lock was walking right beside him and they were talking in low voices. They appeared to be moving down a clean white sidewalk along a row of well cared for houses.

The neighborhood could have been in any town in America, as far as Kat could see. The houses looked to be upper middle class—prosperous without being gaudy. There were luxury cars and minivans in the driveways and the lawns were green and well tended. All the houses were quiet and peaceful...except for the one at the end of the block.

It was a white two story house with green gingerbread trim and a green door to match. But the white gravel driveway was crowded with emergency vehicles, their lights flashing. People in official looking uniforms were swarming over the neatly mown lawn.

"Is that the place?" Lock asked, pointing to the house. "You always see it so much clearer than me in the dreams."

"That's her house." The point of view moved up and down, as though Deep was nodding.

"What's going on?" Lock asked.

"I don't know. But it doesn't look good." Deep sounded grim.

"Maybe we should go back to the HKR building. Come again later. Or send the draft officers for her instead."

"We agreed to come for her ourselves. Those damn draft officers only scare the human females when they drag them out of their homes. And she's already scared enough of me as it is." Deep sounded unhappy.

"Still, it's official procedure." Lock sighed. "Don't worry about the dreams, Deep. She just needs to get to know you. We'll take things slowly during the Claiming period. Very slowly."

"Agreed. If there *is* a Claiming period."

"What do you mean by that?" Lock demanded as they went through the gate of the white picket fence surrounding the house with the gingerbread trim.

"I'm sorry, sir, but this is an official crime scene," a voice said, before Deep could answer. The point of view looked down and Kat saw a human police officer standing there with his thumbs hooked in his belt, frowning and blocking the walkway.

"We're Kindred," Deep said smoothly. "Here on official business."

The cop got a mulish look on his face. "Well, I'm afraid your *business* will have to wait. Crime scene takes precedence."

"Give it up, Murphy." Another policeman, this one a middle aged woman with her black hair scraped back into a ponytail, came to stand beside him. "It's not really a crime scene when she meant to off herself."

"That's not our call to make. The Coroner'll decide if it was suicide or not," the first policeman said stubbornly.

"Suicide?" Lock sounded worried. "What are you talking about? Who—?"

"There they are! Let them through, officers. Let them through—those are the murderers." A young woman with scraggly, brownish-blonde hair came running out onto the front porch. She was pointing to Lock and Deep and sobbing hysterically.

"Murderers, eh?" The first policeman, Murphy, looked at them with considerably more interest. "You gentlemen care to explain that?"

"Officer, I assure you that my brother and I have never even been on this planet until this morning and we—" Lock began but Deep was already pushing past the officers and rushing to the front porch.

"Where is she?" Kat saw his large hands grip the hysterical girl and give her a firm shake. "Where's Miranda?" he demanded.

"You want to see her?" the girl shouted through her sobs. "You want to see what you did to her, you son-of-a-bitch?"

"Yes, I want to see her, damn it!" Deep's voice was fierce now. Fierce and fearful—Kat could hear the dread throbbing in his tone. The knowledge of what he might find if he followed the crying girl into the house. But he went with her anyway, climbing a staircase and going down a hallway to the bedroom at the end.

Kat could hear soft sounds of grief coming from behind one door and there were two paramedics just leaving the far bedroom as they entered it. "Hey, I thought the police didn't want anyone going in there," one protested as Deep and the girl brushed past them.

"Official business," Deep said, but his voice sounded hollow and strained.

At the door to the bedroom, the girl turned to face him, her face pale and blotchy with tears. "So you finally came for her. She said you would. It was all she talked about for the past month." Her voice went high and scared as though she was imitating someone.

"'The dark one—I don't know his name but he won't leave me alone. Every time I close my eyes I see him...coming for me, reaching out to touch me.'"

"Enough. Let me see her," Deep sounded quiet but dangerous. "She's supposed to be our bride—I have a right to see her."

"She was *never* going to go with you," the girl spat. "She made sure of that. You want to see? Fine, have a look!"

She flung open the door, revealing a room that was decorated in cream and pink and butter yellow. A cheerful room with a canopy bed against one wall and set of French doors leading out onto a balcony covered with climbing ivy.

It was cheerful, that was, until you noticed what was lying on the bed. Kat didn't want to see it but somehow she couldn't look away as Deep approached.

At first it looked like a doll. A life sized doll with hair the same brownish-blonde as the crying girl's. But it was clear when you got closer that the doll was broken—its large, china blue eyes were wide and staring at the canopy overhead, its mouth frozen half open, as though it wanted to speak.

Oh my God, Kat thought numbly. *It's not a doll—it's a girl. And she's dead. She's really dead.*

"Gods!" There was a sudden, dizzying shift in the point of view and Kat realized that Deep had fallen to his knees. "Miranda!" he whispered hoarsely.

"I found her like this when I came to get her for breakfast." The crying girl, who had to be Miranda's sister, sounded numb. "She took my mom's pills—all of them. And she left this." She thrust a crumpled piece of notebook paper into Deep's hands. "Read it," she demanded.

Deep bowed his head and the words on the paper came into focus.

They're coming for me and the dark one won't leave until he gets me. I see them every night getting closer and closer. I just want him to leave me alone. I just want the dreams to stop. I'm sorry. I'm sorry...

There might have been more but Kat couldn't read it. The point of view was suddenly blurry. When she heard Deep speak again, she understood why.

"She wrote this?" he asked, his voice shaking. "Before she..."

"Killed herself. Yes," the girl said flatly. "She was so afraid of what you were going to do to her. So afraid she would rather be *dead* than let you get her." She ran both hands through her hair distractedly. "Miranda had her whole life ahead of her. She was in college—she was going to be a vet because she loved animals. Did you know that? Did you know anything about her except that you wanted her?"

"This was never our intention," Deep protested. "We'd been dream sharing for weeks. I knew she was frightened of us...of *me*. But I never thought—"

"That she'd go this far? I didn't either." Her voice began to rise in pitch. "I knew something wasn't right last night. I never should have left her. Never should have—"

"None of this is your fault." Deep stood slowly, never looking away from the dead girl on the bed. "None of it. I bear this blame alone."

"End memory," a soft, mechanical voice said. There was a clicking sound and the liquid crystal screen went black. Then the room was silent except for a low, hoarse sound Kat didn't recognize at first.

She looked away from the screen and saw that Deep had put his head down on the desk, his face buried in his arms. His broad shoulders were heaving. The hoarse, painful sound was coming from him.

He's sobbing, she realized. *My God, he's tearing himself apart.* Despite the way he'd treated her earlier, she had an overwhelming impulse to go to him, to put her arms around him and comfort him, to somehow ease the overwhelming agony she felt coming from him in waves.

But she couldn't touch him—she could only watch helplessly as his misery went on and on. At last the sobbing quieted and Deep raised his head. His face was calm but his eyes were red. "I'm sorry, Miranda," he said in a low voice. "So damn sorry." He sighed. "I cannot take back what happened to you. But I *can* keep it from happening to another. I can stop it before it's too late—before I ruin her life the way I ruined yours. I love her too much, I can't let that happen—I *won't* let it happen."

He's talking about me, Kat realized. *He* ***does*** *care! He thinks he'll hurt me if he stays with me, if he and Lock bond with me completely. That's why he's being such an asshole – he's trying to drive me away. But now that I know –*

* * * * *

"My lady? My lady Kat, I know it's early but we agreed that an early start was best." A gentle hand shook her shoulder.

Kat burrowed deeper into her pillow. *No, can't wake up yet. Have to remember. Have to know...it's so important. It's so –*

"My lady?" The hand shook her again and the last vestiges of the dream wisped away.

Kat sat up, rubbing her eyes. "Is it time to get up already?"

"I'm afraid so." Lock sounded apologetic. "We're supposed to be in the docking bay by o-six hundred."

"Okay, okay, I'm up." She frowned and rubbed sleep from her eyes. Something was bothering her—something important was tugging at the corner of her mind. *What was it?* she thought uneasily. *I told myself not to forget it but what —*

"Would you like the first turn in the bathing pool?" Lock asked courteously.

Kat sighed and gave up the hopeless quest. Whatever it was, it would come back to her if it was important enough. Right now she had to get ready to go. "Yeah, I'll go first," she said, nodding. "But I warn you, I have nothing to wear. Not that I can even begin to guess the correct dress code for exploring an abandoned alien planet and getting a double divorce."

Lock winced and she was sorry she'd been so snarky. "Wear whatever is comfortable and practical, my lady," he said in a low voice. "We're likely to be walking through some dark and dirty areas and the entire planet is polluted."

"Got it." Kat sighed. "Wading through polluted muck. So I guess my favorite pair of kitten heels is out."

Lock gave her a wan smile. "I wouldn't recommend them. Unless you want me to carry you the whole way. I wouldn't mind."

Kat straightened up and lifted her chin. "Thank you, Lock, but I think I've had enough of the damsel in distress routine for a little while." *I got myself into this mess, and I guess I can get myself out of it.* But she didn't speak the thought aloud—she couldn't bear to see the sorrow and loss on Lock's face again. Couldn't stand the thought that by this time tomorrow, she would no longer be bonded to him or to Deep.

*Deep...that was it. It was something about him. Something I was supposed to remember...*But though it seemed terribly important, the memory eluded her as she showered and dressed.

Kat sighed. *The only thing I need to remember about Deep is to steer clear of him until we get this damn soul-divorce. Then he can do whatever he wants and we can all go our separate ways — which is what I wanted in the beginning.*

She only wished it was what she wanted now.

Chapter Twenty-eight

"Land usss in the hidden passageway of the Command Complex," the AllFather directed as their ship approached the dark gray-green world that was the Scourge home planet.

"As you wish," Xairn said tightly. He was struggling to keep his emotions in check — at least until he could get away from his father. After Sanja's death, he had felt hollow inside — empty...emotionless. And he had assumed he would never feel anything ever again. But after his last exchange with Lauren, something was stirring within him — something dark and sinister. Something too frightening to face.

Then don't face it. Push it down. Ignore it!

Trying to follow his own advice, Xairn piloted the ship through the layers of atmosphere until they were just skimming over the surface of the black, oily sea. Once, so he'd been told, this immense ocean had been teeming with life — from tiny, delicate fire fish no bigger than a fingernail to the huge purple-green leviathans, larger than the Fathership. But they were all gone — extinct for hundreds of years. Nothing lived in the vast oily waste now but a few hearty strains of algae that had adapted to the chemicals and pollutants which had poisoned the rest of the marine life.

Finally the brown shore of the beach came into view and shortly after that, the old battlefield and the towering edifice of the Command Complex. Xairn knew the dirty gray towers soaring into the soot-smudged sky were mostly for show. The majority of the

Complex was located underground, in a sprawling warren of tunnels.

Xairn had been to the home world — called *Zlicth* in the Scourge tongue — only once before in his life. But he remembered the visit vividly and had no problem finding the hidden passageway around the back of the Complex. It was so well camouflaged that a person walking on the ground would have fallen into it before they saw it. Xairn guided the ship in smoothly and flew through the tunnel until he came to the back entrance of the large building.

"Very good." The AllFather nodded. "When we disssembark, lock the girl in a holding cell in the medical wing."

"What of you, father? What of your peak?" Xairn hoped his voice didn't come out sounding strained. He didn't want the AllFather to have any idea of the newfound emotions churning inside him.

"It isss not yet upon me. I must ssspend time in my *Sssouda*. A few hoursss or perhapsss a little longer and I ssshall be ready to breed her."

Xairn's hands clenched into fists but he only nodded his head. "As you wish. I will see to the girl but what of your guard?"

"They ssshall come with me." The AllFather nodded to the four massive soldiers who were crammed into the back of the ship. They had been crouching there, unmoving for hours in what looked like extremely uncomfortable positions, but none of them had complained. In fact, none of them said anything at all. They just sat there, staring straight ahead with dead black eyes.

Soulless, Xairn thought. *That's what Lauren thinks of them. Maybe they are. Maybe the vat grown are devoid of real consciousness. Or else they hide their emotions even better than I do.*

Of course, up until a few hours before, he hadn't had any emotions to hide. Now he was full of them—some old, hatred for his father, despair for his joyless life—but some new as well. When he remembered how Lauren had looked, naked and defiant as she offered herself to him, feelings stirred inside him which didn't bear thinking about.

If Father finds out I have feelings again, that he can feed on me... Have to get away from him. Get away and stay away as much as possible.

It was his only thought as he watched the AllFather descend from the ship, aided by his Alpha guard. He still seemed stiff and weak but the moment he stepped foot on the ground, he lifted his hooded face and took a deep breath of the dank, fetid air. "Home at lassst." The words hissed from his lipless mouth and he turned glowing red-on-black eyes to Xairn. "Sssee to the girl. Do not bother me unlesss I sssend for you."

"Yes, Father." Xairn nodded briefly and was relieved when the AllFather turned to go.

"Xairn."

He jerked as his father hissed his name. "Yes?"

"The control wand. Give it to me." One skeletal hand emerged from the shadowy depths of the AllFather's robe, palm up. "Just in case you get any ideasss."

Struggling to maintain a blank expression, Xairn did as he was told. Pulling the tiny silver control wand from the instrument panel, he dropped it into his father's hand. Without it the ship could not be started or steered—without it, he was stuck on this planet with no choice but to do his father's will. *Of course I'm going to do his will. What else would I do? Take Lauren and fly away with her?* Xairn shook his head. Just the fact that he'd even *had* such a thought proved that he was becoming more and more unstable.

The Allfather's burning crimson eyes narrowed. "Are you well, my ssson?"

"Perfectly, Father." Xairn stared straight ahead. "Hadn't you better get to your *Souda?*"

"I ssshall indeed. And I will keep thisss with me at all timesss." The silver control wand disappeared into the folds of the AllFather's shadowy robes. Then, surrounded by his four huge guards, he glided away.

Xairn gave them plenty of time to enter the Complex, watching as the massive plasti-steel doors rolled inward silently and then shut behind them. When he was sure they were gone, he sighed in relief. At least now that his father was out of the immediate vicinity, he could stop worrying about the AllFather sensing the new emotions churning in his gut.

Emotions he could neither defend nor deny—and all of them centered on Lauren.

Chapter Twenty-nine

Deep was suspiciously quiet during their flight to the Scourge home world. He barely spoke except to warn Kat to be sure she was buckled in safely when they went through the deep red fold in space. And since Lock was too sunk in misery to say anything and Kat wasn't feeling too chatty herself, their journey was mostly silent. She still had the nagging feeling that there was something she ought to know or remember and every time she glanced at Deep, it grew stronger. But whatever it was, it stayed in the back of her mind and refused to come forward.

At last Deep broke the silence as he piloted the ship into the smoggy atmosphere of the gray-green planet. "Here we are— *Zlicth.*"

"What?" Kat asked, as the oily black ocean whizzed by under their ship. "What's a zlickt?"

"*Zlicth,* is the name of this planet in the ancient tongue of the Scourge," Lock explained as the ship left the water behind and landed on a brown beach. "The same way you call your planet 'Earth.'"

Oh," Kat said as they all unsnapped their safety harnesses. "But if this is their home world, why did they abandon it?"

"Take a look outside and you'll see." Deep pressed a button and the door of the shuttle slid smoothly open.

Kat stepped out onto the metal steps descending from the small silver craft to survey the planet. Standing on the topmost step, she looked out across a beach of grimy brown and gray sand and put a hand to her nose. "Ugh, what's that smell?" It was like a combination of car exhaust, sulfur, and a cat box that badly needed to be changed.

"The sweet smell of *Zlicth*, of course," Deep said with a touch of his old sarcasm. He came to stand behind her. "The Scourge weren't terribly particular about the welfare of their planet, as long as there was a profit to be turned."

"They ruined their world for gain," Lock explained. "This planet contains vast quantities of *verinium* — which gives tremendous amounts of energy when burned."

"But also releases noxious fumes into the air and chemicals into the water," Deep said, nodding at the oily waves lapping at the brown sand. There was a thin grayish scum on the water that looked toxic.

"It's disgusting," Kat said, still holding a hand over her nose. "I mean—oh!" Her foot slipped and she started to fall from the steps. Only Deep's strong hand under her arm saved her. He pulled her back to her feet and gave her a quick shake.

"Try not to injure yourself while we're here—all right, sweetheart?"

Kat stiffened and lifted her chin. "What do you care what happens to me? You just want to be free of me, right?"

Deep's black eyes flashed. "Just because I don't want to be bonded to you doesn't mean I don't care if you—"

"If I kill myself?" Kat finished for him, without thinking. To her surprise, instead of snapping out a sarcastic retort, Deep turned pale.

"Don't say that." His voice was low and hoarse and for a moment, his eyes looked almost haunted.

"Why not?" Kat stared at him, again having that niggling feeling that there was something important she ought to remember.

But Deep only shook his head, and the moment passed. "This may be a deserted world but there are still plenty of dangerous things lying around — the Scourge weren't very careful where they left their toys."

"Deep is right," Lock said, unexpectedly agreeing with his brother. "This is a dangerous place. Which is why we should leave and go back to the Mother ship right now."

"Nice try, Brother," Deep drawled. "But I don't think so — we're going to do what we came here to do. Besides, don't you have another little job while we're here?"

Lock frowned. "Olivia *did* ask me to see if I could find any clues to her cousin's whereabouts. Although what we can find on a planet that's been abandoned for fifty cycles, I have no idea."

"The prophesy," Kat reminded him, walking carefully down the steps to the greasy sand below. "If we can find out the exact wording we might have a clue as to what they want her for and where they've taken her."

"Possibly," Deep agreed, his boots crunching on the sand. "Although I think we all know what they want her for."

Kat frowned at him. "What do you mean by that?"

Deep shrugged. "What does any Scourge want with a female?"

She shook her head. "I don't know but I take it they're not interested in romantic candlelight dinners and long walks on the beach. Especially not *this* beach." She made a face.

"They're depraved in every way," Lock said, stepping down to join them on the sand. "It's one of the reasons many of our forefathers wanted to block the genetic trade with them."

"Hold on." Kat put up a hand. "You're telling me the Kindred actually made a trade with them? With the *Scourge?*"

"Unfortunately, yes." Deep nodded. "A small faction of Kindred, anyway."

"It was only about a hundred and fifty cycles ago that we came across them," Lock explained as they began to walk up the beach. "We observed them first, of course. They had the physical characteristics and DNA to make a genetic exchange possible. But the majority of the Council was against the trade from the start."

"Why?" Kat asked, fascinated despite herself. Who could have guessed that the Kindred's greatest enemy had at one time been an ally?

"The things they had done to their world for one thing." Lock gestured at the dirty beach and oily black water. "To so pollute and ruin a planet showed a blatant disregard for the blessings the Mother of All Life had bestowed on them in the first place. But more importantly, the forefathers didn't like the way the Scourge treated their females."

Kat's breath seemed to catch in her throat. "How...how did they treat them?"

"They're sexual sadists." Deep's black eyebrows were pulled low, his face like a thundercloud. "They enjoy inflicting pain and they demand complete submission at all times."

Kat raised an eyebrow. "So the whole planet was into BDSM? Kinky."

"Not just 'kinky'—depraved," Lock corrected her sternly.

"Lock's right." Deep nodded. "I've seen vids about your sexual practices on Earth—I know a few of your people are into games of sexual control. But it's no game for the Scourge—it's a dominant gene, hardwired into the genetic makeup of every Scourge male. Dominance and submission isn't play to them—it's life or death."

"They can't take a female unless they're dominating her completely," Lock said quietly.

"And they practice and enjoy forms of sexual torture that would turn your stomach," Deep said darkly. "The Goddess help that girl if the Scourge really do have her. I don't like to think of the torment they must be putting her through."

"Poor Lauren!" Kat suddenly felt for Liv and Sophie's cousin as she never had before. Before she'd been sympathetic to her plight and worried about her, but now she felt Lauren's pain like a fist to the gut. Lock and Deep's words brought home what the kidnapped girl must be enduring in a visceral way that nothing else had. "I don't understand, though," she said. "If the Scourge are so horrible, why did the Kindred trade with them?"

"A small faction disagreed with the ruling of the Council," Lock explained. "The Scourge were the first new species suitable for a trade that we'd seen in hundreds of years. And they argued that the Kindred genes were dominant—a new generation of Scourge could be raised who had no wish to torment or inflict pain. Who loved and revered females, as we do."

"They pointed out that the savages from Rageron had been tamed and taught to worship the Goddess," Deep said. "But the Beast Kindred never had the genetic need to dominate that the Scourge do. It turned out to be impossible to breed that out of them."

"So what happened? How did you guys become mortal enemies?" Kat asked. "Was it because they wouldn't stop mistreating their women?"

"Their continued sexual practices led to a lot of friction, yes," Lock said. "But it wasn't until it became common knowledge that the Scourge were experimenting on and torturing abducted Kindred warriors and their brides that all-out war broke out between us."

Kat made a face. "But why would they do something so horrible?"

"They claimed that they were looking for the connection between the Kindred and their mates—the connection they themselves seemed to be lacking," Deep rumbled. "But nobody really believed that—what they were doing was all about revenge."

"Revenge?"

Lock nodded. "You see, from the genetic trade, the Scourge got the Kindred size and musculature and prowess in battle but they also inherited our greatest weakness."

"Our inability to breed females," Deep clarified. "With our people, only five percent of pregnancies result in female children. But in the Scourge, the trait was worse. Only one fifth of one percent of their pregnancies resulted in girls."

"They hated us for it—they still do," Lock said. "They blame us for the decimation of their race."

Deep made a sound of disgust in his throat. "They had something to do with it too—right here in fact. During the Battle of Berrni. You can see the results."

They were climbing a ridge that ran along the top of the greasy brown dunes as he spoke. What she saw when they made it to the top, took Kat's breath away.

There, on a vast field of barren gray dirt, lay the wreckage and remains of hundreds of space ships. Some of them looked a little like the shuttle they had come in and she assumed they must be of

Kindred design. Others were completely alien with strange, gleaming black skin that her eyes kept wanting to slide away from—apparently Scourge ships.

"This is the Field of Berrni—it was the final testing ground," Lock said quietly, gesturing to the wrecked and abandoned ships. "We had broken into their medical complex and rescued the prisoners they had taken and we were about to wipe them out completely. In desperation, the Scourge deployed a viral bomb designed specifically to cause spontaneous combustion in anyone with Kindred DNA."

Kat put a hand to her mouth. "Oh my God—so they burned them alive?"

Deep nodded. "Look in any of these abandoned ships and you'll see little piles of black ash—all that remains of the pilots."

"But the Scourge didn't count on one thing—they themselves had Kindred DNA," Lock said. "They thought that they had modified their virus enough so that it wouldn't affect them—but our dominant genes are incredibly strong. The survivors of the battle escaped aboard the Father ship but not wholly intact."

"It sterilized them," Deep explained. "All but a few who were completely shielded from the initial blast." He looked grim. "We think the AllFather was one of them."

"So he might be looking for a way to replenish his race?" Kat guessed. "Do you think that's what he wants Lauren for?"

"It's entirely possible," Lock said. "Though we won't know for sure unless we can find the exact wording of the prophesy."

Kat shook her head. "Oh, poor, *poor* girl. I really feel sorry for her now."

"We'll do what we can to help find her," Lock promised quietly. "We're not just here to dissolve the bond between us."

"Of course not," Deep agreed dryly. "We have *much* more noble ambitions in mind than simply separating our souls."

"If you say so." Kat gave him a look. "But are you sure it's safe for us to be here? Especially you two—I mean, with the spontaneous burn-you-to-death-if-you're-Kindred virus running around?"

"Why do you think we landed so far from the Complex?" Deep asked, nodding to the gray spikes and spires rising in the distance. The sprawling building was apparently where they were headed. "Lock and I are both wearing monitors that will detect any stray virus strains that might be harmful long before they become concentrated enough to hurt us."

"The virus has had years to dissipate so we don't expect any trouble," Lock explained. "But we're moving in slowly, just in case."

Kat sighed. "All right—as long as you two are safe."

"Why, Kat." Deep put a hand over his heart. "I didn't know you cared."

Kat refused to rise to the bait. "You know I do," she said quietly. "And just because *you* don't, doesn't mean I can turn it off just like that." She snapped her fingers to illustrate her point.

For a moment, Deep looked stricken. "Kat," he said, stopping in his tracks. "Kat, I..."

"What?" Kat stopped beside him and looked up at him, her heart pounding. Was he going to admit that he cared after all? From the corner of her eye she could see Lock's face filled with hope.

But Deep just shook his head. "I'm sorry," he said in a low voice. "Sorry it has to be like this. But it does."

"All right." Kat nodded stoically and began walking again. Let him do what he wanted—she wasn't going to beg. And she wasn't

going to remain bonded to a man who didn't want and love her—
not even halfway bonded. *It's for the best,* she told herself as they
trudged closer to the monstrous gray building that Deep had called
the Complex. *We all need to be free of each other — it's the only way.*

But her heart was sore and she found she couldn't look at Deep
as they walked. Not if she wanted to keep from crying.

Chapter Thirty

Lauren sat huddled on the tiny triangular seat, crammed into the claustrophobically small holding cell and tried not to cry. *It's going to be all right. Everything is going to be all right,* she told herself over and over. If she gave in to panic now, everything would be lost. She had to believe she was going to get out of this somehow. Even if her best chance of escape—Xairn—seemed to be completely conflicted about his feelings for her. *If he **has** feelings at all,* she thought. He certainly didn't seem to want to admit it if he did. Could she break down the wall he'd built between them and get him to see that she was important to him? That he needed her as much as she needed him? Lauren hoped so.

The ship had decelerated and landed smoothly and then she'd heard murmuring from the front of the cockpit. The deep, quiet voice she recognized as Xairn's. The other voice—high and hissing—made her skin crawl. It belonged to the AllFather—the one who wanted to—*No, don't think about it. If you think about it you'll lose it completely.*

Lauren put her fingers in her ears and hummed softly to herself to block out those hateful, hissing tones. The humming started tunelessly but turned into the lullaby her mother used to sing her when she was little. After a few minutes, she could almost hear the beloved voice murmuring the words in her ear... *Hush little baby, don't say a word. Momma's gonna buy you a mocking bird. And if that mocking bird won't sing, Momma's gonna buy you a diamond ring. And if—*

"Lauren?"

She looked up to see Xairn standing there with a terrible look on his face. She couldn't tell if he was angry or just upset but whatever he was feeling, it wasn't good.

"Xairn?" She stood up and took a tentative step toward him but her legs were weak from sitting in the cramped position so long. She stumbled and started to go down.

"Careful!" Xairn caught her and dragged her out into the main part of the ship before swinging her up into his arms. He held her easily, as though she was lighter than a feather.

"What's going on?" she asked softly, looking into his eyes. This was the closest she'd ever been to him—the most he had ever touched her.

Without answering, Xairn carried her out of the ship and into a long concrete tunnel which appeared to be a hidden landing strip. Despite the tense expression on his face, he handled her gently—as though she might break if he wasn't careful.

As they left the ship, panic gripped Lauren by the throat. "Where are you taking me?" she asked, struggling to keep her voice from wavering.

"To a holding cell." His red-on-black eyes flickered to hers quickly and then away.

"But why?" Lauren begged. "This is the perfect opportunity—we can leave in the ship together. Just the two of us."

"Do you think that scenario didn't cross my mind?" he demanded in a low voice. "Unfortunately, it crossed my father's mind as well. He has the control wand in his possession. I cannot start or steer the ship without it."

Despite the bad news that the AllFather had the key to the ship, Lauren felt encouraged. At least Xairn had admitted wanting to take her away — or at least admitted to thinking about it. That was a definite start. "What are we going to do, then?" she asked.

"I don't know. Stop talking — these hallways are monitored."

Lauren was obediently silent as he nudged a button which opened a huge set of double doors that looked like they were made of some kind of metal alloy. The doors swung open silently, revealing a long central corridor with many smaller hallways leading off from it on either side.

Xairn stepped inside and the doors swung shut behind them with a finality that had the panic clawing at her throat again. Lauren refused to give in to the fear. *Have to keep calm. Keep my head and trust that he wants me enough to keep me from his father. To keep him from...* She cut off that line of thought abruptly and rode silently in Xairn's arms as he walked down the long hallway, his boots echoing in the empty space.

Lauren supposed she could have walked by now — her legs felt fine. But she didn't want to. The echoing, empty corridor was creepy — like some kind of a ghost town — and most of the smaller hallways leading off from it were dark and filled with shadows. The air was musty and foul and the few light panels that were on overhead flickered as though they might decide to go out at any time. It was like Xairn was carrying her into a haunted house — one she desperately wanted to escape from. But the man bringing her into it was her only hope of getting out again alive, so she clung to him for dear life.

At last they came to a slightly larger hallway branching off from the main one at an oblique angle. It was blocked by a set of metal doors exactly like the ones that had led into the building in the first place, only smaller. Xairn stopped and nudged a black button which caused the doors to slide silently into the wall, revealing a dimly lit space filled with glass doors and strange equipment.

"What is this place?" Lauren breathed, forgetting she wasn't supposed to talk.

Xairn closed the door behind them before answering. "The medical wing. We can speak here. This wing is shielded from the rest of the Complex."

"The medical wing?" she asked.

Xairn nodded. Where my father and his chief medical officers used to perform... experiments."

"Experiments? What kind of experiments?" Lauren shivered as she looked around. There were several glassed in rooms — some were bare but one was set up like an operating theater. But the instruments that lay scattered on the floor and the exam table were strange and brutal. Saws with jagged teeth, long, thin picks with razor sharp points at their ends, something that looked like stainless steel barbed wire unwound in a lethal, shining line across the glassy red floor...

"What kind do you think?" Xairn said in a low voice.

Lauren felt sick. "*Torture* — my God, they tortured people here, didn't they?" The fear she'd been trying to hold back suddenly grabbed her by the throat and she couldn't breathe. "Oh please, Xairn. Please, no," she whispered in a low, trembling voice. Clinging to him desperately, she buried her face in his neck. "Please...please don't hurt me."

"You think I brought you here to torture you?" he demanded hoarsely. "To take pleasure in your pain?"

"I...I don't know." The tears were coming now, hot and fast and there was nothing she could do to stop them. "Please, Xairn, please..."

"I won't hurt you," he said roughly. "Lauren, look at me."

Reluctantly, she pulled her face away from his neck and looked up into those burning crimson eyes. "Yes?"

"I won't hurt you," he repeated. "And I won't let anyone else hurt you either."

"Not even your father?" she whispered.

"*Especially* not him. I won't let him have you." His eyes blazed and a muscle in his jaw clenched. "And I won't let him harm you."

"You...you won't?" A rush of relief came over her so strongly she felt faint.

"No." Xairn shook his head grimly. "I don't know how I am going to manage it, but I swear on my honor, I *will* take you away from this place unharmed and bring you back to your home planet. Do you understand?"

"Oh Xairn!" She almost laughed through her tears. "I...I could just kiss you!" Throwing her arms around his neck she leaned forward impulsively and pressed her lips to his. They were surprisingly soft but before she could register much more, Xairn jerked away from the sudden contact.

"Don't." His deep voice was harsh, strained. "Don't *ever* do that again, Lauren. Or I can't be responsible for the consequences. Do you understand?"

Not really? Why did a simple kiss upset him so much? But she only nodded contritely. "I'm sorry. I'm just so glad. So glad you care about me enough to help me."

"Let us be clear about one thing." He held her eyes with his. "You *have* aroused emotions in me—very strong emotions. But that is *not* a good thing."

Lauren stared at him uncertainly. "Do...do you mean that you hate me? Is that what you're saying?"

"Not hate, no." He shook his head. "What I feel for you...let's just say it will be better — far better — if those feelings are never explored or acted on."

"I don't really understand what you're trying to say," Lauren said softly. "But I do want to thank you for promising to help me."

"There's no point in expressing your gratitude yet — I haven't even worked out a plan." He sighed. "Until I do, I must pretend to comply with my father's will. And you're going to have to trust me. Can you do that?"

Biting her lip, Lauren nodded hesitantly. "Yes, I trust you."

"Thank you." He nodded gravely. "That means a great deal to me. And now I have to put you in one of these cells and secure the rest of the Complex before reporting back to my father."

"You're leaving me alone? In here?" She couldn't help glancing at the instruments of torture strewn around the surgery suite room again.

"Nothing will harm you," Xairn said, his rough voice almost soothing. "We are the only creatures alive on this planet. Well — other than a few minor life forms like the black crested lizards. But they live mainly on the beaches and won't come inside." He shook his head. "The point is, you'll be safe, even if I'm in another part of the building."

"But what if...if your father decides he wants to come, uh, see me?" Lauren asked, unable to keep the fear out of her voice. "If he touches me, Xairn, I swear I'll go crazy. I can't help it."

"He often has that effect on females," Xairn said grimly. "But you don't need to worry about him — not yet. He is ensconced in his *Souda* — it's a special room within the Complex which channels the power of the planet directly to his person. Once he enters it, a *dravik* forms."

Lauren frowned. "A what?"

"A *dravik* — a large bubble made of nourishing blood which forms around him. He can move about the Complex while ensconced within it, but until it bursts, he will be unable to touch you."

"But how long will that be?" Lauren protested. The idea of the hideous, skeletal AllFather encased in a bubble made of blood was horrific enough. But the idea of him coming for her after the bubble had burst and he was covered in the stuff — well, it didn't bear thinking about.

"At least a few hours — most likely more," Xairn said patiently. "But you don't need to fear — I will return for you long before that. I promise. I just have to lull my father into believing all is well and we'll make our escape."

"How? I thought your father had the only key to the ship we came in?"

"He does but there are abandoned ships not far from here — many of them — from the last battle that was fought here with the Kindred. We can take one of those — they should still be operational."

"All right." Lauren sighed and nodded. "I trust you to do right by me, Xairn. Just please hurry — this place gives me the creeps."

"It has been the site of untold horrors," he agreed, taking her into one of the empty, glassed in cells. "But they're over and done and in the past. You have nothing to fear now."

"I hope you're right." As he deposited her gently onto her feet, Lauren reached up impulsively and gave him a tight hug. "Come back soon," she whispered in his ear. "I'll be waiting for you."

"I will come as soon as I can." Xairn gently disengaged her arms from around his neck and when his face came into view, it wasn't at all happy. "But you must stop touching me that way, Lauren. It…is not a good thing."

"Because it makes you feel?" she asked softly.

Stiffly, Xairn nodded. "Yes. I must go now."

"All right." She stood with her back to one glass wall and watched as he locked her in. "Goodbye."

"I'll return," he said shortly. "Remember, you're perfectly safe. There is no one else on the entire planet besides the two of us, my father and his guards. And they are programmed to stay exclusively with him and protect him."

"All right." Lauren nodded and watched as he left the medical wing. She listened as the echo of his boots died away to silence and then began to pace. The glass holding cell was small—barely bigger than the one she'd been kept in aboard the Fathership, although thankfully larger than the tiny cramped space she'd been shoved into on the adjunct ship. Still, it only took her five steps to get from one end to the other and eight steps to go across diagonally.

Lauren supposed she ought to conserve her strength but she couldn't help it—she was nervous. She had faith that Xairn would keep his word—or try to, anyway—but she didn't like being locked in a cell on a dead planet with an evil being who wanted to rape her. Not to mention his monstrous, soulless guards. Those things were eight feet tall if they were an inch and she had no idea how Xairn was going to get around them if they got in the way when she and Xairn attempted their escape. Or—

Lauren stopped pacing suddenly and listened. *What's that sound?*

At first she thought Xairn was coming back because the faint noise sounded like the echo of his boots in the hallway. But it was coming from the opposite direction he'd left from and soon she could tell that it wasn't just one set of boots approaching her. There were at least two, maybe more, and the deep, masculine voices she heard murmuring over the tap-tapping of their boots were wholly unfamiliar.

My God, she thought, panic rising in her like a tidal wave. *There are other people here — strangers — and I'm locked in this cell like a sitting duck. They can do anything they want to me and I can't stop them, can't get out.*

She was trapped.

* * * * *

"I thought I told you not to disssturb me." The AllFather floated forward, his skeletal form partially obscured by the round crimson-black orb of the *dravik* which surrounded him in a bubble of polluted blood. In each of the four corners of the *Souda* stood an eight foot tall soldier — the AllFather's personal guard were silent as always. Xairn ignored them.

"I know what you said, Father, but I wanted to let you know that the Complex is secure." He kept his voice neutral.

"I sssee." The shape inside the blackish-red bubble nodded. "Well then, that isss all to the good. Where isss the girl?"

"Securely imprisoned within the medical wing, as you requested."

"Very good. Sssee that ssshe isss ready." The AllFather's voice was a hiss of pure lust. "I'll take her the moment my *dravik* burstsss."

Xairn felt a muscle in his jaw clench and forced it to relax. *Nothing I feel nothing.* But it was no longer true. Lauren had woken something inside him. Something that would have been better left undisturbed.

"My ssson?" The AllFather floated closer, seeming to glide within the confines of the *dravik*. He was always in the exact center of the glistening, blackish-red bubble, no matter which way he moved. "Isss all well with you?" he enquired.

"Yes, Father." Xairn did his best to appear stoic and unconcerned. "Of course."

"I sssense sssomething from you. A disturbance..." Claw-like hands reached out but the AllFather couldn't penetrate the wall of the *dravik,* which was feeding him power, and his fingertips stopped inches from Xairn's face. Thankfully, the bloody bubble also kept his mental powers in check so he couldn't rifle through Xairn's mind — though it was obvious he *could* sense that something wasn't as it should be.

Xairn didn't move. "I yearn for the completion of the prophesy. The fulfillment of our race. Perhaps you sense that."

"Perhapsss." The fingers withdrew and the vast, quivering, slimy bubble moved away. "We ssshall sssee in time. For now, leave me and prepare the girl. My guardsss and I will be in the medical wing presently."

"Of course, Father." Xairn bowed submissively and left the room. As the door to the *Souda* hissed shut behind him, he took a deep breath and pressed the palms of his hands to his eyes.

The feelings were growing stronger. The need to possess, to dominate, was flowering in his heart like an evil bloom. Xairn had always known that the seed was there — it was part of his very DNA. But he had hoped and prayed that it would never sprout, that he would never be tempted to the depravity he had witnessed for so long in his father.

I must be calm. I must repress these feelings for a little longer – until I can get Lauren safely home.

But how safe would she be if she was with him and the feelings continued to develop? Xairn feared to answer that question, even to himself. The need that was growing inside him was already so *strong*. Though he hated to admit it, he knew she would be better off away from him.

I must take her home as quickly as possible, Xairn thought. *The need is too great, the desire already too strong within me. If she is to be kept safe, she must stay away from me.*

The thought of just dropping her off on her home planet and leaving, made his heart ache fiercely. But it was the only way. And besides, what had he thought was going to happen between them? It wasn't like he could stay with her once this was over. They had to go their separate ways and never see each other again.

His life would be empty again without her. Meaningless. But if he cared for her, the best thing he could do was take Lauren home and then chart a course for the farthest star he could find.

Lifting his chin, Xairn continued down the corridor, heading for the medical wing. He had no time for the storm of emotions boiling within him now – there was a plan to carry out.

And if it didn't succeed, they were dead.

Chapter Thirty-one

"Here it is — the psychic knife." Deep pushed open a door and ushered them into a large space that appeared to be set up like some kind of laboratory. To one side was a vast silver cylinder that looked to Kat like a massive oil drum turned up on its end. There were steps leading up to it and a door cut into its side which seemed to indicate that you were supposed to go inside it. *Although I'm sure the people who went in there, didn't go voluntarily,* Kat thought with a shiver.

To be honest, the whole place gave her the creeps. The empty, echoing corridors and the medical complex, which Lock told her was just beyond this room, felt haunted. *This is the place where they did those horrible experiments on the Kindred and their brides,* she thought. *How awful to be trapped down here and know that you were about to be torn away from the man or men you loved forever.*

But wasn't that pretty much what was happening to her right now? Kat pushed the thought away angrily. Yes, she cared for Lock — maybe even loved him. And yes, despite all the hateful things he'd said, she cared for Deep too. But one half of the dynamic duo didn't want her and since they came as a matched set, she was going to have to get over both of them at once. *I just hope it won't be too painful,* she thought, staring uneasily at the psychic knife. The more she looked at it, the less she wanted to get into it, or go anywhere *near* it for that matter.

To one side of the large silver drum was a bank of control panels. Deep went to them immediately and began manipulating the various slide-boards and holo-graphs.

"Good power flow," he remarked as he worked. "Must be running on a longevity source."

Lock frowned as he watched his brother work. "I don't care how good it is, Deep, this is madness. Look at this place — this thing is an instrument of torture. And you want us to risk our lives in it?"

"You won't be risking anything but your pride," Deep snapped. "When you find out what a coward you've been."

"Don't be a dick," Kat said, putting a hand on her hip. "I'm with Lock on this one — this entire place gives me the willies. And how do we know that thing is safe? I mean it has the word 'knife' in its name and it was previously used to torture people. Somehow I doubt it would get the Good Housekeeping Seal of Approval — you know?"

"No, I don't," Deep said coldly. "But I *do* know this is our only option."

"It's *not* our only option." Lock's voice was quiet and tense. "We can go back home to the Mother ship and bond the lady Kat to us completely. Then we can spend the rest of our lives trying to make her happy."

Deep laughed harshly. "*Trying* being the operative word, Brother. Bonding her to us would bring her nothing but unhappiness and pain, no matter how hard you *tried* to do otherwise."

"That's not true," Lock protested angrily. "Or it wouldn't be if you could just stop —"

"Stop what?" Deep raised an eyebrow. "Stop being myself? I'm afraid I can't do that, Brother."

"Don't call me that." Lock's voice was a dangerous growl. "I told you I don't want that relationship with you anymore. I don't want *any* relationship with you."

"Then press your hand to the scanner and get into the machine, damn you." Deep sounded exasperated. "Look." He pressed his large palm to a flat black screen on the control panel which lit up immediately with a low hum. "I've got the damn thing all set up — we just need to activate it and step inside."

"How will separating the two of us from the lady Kat free *me* of *you?*" Lock demanded.

"Stop clouding the issue and just do it." Deep took a step toward Lock who was standing his ground with his fists clenched. "You stupid bastard. If you think —"

"Stop it! Stop it! *Stop it!*" Kat couldn't take any more. She pressed the heels of her hands to her eyes, trying to hold back the tears as their negative emotions filled her to overflowing. More than anything she couldn't stand it when they fought, when they hated each other out loud like that. *Next they'll be throwing things or Dad will hit Mom... No!* She took a deep breath. *They're **not** Mom and Dad. They're Deep and Lock. Get hold of yourself, Kat. Suck it up and deal.*

She opened her eyes to see both of them staring at her with concerned looks on their faces.

"My lady?" Lock asked tentatively. "Are you all right?"

"Fine, I'm sorry." Kat ran a trembling hand through her hair. "It's just...you two shouldn't be fighting. Especially not over me."

"Are you saying you're not worth it?" Deep gave her a penetrating glance. "Because I would have to disagree."

"I'm worth it, all right." Kat raised her chin and glared at him. "But I don't want it. And I don't want to come between you and be the reason you two start hating each other."

"You're not," Deep said shortly. "So don't worry about that."

"I am," Kat insisted. "And it's not right. Twin Kindred aren't supposed to fight like this, are they?"

Lock looked troubled. "It's true that we're supposed to be of one mind on just about everything. We used to be, anyway."

"Well we're not of one mind on this," Deep snapped. "You want to keep the soul bond and I don't. So let's just do this and get it over with." He pointed to the flat black screen which had scanned his handprint. "Go on."

Lock folded his arms over his broad chest. "I won't."

"Well, *I* will." Kat stepped forward and slapped her palm down on the scanner. There was a low humming sound and her hand was briefly outlined by a brilliant white light. "There," she said, stepping back when the process was complete. "I'm sorry, Lock," she said softly, seeing the agonized look on the light twin's face. "But I'm not going to stay with a man who doesn't want me and since you two are a package deal…"

"I understand." Nodding slowly, Lock pressed his palm to the scanner as well. Then he stood back and looked at Deep with real hatred in his brown eyes. "Now what, *Brother?*"

Deep took a deep breath and a look passed over his dark features too quickly for Kat to read. Remorse? Grief? Whatever it was, it was there and gone again, leaving his face perfectly blank. She tried to read his emotions but all she got was a storm cloud of negativity — too thick and black to penetrate or understand.

"Now," he said. "We need to—"

"What you need to do is turn around slowly and keep your hands where I can see them."

The deep voice behind them startled them all. Kat's heart began to pound when she turned her head to see a huge male with glowing red-on-black eyes pointing some kind of weapon at them. He looked horribly familiar and suddenly Kat realized where she'd seen him before. *That's the one,* she thought numbly, staring at him. *The Scourge who kidnapped Sophie and was going to kill her. Oh my God, what is he doing here?*

"Guys?" she whispered as Deep and Lock turned around as well.

"Get back." Deep pushed her behind him and then he and Lock joined ranks, standing shoulder to shoulder to create an impenetrable wall between her and the threat. "What do you want?" Deep said, his voice a low, threatening growl.

"I could ask the same thing of you," the Scourge returned. "What are you doing here on my home planet without invitation?"

"We didn't realize we had to wait to be invited," Deep said sarcastically.

"That's no answer." The Scourge sounded agitated now.

"And you're not going to get one," Deep snapped back.

"We're not here to harm anyone," Lock said, obviously trying to smooth the situation over. "Just let us leave and we won't bother you again, I swear."

"I'm afraid I can't do that." Peeking around Lock's elbow, Kat saw the Scourge warrior wave his weapon menacingly. "Drop your weapons on the floor and march single file into the medical wing. Now."

"What makes you think we'll comply?" Deep demanded. "There are two of us and only one of you. Even if you shoot one, the other will still kill you."

"You will comply because I won't be aiming for you," the Scourge said quietly. "I will set my sights on your female and I promise I *will* wound or kill her before either of you can kill me."

"You son-of-a-bitch!" Deep snarled, taking a step forward. Lock put a hand on his arm.

"Deep, I don't think we have any choice."

"Listen to your friend," the Scourge advised. He frowned. "I do not like to make such dire threats. I wouldn't if I could be sure of you."

"Sure of what? Because you can be *damn* sure we'll carve you to pieces if you so much as *touch* our Kat." Deep sounded like he was going into *rage* and Lock put a hand on his brother's arm again.

"Deep, please." He spoke to the Scourge. "What do you want from us? What's your name?"

The Scourge gave them a level look. "I am called Xairn. And for now I just want to talk."

"You want to talk? Then talk," Deep growled. "I don't see why we have to be disarmed to hear what you have to say."

"Because my father is here in the Complex as well." The Scourge raised an eyebrow at them. "Perhaps you know him—the AllFather?"

Deep swore loudly and Lock said,

"Of course we know of him. What is he doing here?"

A grim look passed over Xairn's face. "Gathering power—soon he will be too strong to stop. If you wish to leave this planet alive you need to listen to me."

"We're listening," Lock assured him. "What do you want to say?"

"Only this—I need your help to leave this place safely and I am willing to offer you mine in return if you'll trust me."

"Trust a Scourge? Not likely," Deep spat. "As if—"

"I think we should trust him," Kat said, stepping out from behind the brothers.

"Are you out of your mind?" Deep demanded. "Don't you recognize this male? He's the same one we saw attacking Sophia during our last joining."

"I recognize him, all right," Kat said evenly. "And I remember what we all saw. But I've talked to Sophie about what happened aboard his ship—he didn't want to kill her. He was going to set her free."

"If you're speaking of the human female with the green eyes, that is true," Xairn said, nodding.

"That's her," Kat said. "She's like a sister to me." She took a deep breath. "Look, we're really just here to use your psychic-knife thingy—we're not trying to start any trouble."

Xairn raised his eyebrows in obvious surprise. "You wish to sever the bond between you?"

Deep scowled. "We were...wrongly and accidentally bonded. This is the only way to sever the bond."

Xairn nodded slowly. "I see. Well, if you actually *want* the connection dissolved..."

"We do," Kat said, throwing a glance at Deep. "Very much."

Xairn shrugged. "You may use the psychic-knife if you wish—it is nothing to me. But my father may be here at any moment. He is in his *Souda* now, gathering strength and power. As soon as he feels strong enough he will be here—it may be several hours or a much shorter time before he appears. I cannot tell you for certain."

Lock had a worried look on his face but he spoke calmly. "This is insane. We can leave and come back later—or possibly rethink the entire thing. But if the AllFather is on this planet, we need to go *now*."

"Deep is right," Kat said, nodding. "As much as we want to be free of each other, staying here is crazy."

Xairn frowned. "But you haven't achieved what you came here for."

"He's right about that in more ways than one," Deep growled at Lock. "Or are you forgetting the secondary mission Olivia set for you, Brother?"

"Secondary mission?" Xairn looked wary. "Why else are you here?"

"We are also here to try and gather information about a missing human female—one we are certain was taken by your father for nefarious reasons," Lock said. "Perhaps you know of her? Lauren Jakes?"

The effect on Xairn couldn't have been more profound if Lock had shoved a double barreled shotgun into his gut and pulled the trigger. "Lauren? You're looking for *Lauren?*" He looked shocked at first, but then his voice dropped to a low, menacing growl and he seemed to grow bigger somehow. It reminded Kat of how Sylvan had looked when he went into *rage* while protecting Sophie. "Lauren is mine. She's *mine,*" Xairn snarled. "And I do *not* intend to surrender her to anyone."

"So you *do* have her." Lock's voice was mild but his eyes were hard.

"You bastard." Deep glared at the Scourge. "What have you done to the poor girl? Or maybe I should ask if there's anything you *haven't* done. Is she even still alive?"

Xairn's red-on-black eyes flashed crimson. "Of course she is! Do you think me some kind of a monster?"

"Actually, we do," Deep said. "We know exactly how you Scourge treat your females."

Xairn lifted his chin. "Not me. I have never touched a female in anger—this I swear."

"What about lust?" Deep raised an eyebrow. "Ever touched a female that way?"

Xairn looked suddenly ill at ease. "I...do not act on those emotions. I do not engage in the practices of my father and the rest of my people."

"We'll believe it when we see it." Deep's black eyes narrowed. "Where is Lauren now?"

Xairn bristled. "Someplace safe."

"Can we see her?" Kat asked. "I mean, can *I* see her? I'm no threat," she went on softly, meeting his strange, burning eyes. "And I think if we could hear from Lauren herself that you haven't hurt her, it would make it a lot easier for us to trust you."

Xairn looked at her appraisingly. "I suppose it couldn't hurt to let another female speak to Lauren. But I will not tolerate another male near her." He glared at Deep and Lock and then nodded at Kat. "Come with me."

She stepped forward to meet him, only to feel an iron grip locked around her upper arm. "Like hell, she will." Deep pulled her back behind him.

"Deep!" she protested angrily but he ignored her.

"We feel the same way about Kat that you do about Lauren," he told Xairn, his voice a low growl. "If she goes, we go. It's as simple as that."

Xairn frowned. "I suppose that is fair. But do *not* attempt to take Lauren from me. I have sworn that I will see her safely back to her planet but until then, I refuse to give her up to anyone."

"Even your father?" Lock said softly.

Xairn's eyes flashed crimson and his hands clenched into massive fists. "Especially him. Why do you think I need your help? He has four massive vat-grown guards with him. If they should catch us leaving I could only defend Lauren until I died. After that my father..." He shook his head. "I will not speak of it."

"Come on." Kat shook free of Deep's grip and gave him a glare which he returned with a blank expression. "Let's go."

It took a little maneuvering as to who was going to go first and who would have what weapon pointed at whom, but finally they entered the set of double metal doors at the end of the lab and found themselves in a long hallway made up of several glassed in rooms on either side.

Huddled in one of the rooms, wrapped in a long black cloak, was a beautiful girl with creamy mocha skin and striking amber eyes. Kat recognized her at once from the pictures Sophie and Liv had showed her.

"Lauren!" She ran to the glass wall of the room at once. "It's really you!"

Hesitantly, the girl came forward. "Do I know you?" Her voice was muffled but understandable through the thick glass.

"No, but I know *you*. Or I know of you, anyway." Kat turned to Xairn. "Please let me in to talk to her. I'm not armed—you can pat me down if you want."

"No, he can't!" Deep's black eyes flashed possessively. "He won't touch you or I swear to the Goddess—"

"I will take her word that she isn't armed," Xairn interrupted coolly. "And I will allow her into the cell with Lauren. She has been missing human companionship. Perhaps seeing another of her kind will make her feel better."

"Thank you." Kat stood by impatiently while he opened the door to the cell and then stepped in at once. "Lauren," she said gently, taking a step forward and extending her hand. "It's all right—I'm a friend."

"I just can't believe...after all this time..." Lauren stepped forward slowly. Hesitantly, she took Kat's offered hand. "Are you real?" she whispered, squeezing her fingers. "Are you *really* real?"

Kat smiled at her. "Last time I looked I was. Large as life and twice as natural."

Tears began to stream down Lauren's face. "I'm sorry," she sobbed, blotting her eyes on the black cloak she wore. "I just...I just..."

"Hey, it's all right. It's okay." Impulsively, Kat pulled her in for a hug. Lauren trembled and cried against her and Kat didn't blame her a bit. *God only knows what this poor girl has been through.* Finally the sobs slowed and then tapered off to sniffs and hiccups.

"S-sorry," Lauren said, pulling away. "Didn't mean to cry all over you."

"It's fine," Kat assured her. "I'm sure if our positions were reversed I would have done the same thing. I'm Kat, by the way. I'm a friend of your cousins, Olivia and Sophia Waterhouse."

Lauren frowned. "Who? I don't have any cousins."

"Yes, you do. Your mom tracked them down and didn't want to tell you until she was sure they wanted to do the whole family reunion thing. And they do, by the way—they can't wait to meet you."

Lauren looked dazed. "Wow...I don't know what to say—I've always wished I had more family. I'd love to meet them too. I'd love to meet *anyone* on Earth right now."

"Oh, they're not on Earth—they're on the Mother ship. Both of them are mated to Kindred warriors," Kat explained.

Lauren's amber eyes flickered to Deep and Lock, standing on either side of Xairn outside the glass cell. "And you are too? Is one of those guys your husband...uh, mate?"

Kat felt a pang of sorrow but she pushed it away and gave Lauren a smile. "Nah. Well—we *do* have a kind of connection but it's not complete. And we're going to get rid of it." She eyed Deep. "Irreconcilable differences, you know?"

"I'm sorry to hear that," Lauren murmured.

"What about you?" Kat asked, trying to phrase the question delicately. "How has, uh, Xairn been treating you? All right?"

"He's been a perfect gentleman," Lauren said quietly. "I know what you're probably thinking about why they took me and it's partly true. The AllFather wants to...wants to..." She shook her head. "I can't think about what he wants to do. It's too awful. But Xairn has promised to protect me from him and take me home."

"Do you believe he really will?" Kat asked in a low voice she was pretty certain couldn't be heard through the thick glass. "Look, it's okay—you can tell me the truth. The guys I'm with are armed—we'll keep you safe."

Lauren got a stubborn look in her amber eyes. "I know how it must sound—like I have the worst case of Stockholm syndrome in history. But honestly, Xairn has never hurt me and I *do* trust him. He's very repressed—I mean, wouldn't *you* be if you had his father for a dad? And I get the idea he went through some pretty bad things in his childhood, though he won't talk about it much."

Kat nodded noncommittally. "Sounds like he has major issues."

"He does. Seriously though, he's one of the good guys. Even though he's one of the bad guys—if you know what I mean."

Searching her eyes once more, Kat and found nothing there but sincerity. She nodded. "Yeah, I know. But this whole idea of him taking you home...don't you think it would be better if you came with us instead? We're going straight back to the Mother ship and from there it's a hop, skip, and a jump to Earth."

Lauren bit her lip. "Probably... But I don't exactly know how..."

"How to talk to him about it? Leave it to me." Kat put an arm around her shoulders. "Right now, we've got to get out of here before we can start dividing up the carpool. Come on."

"Okay." Lauren nodded.

"Good." Kat turned and rapped briefly on the glass. Xairn opened the door and she and Lauren stepped out. "Hey, guys, it's okay. He's all right," she said, nodding at the big Scourge. "Lauren says he's a perfect gentleman."

"I am a what?" A look of incomprehension creased Xairn's stern features.

"It means you've never taken advantage of her," Kat said tactfully. "Or hurt her."

"Of course I haven't." Xairn lifted his chin. "I would rather die."

Deep gave him an appraising look. "You sound like one of us— a Kindred warrior. We also would rather die than hurt our females."

"Physically or emotionally?" Kat gave him a penetrating look.

"We have no time for bickering," Xairn reminded them sternly. "We must leave this place quickly, while my father is still in his *Souda*. I was going to take one of the abandoned ships from the battlefield and return Lauren to Earth. But now..." His red-on-black eyes flickered over Kat, who still had her arm around the shivering Lauren. "Perhaps...perhaps you should take her with you."

Deep raised an eyebrow. "I thought you didn't trust her with another male."

Xairn's eyes flashed crimson. "I don't. But I see now that she needs the comfort of her own kind. And..." He looked at Deep and Lock and back at Kat again. "No matter what you say, I do not believe the two of you have any interest in another female besides your companion."

"You're right about that," Lock said quietly. "We have no interest in Lauren—although we will swear to protect her."

"She has kin aboard our Mother ship," Deep said. "We'll see that she gets there safely and is reunited with her family."

Xairn nodded. "Then she shall go with you. Come." He turned to lead the way out but Lauren called his name.

"Xairn, please," she said softly.

"Yes?" He turned to face her.

"What about you? Will you...come with us?"

His rough voice gentled. "No, Lauren. I cannot."

"But why? What are you going to do?"

"Take a ship and get as far from my father as possible." He jerked his head in the direction of the doors. "Come. Time is running out. My father will not remain in his *Souda* much longer. And if he finds us, none of us will get anywhere."

"True enough," Deep growled. "Let's quit this place. We can come back later when it's deserted again."

"Or not at all," Lock muttered.

Kat felt a great surge of relief. *We're leaving. We're not going to do it. Not going to cut the bond!* Up until that moment, she hadn't realized how very much she *didn't* want to be separated from Lock and Deep. She had forced herself to think it was all right because it was so clearly what Deep wanted. But now that it was no longer an option, she couldn't help hoping that he could be made to see reason. That he could learn to care for her as Lock did and the three of them could be happy together.

Stupid, whispered a little voice in her head. *You can't change how he feels. You need to give up that idea right now because there's no way it's going to work.* But despite the negative self-talk, Kat couldn't help the hope that bloomed in her heart. She kept feeling that there was something about Deep—something standing in his way. And if she could just find that last barrier and remove it, maybe—

"Well, well, how very fortuitousss…it ssseems we have visitorsss."

The soft hissing voice froze all of them in their tracks. Kat turned her head slowly, dreading what she was about to see but completely unable to help looking.

It was the AllFather—or the outline looked like him, anyway—encased in a huge, slimy, blackish-red bubble of blood. And he was surrounded by four of the hugest creatures Kat had ever seen—no doubt the vat-grown soldiers Xairn had mentioned.

Kat couldn't be sure, but she thought the AllFather might be smiling—or maybe it was just his eyes glowing with eagerness and greed as he looked them over.

Oh my God, we waited too long. He's here and now we're trapped—what the hell are we going to do?

Chapter Thirty-two

Xairn felt like the marrow in the center of his bones had suddenly frozen. How could he miss his father's entrance so completely? And how much had the AllFather heard of what they were saying?

"Ssso the Complex is sssecure, is it?" his father demanded, drifting closer in the glistening *dravex*.

"It's about to be." Praying the Kindred warriors would understand, Xairn waved his shocker menacingly and growled, "I told you to hand me your weapons and keep your hands where I can see them."

Deep and Lock exchanged a look and then both of them handed over their blazers and spread their hands, palm up. "No need to get nasty," Deep said. "We were just leaving."

"But now you will be ssstaying, yesss?" The AllFather glided forward, his eyes gleaming with hungry glee. "Of course, it begsss the question—why are you here in the first place, Warrior?"

"They came to find Lauren," Xairn said, still keeping his shocker trained on the two Kindred. He hoped they would trust him. If they all stayed calm and kept their heads, they might still get out of here alive.

"And they *have* found her, haven't they, my sssweet?" The red-black bubble floated over to Lauren who shivered and tightened her grip on Kat. "Sssoon," the AllFather hissed at her. "Sssoon I will have you, my lovely. And you will bear me many, many daughtersss. And I ssshall have them too—until the entire Ssscourge race is replenished, ssstronger than we ever were before."

Xairn wanted to kill him—to break through the fragile, glistening shell of the *dravik* and wring his neck, but he held himself in check grimly. Once released from the bubble of blood and power, his father would be a much greater threat. As it was, all he could do was issue orders for his rather stupid vat-grown guards to carry out. But if the bubble burst…Well, Xairn just hoped it wouldn't until they were well clear of the Complex and on their way into space. In the mean time, he waited to see what his father would do next.

The AllFather drifted closer to Lauren and Kat. "Ssso beautiful," he hissed, looking hungrily at Lauren. The sense of dread and horror in the room was almost palpable—the AllFather carried it with him wherever he went like a nauseating scent that permeated everything. Xairn could see that it affected both the human women but neither of them cried or panicked. Instead, Kat raised her chin and looked his father squarely in the eyes.

"Leave her alone."

"Ah, thisss one hasss ssspirit." Skeletal hands reached out from behind the bubble and Xairn knew if the wall of the *dravik* had not been in the way, his father would have caressed Kat's cheek with his scabrous fingers.

Kat seemed to know it too because she flinched back, ever so slightly, but never broke eye contact. "You're a sick, crazy bastard and you need to step back before I pop that weird blood balloon thingy you're floating around in and you go down like a ton of bricks."

The sense of gleeful lust radiating from the AllFather shifted subtly to irritation. "A bit *too* much ssspirit, it seemsss. And which of these is your mate?" He looked at Deep and Lock—both of whom were poised for a fight. Xairn knew that if his father came even an inch nearer their human female, they would spring and all would be lost.

"They both are," he said, moving subtly to put himself between the AllFather and Kat, while still keeping his weapon trained on the Kindred. "I believe they are Twin Kindred."

"Isss thisss ssso?" The AllFather looked at Deep who nodded shortly.

"It is. Which means both of us are ready to kill you if you so much as lay a finger on her."

The bubble glided backward and Xairn breathed an inaudible sigh of relief. "I will not touch her," the AllFather said, still staring at Deep. "But you will not, either. Ever again, my brave warriorsss."

"What do you mean?" Lock asked.

"You ssshall sssee." The AllFather nodded at Xairn. "Take them to the cutting lab and prepare the psychic-knife. And bring the girl." He nodded at Lauren. "Ssshe ssshall watch as their bondsss are sssundered."

Xairn nodded shortly. "Very well." He looped an arm around Kat's neck and waved his weapon at the warriors. "Do as my father says or your female will pay the price."

Deep's hands curled into fists and the pupils of his black eyes turned red. "Take your hands off her! *Now.*"

"I'll release her when you do as you're told." Xairn kept his voice steady and hoped the dark twin would understand. "I believe I know what my father has in mind—you and your female are going to be taking a turn in the psychic-knife."

Lock touched his brother's arm. "Be calm," he murmured. "He won't hurt her as long as we do as he says."

"Indeed." The AllFather nodded within the *dravik*. "Listen to your twin and behave yourself, warrior. I may even let the three of you go once your bondsss are cut. The thought of having my own bride to breed makesss me feel almossst merciful."

Xairn was sure the two Kindred would have fought to the death for their female — it was the Kindred way. His way too, he thought, looking at Lauren who was standing beside him shivering. But since a trip inside the psychic-knife was what they had come for in the first place, he was fairly certain they would play along. Up to a point. It was going to be up to Xairn to gauge when they should make their move — he only hoped they could do it before the slimy bubble of the *dravik* around the Allfather burst, releasing him in a state of supreme mental power.

"My guardsss and I will retire to the viewing area beside the lab." His father's hissing voice broke into his frantic train of thought. "The girl will come with usss. Alpha — take her."

"That is not necessary." Xairn struggled to keep his voice even as the huge vat-grown guard took Lauren's slim shoulders in its huge hands. Gods, just seeing another male *touching* her was enough to send him over the edge! But he had to stay calm. "I have the situation in hand, Father. I do not need help."

"Of course you do, my ssson." The AllFather's red eyes gleamed evilly. "And even if you do not, I feel better with the girl in my own cussstody. Alpha, come."

Lauren threw a pleading glance over her shoulder as the huge guard marched her away. Xairn could do nothing but watch her go. The muscle in the side of his jaw clenched so hard he could feel his teeth grinding together and his grip on the shocker tightened until he was sure he was leaving fingerprints in the metal itself. He couldn't even say anything to reassure her — though the AllFather had turned his back and was gliding into the cutting lab, he was still within earshot. Xairn felt like he was being torn in two as he watched her go but he nodded at Lauren as reassuringly as he could.

Trust me — I will keep my promise! Gods, how he wished he had a link with her — the same kind the Kindred were said to have with their bonded brides. Some way to communicate his true intentions other than just his eyes.

But Lauren seemed to understand him somehow. She nodded back and the look on her face became a little less desperate.

She trusts me, Xairn realized, feeling like someone had stabbed a thorn in his heart. *Despite the hopelessness of the situation, she still trusts me.*

As he watched her go, he swore to himself not to betray that trust.

Even if it meant his death.

Chapter Thirty-three

The huge blackish-red bubble that floated into the cutting lab through the open double doors reminded Kat of a spider's egg sac. It was slimy and glistening and beyond its mostly opaque surface she could see the skeletal shape of the AllFather moving. It seemed to bulge as it moved, as though it might burst and vomit out some vile abomination at any moment. She just hoped they were far away by the time it popped.

In the mean time, it looked like she and Deep and Lock were going to have the soul bond between them cut after all. She felt her heart sink as they entered the lab and Xairn marched her up to the large silver drum of the psychic-knife. *So this is it. This is how it ends between us.* She felt tears threatening but she didn't want to cry in front of the horrible AllFather.

He and three of his guards had mounted a small platform to one side of the room, separated from the rest of the lab by a low wall. It was like an observation area in a regular operating theater. Standing by the bottom steps of the platform were the huge guard the AllFather had called Alpha, and Lauren.

Lauren watched what was going on with uncertain amber eyes and Kat reflected that she had the same delicate bone structure as Liv and Sophie. She hoped with all her heart that they all made it back to the Mother ship for a family reunion. Already she was sure that her two best friends would love their new cousin.

"We are ready," the AllFather called, breaking her train of thought. "Proceed with the cutting, my ssson."

Xairn motioned to Lock. "Open the door of the mechanism and the two of you climb inside."

The light twin did as he was told but Deep wasn't so easy to persuade. "Send me Kat first. I want to know that she's safe."

"Very well. But if you try anything, she dies." Xairn's big hand tightened on her shoulder and he hissed in her ear, so softly she could barely hear it, "Be ready to fight or flee the second you come out. The AllFather will be off his guard for only a moment. Tell your males." Then he pushed her roughly forward with one hand, keeping his weapon trained on Deep with the other.

Kat knew it was just for show but she stumbled and would have fallen if Deep hadn't caught her. "Come on." He led her carefully up the steps to the door of the silver drum.

She allowed herself to be helped inside the dark, circular space and then she felt Lock's hands on her, gentle and competent. Finding her way forward, she leaned against him and whispered in his ear, "Xairn says be ready to fight or run the minute this is over. He says the AllFather will be off guard, but only for a moment."

She felt Lock nod. "I'll let Deep know."

"Let me know what?" Deep said in a low voice.

There was the soft growl of masculine voices in the dark, too low for Kat to hear, and then Lock positioned her against the curved wall and started buckling her in with some kind of safety harnesses. "What's this?" Her voice echoed emptily in the hollow interior of the drum and she made an effort to lower it. "Why do we need to be strapped in?"

"Because among other factors, the psychic-knife uses centripetal force to cut the bonds between Kindred and their brides." Deep was already strapping on his own harness.

"Seriously?" Kat gave him an incredulous look. "We traveled halfway across the galaxy to cut this damn bond when we could have just found a traveling fair back home and gone on the tilt-a-whirl? I mean, who needs the AllFather's evil inventions when you've got an all day ride pass and a semi-sober carnie?"

"I said among *other things*," Deep growled. "I would not be subjecting you to this if it wasn't absolutely necessary."

"But why?" Kat peered at him, trying to make out his features in the gloomy interior of the silver drum. "Why is this so important to you, Deep? Why do you hate me so much that you can't stand even the *thought* of being tied to me?"

"I don't hate you." His deep voice was suddenly hoarse. "If I hated you, or cared for you even a little less, I wouldn't hesitate to complete our bond, little Kat."

"You told me you felt nothing," she said, her voice trembling despite herself.

"I lied," he whispered.

"Deep doesn't hate you, my lady," Lock said, sounding bitter. "He hates himself. And we all must pay for his self loathing."

"I'm sorry," Deep said in a soft, agonized voice. "Lock is right— forgive me for all I have put you through. But please don't think any of it is because of you, my Kat. I bear this blame alone."

For some reason his last words seemed to echo in her head. *I bear this blame alone...I bear this blame alone...*The words seemed important somehow, like something she had heard before and forgotten. Something she must remember...

And then the door slammed shut and the ride began.

It didn't take Kat long to be glad she hadn't eaten much for breakfast. Earlier that morning, Sophie and Liv had arrived at the docking bay yawning and bearing donuts. Despite the fact that she'd been tempted by a chocolate covered Bavarian crème and a jelly filled glazed donut, Kat had only accepted one plain one. And as the drum of the psychic knife lurched and began to spin, she knew that if she'd eaten more it would have come right up.

Kat loved scary rides but the psychic-knife soon attained a speed and force that put anything she'd ever experienced at any amusement park to shame. Flattened against the wall with her head pressed to the side, she struggled to breathe, her heart pounding frantically.

*Oh God, I'll never go on the tilt-a-whirl again if you just let me live through this. Hell, I'll never even go on the **merry-go-round**. I could kill Deep for getting us into this. This is all his fault...* And again his words echoed in her head. *I bear this blame alone...*What had he meant by that? When had she heard those words before? What...?

Suddenly a picture began to form in her head. Kat didn't know if it was a side effect of the knife or just her mind's desperate attempt to distract her from her fear. But whatever the reason, the vision was clear.

A doll on the bed...a life-sized doll with dull blonde hair and wide blue eyes. But not a doll—a girl and she's dead! She's dead! Deep kneeling by the bed, taking the blame, saying that it is all his fault, swearing that it will never happen again...

And then it all came back. *The dream—I dreamed about the dead girl but it must be real,* Kat realized. *We were dream sharing again last night, just like we were when he took my pain. My God, this is why he wanted us to be separated. He was afraid he'd hurt me—ruin my life or kill me. That I'd die like that poor girl, Miranda, who took her own life rather than be with him. But what would make him think that? He ought to know by now I'm not the type to commit suicide...*

Another thought flashed through her head. The memory of the way she'd almost died before Deep had taken her pain and Mother

L'rin had cured her. And the way she'd fainted during the ceremony on Twin Moons while Deep was making love to her. Surely the sight of her limp body, her illness caused — so he must have believed — by him alone, had affected the dark twin. Could it be that Deep had somehow convinced himself she would die if he stayed with her? If he allowed their bond to become complete and permanent?

That must be it! Kat thought excitedly. *That must be why he —*

And then a pain like nothing she had ever felt before stabbed into her very soul.

Part of her was being removed — and not neatly and cleanly like a knife would cut it either. It felt like it was being pulled out like a tooth by a sadistic dentist with no Novocain. *Psychic-knife my ass,* she thought wretchedly. *More like psychic-pliers.* It occurred to her that the pain was on purpose — that the instrument they were in wasn't meant to sever the bonds between a Kindred and his bride quickly and cleanly, but to draw the process out and make it even worse. Lock hadn't called it a torture device for nothing — he'd been absolutely right.

As the pain grew, Kat moaned in agony. God it hurt! Hurt more than anything she'd ever felt in her life and the worst thing was, the pain wasn't physical. It went deeper than that — into the very core of her being. The part that was being removed from her was something she *needed* — something she had to have to survive. It was like someone was cutting out a piece of her heart and she could feel every cruel stroke of the butcher's dull knife. She writhed against the curving wall, feeling like she was being gutted and turned inside out like a fish. Feeling like she was going to die if it didn't stop...

She wasn't sure how long it went on but from the hoarse cries to either side of her, she could tell that Deep and Lock were experiencing the same thing. She longed to comfort them and to draw comfort from the feeling of their strong arms around her. But would she ever be able to touch them that way again? Would she ever—

And then, as suddenly as it had begun, everything was over. The pain ceased and the machine stopped spinning with a sickening jolt.

"Is...is it over?" Finding that she could move again, Kat raised a trembling hand to her head and then ran her fingers down the front of her body. *Am I all right? All in one piece?* It seemed like she must have some visible, tangible wound after going through such a horrible experience. But her seeking fingers didn't feel anything sticky and warm—she wasn't bleeding. At least not outwardly. She wondered about what was going on *inside* though. And what was going on with Deep and Lock? Instinctively, forgetting that their connection had been cut, she reached out for them, wanting to know how they were feeling. To reassure herself that they were both all right.

"My lady, are you well?" Lock asked in a low, trembling voice. Kat could feel the waves of tension and fear coming from him— pretty much what she was feeling herself.

"I...I think so," she said. "Are you?"

"I will be, when we get out of here."

"Deep?" Kat asked. "Are you okay?"

There was a low rustling sound. "Yes," he said at last. "I'm fine."

"You bastard," Lock said, addressing his brother. "You never said it would hurt like that. I've never experienced such pain. And to put the lady Kat through it too—you're a *monster*."

"I didn't know." Deep's voice was hoarse, filled with horror and pain. "Forgive me—I thought with just a partial bond—"

He said something else but Kat didn't catch it. She was too busy noticing that while she could *hear* the pain in his voice, she couldn't *feel* any of it. Frantically, she tried harder, reaching out with the part of herself that had somehow grown during the time she and the twins had been bonded. But for all her seeking she encountered…nothing.

Oh my God, no…No! Kat knew in the past she would have been overjoyed not to feel Deep's dark, negative emotions crowding her head, but now she felt only dismay and traumatic loss. It was as though she'd looked down and suddenly realized that someone had cut off one of her hands.

"Deep," she whispered, her voice breaking. "What's going on? I can feel Lock but when I try to reach you…"

"It's the same for me." Lock sounded, if anything, even more horrified than Kat. "I can feel you, my lady but when I reach for Deep…nothing." She felt his terror—the sudden sense of loss, the realization that after a lifetime of being half of a whole, he was now just half. "Brother," he said, his deep voice shaking. "What…what have you done?"

"You don't have to call me that anymore." Deep's tone was one of utter desolation. "You got your wish, Lock. Can't you tell?"

"I don't understand." Kat yanked against her safety harness, trying to get free. If she couldn't touch Deep with her mind, she needed to touch him with her hands. To make sure he was still there. She had the absurd but somehow compelling notion that he was a ghost now—something she could hear but would never be able to see again. *I need to feel him under my hands, need to smell his skin, touch his hair…*

The door opened suddenly, making her blink with the rush of light. "Now." Xairn's voice was a harsh whisper.

"Now what?" Deep was the first to recover. Unbuckling himself from the safety harness, he crouched close to hear what the Scourge warrior was saying.

"The AllFather is distracted—the pain from your cutting has filled him to completion. He is satisfied for the first time in weeks—torpid. We must act before he becomes alert again. And most especially before the *dravik* bursts."

"*Dravik?*" Kat frowned as she fumbled to unbuckle her harness. "Is that the weird blood-bubble thing he's in?"

Xairn nodded tersely. "Yes. Come, we need to get Lauren and run for the front entrance of the Complex at once. Here." He passed Deep and Lock the weapons he'd taken from them earlier. "Watch what you shoot—if you burst the *dravik* none of us will get out of here alive. Now hurry."

"Wait," Lock said. "What about the guards?"

"They're slow and stupid—they do only what the AllFather tells them," Xairn said rapidly. "But they're also extremely strong so don't let them get too close. They aren't intelligent enough to be trusted with projectile weapons but the AllFather has armed them with *kusaxs.*"

"What's a *kusax?*" Kat asked, finally getting free of her harness.

"A Scourge knife," Lock answered in a low voice. "The blade is made of the tainted black metal found only here on their home planet. It's said that even a scratch from one it will poison your soul."

"Great," Kat muttered. "Like my soul wasn't messed up enough already." She was trying to joke but in fact, the strange feeling of having had something vitally important amputated continued to grow. She couldn't stop reaching out, feeling for Deep, expecting to pick up his emotions. But every time she tried she felt nothing...nothing...

Then Lock wrapped an arm firmly around her waist and they were leaving the confines of the silver drum. "She's yours now," she heard Deep telling the light twin. "Take care of her. Leave the guards to me."

"Brother—" Lock began but Deep gave him a look fierce enough to shut him up.

"Just do it," he ordered. "And don't call me that anymore—it no longer applies."

Lock nodded. "Very well." He pulled Kat closer to him. "Stay with me, my lady. I will shield you with my life if necessary."

"I know you will." There was a lump in Kat's throat as they exited the interior of the psychic-knife. She kept feeling like she had lost something important—something irreplaceable which was now gone forever.

The first thing she noticed when they stepped out was how silent everything was. The spidery shadow of the AllFather, within the glistening bloody bubble, was still—almost frozen. The three huge guards that surrounded him were silent too, reminding Kat of robots that had been switched off or monstrous toys whose batteries had run down.

What's going on with them? Kat wondered, staring at the silent tableau in the viewing gallery. She remembered Xairn saying something about the AllFather being satiated with pain... *Our pain,* she realized suddenly. *That's why that damn psychic-knife hurts so much. It's not just meant to cut bonds — it generates the maximum amount of agony. Pain is what that sick bastard feeds on.* Looking at the skeletal figure slumped within the slimy bubble, she knew she must be right. *After everything we just went through, he must have sucked down so much hurt he can barely move — like a spider full of flies. He looks like somebody who just finished an entire Thanksgiving dinner all by himself, turkey and all!*

Obviously the AllFather's torpor had spread to his attendants. Even the Alpha guard who was holding Lauren seemed to have loosened his grip and was simply standing behind her with his huge hands resting on her shoulders.

Lauren seemed to have sensed the change too. She was tense — her eyes wide, obviously poised for something. A signal? A word? Kat moved a little back from Lock, ready to reach for her and try to drag her away from the monstrous solider guarding her. Then Xairn said, "Now!" and everything happened at once.

Chapter Thirty-four

"Lauren, to me!" Xairn shouted.

She sprang forward, obeying his command at once. The huge hands that had been resting on her shoulders snapped shut—an instant too late.

"Quickly!" Xairn grabbed her hand. "Before they awaken."

"Too late for that, my ssson." The shape within the bloody black and red bubble moved as the AllFather came to life. "Alpha! The girl—get the girl!" he commanded, the *dravik* expanding with the force of his anger.

The huge guard stumbled forward blindly, clumsy after his doze. He reached out but the female his thick fingers closed on was Kat, who was trying desperately to get out of the way as the other guards came to life.

"Let go of me, you idiot!" She thrashed and kicked, aiming for his shins. But though plenty of her kicks connected, the merciless grip on her shoulders only tightened more.

"Kat!" Lock and Deep both ran forward but at the same time the AllFather was descending the stairs of the viewing area. Worse, Xairn could see the *dravik* expanding and contracting regularly now—beating like a heartbeat. It was a sure sign that it was about to burst and release the AllFather. His father had gorged himself on the pain of the Kindreds' cutting and now he would be more powerful than ever. They *had* to get away before that happened.

I could go, he thought. *I could take Lauren and run while the guards are distracted by the Kindred and their female. We could be safe in space before they even realized we were gone.*

But he couldn't do it. He had pledged his help to the enemy warriors as they had pledged theirs to him. He had no right to leave them now — even if it meant his life. But that didn't mean that Lauren had to die with him.

"Run," he told her, pushing her toward the far end of the lab. "Go straight down the corridor and out the double doors at the end. Keep going and you'll come to a place with many abandoned ships. They should be touch activated so —"

"No." She shook her head emphatically. "I'm not leaving you."

"You have to go!" Xairn was torn between exasperation and admiration. "I cannot leave until the Kindred and their female are free."

"I'm not leaving either." She crossed her arms over her chest. "Give me a weapon — let me help."

The thought that she might want to join the fight had never entered Xairn's head. But from the look of things, they could use every hand they could get.

"Here." He fumbled in his boot for a moment and came up with a slim, finger-sized weapon. "This is a stunner. Point and press the trigger button at the end. Aim for the chest if you can — it's a bigger target. Just don't hit any of us — it's calibrated for the guards."

"Got it." She took the weapon in remarkably steady hands.

"And don't burst the AllFather's *dravik*," Xairn added, as he primed his own weapon and took aim. "It will rupture soon enough on its own."

"All right." Holding the stunner in one hand, she steadied her wrist with the other and took aim. Xairn was impressed to see one of the guards who had been reaching for Deep knocked backwards from the force of the blast. Convinced that she knew what she was doing, he joined the fight.

* * * * *

Kat was doing her best not to freak out but it was pretty hard not to. One minute she'd been reaching for Lauren and the next she was being dragged backward by the massive, dead-eyed guard toward the raving AllFather.

"No, no, you imbecile!" he was hissing angrily at the oblivious Alpha guard. "The other girl—thisss female isss uselesss to me. Get the other!" The weird blood bubble enclosing him was moving in waves, sucking in and out almost as though it was breathing. The strange motion somehow made it even more disgusting than it had been previously—and that was saying something as far as Kat was concerned.

"Get off her, you son-of-a-bitch!" Behind her, Lock was aiming his weapon at the guard but clearly he was afraid to shoot—probably because at this range he might hit her instead of the guard. The guard wasn't paying any attention anyway—he just continued dragging Kat toward the AllFather no matter what anyone said or did.

"Can't risk the blazer," she heard Deep shout. "She's too close."

"I know." Lock sounded desperate. "Watch out behind you!"

Deep turned but just then a blast of energy knocked down the guard who had been reaching for him. Kat looked around to see Lauren pointing some kind of tiny weapon and Xairn running toward them. *Oh good, the cavalry is here.* But she really didn't see what good anyone could do. If no one could make the massive hands let her go, she was on a one way trip straight to the AllFather in his slimy bubble.

Then Deep jumped on the Alpha guard's back. Wrapping one arm around the thick throat, he began to squeeze. At first the guard didn't even seem to notice—then he choked and shifted, as though trying to shake Deep off. But it was obvious the dark twin didn't intend to be so easily dislodged. He tightened his grip on the corded neck and squeezed until the flat, black-on-black eyes bulged in their sockets.

Kat felt one paw-like hand leave her shoulder and the Alpha guard began groping at its belt. *A weapon,* she thought dismally. *It's looking for some kind of weapon.* She squirmed in the guard's grasp, trying to get loose. But though she twisted until it felt like her entire arm was about to break off, she still couldn't free herself.

Deep wrapped both muscular arms around the guard's neck and squeezed harder. At the same time, another one of the guards went down, its limbs jerking and thick boots drumming the floor as though it was having a seizure. From the corner of her eye, Kat saw Xairn taking aim again. She didn't know what his weapon did exactly but the results were impressive—the guard wasn't getting up.

Above the shouting and shooting, she could hear the high, evil screech of the enraged AllFather. She couldn't tell what he was saying but he was coming closer, the floating blood bubble throbbing like a vein in an angry man's temple. *Have to get out of here before that thing pops!* she thought, her skin crawling with fear and revulsion. *If we're still here when he gets free of it, there's going to be hell to pay! And we—*

"Deep, be careful! The knife—it's got a knife!"

Lock's desperate cry dragged her attention back to the dark twin and what she saw nearly froze her heart. In the split second she'd been watching the AllFather, the Alpha guard had somehow managed to draw a knife from its belt. To Kat, a confirmed Lord of the Rings fan, it looked like something an orc might carry. The blade was long and curved like a scimitar and the metal it was made of was gleaming, polished black with rust-red streaks running through it.

The kusax! she thought numbly. *Oh my God! Lock said even a scratch would poison him.* And it looked like the guard was intending to do a lot more than scratch. Though it was obviously getting woozy from lack of air, its grip on her shoulder remained firm—as well as its grip on the knife.

As she watched, the Alpha guard raised its arm, obviously aiming to take a stab at the warrior still clinging to its back. Looking up, Kat could tell that Deep saw it too. But though she and Lock both shouted at him, he refused to let go.

"No," Kat screamed as the knife made its slashing descent. It seemed to happen in slow motion—she saw every inch of the black blade as it entered Deep's side, heard the guard's grunt of effort as it thrust the knife home. Then, at the same time, the soulless eyes finally closed and it slumped to its knees, releasing her.

Lock pulled her out of the way just in time. The huge, heavy body of the Alpha guard came crashing down right where she'd been standing, with Deep still clinging to its back.

Kat didn't care. She shook loose of Lock's restraining hand and ran to Deep. "No...oh no," she whispered as she saw the extent of the damage. Only the handle protruded from his side—the entire wicked, black blade was buried in his body.

Then, to her utter surprise, his eyes fluttered open and he sat up.

"Don't try to move, Brother." Lock was suddenly there too, putting a hand on Deep's arm. "You're badly wounded."

"I'm fine." Deep hauled himself up, swayed, and then steadied himself to Kat's amazement.

"You're not," she blurted. "Lock is right—you're hurt. Look at your side!"

Deep looked down, saw the knife handle sticking out of his body, and shrugged. "Looks worse than it feels. I'll leave it in until we get back to the ship though—keep it from bleeding."

How he could stand and talk, let alone move around and get back to the ship with a foot long blade buried in his guts, was more than Kat could understand. But it didn't seem to surprise Lock as much as it did her. "We have to go." He nodded at the other guards, all of whom were on the floor. "They may be wounded but they'll get back up soon enough."

Indeed, the huge Alpha guard was stirring at their feet already. And the AllFather...*wait a minute—where is the AllFather?* Kat wondered uneasily. Her shoulder ached fiercely and she was still horribly afraid for Deep but the fact that she could no longer see the slimy blood bubble and its foul occupant scared her to death.

Then she heard Xairn's deep voice behind her. "Ware!" he bellowed. "Ware the *dravik*—it's going to burst!"

Turning her head, Kat saw that the ball of black-red blood containing the AllFather had moved out into the middle of the cutting lab floor, directly opposite the psychic-knife. The *dravik* was pulsating rhythmically now—faster and faster. Within it the AllFather had his arms raised and his crimson eyes were blazing with fury.

Deep swore loudly. "Go now! Run—everyone. We have to get out of here!"

Kat didn't see how he could take his own advice with a knife sticking out of his side but he grabbed one of her hands and Lock grabbed the other. From the corner of her eye she saw Xairn take Lauren's hand as well. And then they were running as fast as they could. She knew Deep must be in pain with every step he took, but she felt nothing from him, nothing but Lock's fear for her and sorrow for his twin.

We're going to make it, she thought wildly as they neared the double doors at the far end of the lab. *We're really going to —*

A horrible, wet, popping noise, like a rotten carcass exploding, interrupted her train of thought. At the same time, a gush of putrid air, worse than anything Kat had ever smelled, suddenly rushed over them. That was followed by a wet, splattering sound and she was hit in the back by a wave of something slimy and cold.

"Oh my *God!*" Kat gagged in revulsion. The cold, jellied, foul-smelling slime was coating her back and dripping from her hair. Her first instinct was to stop and try to get it *off* her at once. It was the same way she would have felt if she'd found a spider crawling on her skin. *Unclean! Disgusting! Get it off, get it off, get it off!* screamed the primitive part of her mind. But there was no time — Deep and Lock were dragging her along faster than ever now, even though both of them were coated in the disgusting substance too.

The three of them hit the doors at a dead run, shoving them open and barreling through. At the last instant, Kat turned her head and saw that Lauren and Xairn were right behind them, both of them absolutely *covered* in the ghastly, black-red slime. Behind *them,* the AllFather stood, skeletal arms raised, crimson eyes blazing. His shadowy cloak billowed around him and despite the glistening remains of the *dravik,* which covered the entire room, he himself was somehow dry. He shook back his hood and opened his lipless mouth to speak —

And then the doors banged shut behind them and they were running down the corridor, heading for safety and home.

But will we all make it there alive? Kat thought, casting a frantic glance at Deep who was holding her hand in one of his, while he grasped the protruding handle of the *kusax* with the other.

She didn't know.

* * * * *

"Stop!" the AllFather screeched. His power flowed outward like a tidal wave, engulfing Xairn and Lauren just as they were about to reach the doors the Kindred and their female had just gone through.

Xairn couldn't help it—he slowed his pace and then skidded to a stop. He felt the drag of the words, the power of his father's command as he never had before—not even on the day that Sanja had died. His knees wanted to lock, his body wanted to turn so his legs could carry him back to kneel at the AllFather's feet.

Lauren felt the power too. Xairn felt her freeze beside him. Her hand, already slimy from the noxious remains of the exploded *dravik,* began to slide from his grip as she turned toward his father.

"Yesss...Come to me, my bride...come..." The AllFather was calling her back, forcing her will to bend to his, luring her back to a living death, an existence of pain and madness and never ending suffering and agony.

"No!" At the thought of the female beside him—*his* female, being used in such a way, Xairn felt something growing inside him. A rage so fierce it was like a red curtain dropped over his vision, tinting everything a bloody crimson. *"No!"* he bellowed again, turning to face his father, his hands clenched into fists. "You shall not have her. Lauren is *mine!"*

The AllFather's voice dropped to a soft hiss, sounding reasonable and coaxing at the same time. "Come now, Xairn, thisss is asss it must be. The girl is the future of our race, our destiny. You know thisss."

"Lauren is *not* your destiny. And she's not your property to do with as you please." Xairn glared, his eyes never leaving his father's. "Here and now, I cut the ties that bind me to you. I never wish to see you again."

"But you *will* sssee me. Sssee me now. *Come to me, my ssson.*" The power was doubled, trebled, the drag of it like lead on Xairn's limbs. But this time he had more to fight for than just a pet. Rage and a power of his own filled him — something savage that had been sleeping, or had only just started to stir, suddenly woke fully within his chest.

"*NO!*" Bending, Xairn scooped Lauren into his arms. "I will die before I let you have her. And I will kill you if you threaten her again. I renounce you as my father and I renounce my race. For now and evermore *I am no longer Scourge.*"

Xairn felt the words of power leave him and gloried in the sense of rightness they gave him. He wasn't just saying this to hurt the AllFather, he had given his oath to the universe. It had gone out from him with a finality that could not be refuted or ignored. He had cut the ties that had bound him all his life — he truly was no longer Scourge.

His father said something else, but though Xairn felt the drag of his mental command, it couldn't control him. His heart, so long a cold and shriveled lump of carbon, was a glowing, beating star — a super nova in his chest. He was alive in a way he never had been before. Alive and filled with emotions he had been suppressing for a lifetime.

He wanted to rip the AllFather limb from limb and bathe in his blood. Wanted to throw back his head and howl like an animal scenting prey. But most of all, he wanted to take the woman in his arms right there, filling her with his cock as she writhed beneath him on the cold, hard floor while he pounded into her again and again as she screamed his name and…*No! No, get hold of yourself!*

Xairn shook his head, trying to force the disturbing feelings back, to hide them away and ignore them as he had been his entire life. But the door had been opened and there was no closing it—he was filled with urges he had never known before—urges he had sworn never to act on.

Must get Lauren out of here. Give her to the Kindred—keep her safe, away from me!

The AllFather's eyes glowed. "You feel it, do you not, my ssson? The need to hurt, to dominate, to *breed*. You can renounce your race if you like but those needs within you mark you as Ssscourge. They are your birthright and you cannot essscape them."

"No! I will never be like you—*never.*"

Turning, Xairn carried Lauren through the double doors and out into the long corridor that led to freedom. He had to give her to the Kindred warriors to take back with them as quickly as possible. He had to get her out of his sight.

Before he did something he would regret forever.

Chapter Thirty-five

"Stop for a minute. I need to take care of this." Deep staggered to a halt as soon as they were out of the Scourge Complex.

Kat stopped beside him at once. "How can I help?"

He made a face and she knew he was in pain, though she couldn't feel it the way she ought to. "Need you to...pull it out."

"But I thought you said...what about the bleeding?"

"Bleeding be damned—can't stand it anymore." He looked at Lock. "Hold me steady while she does it."

"Of course, Brother." Stepping forward, Lock pulled his twin close and locked his arms around Deep's broad chest. Then he looked at Kat. "Pull it out as quickly as you can. There's no sense prolonging the agony."

"Of course." Kat felt like she might be sick but she realized that she didn't have time for that luxury. *I wish Liv was here,* she thought, reaching for the handle of the black knife. *She'd know how to do this. I'm not a nurse!*

"Do it!" Deep said through gritted teeth.

Get on with it, girl! Stop stalling. Kat clenched her jaw and took a firm grip. "Here goes," she said grimly and yanked as hard as she could.

The curving black and rust-red blade slid out smoothly. As the final inch came out of Deep's side, he cried out and fell to his knees. Lock went down with him, holding him tight. When he looked up at Kat, there were tears in his brown eyes.

"I can't help him," he said hoarsely as the dark twin slumped in his arms. "I can't feel his pain—can't help him bear it."

"Never mind." Pressing a hand to his side, Deep somehow staggered to his feet again. It seemed to Kat like a superhuman effort—or a superKindred one, she supposed.

"I don't understand," she blurted, looking down at the hateful blade, still clutched in her fist. "How can you just go on like that? I thought even a scratch from one of these things was poison."

Deep's black eyes flashed. "I go on because I have no choice, little Kat. And as for the blade—it's not a *kusax*."

"It's not?" Kat examined it more closely. It still looked like something an evil orc would carry straight to Mordor, only now it was sticky with Deep's blood.

"No." Lock, who was still helping to support his brother, shook his head. "A *kusax* is much smaller than that and it has a short, five-sided blade that ends in a bright green tip. It's the tip that contains the poison—some say the AllFather has a throne made of the same metal."

Kat remembered Liv's description of the black metal throne etched in glowing, neon lines that the AllFather sat on in the Fathership. *That must be it,* she thought. *Maybe it's part of his power source or something.* "So…" She looked back up at Deep and down to the long, curving knife in her hand again. "Does this mean you'll be okay?"

"If we get him back to the Mother ship quickly. Twin Kindred have self-sealing internal organs. Come." Lock jerked his head in the direction of the beach. "We still have to get through the old battleground."

"But what about Lauren?" Kat asked. "We can't just leave her here."

"She and Xairn are right behind us," Lock said. "I saw them as we were leaving. Don't worry, they can meet us on the beach. Until then, Xairn will take care of her."

"How can you be sure?" Kat insisted as they began walking again. The old battlefield was in sight now—she could see some of the wrecked and abandoned ships littering the dusty, barren plain.

"Didn't you see the way he looked at her?" Deep shook his head. "Don't worry, Kat, he'll die before he lets her come to harm."

Kat thought they were trusting the big Scourge an awful lot on such a short acquaintance but then she remembered Lauren's words and the way she'd looked at Xairn. *Maybe it will be all right, after all,* she thought. *And we do need to get moving – need to get Deep back to the Mother ship. Even if the knife **wasn't** one of the poison kind – a kusax – it still nearly went right through him.* Looking down, she realized she was still clutching the bloody blade in one hand. She almost threw it away, but then she tightened her grip on it instead. They weren't safe on the ship yet and who knew what might happen between here and there?

"Come on, Brother, just a little bit further," Lock urged as Deep staggered, one hand pressed hard to his wounded side.

"I'm fine," Deep growled but he made no move to stop his twin when Lock looped an arm around him to give him support. Kat hoped he was all right as he claimed, but she couldn't help worrying. She wished again that she could tell what he was feeling—if she could still feel his emotions, she would have been able to tell if he was lying or not. *Maybe it will all be okay,* she thought hopefully. *We'll get back to the Mother ship and Sylvan can fix Deep up. We can find out why Lock and I can feel each other but not him. And get a shower and wash all this gunk off!*

She shivered in disgust at the feel of the now-drying goo on her back and hair. It must have been the remains of the AllFather's bubble—she wasn't sure. Whatever it was, it smelled worse than anything she could even imagine. She probably would have been happier having rat guts in her hair. Or roaches, or spiders, or pretty much anything else but this disgusting slimy jelly-like stuff.

They were almost all the way through the maze of dead and abandoned ships when she heard a hoarse shout behind them. The three of them turned to see Xairn striding toward them with Lauren held in his arms. He shouted something else, but he was still too far away to hear—just on the edge of the old battlefield.

"See?" Deep said as they stopped to watch the huge Scourge approach. "I told you he would protect her."

"He may be of the AllFather's bloodline, but I believe he must have some Kindred genes as well," Lock said thoughtfully, stepping forward.

"He certainly cares for his female like one of us." Deep sounded approving. "I wonder if his mother could have been one of the rare Scourge-born females? They say there were a few born before the race was decimated."

Xairn shouted again and this time Kat could hear him. "You must take Lauren with you," he said. "Back to your Mother ship. She cannot stay with me."

Kat frowned. The Scourge warrior sounded truly distressed. "Is there something wrong with her?" she yelled, running forward a few steps to meet them. "Is Lauren hurt?"

"No, but she must—"

But whatever else Xairn was about to say was suddenly cut off when a massive hand reached out from behind an abandoned ship and yanked Kat off her feet.

"Wha—?" she gasped as the hand spun her around. She looked up and up and up…into the face of the Alpha guard. But this time its eyes weren't the blank, empty black-on-black she'd come to expect. Instead, the pupils blazed crimson with malice. When the guard opened its mouth, a familiar voice came out.

"Die, sssweet little human," it hissed. "Die ssslowly and know that the daysss of your race are numbered. I will take sssuch revenge on the femalesss of your world asss hasss never been ssseen before."

A knife suddenly appeared in its grip—a tiny one, so small it looked like toy in the Alpha guard's huge hand. The blade was strange, black and many sided, and the tip…the tip was a bright, poisonous green.

It all happened so quickly that Kat had no time to react. She wanted to raise the curving black blade she still carried to defend herself, but her arm seemed frozen in place. Somewhere to her right she heard shouting as the tiny sharp, knife came down, the shining, deadly point coming closer and closer…

And then Deep and Lock barreled into the massive guard, knocking him to the ground. The knife flew out of his hand. Kat tried to see where it went but then she was knocked over too, her legs pinned under the tangle of bodies.

She hit the ground hard, knocking all the wind out of her and a sharp stone sliced into her cheek. *Ouch! Can't…breathe…* Gasping for air, she blacked out for a minute.

When she came to, Deep and Lock were kneeling over her, worried expressions on both their faces. Behind them, the body of the massive Alpha guard was lying completely still. Vaguely, Kat could see the handle of the black blade she'd been carrying since she pulled it out of Deep protruding from its chest. Was it finally dead? *God, I hope so!* She struggled to sit up but four large hands pressed her back down gently.

"Are you all right, my lady?" Lock asked anxiously.

"Did it touch you? Did the blade of the *kusax* scratch you?" Deep demanded at the same time.

"I...I'm fine, you guys. Let...let me up," she demanded breathlessly. She rolled onto her side with some help from Lock and propped herself up on one elbow, still trying to catch her breath.

Deep, one hand still pressed to his wounded side, scanned the area alertly. "Where did the *kusax* go?"

"I don't know. I saw it fly out of the guard's hand—I don't know where it landed. Ouch!" Kat winced at the stinging in her cheek. She put a hand to her face and her fingertips came away bloody. "Damn, that was one sharp rock."

"What's wrong?" Deep was by her side at once.

"Nothing." Kat shook her head, brushing her long hair, still matted with the AllFather's slime, out of the way. "I just got cut with a rock when I fell. I'm okay though, it's just a scrape."

"A rock, you say?" Lock sounded so grim that she sat up and looked at him.

"I guess so, why?"

"Because." Reaching down, he grabbed something off the ground that she hadn't seen earlier—something which must have been covered by her hair.

"No," Deep whispered and there was real horror in his voice. "Oh please, Goddess...*no.*"

Kat already knew what she was going to see, but she couldn't help looking anyway. Gripped in Lock's big fist was the tiny, sharp dagger the Alpha Guard had been aiming at her. On its poisonous, bright green tip was a single ruby droplet of blood — *her* blood.

She was going to die.

* * * * *

"What are they doing? What's wrong?" Lauren strained to see what was going on with Kat and her two Kindred warriors, but they had gone out of sight and there were several abandoned ships in the way of her line of vision.

"I don't know," Xairn said grimly. "But you *must* go with them."

Lauren looked at him uneasily. Both of them were covered in the slimy gook from the AllFather's bubble but aside from that, he looked...*different* somehow. His red-on-black eyes were blazing — it was as though someone had lit a fire within him and it was consuming him from the inside out. *No, not just a fire,* she thought in alarm. *An inferno. God, he looks like he's about to explode.* "Xairn," she said tentatively. "Are you all right?"

"No," he said shortly. He shifted and she could feel his hard muscles bunching with tension.

Lauren wasn't sure what to say. "Am I too heavy? Do you need me to get down? I can walk now."

"Of course not — you're very light." For the first time he seemed to focus on her totally. "And this is the last time I'll ever get to hold you," he added in a low voice. "I would rather not put you down until I have to."

"All right then," Lauren said softly. "I don't mind. I'm just worried about you."

He shook his head and the distance returned to his eyes. "I'll be fine. I just need to be certain you're safe before I leave."

"But I don't *want* you to leave," Lauren protested. "I...I don't like the idea of never seeing you again."

"It's for the best." Xairn began walking rapidly in the direction they'd last seen Kat and her Kindred warriors. "It is better if I don't see you—safer."

"How could it be safer for us to be apart? I don't understand."

He closed his eyes briefly, a look of almost agony passing over his strong features. "I would rather not explain. I don't want your memory of me to be...tainted."

"If you're thinking I'll hold your father against you, you're wrong," she said quietly. "People don't choose their parents. You can't help what he's like or what he did."

"It's not that." He shook his head. "Please do not ask me to explain. I don't wish you to think me a monster."

"A monster?" Lauren looked at him in shock. "Why would I ever think that? How could—"

A sudden sound behind him made both their heads turn.

"Oh my God!" Lauren put a hand to her mouth. "The guards—they're back!"

It was true. Two of the AllFather's immense guards were closing in on them rapidly. Only their great size and bulk kept them from running faster.

"Do you still have the stunner I gave you?" Xairn asked, backing away from the approaching guards warily. "If you do, shoot. I can't reach my own weapon without putting you down and that would not be safe at this moment."

Lauren fumbled in the folds of the black cloak. She'd hidden the tiny weapon in a small pocket sewn on the inside but now she couldn't seem to find it. "I can't...can't find it. God, Xairn, what are we going to do?"

"I don't know." He turned his head to look behind them briefly. "But here comes another one."

"I thought they were all dead!" Lauren looked at the approaching guards fearfully. "Or at least disabled. How can they just get up and walk after the way we shot them?"

"They're probably being animated by my father—he'll stop at nothing to get you back."

Lauren's heart froze in her chest. "No! Oh, no—please, Xairn, don't let him have me!"

"Didn't you hear me before?" His deep voice was fierce. "I'll die before I give you up. Damn it to the seven hells, where are those Kindred?" He craned his neck, obviously looking for Kat and her men, but there was nothing to see but junked and abandoned ships. And in the mean time, the three guards were closing in. One of them opened its lipless mouth and the voice of the AllFather filled the air.

"Come back, my ssson. Return the girl to me and all ssshall be forgiven. You ssshall rule at my ssside as you were always meant to do. Come back and bring my bride..."

"Xairn—they're getting closer!" Lauren clutched his shoulders—they were being surrounded. They were trapped.

Xairn swore blackly in a harsh, guttural language. He looked at Lauren, frowning fiercely. "I am sorry but there is no more time to find your human friend—you'll have to come with me."

Turning, he jogged to the nearest silver ship and slapped his palm to its side. "Open!" he shouted and then repeated the command in another foreign language.

A hatchway slid to one side smoothly, revealing an opening into the ship. Xairn boosted Lauren in and then climbed in after, just as the first of the AllFather's guards reached them.

"My ssson," it began in the AllFather's high, evil voice.

"No longer." Xairn kicked the possessed guard in the jaw, knocking it to the ground. Another was already coming but by then he had closed the hatch and was giving the ship directions in the same, foreign tongue he'd spoken in earlier.

Lauren scrambled into a seat which was much too large for her—it seemed to have been built for people Xairn's size, not humans. Xairn took the seat beside her and began working the controls. "Strap in," he directed. "This will not be a smooth flight."

"All right." Lauren was fumbling with the unfamiliar, too-large safety harness when something big and heavy thumped against her side of the ship. A dent appeared in the metal just beside her thigh. "Oh!" she gasped, jumping away. "What—?"

"They're trying to get in." Xairn was still concentrating grimly on the control panel. "Don't worry, they won't. The Kindred build their ships well."

He did something else to the controls and they started to rise straight up into the air. There was another mighty *thump* which made the small ship sway alarmingly in mid-air, and then they were apparently above the reach of even the massive guards.

They rose higher and higher and Lauren watched in the viewscreen as the dark, polluted planet receded into the distance. When it was no larger than a dirty tennis ball hanging in space, Xairn held the ship still for a moment and sat in silence, staring at it.

Though his face was impassive, Lauren thought she understood what he must be feeling. Reaching out, she rested her hand lightly on his knee. "I'm sorry," she said softly. "It must be hard—saying goodbye to your home planet."

"That place was never my home." Xairn's voice was cold but when he looked at her his eyes were burning. "I have no home. No people. No father. I have nothing."

"That's all right." She tried to smile. "You can come home with me—if you want."

"Eventually." His voice was remote. "But I'm afraid it will be some time before you see Earth again."

"What do you mean?" She tried to keep the fear out of her voice but he was acting so strangely it scared her. "Why—?"

"You will understand in time." He looked down at her hand, still resting on his knee. "I thought I asked you before not to touch me."

"I'm sorry." Lauren removed her hand hastily. "I just thought...I wanted to comfort you."

"I need no comfort. And I do not want your hands on me. It isn't safe."

"Isn't safe? What do you mean?"

He turned his head to look at her and she thought again that his eyes looked like they were on fire. The savage look on his face was like nothing she had ever seen before. There was nothing but hunger in his gaze. No compassion, no pity...just the naked desire to devour. "Please, Xairn," she said, her voice trembling. "Please, you're scaring me."

He took a deep breath and the fire in his eyes died down a little. Some of the tension eased from his broad shoulders and the hunger left his face. "Forgive me, Lauren." He shook his head. "But I wish very much that you were not with me right now. It would have been better if you had gone with the Kindred and their female. Better and far safer."

"I'm safe with *you*." Lauren touched his arm for emphasis and then remembered he didn't want her to and drew back. "It's all right," she said, holding his eyes with hers. "Everything is going to be all right because *I trust you*. And I know you'll keep your promise to see me safely home."

"I did promise that, didn't I?" Xairn pressed a hand to his eyes briefly and took another deep breath. "Yes, I did. And I will keep my word. Even if it kills me to do so."

Lauren didn't understand what he meant by that, but as the small silver ship turned away from his home world, she *did* understand that it would be a while before she saw Earth again.

She didn't know where Xairn was taking her, but it wasn't home—not yet.

Chapter Thirty-six

"Am I going to die now?" Kat tried to keep her voice even and nonchalant but she couldn't help the little tremble that crept in as she stared at the poisoned knife in Lock's hand. "Because I don't *feel* any different."

"The effects of the *kusax* are not immediate," Lock said in a low voice. He threw the dagger away with a quick, jerky motion, like a man getting rid of a deadly snake. "But we should not speak of that now. We need to get back to the ship."

"Lock's right." Deep spoke slowly, a stricken expression on his face. "We...we need medical attention. We must go."

"All right, let's go then." Kat got unsteadily to her feet, shaking off the helping hands of both brothers. She wanted to know that she could still get up and move around on her own—wanted to feel that she was still all right, no matter what they said about the stupid Scourge knife that had scratched her. She headed in the direction of the beach and then stopped. "Wait a minute, what about Lauren?"

There was a suddenly muted roaring sound and a rush of wind. From further down the abandoned battlefield a small silver Kindred ship rose into the air. It hovered for a moment and then shot straight up, disappearing into the smoggy sky.

"There's your answer," Deep said, pointing. "Xairn has gone and he's taken Lauren with him."

"How can you be sure he took her with him?" Kat demanded. "What if she's still here, wandering around in this horrible place?"

"He would not have left her," Lock said quietly. "He loves her, my lady—could you not tell?"

"I know that *Lauren* seemed to be very fond of *him*..." Kat frowned. "But Xairn's still a Scourge. And I don't know if I could tell that *he* loved *her*."

"His heart was given," Deep said. "It was clear—at least to another male who has given his heart."

"And how would you know? When did you ever give anything to anyone but pain?" Lock asked but his voice was more weary than angry.

Kat held out her hands. "Don't start guys, okay? Let's just do a quick search to make sure Lauren's not here and *then* we can assume she went with Xairn. All right?"

"A *very* quick search." Lock frowned. "We need to get you home, my lady. To see if there is anything...anything Sylvan can do for you."

Kat put a hand on her hip. "Do me a favor and stop acting like I have one foot in the grave, okay? For your information I feel perfectly *fine*. In fact I don't have a bit of pain and—"

At that moment the alpha guard sat straight up and began laughing. The black knife blade still protruded from the center of its massive chest—there was no way it could still be alive. But somehow it was—or at least it was moving. The high, eerie cackle that came from its dead, lipless mouth froze the blood in Kat's veins.

"Of course you do not have pain yet, sssweet little human," the thing said. "That comesss later, after the weaknesss has ssset in. After the green linesss reach your heart and delve deep to find your very sssoul..."

"Oh my God!" Kat gasped as the reanimated Alpha Guard began to get up. "It's alive. How the hell—?"

"The AllFather is directing it, just as he was before." Quickly, Lock scooped her into his arms. "Shoot it, Deep, and let's be on our way. We've overstayed our welcome here."

"I think you're right." Pulling his weapon, Deep took careful aim and released a bright red beam of energy.

The deadly laser blast took off the monstrous Alpha guard's head as easily as a knife slicing through cheese. It fell from the broad shoulders and rolled on the ground at their feet, the eyes still blinking and the lipless mouth still laughing. "Die," it whispered, so faintly Kat could barely hear it. "Sssoon you ssshall die, little human...sssoon...sssoon..." Then the guard's body fell to its knees and collapsed slowly, its dead hands still reaching out, the thick fingers grasping the air.

"Crap!" A chill swept over her and Kat felt like she might be sick. "That's...that's the creepiest thing I've ever seen. I can't believe it just kept *moving* and *talking* like that even after..." She shook her head, unable to finish.

"Come on. Let's get the hell out of here!" Deep led the way, his hand still pressed to his side.

"But *Lauren!*" Kat protested. "You promised we'd look for her!"

Lock turned reluctantly and then they saw three more of the massive guards lumbering toward them. "I'm sorry, my lady," he told her. "But we must go now. You and Deep are both wounded. I cannot protect you both and fight off three more guards on my own."

They ran through the ships on the battlefield and crossed the polluted beach, the oily brown sand crunching under the twins' booted feet. The guards behind them were gaining rapidly, probably because none of them was A—wounded or B—carrying a plus-sized woman, Kat thought, staring over Lock's shoulder as he ran. Deep staggered along beside them, his face white and one hand fisted at his side. There was blood leaking down his leg in a dark rivulet. God, she hoped all this running wasn't making his wound worse, though she didn't see how it could possibly be helping any. She still didn't even know how he could be functioning after receiving such a serious injury—did Twin Kindred have extra special healing ability? Lock had said something about self sealing organs but what did that even mean?

Finally they reached their ship and piled inside. "I'll pilot," Lock said, sliding into the driver's seat. For once, Deep said nothing. He only nodded and settled himself carefully in one of the other seats. Kat did the same and started to buckle herself in. She felt terrible about Lauren but Lock and Deep didn't seem overly concerned. *Maybe they're right,* she comforted herself. *Maybe Xairn took her with him and he's so in love with her that he'll take care of her no matter what happens.*

She hoped so. It was going to be really hard to face Liv and Sophie and tell them that she had found their long-lost cousin...and then lost her again. Then again, it was going to be hard to tell them the other news too.

But surely I won't die — not of a tiny little scratch! She touched her wounded cheek gingerly with her fingertips and winced at the sting.

"I'm sorry."

Kat looked up to see Deep watching her with a look of remorse in his black eyes. "What?" she asked.

"I said I'm sorry. All this is my fault. If I hadn't insisted we come here, none of it would have happened. You wouldn't have been cut and—"

"That's true," Kat interrupted, refusing to discuss her impending doom. "But we were looking for traces of Lauren too, so the mission wasn't a complete wash." She frowned. "I still don't understand what happened in the psychic knife though."

"I understand," Lock said grimly as he worked the controls. "The knife is made to cut bonds between people, but it only cuts the bonds the operator stipulates. When Deep set the controls, he didn't program the machine to cut the soul bond between the two of us and you, my lady. Instead he—"

"Cut the bond between the two of us and himself," Kat finished, understanding. "So now you and I are bonded but neither one of us has any connection to Deep."

"That's true." Deep nodded. "I thought...I believed that the two of you would be better off together. Without my interference."

Lock turned to give his brother a fierce look. "That's not right or natural and you know it, Deep. The Goddess formed Twin Kindred to share a female—I never wanted the lady Kat all to myself. I wanted to *share* her with you. And now..." His throat worked convulsively and he shook his head. "And now I don't know what will happen to us. Any of us. Because I cannot live without the two of you and both of you are wounded."

"It's going to be okay. We're going to get through this." Kat tried to sound a lot more positive than she felt. "Once we get back to the Mother ship, Sylvan will patch us up physically. And as for the bonding and soul stuff, we can always go back to Mother L'rin, right? I mean, I know she was pretty pissed at us last time we saw her but surely she won't turn us away when we explain what happened."

"Maybe she *can* help." Deep sounded hopeful. "Hasn't she treated *kusax* wounds before?"

"I don't remember." Lock stared straight ahead at the viewscreen. "But I think it would be best for us to contact her as soon as possible to ask."

"There, see—all better." Kat tried to smile at them but neither brother returned her positive expression. She felt a steady wave of *worry/fear/helplessness* coming from Lock and from Deep she still felt...nothing. *God, I never thought I would miss having his feelings in my head! Now I just wish I could tell what was going on behind those black eyes of his.* But whatever it was, Deep wasn't telling.

It will be all right, Kat told herself uneasily. *We've been through a lot but surely we can fix this, like we fixed everything else. We're all going to be okay...aren't we?*

She hoped so. Oh God, she certainly hoped so.

Chapter Thirty-seven

"I'm afraid you and Olivia need to prepare yourselves, *Talana*." Sylvan's face looked so grave that Sophie's heart skipped a beat.

"Prepare ourselves? For what?" Liv demanded.

"I've examined Kat thoroughly and done everything I could for her. But..." Sylvan hesitated so long that Sophie couldn't wait any more.

"But what? What's wrong with her?"

She was afraid to hear the answer. The minute Deep and Lock's ship had returned to the docking bay, they had requested immediate medical assistance. Deep had been badly wounded and was being examined by one of Sylvan's colleagues. But Kat, well, she'd *looked* all right when they wheeled her into the med station strapped to one of the floating Kindred stretchers. She'd even smiled at them and given a big 'thumbs up.' She'd had some weird stuff matted in her hair and on the back of her clothes but Sophie hadn't seen any blood or obvious wounds. Well, other than a tiny red scratch on her cheekbone, but that was nothing. So what could possibly be wrong?

Sylvan took a deep breath. "Kat has been wounded with a *kusax*."

"A what?" Olivia gave him a blank look. "What's that?"

"A weapon of the Scourge—it poisons the soul."

"The *soul?*" Liv raised her eyebrows. "Seriously?"

"Just because you can't see it on any kind of scan or medical exam doesn't mean it doesn't exist, Olivia," Sylvan said quietly. "And that is precisely why this kind of poisoning is so...difficult to treat."

"But there is a treatment—right? *Right?*" Sophie asked anxiously.

"There has to be," Liv said. "Poison is curable if you catch it in time and they just came back an hour ago. So what's the antidote?"

Sylvan shook his head reluctantly, his ice blue eyes sorrowful. "I'm sorry, Olivia, there is none."

"No antidote?" Sophie fumbled for her sister's hand and gripped it hard for support. "Sylvan, please don't tell me what I think you're going to tell me. Please don't say that Kat is going to...to..."

"To die," he finished for her softly. "I'm so sorry, *Talana*. But there's no cure. Nothing I can do."

"I don't accept that!" Liv declared. "I *can't*. The Kindred have an incredibly advanced system of medicine, Sylvan. *Surely* there must be something you haven't tried."

He shook his head. "Unfortunately, this is not the first case of soul poisoning I've treated—or tried to treat. It starts in the soul but because your spirit is anchored to your body, eventually it affects everything. The symptoms are always the same—at first the victim feels nothing. Then the place where he—or in this case she—was wounded begins to show curling dark green lines, just below the surface of the skin. That's the poison working its way from the soul into the body and ultimately to the heart. As the lines progress, the symptoms progress as well. Weakness, dizziness..."

"And then what?" Sophie demanded.

Sylvan sighed reluctantly. "And finally intense pain and death. But once she reaches that stage there are drugs we can give her —"

"To ease her pain? To help her die? No!" Liv shook her head emphatically. "Kat's our friend — our *best* friend, Sylvan. And she's a young, healthy woman. Don't start talking that hospice shit to me — don't you *dare*."

"There has to be another way — something we can do. There *has* to." Tears were rolling down Sophie's cheeks now but she couldn't seem to stop them. *"Please, Sylvan!"*

Sylvan looked almost as upset as she felt. "Talana —"

"There is something — at least we hope there is." Lock came up behind them, and despite her distress, Sophie thought the light twin looked worse than she had ever seen him. His dark green uniform shirt and black pants were stained and dirty and the expression on his handsome features was one of weariness beyond endurance.

"What? What is it?" She and Liv both spoke eagerly at the same time.

"Deep has gone back to Twin Moons to beg help from Mother L'rin. She healed Kat the first time, we have hopes that she may be able to do it again."

"What?" Sylvan frowned. "Deep has already left the med station? I was told he was gravely injured."

Lock shrugged. "You know how quickly we Twin Kindred heal — Deep was already on the mend, even before we left the planet." He cleared his throat. "It is his heart, not his body, that is broken now. He took a quick shower and left — against the advice of your colleague, I might add."

"Twin Kindred do heal well and cleanly," Sylvan admitted grudgingly. "You're especially lucky your internal organs are self-sealing after any kind of blunt trauma or puncture wound. But I still would have liked to have a look at him myself."

"We felt there wasn't time to waste." Lock spoke in a low voice and nodded at the entrance to the med center where Kat was resting in one of the private rooms. "If there is a cure for soul poisoning at all, it would be better to apply it early rather than to wait until the disease progressed to the...the later stages." He coughed and looked away but not before Sophie saw the glint of tears in his brown eyes.

"True," Sylvan said. "Well then, please let me know what he finds out."

"Can we see Kat now?" Liv demanded.

"Certainly." He nodded gravely.

Liv was already striding toward the med center entrance but Sophie hung back. "Does...does she know? About the poisoning? About how there's no...no known cure?" Her throat was so tight she could barely get the words out.

"She knows," Sylvan said quietly. "I don't believe in keeping such things from patients." He pulled Sophie into a tight embrace and buried his face in her hair. Softly, he spoke through their link. *"I'm sorry, Talana. So sorry there isn't more I can do. I know how very dear Kat is to you and Olivia."*

"She's more than a friend—she's like our sister." Sophie wanted to cry again but she was afraid she would never stop if she did. "I know you're trying," she said aloud, kissing Sylvan on the cheek. "I won't blame you if...if... I won't blame you. No matter what happens."

He drew back, searching her eyes for a long moment. "But I'll blame myself. I want so much to make you happy—I'd do anything I could to keep you from pain. Anything."

"Don't. Don't, Sylvan. I know." Sophie kissed him again. "I have to go, Liv is waiting for me."

He nodded. "Go then. I'll be here if you need me."

"I know." She tried to smile but couldn't quite manage it. She was still swiping tears from her eyes when she caught up to Olivia, who was hovering just outside the closed door of Kat's room.

"I don't know what to say." Liv's voice, so strong a moment ago, was wavery and uncertain.

"I don't know either," Sophie admitted. "I just...what can you say about something like this?"

"You *could* say, 'Hi Kat, welcome home.'" The door slid open to reveal Kat standing there with one hand on her ample hip and a little smile on her face. Her long red hair was damp — obviously she'd just gotten out of the shower. Sophie couldn't see a thing wrong with her except for a tiny green half-circle that looked like the start of a shamrock tattoo on her right cheekbone.

"Hi, Kat-woman." Olivia looked at her uncertainly. "Are you okay?"

"Peachy, aside from the fact that I'm supposed to die in the next twenty-four to forty-eight hours." Kat's voice was perfectly calm but there was something wild in her eyes — a despair that Sophie could see even if their friend wasn't willing to speak it out loud.

"Kat," she choked, holding out her arms. "Oh, Kat..."

Suddenly all three of them were hugging and crying, right there in the hallway of the med center. Sophie held her friend tight, feeling like if she could just hold her close enough, she might never have to let go.

Surprisingly, Kat was the one to recover first. Sniffing, she pulled back from the little huddle of misery they had formed and blotted her eyes on the sleeve of the hospital gown she was wearing.

The Kindred version of the gown was made of much nicer fabric and came in a variety of stylish colors but unfortunately still gaped open in the back.

"Okay, that's enough of that," she said, wiping her eyes one last time. "I don't have time to waste getting all emotional."

"Sorry," Sophie whispered, blotting her own eyes. "I just...I can't believe it. It can't be true."

"It doesn't feel real to me either." Kat lifted her chin. "But I guess it is. Sylvan's the best and if he says there's nothing they can do..."

"Don't give up hope yet," Liv said, sniffing fiercely. "We just saw Lock and he said Deep was on his way to Twin Moons to find Mother L'rin. She healed you before—I'm sure she can help this time, too."

"Yeah, that's what we were talking about on the way up here." Kat frowned. "But should Deep be going such a long distance after the wound he got? I mean, you should have *seen* the knife he got stuck with. It was practically as long as my arm."

"Lock said he felt he was healed well enough to travel," Sophie said. "And Sylvan said something about the Twin Kindred having self healing or self sealing organs or something, I think. Anyway, Lock said they didn't want to waste any time in case...well, you know."

"I know." Kat nodded.

"I don't understand why *Lock* didn't just go and let Deep stay here and recuperate," Olivia said.

"He probably wants to apologize in person," Kat murmured.

"Apologize? For what?" Liv said. "Was it his fault you..." She motioned to the tiny green mark on Kat's cheek.

"Oh no, that was just bad luck." Kat swallowed. "Really, *really* bad luck. But Mother L'rin was extremely angry at us the last time we saw her—especially at Deep because he was the one who insisted we cut our bond."

"And did you?" Sophie asked. "Did you get it cut?"

"In a way." Kat sighed. "Look, it's a long story and I don't want to tell it here. Hang on while I get dressed—I had Lock go get me some clothes. Just give me a second and then we can go back to my suite and talk."

"Wait a minute." Liv frowned. "You can't just leave AMA, Kat."

"Watch me," Kat said grimly. "You think I'm going to spend my last day or days cooped up in here wearing a hospital jonnie? I don't *think* so. If I'm going to die I need chocolate STAT. And I want to wear my favorite dress—you know, the green one I spent a fortune on and keep in the back of the closet? I've never dared to wear it out because it's too low cut so I feel like my boobs are falling out of it. But I'm going for it now. And I also want to...to..." Her voice began to waver. "Oh hell, I want to talk to my Grandma. I think...I guess I'd better warn her what's going on. What's going to happen."

"Kat..." Sophie and Liv reached for her again but she shook her head and took a deep breath.

"Nope, not gonna cry. I am *not* going to spend the time I have left whining." She squared her shoulders. "Hang on, I'll be out in a minute and then we're going to paint the town red. Or the Mother ship. Or whatever."

As the door shut behind her, Sophie looked at her sister. Olivia shrugged. What could they do but comply with what might be Kat's last request? *It's so like her,* Sophie thought, listening to the determined sounding humming coming from behind the door as

Kat got dressed. *Not to complain or waste time crying. She's so much braver than I could ever be.* It was one of the reasons she loved Kat—why she and Liv *both* loved her. But to see her friend's courage tested in such an extreme way was almost beyond what Sophie could stand.

Liv must have seen the look on her face because she squeezed Sophie's hand. "I know," she whispered. "It's hard."

"It's *awful*," Sophie whispered back. "Poor Kat."

"She doesn't want us to pity her." Liv sniffed and straightened her shoulders. "So we won't. We're going to make this the best time she ever had—however long we have to do it."

"You're right." Sophie blotted her own eyes and tried to be brave. After all, how could they deny their friend's request to have a little fun before she died? *But please, God, don't really let her die. Don't take Kat away from us,* she prayed fervently. *Let Deep find the solution, let him bring back hope that everything is going to be okay.*

Then Kat came out of her room, dressed and smiling and Sophie forced herself to smile back. Everything was going to be all right because it *had* to be. Losing Kat was unthinkable so she wasn't going to think about it.

Not yet. Not until she had to.

Chapter Thirty-eight

"I am sorry, Warrior, but I can do nothing for you." Mother L'rin stood wreathed in the pink and gold and green plants of the Healing Garden, looking almost like one of them herself. She had agreed to see him on short notice which was good since Deep hadn't intended to wait for anyone. He'd folded space and gotten back to his home planet in record time—less than an hour from when he'd left the Mother ship. And now it seemed his entire trip had all been in vain.

"Please." He struggled to keep his voice even. "Please, Mother L'rin, I'll do anything. *Anything*. Look..." He tore off his shirt, baring his back for her. "Use the whip. Lash me until my skin peals from my body—I don't care. Only please *heal* her."

She spread her wrinkled hands. "I have already told you—I cannot."

Deep wanted to tear his hair in frustration. "Please don't punish Kat for *my* arrogance. I know I have been disrespectful and rude and foolish..."

"You have been all those things." Mother L'rin nodded gravely. "But worse than anything else, you have blasphemed against the Goddess. It was *she* who put you and your brother together with the lady Kat. It was *her* will you broke when you cut the bond she had forged between the three of you."

"Then I'll go to the sacred grove," Deep began pacing wildly. "I'll get on my knees and I'll pray for forgiveness."

"You may do that if you wish and I am certain that the Goddess will forgive you—she is merciful in all things," the old healer said quietly. "However, that does not mean she will heal your lady. Some things cannot be undone, Deep."

"But there has to be a way. There *has* to." He fell to his knees before her. "Please, Mother L'rin—you healed her before. I know you can heal her again. I am *begging* you."

"*I* did not heal her," she corrected him gently. "*You* did. You and Lock. By forging the soul bond with her in the first place."

"And then we cut it." Deep slumped back on his heels. "Or I should say, *I* cut it. Or insisted on having it cut."

"That you did." Mother L'rin nodded. "There is nothing you can do for soul poisoning but dilute the poison. If you and Lock both were still bonded to the Lady Kat, you might have been able to save her by completing the bond and each taking a little of the taint into yourselves."

Deep felt like an iron fist was gripping his heart. "So...we might have saved her if I had not cut the bond between us?"

"It is not certain but you would have had a chance. Now, I fear...there is none. No chance."

"No chance," Deep echoed. "Gods, what a fool I am! In trying to save her I have damned her instead. Oh, Kat..." Rage and frustration rose within him along with a grief too terrible to be born. He had condemned the woman he loved to die. Then he had a new fear. "But Lock still *is* bonded to her. Does...does that mean they both will die?"

Mercifully, Mother L'rin shook her head. "If what you have told me is true, the bond between them is not complete. And it never can be."

Deep frowned. "Why not? Other than the fact of Kat being...being poisoned?"

"The poison cannot seep though an incomplete or partial bond," the old healer said. "And a Twin Kindred cannot form a complete bond on his own without his brother. Be at peace, Deep—you will not lose your twin as well as your lady."

"I've already lost him. As surely as I've lost Kat. Lock hates me now and I don't blame him." Deep looked down at his hands. "Gods, how could I have been so stupid? So...so..."

"Prideful," Mother L'rin finished for him. "You chose to withdraw yourself from the will of the Goddess. You refused to trust her when she brought a new female into your life."

"You didn't see her lying there," Deep said in a low voice. "Miranda. Just lying there, her eyes open, staring at nothing. Dead. And all because of me."

"I know about your past." Mother's L'rin's voice was unexpectedly gentle. "It was a tragedy. But far sadder is the fact that you have cut yourself off so thoroughly that you could not see the lady Kat for what she truly is—a courageous female who would never take her own life."

"She may wish to if the soul poisoning progresses much farther," Deep said grimly. "I'm told the pain can be intense." He pressed the heel of his hand to his eyes. "And it's all my doing. Don't you see, Mother? This is why I wanted to cut her from me in the first place—to spare her pain. But my plan backfired and made things worse. So much *worse.*"

"I'm sorry there is nothing I can do for you or for that sweet child you and Lock both care for so much." Mother L'rin touched his shoulder gently. "Go home and make your peace with her and with your brother before the end."

"Neither Kat or Lock is going to want to make peace with me." Lock took a deep breath and stood up. "I bring them nothing but tragedy and pain—as I have always done."

"You are a dark twin," Mother L'rin said. "Your path is not the easy one, Deep."

"No, it is not." Slowly he turned to go. "I have been the worst kind of fool. Truly, I should be the one who is dying—not my little Kat. If I could give my life for hers, I would."

"It is not for you to say who lives and who dies," Mother L'rin said. "That is a task for the Goddess."

"Maybe so," Deep murmured. "But even the Goddess must recognize justice when she sees it." He knew now what he had to do. He might not be able to heal Kat or stop her demise, but at least he could make a proper atonement for the role he had played in her death. It was only right.

Chapter Thirty-nine

"I'm sorry, Grandma. Really sorry." Kat wiped away a tear that she couldn't help shedding. As much as she was determined to stay positive, it was impossible to tell the woman who had raised her that she was about to die without tearing up.

"And you're sure you can't come back to Earth and see me?" Her grandmother asked in a quavering voice. She was crying too but also oddly calm.

She's still in shock, Kat thought. *She can't really believe it. Well that makes two of us.*

"I'm sorry Mrs. O'Connor, I know you want to see Kat but she needs to stay here on the Mother ship," Liv answered for her. "She needs to have access to the special drugs that will help when she…when the poison…drugs that help," she ended lamely.

Grandma nodded her silver-haired head. "I understand. And if you truly have such a short time, I won't keep you. But I will say this — I love you, Kat. More than I can say."

"I love you too, Grandma. Thanks for always being there for me after Mom and Dad split up."

"They love you too, you know — your parents," Grandma said. "They just never knew how to show it."

That's because they were too busy hating each other to show that they loved me. But Kat didn't say it aloud — there was no point in bringing up bad memories at this point. "You tell them what's happening and that I love them, okay?" she said.

Her grandmother nodded. "I don't know how but…yes, I'll try."

"Thanks, Grandma." Kat felt like she was about to burst into tears and she was afraid if she really started bawling, she wouldn't be able to stop. She didn't want to spend her last two days having a pity party. "I, uh, think our time is up," she lied gently. "There are other people waiting to use the viewing room."

"Of course." Her Grandmother blew her a kiss. "Remember, Kat, I'll always love you, no matter what."

"Thanks Grandma. Goodbye." Kat watched as her grandmother's image faded to a single bright dot in the middle of the viewscreen and then went completely black. Olivia, sitting on her right hand looked grim and Sophie, on her left, was openly sobbing. "Okay, guys, come on," she said with an effort. "Let's get going. We can't paint the town red of we're crying our eyes out."

"I'm sorry," Sophie whispered brokenly, trying to control her tears. "I just...don't want to lose you, Kat."

"I don't want to lose me either," Kat said grimly. "But I'm not lost yet so if you don't mind —"

Suddenly the viewscreen popped back to life. "Forgive me for interrupting your privacy," said the Blood Kindred warrior, whose face had appeared on the screen. "But there is an incoming call for Miss Waterhouse from a woman who says she is your aunt. Do you care to accept it?"

"Oh my God! Aunt Abby! That detective must have told her what we said about Lauren." Sophie turned to Liv. "Should we take it?"

Liv frowned. "It's likely to take a little while and we might not have much time to, er, have fun. Maybe we should ask her to call back later."

"No." Kat swiped at her eyes and shook her head. "Take the call. I want to talk to her."

"All right, if you're sure…" Liv looked up at the Blood Kindred communications officer. "Fine, we'll take it."

"As you wish." His image disappeared to be immediately replaced by the distraught face of Liv and Sophie's Aunt Abby.

"Detective Rast told me that Lauren's been taken by the Scourge," she said without preamble. "He said you knew all along. How could you lie to me, Olivia, Sophia? How *could* you?"

"We didn't want to," Sophie said at once. "But we thought it might be easier for you to just think she was missing rather than to know…to know…"

"That the Scourge had her," Liv finished for her. "Aunt Abby, we're sorry, really we are. We thought not knowing would be better than, well, knowing."

"And you're sure they have her?" Aunt Abby looked almost wild. "Truly certain?"

"Beyond the shadow of a doubt," Liv said quietly. "I'm sorry."

"They don't have her any more." Kat spoke for the first time, stepping forward. "At least, the AllFather doesn't."

"What do you mean? What do you know?" Liv and Sophie's aunt demanded wildly.

"I don't know exactly where she is right now but I saw Lauren just a few hours ago and she was fine," Kat assured her. "She hadn't been molested or abused in any way—just held prisoner."

"But where? Where are they holding her?"

"She was on the Scourge home world when I saw her." Kat shifted uncomfortably. "But I *think* she escaped." She wished again that they could have made a more thorough search for Lauren before leaving the deserted planet.

"You *think?* So then she'll be coming home soon?" The hope in Aunt Abby's eyes—the same clear amber as Lauren's—nearly broke Kat's heart.

"I don't know," she admitted. "I do know she had a protector— one of the Scourge was taking care of her, making sure she was safe and no one hurt her. We...had to leave the planet in a hurry but we saw another ship take off right before we went. I *think* he and Lauren must have been aboard."

"But will he bring her home? Will I see her again?" Aunt Abby demanded.

Kat bit her lip. "I wish I could answer your questions but I really can't. All I know is that Lauren seemed safe and well when I saw her and she did say that Xairn—the Scourge who was keeping her safe—had promised to take her home."

Aunt Abby took a deep breath and nodded. "All right, thank you..."

"Kat," Kat supplied.

"Thank you, Kat. At least I know she was well and healthy a few hours ago. If only I knew where she was and if she was heading home..." She blotted her eyes and looked at Sophie and Liv. "If you find out anything else will you please, *please* let me know, girls? Lauren is my daughter, I'd like to be kept in the loop."

"Of course, Aunt Abby." Olivia looked chagrinned. "And we're really sorry for not telling you in the first place. "We just thought...well, obviously we thought wrong."

"Obviously," Aunt Abby agreed. "Oh, and you can expect a visit from Detective Rast. He's going to be coming up soon to see what other information he can get."

"Of course, he's welcome to come." Sophie nodded eagerly.

"I'll talk to you later. If you get any more information about Lauren or her whereabouts, I'm always available." Aunt Abby nodded once more and was gone.

"Whew." Sophie put a hand to her head. "That wasn't so good. I guess we should have told her in the first place."

Liv frowned. "We agreed not to for her own good. Though I guess I can understand how you'd want to know any information you could about your child." She cupped her still-flat belly protectively.

The maternal gesture caught Kat unawares and she nearly started crying again. *I'll never get to meet Liv's little boy,* she realized suddenly. *Never get to hear him call me 'Aunt Kat' or have any babies of my own. Oh God...*

A knock on the viewing room door interrupted her morbid thoughts. She looked up to see Deep standing there, his broad shoulders slumped wearily.

"Yes, what is it?" Olivia asked him at the same time Sophie chirped,

"Did you find it? Did you find the cure?"

"Forgive me," he said heavily. "But could I please speak to Kat alone?"

Liv and Sophie exchanged glances that held a world of silent communication. They nodded at the same time. "Of course," Liv said quietly. "We'll be outside in the hallway if you need us." They stepped out together, the door *whooshing* shut behind them.

"Did you find anything? What did Mother L'rin say?" Kat tried not to sound too eager but she couldn't help herself. Surely the wise little healer would be able to help her. Surely...but Deep was shaking his head.

"I'm sorry, Kat but she says there's nothing she can do."

"Nothing? Nothing at all?" Kat could scarcely believe it. "No magic plants or herbs. No spells? Just...*nothing?*"

"Forgive me." Deep bowed his head. "I have failed you in the worst possible way."

"No." Kat shook her head, trying to keep back the wave of despair that was threatening to drown her. "No, it's not your fault."

"It *is* my fault," he said forcefully, looking up. "*I* was the one who insisted we cut the bond between us. *I* was the one who pretended I didn't...didn't love you so that you would agree to our separation."

Kat's breath caught in her chest. "What are you saying?"

"That I *do* love you. Oh, Kat...I've been such a fool. Such a Goddess damned fool when it comes to you." His voice was hoarse with emotion.

"Deep—"

"I've always loved you," he went on, taking her hand. "From the moment Lock and I first laid eyes on you. He was male enough to admit how he felt but I...I was afraid. So afraid that what had happened once before might happen again."

"I know about that," Kat said quietly. "About Miranda. I saw it when I was dream sharing with you. I know how deeply it affected you."

"You didn't seem to want us at first," Deep said, examining her small hand in his big one. "I hardened my heart against you then. I told myself I wasn't surprised that such a gorgeous elite female wasn't interested in joining with Lock and me. After all, we'd already had our chance once and failed miserably. Or I should say, *I* failed miserably."

"It wasn't your fault Miranda killed herself," Kat protested.

"Yes it was. Just as it's my fault you're going to...to..." Deep shook his head, apparently unable to go on.

"You don't have to say it." Kat squeezed his fingers. "And it's not all your fault. I *was* against being with you and Lock to start with. It was scary—the idea of being with two guys at once—really big guys too. And having your emotions in my head all the time, at first it was awful. Now...now I kind of miss it. Miss *feeling* you, Deep."

He raised his head. "When did you change? I thought you seemed different while we were on Twin Moons but I didn't let myself believe. I was too afraid. And then you collapsed after we made love and I told myself it was for the best if you didn't want us. I was so afraid, you looked so much like *her* at that moment."

"I understand," Kat said quietly. "I thought it might be something like that. But as for when I changed my mind about you and Lock, It was so gradual it's hard to say. I think it was on Twin Moons, before we were captured by the natives, when I first realized how *nice* it could be feeling you and Lock inside me." She blushed. "Uh, you know what I mean."

Deep smiled sadly. "Yes. Don't worry, I won't mock you."

"That's a change." She gave him a tiny smile back. "Anyway, I noticed that when both of you were in harmony, when you were loving each other and...and caring for me, it was *wonderful* feeling your emotions. Like being filled with sunshine. I think that's when I began to feel less opposed to the idea of being bonded to both of you permanently, even if it was an unconscious rather than a conscious decision."

Deep sighed. "Lock and I haven't had many of those brotherly moments lately. I've made him hate me—just as I tried my damndest to make you hate me, Kat."

"Well, you never really succeeded." She squeezed his hand. "Although I certainly thought you were an asshole."

"I was," he said seriously. "And a bastard and any other Earth vernacular names you can think of to call me. But worst of all, I was a fool. Lock and I could have had you in our lives forever if I hadn't been so arrogant and cowardly. Now...there's nothing I can do except admit my faults to you and say goodbye."

"Deep—" she started to protest but he shook his head.

"I do not ask for your forgiveness. I know full well I am beyond redemption." He sighed and looked into her eyes. "But please let me say it once more—*I love you, Katrina O'Connor of Earth*. I love you with everything that is in me. I will never forgive myself for the way my foolish actions have harmed you. And for this..." he brushed her wounded cheek with his fingertips. Kat felt the tingle and knew the curling green lines must have progressed. But she didn't pull away from his touch.

Deep studied her eyes for a long moment. *Searching for something*, Kat thought. *But what?* If he was searching for hatred or recrimination he didn't find it. Even though she was going to die, Kat couldn't bring herself to hate him. He had acted horribly but in the end, it was her best interest he'd had in mind. *He was trying to save me...save me from himself. And now it's too late.*

"Kat..." Deep's voice was filled with need. He pulled her close and Kat didn't fight him. She expected a desperate, burning kiss filled with passion and Deep didn't disappoint her. But then, suddenly, the kiss turned gentle and his touch was soothing rather than demanding. *This is how he could be all the time, if only he let himself*, she thought as he deepened the kiss, sucking her lower lip tenderly before exploring her mouth. *If he could let go of his past, his bitterness, his fear. If he could have let himself admit he loved me before it was too late...*

She clung desperately to him, her heart drumming in her ears, feeling like she was going to die if he let her go. *But you're going to die anyway, no matter what,* a little voice in her head reminded her. Kat pushed it away. She didn't want to think of that right now. She just wanted to let herself melt against Deep and know, finally truly *know* that he loved her.

Even if it was too late.

At last he pulled back and studied her face. "Thank you." His voice was hoarse and there was a bright sheen of tears in his bottomless black eyes. "Thank you for not hating me."

"Deep, I could never—"

"Forgive me, but we need to use the viewing room." Two Beast Kindred officers came in with Olivia and Sophie trailing behind them.

"Sorry," Liv said. "We tried to stop them."

"That's all right." Deep straightened and nodded at them. "I think we're finished here. Aren't we, little Kat?"

"I...I guess so." She wasn't sure why but she had the feeling that she needed to say or do something else. But what? What else could she do but let Deep go as he seemed intent on doing. *There is one thing I can do, though,* she thought. "Deep," she called as he turned for the door.

"Yes?" He turned back for a moment.

"Please, if you meant what you said, tell Lock everything you just told me," she said quietly. "He needs to hear it as much as I did. Maybe even more."

A grim look crossed his face. "Don't worry, little Kat. That's exactly what I'm going to do." Then he turned again and was gone, through the doorway as silent as a ghost.

Kat watched him go, strangely troubled. But then Sophie and Liv were taking her by the hand and leading her out of the viewing room. *I'll see him again,* she promised herself. *Before it's too late, I'll see him one last time.*

* * * * *

Lock packed slowly, putting his clothing into the compressor and watching as the machine minimized each item and spit it neatly into the waiting box. Using the handy little contraption, an entire household full of items could be packed in one or two small crates, making moving out much easier. Physically, anyway. Emotionally, he was torn.

He had taken a long shower, washing the AllFather's muck from his body and it was there, with the hot water pounding on his head, that the idea of leaving had presented itself. Lock wasn't sure where he was going, only that he needed to get away.

Living with his brother had always been the most natural thing in the world. But now that the connection they had shared since birth was cut, it didn't feel right any more. Even if he and Deep had still been getting along, it wouldn't have worked. And since they'd declared open warfare on each other, the idea of continuing to live in the same suite and share the same bed as they had since they were babies was completely unthinkable.

I'm an island now. A single that used to be a double. It was something he had secretly wished for sometimes as a child. Deep had always been abrasive and argumentative, making it hard to make and keep friends. Sometimes Lock had wished he was a different kind of male, a Blood or Beast Kindred instead of a Twin. Someone who could live life on his own instead of always being tied to another.

But now that he had his wish he just felt...empty. *I don't even hate him anymore,* he realized tiredly as he packed. *Because he's not my brother now that the tie between us has been cut. He's just a stranger. And I'm alone...all alone for the first time in my life.*

He would be even more alone once Kat died but he didn't want to think about that. He wanted desperately to go see her, to tell her how he felt one last time before it was too late. But something kept holding him back — maybe it was the fear that once he said goodbye the whole situation would finally be real. Lock knew it wasn't logical to delay for such a reason but he couldn't help himself. He didn't want to admit the woman he loved — the only woman he had ever loved — was going to die.

Oh my lady...Oh Kat...

"I'm back, Brother."

The sound of Deep's voice behind him startled Lock and he turned to face his twin.

"What did Mother L'rin say?" he demanded. "Did she give you any hope?"

"None. I'm sorry." Deep's shoulders slumped. "She did say there might have been hope — if we were both bonded to her. We could have diluted the poison — shared it between us until it was no longer deadly. We *could* have saved Kat's life."

A swell of fury and despair threatened to overwhelm Lock but he stood his ground, his hands clenched into fists. "But we can't now, is that it? Now that you're no longer bonded to either one of us?"

"We can't," Deep acknowledged heavily. "Because of me. Because of my foolish pride, my fear, my arrogance. I'm sorry, Brother. This is all my fault."

Despite the emotions tearing him apart inside, Lock couldn't help looking at his twin in surprise. "What a shock—the infallible Deep finally admitting he has some faults. But saying you were wrong now won't help anything. It won't save Kat's life...or keep me from leaving."

"I noticed you were packing." Deep nodded at the compressor and the half full box. "Where will you go?"

"I don't know," Lock said tiredly. "I'll stay here until Kat is...until she's gone. But after that..." He shrugged his shoulders. "Who knows?"

"Anywhere away from me, I guess," Deep said in a low voice. "I can't say that I blame you, Brother."

"Don't call me that," Lock said, but without heat. "As you pointed out, it no longer applies."

"Lock..." Deep came forward and put a hand on his shoulder. Lock wanted to shrug it off but he was too tired. He looked into his twin's eyes instead...the eyes of a stranger.

"What?"

"I know I've made a mess of everything. I've ruined all three of our lives and cost Kat hers. But I need a favor."

"A favor?" Lock raised an eyebrow at him. "After all you've put us through, you have the nerve to ask me for something?"

"It's easy. And small. It will only take you half a second—less. I swear." Deep looked at him earnestly. "Please, Brother, if you ever loved me, grant me this one thing."

Lock sighed. "All right, I should say no but...what is it?"

"First swear you'll do it." Deep's grip on his shoulder tightened. "Swear on our fathers' graves."

"Our fathers were buried at sea," Lock reminded him. "But I know what you mean. Yes, I swear it."

"Thank you." Deep breathed a sigh of relief and took a step back.

"Well?" Lock frowned at him. "What is it? And when do you need me to do it?"

"The sooner the better." Deep drew his blazer and pressed it into Lock's palm. "Here."

Lock looked down at the deadly weapon, uncomprehending. "Why are you giving me this? What do you expect me to do?"

"I expect you to honor your promise, Brother," Deep said calmly. "And kill me."

Chapter Forty

Kat stared at herself in the bathroom viewer, tracing the curling green lines that swirled around most of her right cheek. *So this is how it ends. Done in by what looks like a really bad Saint Patrick's Day tattoo.* It seemed so unfair — so unbelievable — that something so small should end her life. But Kat knew it was true. Even now she could feel herself getting weaker. *At least I don't have that awful pain anymore. No more rusty spike in my brain – that's an improvement.*

An improvement but little consolation, considering that she was dying.

She frowned at her image in the viewer. She was doing it again — having a pity party when she had promised herself not to waste her last hours whining. Liv and Sophie had wanted to take her dancing or drinking at one of the clubs on the ship but Kat had vetoed that idea. Instead they'd decided to go back to her suite for brownie sundaes and girl talk — possibly the last girl talk they'd ever get.

But as much as she loved spending time with her friends, Kat yearned for something more. If these were her final hours she wanted to spend them doing something exhilarating. Something incredible...but what?

Suddenly a memory came to her — the feeling of flying like a weightless, invisible bird, the sight of suns and planets and galaxies rushing past her, the incredible exhilaration of being joined to two other minds as they swooped through space at impossible speeds... It was the sensation she'd gotten the last time she'd done a joining with Lock and Deep, when they were searching for Sophie after she'd been kidnapped by the Scourge. By Xairn, in fact — the same warrior who was now holding Lauren.

That's what I want to do, Kat realized with a surge of excitement. *I want to feel that joy one more time. And maybe we can help locate Lauren while we're at it. That way it will be like I'm doing something useful before I die...leaving things better than I found them.* Of course, it was joining with Lock and Deep that had started this whole mess in the first place. But what did she care now if the pain came back? She was going to die anyway. *If I could get Lauren's mom even just a little bit of hope it would be worth it.*

Kat nodded at her face in the viewer. "I'll do it."

Turning, she headed out of the bathroom to tell Sophie and Liv her decision. Then all she had to do was convince Deep and Lock.

* * * * *

Kat let herself into the twins' suite without knocking. The door recognized her and let her in with no problem, *whooshing* quietly shut behind her. She was rehearsing her argument when she came to the bedroom...and stopped in her tracks.

Deep and Lock were standing in front of the huge bed, neither one of them moving. But Lock had a blazer pointed straight at Deep's heart.

"Take the shot," Deep urged, baring his chest. "One quick, clean shot and you're done."

"I don't want to." Lock's voice trembled and so did his hand, holding the weapon. "I probably *should* after everything you've done but...I don't. I can't lose my brother and the woman I love at the same time. I *can't.*"

"You've already lost me." Deep's voice was desolate. "And we're both going to lose Kat. I deserve to die for the part I played in that—you know it's true."

"That doesn't mean I have to be the one to kill you!" Lock threw the blazer down and it *clunked* harmlessly on the carpet. "It's not fair for you to even ask me."

"I thought you'd want to," Deep said quietly. "You hate me, don't you? I thought it would give you satisfaction."

"How could I take satisfaction in killing my brother? The other half of my soul." Lock grabbed him roughly and pulled him into a hard embrace. "I don't hate you, Deep," he muttered into his brother's shoulder. "Sometimes I wish I could but I don't, no matter what you've done."

"I don't hate you either," Kat said quietly. "I never could—which is what I was trying to tell you before we were interrupted in the viewing room." She stepped forward. "In fact, I...I love both of you. Very much."

Tears stung her eyes as two sets of muscular arms enfolded her. "Kat, little Kat," she heard Deep murmur as Lock whispered, "My lady…" into her hair.

"I've come to ask you for something," she said at last, pulling out of the sweet, three-way embrace and looking up at them. "Kind of a last request."

"Anything," Lock said at once and Deep said, "Name it."

"A joining." Kat spoke rapidly as both brothers opened their mouths to protest. "Just hear me out. I want to act as your focus so we can find Lauren. I spoke to her mother earlier and she's distraught. If I could give her any information about where Lauren is and if and when she's coming home, it would mean a great deal to her. Will you help me?"

"Mother L'rin told us to never use you as a focus again," Lock protested. "She said that it was very dangerous for you."

"She also told Deep there was no hope to save me from the soul poisoning," Kat said flatly, pointing to her cheek. "So what have I got to lose?"

"The Scourge home planet is three times as far as Twin Moons," Deep said thoughtfully. "Such a distance has never been attempted before. Even if we could cast a net so far, it could be all for nothing if they've folded space. Attempting such a distance might be the end of all three of us."

"Oh." Kat shook her head. "I...I didn't know. Then of course I withdraw the request. I wouldn't want to put you and Lock at risk."

"Risk be damned," Deep growled. "I don't care how dangerous it is at this point."

"I agree with Deep," Lock said quietly. "There is no life for me without you, my lady. I too, will take the risk."

"I can't let you sacrifice yourself for me," Kat protested.

"We're not. Or not *just* for you," Lock said. "It's for Lauren and her mother too, remember?"

"Well, yes..." she said hesitantly. "But—"

"I would rather burn brightly for an instant and bring some light into the universe in my last moments than live a thousand years in darkness," Deep said softly. "And I want to be joined with you again, Kat. I think Lock feels the same."

"I do." Lock nodded. "So very much, my lady."

"Well then..." Kat knew she shouldn't let them do it but the lure of being between them again, feeling their minds joined to hers, was too tempting. Then she had a new thought. "But...can we even do a joining now that you two aren't connected anymore?"

"Severing the bond between us won't have affected our abilities as seeker/finders," Lock said. "Though it may mean we'll need a great deal of…contact in order to achieve a good link."

"We'll need that anyway, casting a net such a distance away." Deep stepped closer and brushed Kat's cheek lightly with his fingers. "How do you feel about that, Kat?"

Kat's breath caught in her throat. "What exactly are we talking about here? Complete nudity?"

"At least." Lock cleared his throat. "And quite possibly penetration as well."

"By both of us. At the same time." Deep searched her eyes with his. "Now how do you feel about it?"

Kat lifted her chin. "I say I'd rather go out with a bang than a whimper. Although…" She bit her lip. "It *has* been awhile since I ate the bonding fruit."

"Wait here." Lock disappeared and came back a moment later with a lovely blue crystal bottle etched in flowing designs and a small crystal goblet to match. "Here." Handing the cup to Kat, he poured it about half full of a shimmering, clear liquid.

Kat raised the goblet to look at its contents and a familiar scent wafted up. *Fresh pineapple…ripe raspberries…buttered popcorn.* "Bonding fruit." She looked up at Lock. "Is it made from bonding fruit?"

"It is distilled from the *Kala* fruit, yes." He nodded. "I found it in my things when we came back from Twin Moons. I think our mother put it there." He gave Kat a sad smile. "She likes you a lot, you know."

Kat felt a lump in her throat. "I liked her too. I just…I wish I could have gotten a chance to know her." She took a deep breath. *Okay, I can't do this if I'm bawling like a baby. Get hold of yourself, girl!*

"My lady, don't—" Lock started to say but Kat didn't wait for him to finish.

"Bottom's up!" Lifting the goblet, she tossed down the contents in one gulp. The sweet, innocent-smelling liquid lit her insides on fire. "Wow!" Kat gasped, her eyes watering. "What the hell is in that stuff? I don't remember the bonding fruit tasting like that."

"That's because this 'stuff' is the distilled and fermented essence of the bonding fruit," Deep said dryly. "It's incredibly potent."

"I was about to tell you not to drink it too quickly." Lock gave her a worried look. "Most females just sip it."

"Just sip it, huh?" Kat looked ruefully at her empty glass. "Sorry. I guess my history of bonding fruit abuse continues. I'd offer to go to rehab if I had the time."

"Let's not talk about time right now." Deep pulled her into his arms and Lock came up close behind her, pressing against her back. "Let's talk about pleasure…and building enough power to cast our net."

Kat had one more fear. "Before we do this…is it going to cause a bond?"

Deep raised an eyebrow at her. "Are you *still* afraid of being bonded to the two of us?"

Kat frowned. "Not at all. I just don't want to drag either one of you down with me—if the joining itself doesn't do us all in, that is."

"I don't think that's possible, my lady." Lock sounded sad. "With the bond cut between the two of us and Deep, I don't see how we could form a bond with you—even half a bond as we did before."

"All right then." Kat relaxed. "I just wanted to be sure."

"What you can be sure of is that we want you," Deep rumbled in her ear. "And right now, we want you naked."

Kat bit her lip but allowed them to undress her. She knew she ought to have lost her body consciousness by now — they saw her ample curves as beautiful and alluring, after all. But she didn't know if she'd ever get used to being naked with two gorgeous guys staring at her. *You don't have time to get used to it,* a nasty little voice whispered in her head but Kat pushed it away. As Deep had said, it was better not to talk about time.

True, little Kat. Better we should speak about desire. Deep looked down into her eyes, a faint smile on his sensuous lips.

Oh, I can hear you again!

And I can hear both of you — though Deep's mental voice is very faint, Lock said in her mind.

That means we need to get closer, Deep sent.

All right. Reaching up, Kat cupped his scratchy cheek. With her other hand, she laced her fingers with Lock's. It was surprising how good it felt to be able to hear both brothers inside her head again. She had thought during their first joinging that she would never get used to having two sets of alien thoughts and emotions filling her all the time...but apparently a girl could get used to almost anything. *What about having two cocks filling your pussy?* Kat blushed but neither Deep or Lock reacted so apparently she'd managed to keep the thought to herself.

Not quite, Deep sent through their link. *But that's all right...we won't get to that for awhile.*

We want to see you first, to touch you and bring you pleasure, Lock murmured in her mind.

That sounds wonderful, Kat sent. *But you two are **always** the ones giving the pleasure.*

Meaning what? Deep frowned.

Meaning that I want to be in charge this time. Kat nudged them toward the bed. *At least to start with.*

What would you have us do, my lady? Lock asked.

First I want to undress you. Turning to him, Kat began to suit actions to words. Off came the green Kindred uniform shirt, baring a broad, smooth chest with golden tan skin. Kat ran her fingers down it and pinched Lock's nipples lightly until he moaned low in his throat. Then she reached for his pants and peeled them down. Lock toed off his boots for her and, as she rose from pulling the pants all the way off, she saw that his cock was already more than half hard. His bonding scent, the hot coffee/clean linen aroma she found so soothing, was beginning to manifest as she touched him.

My lady, he sent breathlessly as she took him in her hand. Hot and silky smooth against her palm, his shaft was long and thick. It was hard to believe that it would ever fit inside her — let alone it and another just like it at the same time. But already Kat could feel the familiar tingle in her nipples and pussy that let her know the bonding fruit drink was working on her.

Fast stuff, she thought to herself. Either it was working faster because she'd had bonding fruit before or the distilled essence was just more potent.

Both, Deep sent her, apparently hearing her thought. His coal black eyes watched hungrily as she stroked Lock's shaft.

Kat was intrigued. *Do you like to watch, Deep? You like to see me touch your brother this way?* she sent, giving him a naughty little smile.

Deep raised an eyebrow at her. *Kinky, little Kat. But yes, it does give me pleasure to see my twin receive your ministrations.*

Just as it gives me pleasure to watch you with Deep, Lock sent. *That's the way it is with Twin Kindred — otherwise we would be jealous of each other instead of being willing to share a female.*

Then I guess it's your turn to watch, Kat sent him. Letting go of Lock, she turned to Deep. *Time to strip, lover.*

Lover...I like that. He gave her a half-lidded gaze and a sensual smile as he spread his arms. *I'm all yours, little Kat. Strip me.*

With pleasure. Kat wasn't lying — she enjoyed herself immensely as she pulled away Deep's shirt, baring his muscular chest. It was just as broad as Lock's but he had a small patch of wiry black hair between the flat copper disks of his nipples. *Mmm...* Daring greatly, Kat leaned in and took his right nipple lightly between her teeth.

Deep sucked in a breath and his hands clenched into fists as she teased the tiny nub with her tongue. *Gods, little Kat. You have no idea what you're doing to me.*

Let's find out then, shall we? Continuing her exploration, Kat unfastened his black flight pants and pulled them down. Deep's shaft came into view at once, rampant and rock hard, thrusting up from between his muscular thighs.

Mmm... Kat couldn't get finished pushing his pants and boots down fast enough. She wanted to touch that long, hard shaft, to hold Deep in her hand. Already she could smell his bonding scent, that dark chocolate and sex spice that put all her senses on full alert.

Deep groaned as she stroked him, his shaft throbbing and hot between her fingers, like a bar of heated iron from the forge. *Kat, little Kat...you're driving me crazy!*

I enjoy driving you crazy. Kat smiled up at him. *And I hope you like taking the scenic route because I'm not nearly done yet.*

What else do you have in mind for us? Lock asked, his chocolate brown eyes glued to the way she was slowly stroking Deep's shaft.

I want to suck you. Kat smiled as the two of them looked at her in obvious surprise. *Both of you.*

I can't wait to feel your sweet lips wrapped around my cock. Deep's eyes were blazing with desire. *But first I want to do something.*

What? Kat asked but the dark twin didn't answer. He left the room for a moment and then returned with something under his arm.

"What's that?" Kat asked aloud, intrigued as he set it up next to the bed.

"A portable, expandable viewer. I want you to be able to watch while you suck us…and while we fuck you, little Kat."

Kat raised an eyebrow at him. "Who's kinky now?"

"Does it bother you?" Lock asked, looking at her anxious. "Because if it does…"

"No…no I don't think it does." Kat looked into the viewer thoughtfully. She didn't look at herself naked much because when she did, she was usually cataloguing her faults. Not this time, however. This time she made an effort to see herself as Deep and Lock saw her.

So beautiful, Deep whispered in her mind. *Your full breasts, your curving hips, your ripe nipples.*

Truly, my lady, you look like a goddess, Lock assured her.

A goddess? Kat wasn't sure about that but she *did* think the girl in the viewer looked pretty. Her long, auburn hair fell around her shoulders like a silky curtain and her pale, creamy skin seemed to highlight how tight and pink her nipples were. The small thicket of red curls at the top of her sex led down to the tender slit of her pussy — innocent and tantalizing at the same time. The men on either side of her were handsome and muscular — one light and one dark — completely different except for the identical expressions of need and lust on their faces. *They want me,* Kat realized. *As much as I want them.*

Even more, Lock assured her, dropping a kiss on her cheek. *Where do you want us, my lady?*

Right here in front of the bed will do to start, Kat decided. She smiled at both of them and then turned to Lock. *I think it's your turn again, isn't it?*

Before the light twin could answer, she had dropped to her knees before him and was rubbing her cheek against his shaft. His mating scent was very strong here. Warm and comforting, it seemed to beckon her. Kat nearly purred as she placed a gentle kiss on the head of his shaft.

Lock moaned gently as she took him in but he held rigidly still, obvious afraid he would hurt her if he thrust. *It's okay,* Kat sent him as she sucked. *You can move a little bit – I don't mind.*

My lady... His mental voice sounded hoarse as he began to slide hesitantly between her lips. Kat helped him by dropping her jaw and angling forward to take in more of his shaft.

Gods that's so incredibly hot, Deep murmured in her head. Kat looked up as well as she was able to see the dark twin watching hungrily as she sucked Lock.

You really do like to watch, she murmured.

Of course I do. I can't imagine a more arousing sight than watching Lock fuck your sweet little mouth.

Except maybe watching yourself do it. With a last, loving suck, Kat pulled away from Lock and turned to Deep. *Get ready...*

Before you start, watch. He angled himself to one side and motioned Kat to do the same. At first she couldn't understand why but then she caught a glimpse in the viewer and understood. Deep wanted her to watch as she sucked his cock, wanted her to see his thick shaft sliding between her lips as he fucked her willing mouth.

The tingling in her nipples and pussy grew as she took him in her hand once more. She was beginning to feel wet and swollen between her legs and she knew she needed to be penetrated soon. But for now, she wanted to enjoy this, enjoy making love to the two men she loved most in the universe.

Slowly she leaned forward, watching as the red-haired girl in the viewer did the same. Deep was standing rigidly still, his thighs spread to give her easy access. It was clear he expected her to take him in her mouth right away. But Kat didn't like being predictable.

Leaning a little lower, she cupped his balls in her hand, rolling them gently with her fingers. Deep gasped in surprise as she covered them in feather-light licks, her tongue flicking quickly over his sensitive flesh as he watched. Before he could say anything, Kat turned her attention to his cock.

It was long and, if possible, even thicker than Lock's. But somehow she managed to take at least half of him in her mouth on the first try.

"Gods, Kat!" Deep groaned aloud as she bobbed her head in a hot, sucking rhythm.

From the corner of her eye, Kat watched as the red-haired girl in the viewer gave the muscular, dark haired male an excellent blow-job. It wasn't a skill she'd practiced often and certainly she'd never sucked anyone as big as Deep or Lock but she seemed to be doing great now. In fact, she was disappointed when Deep pulled away and gently helped her to her feet.

No more, little Kat, he sent, stroking her cheek. *Now it's our turn to pleasure you. And I want you to watch everything we do in the viewer.*

All right, Kat sent, rather breathlessly. Her nipples were so tight they ached and her pussy felt like it was on fire. The bonding drink must really be working because she felt incredibly hot, incredibly needy.

You're feeling the same effects you did when you first ate the entire bowl full of bonding fruit, Deep told her.

Only multiplied because of the potency of the drink, Lock sent.

Multiplied? Kat began to feel alarmed. *Seriously? Because last time I thought I was going to go crazy.*

Last time you wouldn't let us fuck you and fill you with our seed, Deep reminded her. *That's what you need, sweetheart — to have our cum painting the inside of your pussy, filling you to overflowing. Only then will you feel better...but I want to taste you first.* He looked up at his brother. *Lock, tend to her nipples. I want to lick her sweet pussy.*

Of course. Lock bent his head and took one of Kat's aching nipples between his lips at once. As he began a strong but gentle suction, Deep dropped to his knees before her and spread her thighs.

Open for me, little Kat, he demanded, looking up at her. *Spread your thighs so that I can lick your creamy pussy.*

Kat couldn't refuse, even if she had wanted to. She needed this too much. Wanted to feel his hot breath and talented tongue stroking the inside of her pussy and teasing her clit.

That's exactly what I want to do to you, Deep murmured, stroking her thighs. *But first I want to look at you.*

Kat bit her lip to keep from moaning as he spread her swollen pussy lips gently with his thumbs, baring her slippery inner folds for his pleasure.

Gods, he murmured softly in her mind. *Look how wet she is, Lock. The bonding drink must really be affecting her.*

Kat was torn between embarrassment and pleasure as both brothers stared at her spread pussy. It was true she was wet—her inner cunt was slippery and glistening with her juices and her clit was throbbing like a pink pearl in the center of her folds.

Beautiful, Lock agreed, pinching her nipples gently. *Lick her, Brother. Eat her sweet pussy. It's what our lady needs.*

With pleasure. Bending his head, Deep pressed a soft, hot, sucking kiss to her sensitive clit, making Kat moan breathlessly. Without meaning to, her hands slid down and buried themselves in the thick silk of Deep's black hair. *That's right, little Kat,* he growled softly inside her head. *Hold on to me. It's going to be a wild ride.* Then he spread her even wider with his thumbs and took a long lick upwards, starting at the entrance of her pussy and bathing her entire cunt with his tongue.

"God!" Kat gasped. Her fingers tightened in Deep's hair involuntarily and her eyes were drawn inexorably to the viewer. The red-haired girl was standing with her legs spread, moaning with obvious pleasure. The blond man behind her was pinching and twisting her nipples while the man with black hair knelt between her legs, splitting her thighs wide with his broad shoulders and lapped her pussy as though he couldn't get enough of her sweet honey.

"Oh!" Unable to help herself, Kat tilted her pelvis forward, giving Deep greater access to her pussy. But it wasn't enough for him. With one sudden move, he shifted one of her legs up to his broad shoulder, spreading her thighs even wider for him and opening her completely.

Kat moaned and jerked against him as she felt Deep enter her with two thick fingers as he lapped her cunt. Behind her, Lock continued to pinch and twist her nipples while he kissed and nibbled her neck.

"Does it feel good, my lady?" he murmured hotly in her ear. "Do you liked being spread open so Deep can taste your sweet pussy?"

"Yes, God, yes!" she moaned, unable to lie. She could feel the orgasm building within her, threatening to wash her away with its intensity but she couldn't stop reaching for it just the same. She needed to come, God how badly she needed that!

Not yet. Much to her frustration, Deep pulled away just when she was tilting over the edge.

Deep! she protested but he shook his head.

I'm sorry, little Kat but we need the energy of your orgasm to propel us across the vast distance to the Scourge home world. So you can't come yet.

But I'm about to go crazy! I need —

You need to come, my lady, Lock murmured soothingly. *And never fear, you will. But you must come with both Deep and I inside you.*

Only when we have both our cocks buried to the hilt in your sweet pussy can we let you orgasm, Deep sent. *Because only then will the three of us be fully joined.*

Kat bit her lip. Bonding drink or no bonding drink, this part still made her a little bit nervous. They were both so freaking *big* and the idea of two of them at once...

Don't worry, my lady. Lock stroked her hair gently. *I can feel your apprehension but when Deep and I come together, our shafts will fuse into one symmetrical shape — much like the phallus we used on you the night after you ate the bonding fruit.*

It makes for greater ease of penetration, Deep added. *As though you're being filled by one cock instead of two.*

*Except that **one** is freaking huge,* Kat pointed out. *Will you still be able to do that – to fuse together that way with the bond between you cut?*

Deep frowned. *We should be able to. The bond affects our emotional connection – not our physical abilities. But we won't be filling you together to start with.*

You won't? She looked at both of them. *Then what are you going to do?*

We'll take things slowly, Lock assured her. *Each of us will take a turn. Having one shaft at a time inside you will stretch you open gradually.*

And it will make us wet enough to enter you together, Deep said. *Both our cocks need to be coated with your juices so that we can slide easily inside you when we fuse together.*

All...all right. Kat felt like her heart was trying to pound its way out of her ribs with a mixture of apprehension and excitement. God, was she really going to do this? It certainly looked like it. *How do we get started?* she asked.

I think it's time we all moved onto the bed, Deep said. *I'll adjust the viewer so you can keep watching while Lock and I fill you.*

Kat allowed herself to be helped onto the vast, broad bed thinking that it was odd he'd said "fill" instead of "fuck."

That's because it's not really fucking until we're both together inside you, Deep sent, apparently hearing her thoughts. *Not by Twin Kindred standards, anyway.*

Oh. Okay. Kat cuddled with Lock on the bed while Deep adjusted the viewer. Her eyes strayed to the image of the red haired girl and she saw that her cheeks were flushed and her eyes were bright from the pleasure she'd already given and received. She also couldn't help noticing that the spiraling green lines of poison had grown until they nearly covered her right cheek but she refused to dwell on that. She was going to squeeze as much love and pleasure and joy into her final hours as she could and not think about anything morbid. Still...a tear dripped down her green-stained cheek despite herself.

"My lady..." Lock whispered aloud, his voice husky with sorrow. Kat felt his pain and loss as she felt her own and for a moment the shared emotion was almost her undoing. She leaned her head against his broad chest and breathed deeply, trying not to cry. Trying not to spoil what little time she had left.

"Kat?" Deep climbed into bed beside her and nestled close, his broad chest pressed to her back. "Are you all right?"

"Fine," she whispered in a muffled voice. "I'm just...I'm fine. Really." And the strange thing was that after a minute, she was.

It was the warmth and reassurance of their bodies against hers that did it. Kat felt completely surrounded by them, cocooned in comfort. And though she couldn't feel Deep's emotions as she felt Lock's, she knew he cared for her just as much as his brother. She could feel his love in the gentle way he touched her, the soothing way he caressed her hair.

Finally, she sat up and swiped at her eyes. "Sorry, guys. Didn't mean to kill the mood."

"You didn't," Lock said quietly. "We feel as you do, don't we, Deep?"

"Indeed." Deep stroked her arm, his eyes bleak. "The idea of losing you just as we're really getting together is agony, little Kat. Unbearable."

Kat sniffed and lifted her chin. "Well we're just going to have to bear it. We need to do this for Lauren. And..." She snuggled back down between the two of them. "If I have to go, I want to go out on a high note, you know?"

"A high note?" Lock frowned.

"I mean..." Kat could feel her cheeks heating in a blush but she made herself continue. "I want to feel you in me, both of you, before the end."

"And we want to fill you, little Kat. And fuck you," Deep murmured. "But first we must wet our cocks in your pussy. Are you ready to let us do that?"

Kat felt a twist of desire in the pit of her stomach. God, just the idea of spreading her legs and letting them fill her, one at a time was making her hot. The bonding drink was still in her system and her pussy ached with the need to be penetrated. But even beyond that, the love she felt for both of them drove her on. *Yes,* she murmured, using the mental link of the joining to answer. *Yes, go ahead. I want you to. Uh...*she looked at them doubtfully. *Which one of you wants to...?*

Fill you first? I will, Lock murmured, his brown eyes half-lidded with lust. *The last time I entered you, my lady, I never allowed myself full penetration. This time...*

This time he needs to thrust hard and deep inside your sweet pussy, Deep finished for his twin. *Come here, Kat.* He held out his arms and she crawled into his lap. He kissed her urgently for a moment, then urged her up onto her hands and knees. *Lean your head against my chest and spread your legs as wide as you can,* he directed as Lock got into position behind her. *That will open your pussy enough to let Lock get deep inside you.*

Kat shivered slightly as she felt the broad head of Lock's shaft brush her wet folds. She moaned softly as he slid over her sensitive clit and Deep stroked her hair soothingly. *Watch him,* he directed, indicating the viewer. *Watch Lock penetrate you, little Kat. Watch him fill your sweet pussy with his cock.*

Turning her head, Kat did as he demanded. It was an incredibly erotic sight. The red-haired girl, on her hands and knees, trembling and leaning against the black haired man who was propped up against the head of the bed. Behind her, the blond man knelt, slowly thrusting his thick shaft inch by inch into her wet, open pussy.

Now, Lock whispered through their link as he stretched her open, his cock finally sliding home inside her. *Do you feel that, my lady? Do you feel me in you?*

Yes... Kat moaned and tilted her pelvis, trying to get even more. The penetration was good — was wonderful — but the bonding drink in her system was telling her she needed more. So much more... *Good...so good.* If only she could get Lock to fuck her, to thrust just a little bit, she was sure she could go off like a rocket...There was some reason she wasn't supposed to come yet but it slipped her mind. Her thoughts seemed to be blurring, her rational mind consumed with the need for pleasure and penetration.

But though she came close, she couldn't quite tilt over the edge of orgasm. All too soon it was over — Lock withdrew slowly, as though reluctant to leave the tight, hot confines of her pussy. Kat almost cried with the feeling of emptiness. But there was another shaft right in front of her, she realized, looking down at Deep's lap. And it was even thicker than Lock's.

Now, Deep was saying. *It's my* —

Kat didn't give him a chance to finish. With a little cry, she sat up and straddled his narrow, muscular hips. Taking his shaft into her hand, she positioned the wide head of his cock against the opening of her pussy and sank down on him before Deep could say a word.

Both of them moaned at the sudden intimate contact and Kat gasped in pleasure as the thicker shaft stretched her wide.

"Gods, little Kat," Deep murmured hoarsely. "I've never known you to be so forward."

"I need it," Kat told him, raising her pelvis so that a few thick inches slipped free and then thrusting back down again to impale herself once more. "I need *you*. God, Deep, please…fuck me!"

"Gently, Kat. Gently," Deep cautioned. He looked over her shoulder at Lock. "Brother, I know we wanted to take things slowly but I think the bonding drink is having an even more pronounced effect on her than we thought. Our little Kat needs to be fucked very badly. *Now*."

"I think you're right." Lock nodded. "So how…"

Lie down beside us on the bed, Deep directed, switching back to the mental exchange of the joining. *I'll withdraw for just a moment and then we'll fuse and enter her together.*

Yes, Kat sent urgently. *Yes, that's what I need — both of you in me. Now. Right away — please!* She was no longer afraid or uncertain. This was what she needed — both of their thick cocks filling her at once. Filling her, fucking her…and coming in her. She was certain of it. *Please,* she whispered and then gave a soft cry of protest as Deep withdrew from her slowly. God, she felt so empty without him and she needed so badly to be filled…

It's only for a minute, sweetheart, he promised, stroking an errant strand of hair out of her eyes. *Only for a moment and then Lock and I will fill you properly — the way you need to be filled.*

He urged Kat to lie on her side, propping a pillow under hear head. *Relax, little Kat,* he murmured. *Gods, I love you! You're so beautiful and so brave, spreading your sweet pussy for Lock and I to fill you at the same time. I never thought you'd be willing to do this with us. To love us both at once.*

You thought that because of what happened in the past, Lock told his brother. *I always knew the lady Kat had courage.*

It's not just courage, Kat protested, trying to think past the haze of lust that was clouding her mind. *It's need — please, I need you both so badly!*

We know, my lady. Just a moment while we fuse, Lock responded, kissing her shoulder.

Lock and Deep were conferring in low voices but she only heard about half of what was said and she comprehended even less. All she knew was that she was consumed with a burning desire and only being filled and penetrated could slake her sexual thirst.

"Press your shaft to mine," Deep murmured to Lock. "I know we cannot feel each other's emotions as we should at this moment so we must let our bodies do what is necessary."

"Here. It's not…Ah, there." Lock's voice was strained at first but then he sounded relieved. "Do you feel that, Brother? I think we're ready to fill our lady."

"Yes," Deep responded. "And our little Kat is more than ready to be filled…and fucked."

Lock, who was behind Kat, raised her top leg, opening her pussy for their penetration. Both of them pressed very close to her, their hard chests bracketing her own until it felt like all three of their hearts were beating in the exact same rhythm.

Together, Deep murmured. *I'll guide us…now!*

Kat gasped in pleasure as she felt the single, thick cock begin to push into her pussy. First she felt the slippery, broad head press against her entrance. Then, with a slight stretching sensation, the brothers breached her entrance and began to enter her.

She moaned softly and bit her lip as the sensations became incredibly intense. She could feel her body opening for them, taking them in, but the feeling was of a tightness that was almost but not quite painful.

God, so much, so deep, she thought, writhing between them. *Almost too much…*

It's all right, Kat. You're all right, Deep sent, searching her eyes anxiously. *I know it's hard to take the first time. But I swear to you, in a moment you'll adjust.*

Slowly, my lady. Gently, Lock sent as they continued to thrust slowly into her. *Once we touch bottom inside you, the bonding drink will take its full effect and you'll feel nothing but pleasure.*

I hope you're right, Kat sent, biting her lip. *Because…Oh!* Just at that moment, she felt them press hard against the end of her channel and a wave of pleasure overcame her. "God," she gasped deliriously. "Deep…Lock… Please, I'm close, I'm *so close…*"

Gently but with power, Deep directed, obviously sending to his brother. *Just a few thrusts should do it. The moment Kat comes, we'll be launched.*

The feeling of their long, thick cocks pulling out and thrusting back in again was too much for Kat. With a low moan, she felt herself coming, finally tilting over the edge as the orgasm that had been building so long finally came crashing down on her.

God, yes! she thought again and then the world around her melted away and the air was suddenly full of stars.

Chapter Forty-one

The peak of orgasm faded gradually to be replaced by the familiar rush of pleasure and the sensation of being a swift, invisible bird. Kat looked around in delight at the sight of the blue-white ball of Earth floating in space and the stars surrounding it.

Hold on, she heard Deep say. *We're going to be going faster and farther than we ever have before. Whatever you do, stay together and don't get lost.*

Kat had a moment of concern—she hadn't known it was possible for them to get lost from each other during a joining. *How could we possibly*—she began and then everything became a blur.

During their previous joinings, Deep had taken his time, allowing her to see her solar system first hand—or as first hand as they could get on the astral plane, anyway. This time, apparently they had no time to linger. Stars, planets, entire constellations rushed by in the blink of an eye. Suns so massive they blotted out the blackness of space with their fiery brilliance rose up and vanished so fast they seemed like wild illusions.

We have to hurry, Lock explained in her mind as they flew. *We have to use the power of your orgasm quickly, my lady, before it dissipates.*

Not to mention that the longer we wait, the more likely it is they'll fold space and be gone beyond our reach, Deep growled. *Have you got the net ready, Lock? Moving at this rate we'll be there before we know it. I just hope I can hold us in place long enough to find them and see what they're up to.*

I've got the net. Don't worry, Lock responded.

Good. Are you picturing Lauren in your mind? Deep asked Kat. *I hope you know her well enough to find her.*

I didn't have much time to get to know her, but she made a big impression on me, Kat said, watching as the stars and planets whizzed by them. *She's so beautiful and so brave – I really felt for her. Yes, I'm certain I'll be able to locate her if we can catch them in the net.*

Let's hope they're not far from the Scourge home world, then, Deep said grimly. *If they've gone too far we'll never find them.*

I have a net big enough to cover three sectors. Lock sounded confident. *Unless they've folded space, we'll find them. Never fear.*

Are we almost there yet? Kat asked, feeling like a little kid. As fast as they were traveling, she had the strange sensation that they already had been on the astral plane longer than on any of their two previous joinings.

It's just ahead. Look, Lock murmured.

Their incredible speed slowed until the white and black blurs rushing past them became planets and stars again. It reminded Kat of how space looked when the Millennium Falcon was coming out of light speed in the *Star Wars* movies. Just ahead she saw the dirty, gray-brown ball of smog and pollution that she recognized as the Scourge home planet. It was only about the size of a billiard ball in the sky but it was getting closer by the minute.

I don't see their ship, she sent, feeling disappointed.

Don't worry, Lock told her. *I'm casting the net wide and far.*

Kat felt a moment of intense concentration from him, as though he was preparing to do some hard physical labor. Then the Scourge home world and all the space around it in every direction was blanketed in a silvery, shimmering net so beautiful and vast it took her breath away.

Oh Lock, she whispered, totally awed. *This is your finest work yet. It's gorgeous.*

Let's just hope it does its job, Deep said. *Open your mind and feel for the tugging, Kat. Is Lauren anywhere near here?*

Kat deepened her concentration. *Well, she's not on the planet,* she sent with relief. Despite being ninety-nine percent certain that Lauren and Xairn had left in the small silver ship they'd seen blast off, she'd had a nagging fear that Sophie and Liv's cousin had somehow been left behind. But apparently that wasn't so — she didn't feel Lauren anywhere on the surface of the deadworld. She made one more sweep to be sure...and her mind touched something new — something so shocking and harsh she drew in a ragged gasp.

What? What is it? Deep demanded, sounding concerned.

Something on the planet. Something dark. Burned me...shocked me, Kat choked. Her astral form was tingling all over. It was as though she'd grabbed a live electrical wire with her bare hands.

The AllFather, Lock sounded grim. *He must still be there.*

Did he feel you, Kat? Deep asked urgently. *Does he know we're here?*

I...don't think so. Kat shook herself mentally, trying to regain control. *He's angry though. So much rage...hatred...betrayal.*

No doubt because Xairn flew off with the only female who could fulfill their twisted prophesy, Lock sent. *This changes things, we have to hurry. If he feels us out here...*He let the sentence dangle ominously and Kat had an idea she didn't want to know what might happen if the leader of the Scourge found their vulnerable spirits wandering so far from their physical bodies.

We have to hurry anyway. Deep sounded strained. *Taking us this far and holding us here is almost beyond my power. Quickly, Kat, avoid the planet and feel for the tug of Lauren's mind in the space around it.*

Got it, Kat sent. *Just give me a little time.*

Time is what we don't have. Hurry!

She didn't bother answering. Taking a deep breath she pictured Lauren in her mind's eye. The delicate features, the long, silky black hair and warm mocha skin, the high cheekbones so like Sophie and Liv's. And of course her striking amber eyes. *Lauren,* she thought, feeling her way along the net, searching with every ounce of concentration she could muster. *I haven't known you long but I can tell you're strong. Brave. You've been through so much but your spirit shines through it all. Let me find you so I can give your mom some hope. She loves you so much! Please let me tell her that her daughter is coming home soon...*

At last she felt the faintest tug imaginable from the far distant corner of the great net. It was so miniscule Kat nearly ignored it, almost waved it away like a tiny mosquito buzzing near her ear. But then the feeling began to grow and she knew it wasn't her imagination—the tug really was Lauren, and she was somewhere on the edge of the shining net Lock had cast.

This was the part Kat liked the most. As the seeker, Deep provided the power to get them to their destination and hold them in place. Lock, as the finder, wove and cast the net. But as their focus, it was Kat's job to track down the person they were looking for and fly the three of them to the exact spot where that person was.

Hang on boys, here...we...go! She spread invisible wings and lunged forward, slicing cleanly through space as a swimmer diving into a pool slices through water. The feeling of speed, the exhilaration of finding what they were looking for as she followed the tug forward, grew stronger and stronger within her...

Kat, watch out! Lock sounded more alarmed than Kat had ever heard him.

What? What's wrong? She wanted to look behind her but they were moving too fast.

It's coming...he's coming for us. Look to the planet! Look to Zlicth!

Finally managing to backpedal, Kat turned her gaze to the quickly receding Scourge home world...and saw something that nearly stopped her heart.

A finger of darkness was extending from the planet. A searching tendril of black slime which made even the blackness of space seem faded and pale in contrast. But this finger was huge—a tentacle of pure evil big enough to engulf them completely like a snake swallowing a mouse.

If it touches us, Kat thought, her blood turning to ice. *If it even brushes us we'll be caught. I just know it!*

The AllFather, Deep sent. *He must have felt your probe after all.*

What can we do? Kat sent back, trying not to panic. *How do we get away?*

We can't. Not unless we leave now, Lock sent.

But I don't want to leave! We're so close. I can feel Lauren and we're almost to her.

Then we can tell her mother that she's safe, Lock sent back. *But if we stay here and the AllFather catches us in his web, we'll never get back to our physical bodies and be able to tell her anything at all.*

Kat wanted to cry. To come so close and then not be able to finish what they'd started was too much, too awful. *I don't—* she began but Deep interrupted her.

Kat's right – we shouldn't leave without seeing this through.

I agree but I don't see how, Lock argued. *If we don't leave now –*

There is another way. Deep sounded determined. *Go on Kat, take us there. If the AllFather traces us I'll...distract him.*

That was all Kat needed to hear. She dived forward again, following the tugging which was growing stronger in her mind. *Find me,* Lauren's life force seemed to be saying. *Find me, find me, here I am!*

There! Kat couldn't keep the triumph out of her voice as a small silver spaceship came into view. *There she is! I knew it.*

Quickly, then Lock urged. *The AllFather is just behind us. His arm grows long and if he catches us...*

Too late. Deep sounded so grim that Kat turned her attention from the spaceship to look behind them again. Rolling toward them like a black, oily cloud that smudged and dirtied the very space it moved though, was the AllFather's trap. Kat could feel the tingling, burning sensation again even though she wasn't touching it...yet. A sudden , awful thought filled her mind.

What were we thinking? We'll lead him right to them!

Lauren and Xairn aren't on the astral plane, Lock told her. *So while the AllFather might sense them, he won't be able to hurt them. Not physically, anyway. Hurry, Kat, we have no time to spare.*

He's getting too close, Deep sent. *You two stay together, I'll distract him.*

Stop! Lock's mental voice was urgent. *Don't you think I know what you mean by 'distract' Deep? You can't sacrifice yourself for us – I won't allow it.*

What makes you think I'd sacrifice myself? Deep's voice was filled with mocking laughter but it sounded hollow to Kat. *Don't be foolish, Lock. The AllFather won't know there's more than one mind wandering the astral plane. If he gets me, he'll think he has us all. But he won't get me – I'm just going to lead him a on a little chase while you two look in on Lauren. So hurry!*

Kat wanted to protest but there didn't seem to be any way to stop him. *I love you, Deep!* she sent as strongly as she could. *Be safe and come back to us or I swear the AllFather won't have to do a thing to you – I'll kick your ass myself!*

You and your Earth vernacular. I don't see how you could hurt me by planting your sweet little foot on my posterior. Deep laughed again in her head. *But I'll be sure to come back so you can demonstrate.*

Do that, Brother, Lock sent. *I love you too.*

And I love both of you. Goodbye. And then there was sudden silence from the spot where Deep had been. Looking over her invisible shoulder, Kat saw something bright whiz daringly close to the foul finger of darkness. The inky black tendril hesitated and then seemed to make a decision. It swooped after the bright thing so fast it was a blur in space.

God! Kat's heart was in her throat. She hadn't realized the AllFather was so *fast* on the astral plane. Watching him chase after Deep's spirit was like watching a striking cobra after a mongoose.

Don't waste time watching, Lock told her, sounding stern. *Deep is playing the decoy so that we can get the information we need. Hurry, Kat. Hurry!*

You got it. Forcing herself to look away from the horrifying spectacle, Kat turned her attention toward Lauren and gave their mission her whole concentration again.

There was nothing else she could do.

Chapter Forty-two

Slicing through space, Kat dived straight at the silver ship and passed through its skin easily. She could feel Lock behind her but he said nothing as they looked around the cockpit they suddenly found themselves in.

Xairn's massive form was hunched over the controls and he seemed to be concentrating fiercely. Kat felt a stab of panic as she realized she didn't see Lauren. *But I feel her here! Where is she? Where —*

"Oh, that feels *so* much better." Lauren came forward from a hidden compartment at the back of the ship. She was wearing one towel draped around her body and blotting her still-damp hair with another. Kat guessed she must have just come out of the shower. *Who knew they had showers on these ships?* she thought as she watched.

It was a standard feature on the older models, Lock murmured. *Warriors used to have to stay away from the Mother ship for much longer — each ship had all the comforts of home. Well, as much as it was possible to have in deep space, anyway.*

"I am glad you're feeling better." Xairn glanced up, his red-on-black eyes widening briefly as he took in the way the thin towel draped over Lauren's curves. Then he looked back at the controls hastily. "It must be a relief to get the remains of the *dravik* off your skin."

"It certainly is." She settled in the passenger seat beside him, still patting her hair. "I just wish I had some other clothes to wear. I'm afraid your cape is ruined."

"That's quite all right." Xairn's deep voice sounded slightly strangled. "I'm certain we can find you something…suitable to wear in the place we are headed."

"Where is that? Where are we going? Are…are you still going to take me home?"

He nodded stiffly, still not looking at her. "I have sworn to do so and I will keep my promise. But it wouldn't be safe for us to go back to Earth now—not before we make a few minor adjustments."

"Adjustments? To what—the ship? So your father can't trace it—right?"

Xairn shook his head. "That is not what I am referring to at all. We'll need to adjust our DNA—both of us—before I can safely take you back to your home planet."

"Our *DNA?*" Lauren sounded horrified. "What are you talking about, Xairn? I don't want my DNA adjusted!"

"I'm sorry but it's necessary." He stared straight ahead as he spoke, his broad shoulders tense. "Which is why we're heading to the Maw Cluster at this very moment. The best genetic manipulators live there. They can help us reach our destination safely."

"But…" Lauren made a helpless gesture. "How far away are they?"

"About a hundred thousand light years from Earth."

"*What?*" Lauren demanded. Then she took a deep breath and put a hand on his muscular arm. "Xairn, I'm trying really hard not to get upset or excited here. But it sounds to me like we're going in the opposite direction of where we need to be."

"Lauren..." Xairn looked pointedly at her hand on his arm and Lauren withdrew it hastily.

"Sorry. But look, how can you even get us so far away and back again before we get old and die? I mean, I'm a cupcake baker, not a physicist but I don't see how it's possible."

"It's possible, all right. Using *that*." Xairn nodded at the viewscreen and Kat followed his gesture involuntarily. What she saw was incredibly strange. There appeared to be a dark silvery-blue, swirling hole somehow cut into the fabric of space. *Not just a hole,* she thought, still staring. *It's like a funnel or a spout. Like water circling the drain in a bathtub – the biggest bathtub in the universe.*

"What's that?" Lauren sounded as awed as Kat felt. "Is it a black hole?"

Xairn made a strange, deep rumbling sound from low in his chest that made Kat drag her eyes away from the strange sight on the viewscreen. After a moment, she realized the big Scourge warrior was laughing. It was a rusty sound, as though he didn't laugh very often, but kind of nice anyway.

"Of course not," he said, one corner of his mouth twitching with amusement. "If it were, our ship would have been broken to bits and sucked in by its huge gravitational pull even before we saw it. That, Lauren, is an inter-dimensional gateway. A wormhole."

"A wormhole? And you're going to fly us *into* it?"

"Through it," Xairn corrected. "We'll be at the Maw Cluster instantaneously. After we conduct our business there, we can find another to take us home—your home anyway. That sector is full of them and the star charts indicate several that will bring us back to your solar system."

"I don't know..." Lauren looked doubtful.

"I do." Xairn closed his eyes for a moment and his entire body tensed. "Can't you feel that? My father is out there somewhere, not far behind. He's seeking someone or something else now, but the moment he captures it he'll turn his attention to us."

Lauren looked over her shoulder fearfully although there was nothing but the back of the ship to see. "He's after us? You mean in a ship?"

"He's pursing with his mind." Xairn made a face. "I can hear him whispering to me. Urging me to bring you back to him... Gods!" He pounded one huge fist on the steering yoke. "We *have* to get away before it's too late."

"All right." Lauren's face had gone pale but she began strapping herself into the safety harness with determination. "All right, Xairn. Get us out of here."

His grip on the controls tightened and the look of concentration on his face was frightening in its intensity. "Hold on. Traversing a wormhole is rough business."

We have to go! Lock's voice in Kat's head startled her. She'd been so caught up in the interaction between Lauren and Xairn that she'd almost forgotten what was going on. *Kat, we have to go,* Lock said again. *If they take us with them through the wormhole, we might never get back to our physical forms.*

Got it. Kat gave herself a mental shake. *Let's get out of here, grab Deep and go.*

Rising up through the skin of the ship, she found herself in the darkness of space once more. *Deep? Where is he?* She felt a moment of panic and then she saw the bright silver streak of his spirit zipping around, just inches away from the seeking black smudge of the AllFinger's tentacle. God, how was he doing that? Staying one step ahead of the evil like that? Kat felt her heart, thousands of light years away, jump in fear as she saw the tendril of darkness almost catch him just before he skipped away.

Deep, she called. *Deep, come back to us! We know what's going on with Lauren. Let's go home.*

Can't. His mental voice was hoarse with exhaustion. *He'll feel it. He'll know there's more than one of us if I join you two. Can't risk it.*

Yes, you can, Brother! Come! Lock demanded, but his command had no effect on the brilliantly darting light that was Deep's spirit.

You'll have to go without me. I can't distract the AllFather and hold you here much longer anyway.

Don't you dare let us go while we're still separated! Kat raged at him. *We need you, Deep.* **Lock** *needs you and he's going to need you even more after I'm gone.*

I'm sorry, little Kat. But I —

Just then there was a blast of light from the direction of the wormhole. Momentarily distracted, Kat turned her attention to it just in time to see the small silver ship circling the wide funnel like a toy boat being sucked down a vast drain. *My God,* she thought. *Can they survive that? They're going to —*

Deep! Lock's mental voice was filled with such anguish that Kat felt it like a knife in her heart. From the corner of her eye she saw something that made her scream in sorrow and disbelief.

The bright, flitting light had flown too close to the black tentacle of darkness. As she and Lock watched, an oily, black, many-armed cloud erupted around it and began to engulf it, like an octopus snaring its prey. For a moment the light seemed to be straining to pull free, struggling away from the tentacles until only one of them had a grip on it. *No, not just a light — that's Deep,* Kat thought numbly. *Deep, please no! Not now. Not when I finally know that you really do care for me. That you love me the same way I love you! Please!*

But her mental plea did no good. As they watched, a thousand more tentacles exploded, like a nest of writhing snakes. They covered the light, drawing it inexorably inward...until the darkness ate it completely.

No! Kat howled with anguish. *No, Deep! No!* She felt Lock's grief too—an agony so intense it was almost unbearable...and then, suddenly, they were flying backwards, away from the darkness and the vanished light. Away from Lauren and Xairn and the wormhole and the polluted Scourge home world at a tremendous speed until everything was a blur.

Stop! Kat was in a panic. *Stop! We have to go back for him! We can't just leave him there.*

He is already lost. Gone beyond our reach. Lock's voice was quiet with despair. *And we cannot go back. It was Deep's power that brought us out so far and held us in place. Without him, we can't help being pulled back.*

Even as he spoke the incredibly fast, intense journey was over. Kat felt herself reenter her physical body with an almost audible *thump.* Her eyes flew open and she found herself looking into Deep's face.

The coal black eyes she'd grown to know so well were open but unseeing. His broad chest rose and fell but the rest of his big body was limp.

"Deep?" Kat patted his cheek eagerly. "Deep, can you hear me?"

"My lady, he's gone. He cannot hear you where he is." Lock's voice was thick with sorrow.

"What do you mean?" Kat demanded. "Where is he?"

"Gone," Lock repeated. "His spirit is untethered from his body, lost forever to the AllFather. Only a shell remains."

Kat looked in horror and disbelief at the familiar, sharp features of the dark twin. Deep had made her completely crazy at times, he had even managed to make her believe he didn't care anything for her even though he was madly in love with her. But despite his contrary nature, she'd grown to love him dearly. And now…

Now he's gone, she thought numbly. *Gone forever and there's nothing I can do about it.*

A sob rose in her throat. A sound of pure longing and loss and grief.

Gone…forever gone. Oh Deep…

Chapter Forty-three

Deep was so far past exhaustion he could barely feel. The power it took to keep the three of them at a spot so many light years from their physical forms, as well as the energy to dart around, keeping one step ahead of the AllFather, was draining him rapidly. He felt like he was running a race without oxygen, like his lungs were burning and the big muscles in his thighs were quivering with fatigue until he might collapse at any moment. But that was all right—as long as Kat and Lock got to safety. That was all he cared about, all that mattered.

When he felt the AllFather catch him, like a corpse-cold hand closing around his ankle, dragging him down to the bottom of a lake of darkness, it was almost a relief. Still, he tried to get away. Straining, he pulled with all his might. He wouldn't leave Kat and Lock alone if he could help it. Couldn't leave…And then the darkness erupted around him and he lost sight of the stars and planets and space. There was nothing but greasy black nothingness wherever he looked.

Sssooo, he heard a familiar voice whisper in his mind. *I did not know you had sssuch ssspecial talentsss, Warrior. How fortuitousss, especially when I am ssso very hungry…*

He'll eat me, Deep thought with despair. *He'll suck down my spirit like a fine wine — he won't even have to extract it from my body. I've handed it to him on a silver platter.* That was an Earth vernacular saying which he had learned only recently but he'd never imagined he would be able to apply it to himself. *Kat,* he thought as the cold, oily tentacles slid around him, suffocating him, making it hard to breath. *Lock, I'm so sorry. I loved you both so much. But if my death can set you free, it's worth it.*

Sighing, he released the tension inside himself, the psychic anchor which had held them all in place in this particular part of space. He thought he heard cries of sorrow as he let Kat and Lock's spirits go, allowing them to slingshot back to their waiting bodies on the Mother ship. But they were so faint he couldn't be sure. The AllFather didn't seem to notice them at all—he was too busy preparing to devour.

So this is how it ends, Deep thought, feeling oddly at peace. *I just hope it goes quickly.*

Not quick, Warrior, the AllFather hissed in his head. *Not too quickly at all. You helped my ssson to sssteal my bride. And sssince he is gone beyond my reach for the present, I want to sssavor your pain. Ssslowly...oh, ssso ssslowly... I —*

No. You shall not have him. A sudden flash of light, like a stroke of lightening splitting the darkness, cut off the AllFather's words. Deep was momentarily blinded. *What – ?*

Not what, Warrior. Who. The voice in the darkness was filled with authority and distinctly feminine.

Who, then? Deep thought at it, feeling disoriented and confused. Where was the AllFather? What was happening to him? And who was this new entity he was speaking with?

Do you not know me? The voice was gentler now, almost laughing. The dark, oily tendrils suddenly shrank back at the sound and then disappeared altogether. **You have worshiped me your whole life,** the voice went on. **Or pretended to, anyway.**

Goddess? Mother of All Life? Deep could barely believe it. Like his brother and all other Kindred, he had been raised to show deep

respect to the female deity they worshipped. But deep in his heart
he had always harbored doubt as to her actual existence.

Doubt no more, Warrior. The light around him was growing. A
soft glow that seemed to be the exact opposite of the AllFather's evil
black cloud.

I do not doubt, Deep sent, wishing he could see the being he was
addressing.

**To see my face is to die. No mortal can look upon my true
visage and live,** the Goddess sent gently. **But I have provided a part
of myself to you, Deep—a part you rejected.**

To Deep's surprise, out of the glowing white light stepped Kat.
Or the image of her, anyway. She was wearing the deep green gown
Lock had gotten her for the party on Twin Moons and her long
auburn hair was loose around her shoulders. She was so beautiful
his heart ached, yet he was confused.

*I don't understand. Are you saying that Kat is actually you? That's
she's a goddess?*

No, of course not. Musical laughter like chimes filled the air
around him. **But I place a little piece of myself in every female that
I match with my males. That piece is what calls to you—what
starts the dream sharing and causes the attraction between Kindred
males and their chosen brides. Do you see now why fighting your
love for Kat was useless from the start?**

I see. Deep nodded respectfully. *Forgive me, I beg. Truly, I have
misused your gift to me most shamefully, Goddess.*

You certainly have. The voice was stern. **For that willful misuse
you deserve to die, Deep. As well you know.**

I know. He bowed his head submissively.

**But there are others who would miss you if you were gone. Your
brother Lock, for instance. Though you have treated him cruelly,**

still he loves you. And Kat, of course. She too would grieve your loss, though you have done your best to turn her against you.

*Kat...*Deep almost couldn't continue. *Forgive me, Goddess, but Kat will not have long to miss me. She has soul poisoning. I fear she hasn't long to live.*

I am aware of the situation with your lady, Deep. The voice was gently reproving. *Tell me this, would you trade places with Kat? Would you take her pain and the certain death that comes with the wound of the kusax if I allowed her to live?*

In an instant! Deep felt a surge of hope. *Please, Goddess, I know now that you're capable of all things. Please, if I could give my life for Kat's, how gladly would I do so.*

I feel the sincerity of your words. The voice sounded approving now. *And so I will honor them in the spirit in which they are spoken. I will give to you, my errant son, what I have given to few others.*

What do you give? Deep asked after a moment when the voice appeared to have finished speaking. *Do you mean you'll allow me to switch places with Kat? Please, Goddess, please, let it be so.*

Remember my words, the voice whispered, not answering his question. *Listen carefully that you may hide them deep in your heart. A war is coming—a conflict that will make the battles you have had with your enemy thus far seem like the battling of children at play with their toys.*

Am I to play a part in it? Deep's heart sank. *Does that mean you won't allow me to die in Kat's place?*

Many will have a part to play. Not least of all this one. The image of Kat melted away to be replaced by one of Xairn.

Him? Deep couldn't help feeling doubtful. *But he's one of them — a Scourge.*

Has he not conducted himself as a true Kindred would? the Goddess demanded. *I tell you, Deep, this male is close to my heart. Much grief and pain has he borne, yet he remains bowed but not broken.*

He did seem to revere Lauren as a proper male should his female, Deep admitted grudgingly. *Still, I don't see —*

His heart is in conflict, the Goddess continued. *Though I have planted light within him, there are seeds of darkness as well. The outcome of the conflict I spoke of will hang upon his will.* Her voice grew stern again. *I charge you, Warrior, that you give him aid if he asks it of you. That you help him in any way you can. And that you not speak of this until the time is right. Do you understand?*

I understand. Deep wanted to ask how he would know when the time was right but he had a feeling the question was unnecessary. The Goddess would let him know when it was time to reveal what she had showed him. Until then, for however long he had, he would keep the secret in his heart.

A long, lonesome time, he thought, feeling an ache when he thought of Kat. *An eternity without my Kat. Unless I am given the opportunity to speak at once and then I die in her place.* Anything was possible, he supposed. He only hoped he wouldn't have to live without the woman he loved and the brother that was still so dear to him—even if the emotional bonds between the three of them were cut.

It is time for you to return, the voice murmured in his ear. *Remember all that I have told you. Remember that I give to you what few others receive.*

But what...What

"Is it?" he finished aloud.

"Wh-what's what?" Kat was sobbing uncontrollably and Lock was holding her in his arms with a look of pure misery on his face.

"Forgive me, my lady," he murmured. "But I said nothing."

"Yes you did." She looked up at him, sniffing. "You...you said 'what is it?'"

Deep cleared his throat. "Actually, I said that."

The expressions on their faces when they looked at him made Deep wish he had a recording device. Shock and dismay were followed by fear, disbelief, and finally, burgeoning hope.

"D-deep?" Kat whispered, her voice scratchy from crying. "Deep, is that you?"

"It certainly looks like it." Glancing down at himself, Deep saw that he was still nude, though he and Lock were no longer fused or joined to Kat.

"Are you all right, Brother?" Lock's voice sounded strained and hoarse. He put out a hand as though he could scarcely believe it. "Are you...really all right?"

Deep seized his hand and squeezed it tightly. "I feel fine, Brother. Never better."

"Yes..." Lock looked at him in wonder. "You *do* feel fine. I feel it in my bones—your wellbeing. Your happiness to see us again."

"What are you talking about?" Kat asked uncertainly.

"The bond. The emotional bond between us," Deep said slowly. "I don't know how it's possible but it's back. It's been restored."

"I...I think I can feel him too," Kat said hesitantly. "Only I can hardly tell if it's just me or both of you. I feel...I'm so filled with joy. And gratitude. Oh, Deep!" She threw herself into his arms and he caught her and held her tight. "You're back. You're really back and all right!" Her voice trembled with emotion.

"Yes, I am." Deep stroked her shining hair gently, so filled with joy he could barely speak. But then he had a new thought. If he was back in his physical form with not a cut or a scratch on him, did it mean that the Goddess had decided *not* to let him trade places with Kat?

Surely she wouldn't be that cruel, he thought, carefully shielding his thoughts. *To bring me back and let me hold the woman I love and then take her away again. Oh, please Goddess...*

Kat, who had had her face buried in his chest, pulled back to look up at him. "You're upset now. What's wrong?"

"Yes, what is troubling you, Brother?" Lock leaned forward, frowning.

"This." Lifting Kat's chin, Deep brushed his fingers over her right cheek...and then realized that it was smooth and unmarked. Had he mistaken which cheek had been wounded with the *kusax*? Quickly, he turned her chin to look at the other cheek—nothing. So the Goddess *had* honored his request. Knowing what he would see, Deep turned to look at the viewer which was still humming beside the bed. He examined the angular planes of his own cheeks and found...nothing.

So he wasn't to trade places with Kat after all. Instead, they were both to live. The soul poisoning was gone. Healed. And the Goddess had restored their bonds. *Oh thank you, Mother of All Life. Thank you so much!*

Lock, who had been watching him and Kat in the viewer, seemed to realize what was going on at the same time. "My lady..." His voice trembled with joy and disbelief. "Kat, your cheek."

"What?" She put a hand to her right cheek, frowning. "Has it spread some more?"

"No," Deep brushed her hand aside and pointed at her reflection in the viewer. "It's gone, little Kat. It's completely gone."

"Oh my God. What does that mean?" She examined her unblemished cheek in the mirror. "Has it moved somewhere else?" She looked down at the rest of her body and then examined herself in the viewer, looking for the green spiral of the soul poison.

Deep already knew she wouldn't find a thing. A puff of air so soft that no one but him could hear it blew gently against his ear. *I give to you what few others receive, Deep*, it whispered. *A second chance. Use it wisely and well. Love your lady and your brother and treat them with respect and kindness as a true Kindred should. And do not forget your promise.*

I won't, Deep sent, his heart filled to overflowing with gratitude. *Thank you so very much, Goddess. I won't forget.*

"You won't forget what?" Lock was frowning at him and Kat was still searching her body uncertainly.

"Stop." Deep, lifted her chin and kissed her gently on the forehead. "Stop looking, little Kat. You're not going to find anything—you're cured."

"Cured? Are you sure?" The light of hope shone in her eyes. "But how? By who?"

"By the same one who sent me back to both of you." Deep hugged her tightly and then beckoned with his free arm to Lock. "Come here, Brother."

Lock joined their embrace with tears in his eyes and they held Kat tightly between them in the way of the Twin Kindred when they find their true bride.

You're ours now, little Kat, Deep sent her through the new and very permanent bond that had been formed in their joining. *Mine and Lock's forever.*

You mean…we're bonded? Completely bonded this time? She looked up at him, uncertainty filling her lovely blue eyes.

I hope you don't mind, my lady, Lock sent anxiously. *But it's true — feel the depth of the bond between us. This connection is to the soul bond we shared previously as a rope is to a thread. It binds us tightly and permanently together.*

Lock's right, Deep told her. *I'm afraid there's no going back.*

No going back? You idiots! Kat was laughing and crying at the same time as she pulled them both close again. *I don't **want** to go back! I just want to spend the rest of my life with the two most wonderful guys in this or any other galaxy.*

Oh? Deep raised an eyebrow at her. *And who are they? Have we met them?*

*You…*Kat shook her head, still laughing through her tears. *I swear one of these days I'm going to kill you, Deep.*

I've already died. He made his mental voice serious as he looked into her eyes. *But I came back for you, little Kat. You and Lock. And to keep a promise.*

"A promise?" Lock said aloud, frowning. "A promise to who?"

"Never mind." Deep shook his head. "I'll tell you when the time is right. And it isn't yet."

"*I* know what the time is right for." Kat's eyes were suddenly half-lidded with desire as she smiled up at him and Lock. "It's time for another session of bonding sex between the three of us. I want to feel both of you in me again."

Deep smiled. "You want to 'renew our vows' as they say on Earth, already?"

"Absolutely." She smiled. "And do you think this time we could manage to do it without anybody being dead for a couple of minutes and giving the rest of us heart attacks?"

"I think that can be arranged, my lady." Lock smiled and stroked a strand of silky red hair out of her eyes. "And this time I want to be in front."

"You can both take turns being in front and back all night long." Kat smiled and gave them each a long, slow kiss. "I drank a whole glassful of that bonding juice, remember? I don't think the effects will be wearing off any time soon."

"I hope not, little Kat," Deep murmured as he and his brother lowered their bride gently to the bed and prepared to bond her to them all over again. "I certainly hope not."

Epilogue

"So Sylvan gave you and Deep both a clean bill of health?" Olivia chose a homemade soft pretzel from the tray and added a tiny dollop of horseradish mustard before taking a big bite.

"Yup. We're good to go—not a trace of soul poisoning anywhere." Kat smiled happily.

"But how?" Sophie asked. "What healed you?"

"Mother L'rin told Deep that if the three of us had a bond we could dilute the poison. We didn't think a bond was possible when we, *ahem*, had bonding sex, but apparently we formed one anyway. So that's the official theory. But Deep seems to think there's more to it."

Like what?" Liv asked

"I don't know and he's not telling. I guess the important thing is that we're all healthy and together." Kat sighed happily. "I'm just so glad everything's okay. And I can even act as their focus as often as I want—now that we're bonded it's safe. So it looks like I have a whole new career in front of me."

"I thought you wanted to go to law school," Sophie said.

"Nope. Having hot three-way sex in order to find missing persons is way more fun than torts and tax law." Kat grinned.

"My, my. You're grandmother will be *so* proud," Liv said dryly, adding more mustard, a splash of soy sauce, and some creamy peanut butter to her next bite of pretzel.

"She's just happy I'm not going to die," Kat said seriously. "I don't think she cares what I do for a living as long as I *live*." She made a face as Liv added even more condiments to her pretzel. "Uh, don't take this the wrong way, hon, but that looks disgusting."

"It may look awful but it tastes like *heaven*." Liv smiled.

"She's been craving salty instead of sweet lately," Sophie explained taking a dainty bite of her own soft pretzel. "I swear I'm going to become a master baker just trying to keep up with her pregnant whims."

"You're the best sister ever." Olivia smiled at her gratefully. "And *you're* the best friend," she told Kat. "Although you *should* have told us the minute you knew you weren't going to die instead of spending the rest of the night having wild three-way sex with your men." Her gray eyes filled with tears. "Sophie and I sat up all night talking about how much we were going to miss you. And...and..." She sniffed. "Sorry. Hormones again."

"Aw, Liv, I'm so sorry. Really I am!" Kat leaned over and hugged her. "I know it wasn't very nice of me but I was so happy that Deep was back from the dead and I wasn't going to die. Plus, I drank like a whole glass full of horny juice—you know, from the bonding fruit? And it kind of...clouded my judgment."

Sophie shook her head. "You and that bonding fruit. I honestly think you're addicted, Kat."

"Better addicted to bonding fruit than pretzels with horseradish, soy sauce, and peanut butter," Kat pointed out, laughing.

"I guess so." Liv stopped eating and stared at her pretzel thoughtfully. "You know what this needs? Some hot sauce. Do you have any?"

"I don't think so." Sophie got up to look. "Tranq Prime food is pretty bland...except when it's completely disgusting, which is most of the time. Sylvan doesn't care much for condiments."

"I can run get some from our suite if you want. I think I have a tiny little bottle of Tabasco somewhere," Kat offered.

"No!" Sophie yelled at the same time Liv said, "Not on your life."

Kat looked at them in surprise. "What? You changed your mind?"

Sophie came back to the couch looking sheepish. "No, it's just that Liv and I made a pact not to let you out of our sight for a little while. Since every time you leave you wind up doing crazy things like getting soul bonded or poisoned."

"We'd just feel safer if you stayed right here with us for awhile." Olivia smiled and squeezed her hand.

"Fine with me," Kat smiled and settled back against the comfortable cushions. "But if you want to keep me in your line of vision every single minute I'm afraid you're going to have a fight on your hands. Deep and Lock are expecting me back in time for dinner...if we even manage to eat. I swear those two are insatiable."

"Said the girl who can't get enough kinky threesome sex," muttered Liv.

"Liv!" Sophie nudged her sister and grinned. "We agreed we weren't going to keep on teasing her all the time about that. We have better things to talk about."

Olivia raised an eyebrow. "Than sex? I don't think so."

"How about how Lauren's mom reacted to the news that her daughter is headed for the Maw Cluster—wherever that is," Kat said soberly. "Do you guys think I was able to give her any hope at all? I feel so bad about the whole thing."

"I think she took it reasonably well," Sophie said thoughtfully, breaking off another piece of pretzel and popping it into her mouth.

"You told her that her daughter was safe and with a male she trusted. And that she'd be coming home eventually," Liv spoke distractedly, busy with doctoring another pretzel into submission. "What about maple syrup, Sophie? Got any of that?"

"Actually, I do." Sophie popped up again. "But *please* tell me you're not going to mix it with soy sauce and horseradish."

Liv gave her a mock glare. "Just get it. Anyway, as I was saying, Kat," she continued. "You did the best you could. I mean, you risked your life to get that information. And I think Aunt Abby was grateful that you tried." She sighed and took the maple syrup Sophie was offering her. "Thanks. Detective Rast is still coming up in a couple of days to check things out, though. I think he wants to make sure we're not hiding Lauren somewhere on the ship or something."

"What? Why would we do that?" Kat protested.

Liv shrugged as she added the syrup to her nightmare of a pretzel. "Dunno. I get the feeling he doesn't quite *trust* the Kindred."

"That's because he doesn't know them like we do," Sophie said, watching as her twin took a big bite of the dripping concoction in her hand. "I swear I'm never going to bake for you again, Liv— you're *ruining* my perfectly good pretzels."

"I'm *improving* them," Olivia corrected, licking her fingers. "God, that's good! Anyway, Rast should be here on Friday."

"What? You never told me that!" Sophie put down her pretzel and frowned. "He's going to be here right in the middle of my bonding ceremony."

"You're *bonding ceremony?*" Kat and Liv said at the same time.

"When were you going to tell us? Where are you going to hold it?" Kat demanded.

"And how do you think you'll get an entire wedding together in just a few days?" Liv asked.

Sophie blushed. "It's not going to be a big to-do, you guys. Just something small and intimate — only friends and family. And since Nadiah is on her way, we thought this would be the perfect time."

"So she finally came of age?" Kat remembered the way Sophie had described Sylvan's cousin, who had helped her out considerably on Tranq Prime. With her bubbly personality and multicolored hair she sounded like fun.

Sophie nodded. "Yup. Her mother is having a fit, too. Apparently she wants Nadiah to settle down and marry some stodgy full-blooded Prime guy they have all picked out for her. In fact, I think there was some kind of childhood engagement or something and she's claiming Nadiah has no choice."

"Is that true? Will she cave and marry him?" Olivia raised her eyebrows.

"Anyone else might but not Nadiah." Sophie laughed. "She told me all that from Tranq Prime and then the next time I heard from her, she was aboard a cargo carrier bound for the Mother ship. So I'm guessing the Prince Charming dear old Mommy picked out is going to be left standing at the altar."

"Well *you* won't be." Kat kissed her cheek impulsively. "You're going to make a *gorgeous* bride, Sophie."

"Thanks." She smiled. "I just wish there was someone Nadiah could do the luck kiss with during the ceremony. I know it would give her such a thrill, but all of Sylvan's brothers and second brothers are spoken for now."

"Isn't there *anyone?*" Liv asked, eyeing the last pretzel.

"Well, Sylvan *does* have an old friend he wants to ask but he's having trouble getting hold of him. Apparently he's doing some kind of religious retreat back on the original Kindred home world. You know—wearing special clothes, eating special foods, purifying himself. That kind of thing." Sophie shrugged. "We're hoping he'll come but it's kind of iffy right now. I told Nadiah not to expect too much but she says she's just happy to be in the ceremony—even if she doesn't get to kiss a Kindred."

"She has a real thing for the Kindred, huh?" Kat smiled.

"Mmm-hmm." Sophie nodded. "Especially the Blood Kindred. I think it's kind of a rebellion thing because her parents are so against them."

"Well, she can have her pick here," Liv said. "Better keep her away from the unmated males area though—that can get kind of hairy." She shivered and Kat knew she was still remembering her own 'adventure' there, back when Baird had first called her.

"I don't think she'll have to look far to find a male—she's really pretty." The timer dinged and Sophie jumped up. "Hang on, that's my second batch of pretzels."

Kat groaned. "Another batch? I'm already so full you're going to have to roll me out of here."

"Well, it's not like you have to go on a diet," Liv pointed out. "Since Deep and Lock love you in all your curvy glory."

"That's true." Kat couldn't help smiling. "After a lifetime of Weight Watchers and Slim Fast it's nice not to feel horribly guilty if I want a donut now and then. Not that I'm totally letting myself go," she added hastily. "But now I feel, I don't know…"

"Beautiful, just the way you are?" Sophie suggested, smiling from across the room. "Honestly, Kat, that's what we've been telling you all along."

"Yeah, but having your best friends tell you is one thing. Having two hot guys panting after you is something else entirely." Olivia grinned.

"She's right." Kat grinned back and then sighed.

"What is it? What's wrong?" Sophie asked anxiously. "You look so sad all of a sudden. What are you thinking about?"

"More like 'who,'" Liv said. "Is Deep already giving you problems again?"

"Deep? Oh no, he's fine. More than fine—incredible, actually." Kat smiled. "I don't know exactly what happened to him while he was, uh, gone for those few minutes and he won't say either. But whatever it was, it really changed him."

"Then why the long face, Kat-woman?" Sophie asked, piling hot pretzels onto a platter.

"I was just thinking of Lauren again," Kat admitted. "There's something that worries me. Something...well, something I didn't tell your aunt."

"What?" Olivia frowned and Sophie said, "Oh dear."

"I'm sorry," Kat said. "I know you two agreed to do full discloser with her from now on but I didn't want to upset her."

"What could upset her more than knowing her daughter is flying through wormholes with a huge Scourge warrior a hundred thousand light years from Earth?" Liv asked practically.

"Believe me—this could upset her more." Kat sighed again. "It was something Xairn said when Lauren was asking when he would take her home. He said..." She stopped, biting her lip.

"Well, go on," Liv said impatiently. "Spit it out."

"Yes, Kat, give!" Sophie demanded.

Kat frowned. "Okay, but you're not going to like it. Xairn said that the reason he was taking Lauren to the Maw Cluster was so they could change their DNA before he took her back to Earth."

"What?" both Sophie and Liv shrieked at once and Sophie almost dropped the pretzels.

"Change her DNA? That's *crazy*," Liv said.

Kat nodded. "I know—I thought so too. What do you suppose he meant by it? Is he going to turn Lauren into something else…some other life form he can smuggle back to Earth without anyone knowing?"

"I hope not." Sophie looked worried. "Oh, poor Lauren! I wish Liv and I had gotten a chance to meet her."

"I think you'll get your chance." Kat straightened her shoulders. "I will say this—I think Xairn had her best interests at heart. And I don't think he'd hurt her…not on purpose anyway."

"I hope he won't hurt her at all!" Olivia exclaimed. "And when do you think he'll bring her back home?"

Kat shook her head. "I just don't know. But I hope she's being careful and safe—as safe as she can be, anyway." She smiled. "Deep and Lock think that he loves her, you know. And that he acts more like a Kindred than a Scourge."

"I hope they're right about that. I've heard what the Scourge like to do to their women." Sophie shivered. "Whips and chains and God knows what."

"Supposedly they're into domination and bondage," Kat said. "But believe me, girls, Lauren has backbone. I don't think Xairn will find it easy to dominate her—if he even tries."

"Let's hope he doesn't." Liv frowned and looked at Sophie. "Hey, why are you standing way over there with the fresh pretzels when I'm sitting over here?"

"Sorry, your pregnant majesty," Sophie said sarcastically, but she was smiling as she brought the platter. "Here you go—have some."

Kat looked down at the fresh batch uncertainly. "Uh, Sophie? What did you put on these things? I've never seen pretzels that look like this before."

"That's because these are the sweet ones." Sophie pointed. "See? These are the s'mores pretzels with crushed up graham crackers and marshmallows and chocolate. These are the blueberry ones. And these are cinnamon raisin."

"Mmm, they look delicious. Thanks, womb-mate." Olivia picked up a blueberry pretzel and raised it to her nose. She inhaled deeply. "Wonderful!"

Kat frowned at Sophie. "I thought you said she was craving salty things now."

Sophie shrugged. "It changes daily—sometimes hourly. I'm just trying to keep up."

"Salty is good too." Liv stopped with the blueberry pretzel halfway to her mouth and looked up. "Hey Sophie, got any ketchup?"

The End

If you have enjoyed this book, please take a moment to leave a review for Sought *at www.amazon.com/dp/B005BT583Y Good reviews means new readers which allows me to keep writing for a living and bringing you your favorite books. :) And read on to find out about Brides of the Kindred 4, Found, Xairn and Lauren's story.*

Brides of the Kindred – Sought

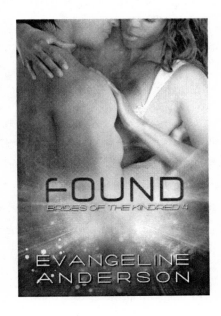

A warrior with a scarred heart who doesn't know how to love. And the woman who must teach him how before it's too late...

The son of the evil AllFather, Xairn is filled with conflicting emotions. On one hand, he has finally gained his freedom and cut the ties that bound him to his race and the sadistic male who is his father. But doing so has unleashed feelings in him Xairn would rather keep buried. Desires that he prayed would never manifest now rage through him and they are centered on one woman alone...

Lauren Jakes is the long lost cousin Liv and Sophie never knew they had. Abducted by the Scourge, she formed a connection with Xairn more meaningful than any other in his life. But though Lauren thinks she knows him, there is more to the huge Scourge warrior than she comprehends. A nightmare childhood and a cruel father have scarred Xairn's heart almost past the point of healing. But that is nothing to the secret inside him—the forbidden desires coded into his very DNA itself, which urge him to commit unspeakable acts in order to sate his newly awakened hunger.

Now a conflict is brewing—both in Xairn's soul, and aboard the Fathership where the twisted AllFather has hatched a new, malicious plot to bring his estranged son home. Can Xairn resist the brutal lust growing within him? Can he fight against his very nature which urges him to dominate and control any female he mates? Can Lauren heal his heart before the AllFather's trap closes on both of them?

And can she teach him how to love before it's too late?

You'll have to read *Found,* Book 4 in the Brides of the Kindred, to find out.

Chapter One

Lauren Jakes was bored.

Although how it was possible to be bored when she was a hundred light years from Earth on a strange planet in a far off galaxy where no other human had ever set foot was beyond her. By all rights she ought to be soaking in the exotic sights and immersing herself in the fascinating alien culture. It was certainly better than the tiny metal cell she'd been kept in on the Scourge Fathership.

The Scourge were a menacing alien race which had come to Earth searching for the one female they believed could mate with their evil overlord, the AllFather. She and she alone would be able to revitalize their race by bearing daughters. Lauren was that female and she had been taken and held within their immense ship for weeks.

While she was there, however, she'd made a connection with Xairn. The huge alien with the burning red-on-black eyes was the AllFather's son, but he had severed his ties with both his father and his race in order to free Lauren and take her home. Of course, first they had to travel through a wormhole to another galaxy in order to get their DNA modified which, according to Xairn, was the only way they could go back to Earth safely. Lauren wasn't thrilled with that but if he said it was necessary, she believed him. So she'd been prepared for danger and adventure and excitement...but not for boredom.

Because in order to soak up exotic sights and immerse herself in the alien culture, she would have to leave the small silver Kindred spaceship where Xairn had left her. And the enormous Scourge warrior had made it very, *very* clear before he left that she wasn't to do that. Sighing, Lauren remembered their conversation...

"Under no circumstances should you step foot outside the ship," he told her sternly as he was about to leave himself.

"Why?" Lauren looked out the viewscreen apprehensively. Xairn had landed them in a dark alleyway in a city he'd said was called *O'ah* but she could catch glimpses of the street beyond which seemed to be the site of a busy marketplace. "Are the native people dangerous or hostile?" she asked.

"Anyplace is dangerous if you don't know the language and customs," he replied obliquely. "I'll be back in one of your Earth standard days. Until then, stay in the ship and speak to no one."

"All right," Lauren agreed. After everything they'd been through together on the Fathership and the Scourge home world, she trusted Xairn implicitly to keep her safe. Still... "I know you're going to find the uh, DNA, guy," she said, looking up at him. "But I still don't understand why I just can't come with you. Wouldn't that make it easier—save you a trip? After all, you got me some decent clothes."

She nodded down at the voluminous robe that reminded her of the muumuus her elderly neighbor, Mrs. Goldman, liked to wear back on Earth. It wasn't very pretty, and the silver-blue material it was made of was extremely scratchy, but it covered her from neck to ankles which was all Xairn seemed to care about. After the cloak he'd loaned her had been ruined, Lauren hadn't had a thing to wear but the thin towels she'd found in the small ship's bathroom—a fact that had seemed to bother the large warrior greatly. So much so that the first thing he did when they landed in *O'ah* was to go out and buy her the silver-blue muumuu dress.

"It wouldn't be safe for you to come. The splicing quarter is too rough for a female like you," Xairn growled.

"What do you mean 'a female like me?'" Lauren put a hand on her hip and frowned at him. "Do I need to remind you that I helped when we were fighting your father's guards? I may not be as strong as you but I'm not stupid, Xairn. If you give me a weapon I can take care of myself. I won't slow you down."

"I didn't mean that you were stupid or weak." He sighed and ran a hand over the thick, glossy black hair he kept in a club at the nape of his neck. Lauren had been dying to see his hair let down from the moment she'd met him. With his stern, proud features he would have looked almost Native American if not for the strange coloring of his skin and eyes.

"What *did* you mean then?" Lauren demanded.

"Your kind has never been seen here. You'll be considered very...exotic." His red-on-black eyes flickered over the faint outline of her body under the voluminous muumuu, making her feel warm all over. "Many males will want you."

Lauren was getting exasperated. "Xairn, are you trying to say I'm too *pretty* to go with you?"

"That word does not describe you accurately." He looked away from her, frowning. "It doesn't do you justice."

Lauren found herself unexpectedly touched by the oblique compliment. Up until a little while ago Xairn had claimed to have no sexual urges at all toward her or anyone else. Even now, when he had admitted to her that she had woken new and unfamiliar emotions inside him, he still seemed hesitant and uncertain about expressing those emotions. Lauren thought it was because he'd never been given any love as a child—how could he learn to show affection for anyone else when he'd never received any himself? She was determined to work on that, to try and help him as much as she could. But now wasn't the time for a therapy session.

"That's very sweet of you, Xairn," she said. "But I'd still like to go with you."

He shook his head. "You don't understand. Your beauty makes you priceless here in *O'ah*. Any splicer would give his left hand for a chance to replicate your flawless skin and lovely eyes. I am only one male and there are gangs that search for exotics. If they set on us all at once, I don't know that I could protect you." He lifted his chin. "I would die trying, of course. But that would be of little comfort to you if they killed me and took you away to a stripping shed."

"A *stripping* shed?" That sounded bad to Lauren.

"A laboratory where candidates with good or unusual DNA are rendered into their component parts for maximum cloning potential."

Lauren felt sick. "So they kill you and cut you into little pieces?"

Xairn nodded. "Essentially. But that's only in the splicing district. Not here in the main part of *O'ah*."

"But how do you know this...this splicer person you're looking for won't want to do the same thing?" Lauren demanded. "How do you know he won't just kill me and strip me down for parts like a stolen car?" She shivered at the thought.

"Because the DNA specialist I am searching for is one I have had dealings with before. His name is Vrr and he will not betray me." Xairn reached out one large hand awkwardly as though he wanted to comfort her somehow.

Lauren leaned toward him— after hearing about the grisly things they did on this planet she needed all the comfort she could get. "Xairn," she whispered.

His long fingers almost brushed her cheek, but then he drew back without touching her. His hand flexed into a fist at his side. "I've been thinking about this for a long time, Lauren," he said in a low voice. "Planning it. I've wanted to get away from my father almost my entire life. This is the only way to get away from him forever—for either one of us. Only by changing our DNA will we make it impossible for him to lock onto either of us with the molecular transfer beam."

Lauren shivered. "Was that the way he kidnapped me in the first place?" She well remembered the way it had felt to be turned into a million tiny pieces and sent flying through the air. It was *not* a pleasant sensation at all.

Xairn nodded. "We have to alter ourselves enough that he can never transport either of us again."

"And you can do that?"

"The Alteration house can. I built the beam for my father—I know exactly which sequences have to be altered in order to make us untraceable and untransportable."

She sighed. If Xairn really had been planning his escape for as long as he said, then he must know what he was doing. "All right," she said at last. "I told you before that I trusted you, Xairn, and I still do. But please...don't take too long."

"No more than one of your Earth standard days," he promised, nodding. "Two at the very most."

That had been three days ago...

Lauren frowned moodily and looked out the front viewscreen at the busy alien marketplace. Though she didn't want to admit it to herself, it wasn't boredom that was really bothering her.

It was fear.

What if something happened to him? What if he's dead or hurt somewhere with no one to help him? What if he never comes back?

She tried to push the troubling questions to the back of her mind, but she could no longer manage it. Xairn was gone and she was all alone on an alien planet a hundred lightyears from home.

What was she going to do?

There was plenty of food, at least. The Kindred ship was stocked with tiny food cubes which expanded into a full sized meal when they were put in the rehydrator. Xairn had showed her how to work the microwave-like machine before he left and Lauren estimated there were hundreds of the sugar-cube sized meals stored neatly in a cabinet at the back of the ship.

True, some of them were pretty strange — she'd rehydrated one which contained what looked like a writhing nest of worms. Lauren had thrown it away — she didn't like to waste food but there was no way she was eating anything alive. Just thinking of it made her feel queasy. But the other meals seemed edible enough and the portions were so large she could often eat an entire day off a single cube — probably because they were intended for huge Kindred warriors and not Earth females.

"So at least I won't starve to death," she muttered, staring out the viewscreen some more. She wished Xairn had parked a little closer to the entrance of the alley. The light in *O'ah* was a dim, dusky violet which never got much brighter than twilight on Earth. She could make out shapes in the weak, purplish light but it was hard to tell for sure what the alien inhabitants of the city looked like. Lauren wondered if they were humanoid at all or something completely different — huge insects maybe. Or amphibians or reptile-like creatures with claws or beaks or —

"Stop it Lauren," she told herself firmly. "You're just giving yourself the heebie-jeebies. So just stop right n—"

Before she could finish the sentence something hopped right in front of the viewscreen. Lauren let out a startled squeak and nearly fell backwards off the black leather seat she was sitting on. "What the—?"

There it was again. The thing hopped up, obviously tying to get her attention on purpose. With one more hop, it finally managed to scramble onto the nose section of the silver Kindred ship. Then it stood up and waved its hands in the air...only they were more like...

"Paws," Lauren murmured to herself. She pressed a hand to her chest. Her heart was beating like a drum because she'd been certain at first that she was being attacked. But now she wasn't so sure.

The alien hopping and waving in front of the viewscreen didn't look the least bit menacing. In fact what he looked like was a very large...

"Bunny rabbit." Lauren finished the thought aloud. "Oh my God, he's the spitting image of Mr. Kittles!"

Mr. Kittles had been the brown and white lop eared bunny her mom had bought her for her twelfth birthday. He'd been Lauren's favorite pet and had slept in her bed every night. Extremely intelligent for a bunny, Mr. Kittles had learned to use a litter box just like a cat and had begged for carrots on his hind legs like a dog. Lauren had been heartbroken when he'd gotten out of the house and been run over by a careless driver in a huge SUV when she was seventeen. And now, here he was again—almost ten years later and a hundred thousand light years away...how was it possible?

"Well, he's not *exactly* like Mr. Kittles," Lauren murmured doubtfully. Which was true. For one thing, Mr. Kittles had never worn clothes and this bunny—or the alien who looked like a bunny—was. His short, furry frame was draped in a shimmering purple cape and he wore soft brown boots on his hind feet. He was still waving frantically as though he wanted her to let him inside.

Lauren was tempted to do just that from sheer boredom but she remembered Xairn's warning and decided against it. "Sorry, little fellah," she said, watching the caped and booted bunny hop around like crazy. "No can do. No matter how cute you look, you might be bad news and I can't take the risk."

No sooner had the words left her mouth than an earsplitting roar shook the ship. Lauren had the speakers on the viewscreen turned down but even so, she covered her ears and winced. What the hell was *that?*

The answer wasn't long in coming. Suddenly the narrow entrance to the alley was filled with an enormous red reptilian face. It had fierce white eyes outlined in black and a square snout, reminding Lauren of the stylized paper dragons that appeared around the Chinese New Year.

The bunny rabbit's huge brown eyes suddenly widened with fear and it hopped up and down even more frantically. Its whiskers trembled and it seemed to be mouthing a plea at the viewscreen.

The dragon-like creature saw it and roared again, its jaws gaping open to reveal rows and rows of jagged pale blue teeth. It was a tight squeeze but it began pushing its massive head into the alley. A forked tongue licked out of its mouth and slithered over the rabbit's right boot before cinching tight. With a jerk of its head, the dragon lifted the terrified rabbit into the air and for a moment it seemed certain that it was going to eat the helpless little creature right before Lauren's horrified eyes.

Then, at the last minute, the boot came off and the rabbit fell back onto the Kindred ship with a hollow thump. The scrap of brown leather disappeared into the dragon's gaping maw and it roared angrily when it found its prey had eluded it. The tongue snaked out again...

But by this time Lauren had already slapped a palm over the door release mechanism and was beckoning for the frightened rabbit-thing to come in. "Hurry!" she urged, waving at it. "Come on—get in here quick!"

She had no idea if the rabbit could understand her or not but it seemed to comprehend her gestures. Barely eluding the seeking tongue again, it slid across the slick silver surface of the Kindred ship and right into her arms.

Lauren pulled it tight to her chest and slammed the door just as the forked black tongue was curling toward her. The very tip of one fork caught in the ship's door and was amputated in a gout of slimy black blood as the silver panel shut. It fell to the floor with a wet *smack* and lay twitching at Lauren's feet like a snake that's been cut in half but doesn't have the sense to die.

"Ugh!" Lauren took a step back, still clutching the bunny creature to her chest. From the pained roaring outside the ship, the dragon was even more upset than she was. She wondered uneasily if it could force its way into the alley and get her. Would the Kindred ship protect her from something with the size and strength of an angry T-rex?

"Don't worry." The piping little voice from between her breasts startled her and when Lauren looked down, she realized she was still hugging the bunny tight—like a little girl clutching a stuffed animal.

"Wh...what?" she managed to stutter. "Who...how...who are you and how can you speak English?"

The rabbit shook itself free of her and hopped down. Then is shimmered and suddenly began to glow and grow.

Lauren watched in horrified amazement as it doubled and then trebled in height and mass until it was a pillar of brilliant light higher than her head. She blinked, trying to get used to the bright glow but almost at once the light solidified into the shape of a blond man wearing a purple cape, black pants and brown boots.

He was tall—almost as tall as Xairn though not quite so broad in the shoulders. Still, he was large and muscular enough to be a threat and Lauren took a step back when he raised his head. His eyes were a pale, silvery-purple and they gleamed strangely when smiled at her.

"Hello, Lauren," he said. "Welcome to *O'ah*."

* * * * *

Deep in the bowls of the splicing district, Xairn raised his bloody head.

He'd spent more time than he liked looking for Vrr only to find that the DNA specialist had retired and given the business over to his son, Slk. The Alteration house he ran still appeared reputable, however, though the price for what Xairn needed done was considerably more than Vrr would have charged him.

Indeed, he wasn't entirely sure how he was going to pay the fee that Slk demanded. But somehow he had to if he and Lauren were ever going to be free of the AllFather's influence and get beyond his reach. And at least he'd gained permission to access their secure parking area. To bring a ship to the splicing district without secure accommodations was asking to have it stripped in a matter of minutes.

He'd been making his way back through the narrow warren of arching plasti-glass tunnels built high above the skyline of *O'ah* when a pack of splicers had jumped him.

He hadn't been expecting the attack because it didn't make sense. Everyone knew that Scourge DNA was flawed—their stubborn intractability and volatility made them useless as slaves except to other Scourge and their pearlescent grey skin and red-on-black eyes weren't considered beautiful enough to replicate for cloning. So why would splicers attack him? Putting the question aside, Xairn had fought them off one by one, despite the fact that his weapon was out of charge. But the splicers were very determined and it was a long, messy business—mostly knife work which left him covered in gore.

Five splicers lay dead at his feet, their red-black blood splattering the smudged plasti-glass tunnel before he was done. Only one remained alive and in the state he was in, he wouldn't last for long.

Xairn knelt on the male's narrow chest and stared into the pale purple eyes. "Why did you attack me?" he demanded hoarsely, gripping the neck of the splicer's cloak and twisting. "Is Scourge DNA suddenly in vogue on this benighted planet? I thought we had too many flaws to be of much use to a splicer."

"Don't...don't want your DNA," the male choked, a thin trickle of reddish-black blood spilling from the corner of his mouth. "Scourge DNA is shit."

"Why then?" Xairn twisted harder until the male's face turned as purple as his cloak. "Tell me now and I'll give you a painless death."

"T-too late for that." The male broke into a cracked laugh that turned into a sob. "Gods...think my spine is broken. Can't feel anything...below my waist."

"Lucky for you," Xairn said coldly. "You can't feel pain in the lower half of your body. But if you don't want the top half of your miserable carcass to be in absolute fucking agony, you'll tell me what you know, *now*."

"Spider sent us." The splicer coughed weakly, spewing black droplets from his thin lips. "He wanted us to kill you so he could have your ship."

"My ship?" Xairn frowned. "What the hell does he want with a Kindred Outrider? The damn thing is fifty cycles old if it's a day — surely he could see that."

"He doesn't...doesn't want the ship itself." The light in the pale purple eyes was dying and the splicer's voice was growing faint. "He wants...what's inside it." He coughed again. "Treasure..."

"Treasure? I don't have any fucking..." Xairn's voice trailed off and his eyes widened. "Gods, Lauren!"

He shook the splicer hard. "What was he going to do to her? Where was he taking her?"

But the light in the splicer's pale purple eyes had gone out — he was talking to a corpse.

Dropping the lifeless body, Xairn leapt to his feet and took off down the warren of smudged, plasti-glass tunnels at a dead run. If he didn't get back to Lauren soon, there would be nothing to get back to. And if he was too late to save her...

Xairn didn't let himself think about that. Didn't allow himself to explore the new emotions exploding inside him. Rage...possession...desperation...

Please, he prayed, not knowing who he was praying to. *Please don't let me be too late. Oh Lauren...*

Want to read more? You can find Found at www.EvangelineAnderson.com*

Brides of the Kindred Glossary

AllFather—the evil head of the Scourge, a race that are the byproduct of a failed genetic trade. The AllFather is one of the Old Ones and has the power to reach into a person's mind to harvest emotional pain and trauma. He lives for the fulfillment of the Scourge Prophesy.

Bespeak—to contact someone mentally using a Think-me device. It is considered rude to bespeak someone you don't know intimately.

Beast/Rager Kindred—come from Rageron—a jungle planet full of beautiful but deadly flora and fauna. They have dark hair, golden eyes, and hot tempers but their most defining characteristic is the mating fist. The mating fist is an area at the base of the Beast Kindred's shaft which engages fully only during bonding sex with his chosen mate. When engorged it swells to keep the Beast Kindred and his bride locked together until she is completely bonded to him. This ensures sex that is both extremely long lasting and multiorgasmic for both partners.

Blood Fever—a condition suffered by unmated females on Tranq Prime, the home world of the Blood Kindred. Blood Fever or Burning Blood as it is often called, is caused by a parasite living on the icy world that affects only women. The parasite—found in the *fleeta* or blood beetle—reacts with a compound in the Tranq Prime water supply to cause the fever. Symptoms include chills, increased sexual need and the feeling of the blood heating in the veins as well as increased coloration of the nipples and sex. If the fever is not treated in forty-eight hours, it will result in death.

Once a Kindred male has had a female's blood, he forms a natural antidote to Blood Fever which he can pass on by sharing body fluids with her. The most effective way to get the antidote into the female's system is for a Blood Kindred to bite her, thereby injecting it along with his essence. However, it is also possible to pass along the healing fluid through sex.

Blood Fever used to be very common on Tranq Prime which is what prompted the cold, proud natives to initiate a genetic exchange with the Kindred in the first place. A recent vaccine has nearly eradicated the disease, however, and the original inhabitants of the ice bound planet have little reason to continue the trade. A faction calling themselves Purists are against any further trade with the Kindred.

Blood/Tranq Kindred — are blond with pale blue eyes and come from Tranq Prime where ice, snow, and arctic-like temperatures are the norm. To combat the severe weather conditions, the Blood Kindred have higher than normal body heat with double the human amount of red blood cells. They have developed specific biting rituals to share their supercharged blood and take the blood of their mates during their own version of bonding sex. They have a set of double fangs located where a human's canine teeth would be. These fangs do not develop fully or become sharp enough to pierce flesh until a Blood Kindred is with a woman he wishes to mate and bond with.

Bonding Ceremony—a wedding-type ritual which takes place after the Claiming Period if the bride chosen by a Kindred warrior has allowed him to have bonding sex with her and joined her mind to his.

Bonding Sex—the extra step a Kindred warrior takes to bind his bride to him permanently during intercourse. For the Beast Kindred, it is the use of the mating fist. For the Blood Kindred, bonding sex means sex during penetration. Twin Kindred bind a bride to themselves by entering her and coming in her at the same time.

Claiming Ceremony—a sort of engagement service that takes place when a bride is first claimed by a Kindred warrior. He declares his intentions toward her and she vows to obey the laws of the Claiming Period.

Claiming Period—women who are drafted are required to go up to the Kindred Mothership and spend a thirty day "claiming period" with the warrior who has chosen them. If, at the end of that time, they have managed to resist the charms of their Kindred mate, they are allowed to go back down to Earth and resume their normal life. However, if they succumb to their Kindred male's seduction, they are mated for life and must move to the Kindred ship to live, leaving everything else behind and seeing their family and friends on Earth only infrequently. Of course, many women are unwilling to give everything up at the drop of a hat, draft or no draft. But the Kindred have a secret weapon—devotion to their female's pleasure and attention to detail during incredibly hot sex.

Claming Period Rules—The Claiming Period lasts for four weeks during which the Kindred warrior attempts to seduce his chosen bride and she tries to resist him:

The Holding Week: the Kindred warrior may hold his bride.

The Bathing Week: the warrior and his bride bathe together and he is allowed to massage her with scented oils and make her come.

The Tasting Week: the warrior is allowed to perform oral sex on his bride.

The Bonding Week: sex is allowed but it is completely up to the bride whether she will take things a step further and allow bonding sex which is a special and specific process to the three different types of Kindred males. (Most women have given in well before this point but a few do resist.)

The only way out before the claiming period is up is a breach of contract. This can happen if the Kindred warrior does not strictly follow the rules and tries to skip forward in the order of allowed events or by breaking one of the rules laid down by the Kindred High Council. These rules—mostly to do with restrictions on communication with Earth—are for the safety of everyone aboard the Mothership and are nonnegotiable. Ignorance is no excuse for breaking them and will result in immediate termination of the claiming period.

Convo-pillar— A half inch long insect which resembles a brightly colored caterpillar. Convo-pillars were genetically engineered by traders on the fringe colonies around Rageron to translate alien languages by communicating via thought waves to their wearer's brain. They have been outlawed by the Kindred High Council because their notoriously unreliable translations cause more conflicts than they solve.

Dream Sharing — occurs when a Kindred warrior's mind aligns with that of his bride and they begin to see each other's day to day activities and memories in their sleep. However, the alignment of the two (or three in the case of the Twin Kindred) minds can take several forms and is not limited to sleep.

Fireflower Juice — an alcoholic beverage made from the Fireflower plant native to Rageron. It resembles milk in appearance but has the flavor of honey, vanilla, lavender and blueberries.

Kindred — a race of genetic traders who have traveled the universe for centuries looking for viable matches to expand their gene pool. Since a genetic anomaly ensures that their population is ninety-five percent male, they are specifically looking for women.

The three genetic trades the Kindred have already made have resulted in three very specific types of men. But though they take on some of the physical characteristics of the race they are trading with, the Kindred gene always ensures three things: physical prowess, extremely large and muscular body structure, and undying loyalty to the female of their choice.

Krik-ka-re — a Scourge tradition in which the mind life of one being may be traded for or ransomed by another.

Kusax — a special knife made from the tainted metal at the core of the Scourge home planet. One scratch can be deadly as it infects the wounded person with a soul poison which ensures a slow, agonizing death.

Law of Conduct – the Kindred law which says every warrior is responsible for the good behavior of his bride and gives him the right to punish her – within reason. Often the "punishment" is sexual in nature and some brides become serial offenders simply to experience their Kindred warrior's particular form of discipline. ;)

Luck Kiss – a kiss performed by the best man and maid of honor at a Kindred Bonding Ceremony in order to bring the happy couple good luck.

Mate of my kin – the way Kindred warriors refer to the brides chosen by their brothers. It is analogous to the English term sister-in-law.

Mother of All Life – the main Kindred Deity, a kind and benevolent goddess whose teachings include respect and reverence for all things female.

Numala – a Blood Kindred name which means "liquid pussy." It refers to a female who produces more than the regular amount of lubrication when aroused. *Numalas* are much prized by the Blood Kindred and sought after as mates because they are more likely to be able to accommodate a Blood Kindred warrior's larger than average cock.

Psychic-Knife — a torture device developed by the Scourge which is able to break the mental and emotional bond between a Kindred and his bride.

Rage — *also Protective Rage or Berserker Rage* — a state of altered consciousness that comes over a Kindred warrior when his bride is threatened. It floods the bloodstream with endorphins and causes such intense anger and aggression that a Kindred in this state becomes a killing machine who will die to protect the woman he has claimed.

Sacred Grove — an area of green and purple trees that houses the temple of the Mother of All Life. The Kindred Mother ship has been equipped with an artificial green sun like the one on their home world in order to allow these holy trees to grow and flourish.

Scourge — a genetic trade gone wrong, these menacing outsiders have twisted desires and sexual needs fierce enough to frighten away even the most adventurous. Their need to dominate and possess their women completely has led to a strange prophesy that they must fulfill…or die trying.

Scourge Prophesy — "One of two, alike and yet different — the double fruit of a single womb from the third planet of a yellow sun. She shall be marked with a white star between her breasts." These words were spoken by Mee'ah — the last living female of the Scourge race who was believed to be a great seer. The Scourge are a dying race, forced to create new members in artificial wombs called flesh tanks or vats because they have no females. Yet, because they have some of the same genetic characteristics as the Kindred, they are able to create only male children and each new generation is weaker than the last. The prophesy refers to the woman the Scourge believe will be able to mate with the AllFather and bear only daughters to rejuvenate their race.

Take-me—an animal native to Twin Moons that has been domesticated by the Kindred for transportation aboard their ship. The Take-me has green fur and two heads, one on either end. Each head has three purple eyes. The Take-me has the unique features of being to expand and compress its mass which makes it ideal for storage. Because they originally lived in caves, most Take-mes stay very contentedly in small dark areas in the Kindred food prep areas where they live off the scraps and leavings of their master's meals. They can eat almost anything except banana peels which they are allergic to.

Tharp—an animal that looks very much like a thin fur blanket which can be worn as a garment. *Tharps* are cultivated on Tranq Prime and prized for their ability to multiply their host's body heat and keep them warm in even the most frigid conditions. A *tharp* can be worn by only one person— as a neophyte or youngster it imprints upon a host and will slowly starve if parted from them. *Tharps* are intelligent and capable of limited movement. They live as long as their host and subsist only on body heat, needing no other form of sustenance to survive.

Think-Me—a thin silver wire worn around the temples which facilitates mental communication between people who already have an intimate connection.

Touch-U—a flat black mat-like animal native to Tranq Prime which the Kindred have adapted to be a home health appliance. The Touch-U is capable of giving a gentle massage or an all-out erotic experience depending on which button is pushed.

Twin Kindred—come from Twin Moons—a world of vast, stormy oceans dotted with craggy but beautiful islands. True to their namesake, Twin Kindred always come in pairs. The brothers are not identical, however. There is always a light twin and a dark twin. These labels refer not just to skin, hair, and eye coloring but to the twin's moods and perceptions of the world. The dark twin in the pair is usually more moody and withdrawn while the light twin takes a substantially brighter view of life. The twins are closely linked and able to sense each other's emotions. They cannot be separated by long distances or for long periods of time without severe pain. They must also share a woman, linking her into their mental and emotional exchange for very intense ménage sex.

Urlich—a type of dog bred by the Scourge. At maturity they are modified with machinery to heighten their sense of smell and intelligence which results in a cyborg-type animal. Once in pursuit of whatever scent has been programmed into their brains, the *urlich* are utterly single minded and incapable of stopping until their prey has been cornered and captured.

Wave—a Kindred cooking appliance which emits thousands of finely collimated beams of heat to cook food in under a minute.

Zichther—an animal native to the jungles of Rageron, the zichther resembles a small bright blue teddy bear in appearance until it opens its mouth and reveals three rows of incredibly sharp, shark-like teeth.

Also by Evangeline Anderson

You can find links to all of the following books at my website: www.EvangelineAnderson.com

Brides of the Kindred series

Claimed (Also available in Audio and Print format)

Hunted   (Also available in Audio format)

Sought   (Also Available in Audio format)

Found

Revealed

Pursued

Exiled

Shadowed

Chained

Divided

Devoured (Also available in Print)

Enhanced

Cursed

Enslaved

Targeted

Forgotten

Switched (coming 2016)

Mastering the Mistress   (Brides of the Kindred Novella)

Born to Darkness series

Crimson Debt (Also available in Audio)

Scarlet Heat   (Also available in Audio)

Ruby Shadows (Also available in Audio)

Cardinal Sins (Coming Soon)

Compendiums

Brides of the Kindred Volume One

   Contains Claimed, Hunted, Sought and Found

Born to Darkness Box Set

   Contains Crimson Debt, Scarlet Heat, and Ruby Shadows

Stand Alone Novels

The Institute: Daddy Issues (coming Feb 14, 2016)

Purity (Now available in Audio)

Stress Relief

The Last Man on Earth

YA Novels

 The Academy

About the Author

Evangeline Anderson is the New York Times and USA Today Best Selling Author of the Brides of the Kindred and Born to Darkness series. She is thirty-something and lives in Florida with a husband, a son, and two cats. She had been writing erotic fiction for her own gratification for a number of years before it occurred to her to try and get paid for it. To her delight, she found that it was actually possible to get money for having a dirty mind and she has been writing paranormal and Sci-fi erotica steadily ever since.

You can find her online at her website www.EvangelineAnderson.com

Come visit for some free reads. Or, to be the first to find out about new books, join her newsletter.

Newsletter – www.EvangelineAnderson.com

Website   – www.EvangelineAnderson.com

FaceBook   – facebook.com/pages/Evangeline-Anderson-Appreciation-Page/170314539700701?ref=hl

Twitter   – twitter.com/EvangelineA

Pinterest – pinterest.com/vangiekitty/

Goodreads – goodreads.com/user/show/2227318-evangeline-anderson

Instagram – instagram.com/evangeline_anderson_author/

Audio book newsletter – www.EvangelineAnderson.com